Acclaim for Julie Winter's

Dancing Home

In this book, Julie Winter touches on   ......an experience that I have read nowhere else in any literature anywhere. Serena is a unique character, and this is a unique book. A must read for anyone interested in the journey inward.

— ALAN ARKIN
Academy Award Winning Actor, Author, Writer, Director

Dancing Home is a collection of linked stories, written by Julie Winter, that draws on her years of experience of meditation, spiritual practice and teaching. The stories are held together by a cord that vibrates with a life lived in her home, Manhattan, NY. Winter speaks eloquently of a universe inhabited by guardians and animal spirits that infuse the hearts and souls of her characters. The rituals are here: "You are going to be born, going to be our baby," spoken by her mother after the loss of a daughter at birth; funerals—the loss of an adored father; family feasts and celebrations and the change of seasons. She offers each reader the possibility of a personal journey that her most practical character refers to as, "The way to do." Perhaps for us, it is "The way to be."

Read this book slowly . . . Savor it. Like Julie, it is a treasure.

— PAUL BINDER
Founder of *The Big Apple Circus,* Author

Julie Winter has created a world of vivid detail where beauty and suffering are gracefully intertwined. Serena's haunting vulnerability and courage to pursue her purpose and to seek what lies beyond our limited perceptions in a world that may be in opposition more often than not is a beautiful reminder for us to stay curious and trust our own journeys as they unfold.

We experience Serena's joys and pain which reflect the duality of the human experience. In her story, we realize that both can exist as healing takes place.

— ASHLEY TORRENT
Writer, Psycho-spiritual Counselor, Reiki Practitioner

Julie Winter, well known as a brilliant teacher, healer and psycho-spiritual therapist for many years, gifts us with her talents as a storyteller. With this quintessential New York love story, she evokes the bravery of a young girl's emergence into of the joys and pitfalls of womanhood. What's more, we are allowed to follow the extraordinary woman she becomes as she navigates the complexities of lovers, friends and community while encompassing an astonishing spiritual awakening.

— IONE
Author, Playwright, Director

Such a beautiful book! Julie Winter has a rich inner life!

— PHILIP CORNER
Composer, Visual Artist

Reading this book is an invitation into a world rich with texture, vivid descriptions, emotional aliveness. It offers a journey into a life touched by the magic of a mind open to adventures in consciousness and also a rich dive into the complexities, joys, and challenges of navigating deep human relationships. I found myself wanting to keep reading, to continue immersing myself in the beautiful writing that painted pictures in my imagination.

— Nancy J. Napier, LMFT
Author, Sacred Practices for Conscious Living

DANCING HOME

Linked Stories
Julie Winter

For Virginia,
A compassionate,
creative, wise and
inspired woman.
With love and
admiration,
Julie

The Ministry of Maåt
156 Hunter Street
Kingston, NY, 12401
www.ministryofmaat.org

ISBN# 1-889-471-33-4

Disclaimer

Dancing Home is a work of fiction. All incidents and dialogue, and all characters with the exception of some well-known historical and public figures, are products of the author's imagination and are not to be construed as real. Where real-life historical or public figures appear, the situations, incidents, and dialogues concerning those persons are entirely fictional and are not intended to depict actual events or to change the entirely fictional nature of the work. In all other respects, any resemblance to persons living or dead is entirely coincidental.

Notes and Acknowledgments

Dancing Home began as a story I wrote purely for my own pleasure. When it was finished, I began another story, new characters appeared and I continued to write. The characters gave suggestions and then directions and after a while I had a book that I wanted to publish. I contacted Ione, of The Ministry of Maåt press and asked if I could send some sample stories. She liked them and agreed enthusiastically to print the book and that opened the door for it to go out into the world. There are so many people to thank. Friends and colleagues, students and teachers, whose very being contributed to my efforts as a writer. I offer my gratitude to them here.

To Genna Brocone, for her patient, intelligent and insightful proofreading and copyediting, and for being a loving, motivating force, to Al Margolis for his astute proofreading, to Jon Child for his organizing vision and to Detta Andreana for her design skills and organizing ability. Much appreciation.

Heartfelt gratitude to the people at the Ministry of Maåt, especially Ione, who, after opening the door for this book, read the manuscript and added unique, invaluable notes that sparked my creativity.

Joyful thanks to the people who inspired and supported me. Judith Taylor: for her perceptive reading and creative ideas. Philip Corner: who taught me to fearlessly express my artistic vision. Madeline Gleich: for the indescribable depth of our friendship. Jeanette LoVetri: companion on the path of exploring the wider realms. Paul Binder: for the light he brings to my life and to the larger world. Bob Gittlin: for his straightforward, dynamic intelligence and his generosity. And to my sister in Spirit, Nancy Napier, whose wisdom and guidance gave me strength to meet the challenges of writing.

Appreciation for my cherished Thursday Healing Circle for their sustained love and encouragement through my process of writing.

Thanks to the late Michael Sahl, for his shrewd humor and his staunch belief that I could write and to the late Susan Hartung, dear friend, for her articulate mastery and her inspiring bravery. To the late Rachel Child, for her intelligence, insight and love, and because she always called me her sister.

The most profound thanks to the late Dr. Eric Pace, my friend and spiritual teacher, for transforming my life and being with me as a guide until his death and beyond.

To my mother, Eve, for her ferocious love and excellent life training.

And to my husband, Jon Child, for a depth of love beyond description.

To Jon Child, my beloved. Forever.

"Did I know you before
You walked through the door . . ."

Yes, I did; yes, I did. Yes I did.

If Light is in your heart, you will find your way home.

—RUMI

Table of Contents

Born. Again.

Serena was born in a blizzard. Implacable, it raged through New York, surprising in its ferocity. The wild fragile flakes were magical, slowing time until it seemed suspended, insulating the earth and blurring the traffic sounds, making the city dangerous and delightful. Wars raged across two oceans. Bodies were burning; blood was everywhere, in frozen Europe and in the tropics. In the time before Serena's birth and after it, millions of souls left their bodies, passing from realm to realm, crossing unmarked borders.

Serena waits in Ruby's womb, the wet space dense and encompassing, the heat of her mother's blood nourishing her. She understands that she is caught, cannot move and position herself for the journey down the waiting canal. This womb will deliver her or be her burial ground. For all the time Serena has gestated, she has been aware of Ruby's voice in the roundness of this temporary home. "Live, live," Ruby said, the words reverberating when she spoke aloud, commanding her to survive. "You are going to be born, going to be our baby." Serena hears Ruby's compelling inner voice—a rhythmic determined stream that is with Ruby, even in her dreams, probably in her pulse. What need created these words? Such powerful incantations. Serena could not yet fully know, but the sense that she's in danger, might die through her very efforts to be born, enfolds itself in Serena's cells. Perhaps she will never take life for granted.

The snow fills the streets and roads and the doctor is in Westchester. Serena's Aunt Marion, one of her father's stylish iron-willed sisters, goes to the hospital; she does know what the danger is. Tall, in her good wool coat and fine hat, her umbrella neatly folded, her galoshes over smooth black shoes, she has come to oversee matters. She has already called the physician to insist that he come immediately, snow or not. "We don't want a repeat of last time," she said. Dressed and in command, Marion probably saves both Ruby and Serena. But a repeat? A repeat of what? Years will pass before Serena hears the entire story of her birth and the events that preceded it, but it is a mystery she senses, strips of dark mist floating around her beginnings.

Her handsome father, Alexander, waits at the hospital. A charismatic man, with his hazel eyes and luxurious social gifts; a troubadour, a magician. People always wanted to be near him, wanted to listen to his clever stories, to laugh with him and absorb his warmth. A tall man, who appeared to be so strong, with his large graceful hands and broad back, a witty man whose shadows were artfully hidden,

1

whose generosity could be a danger to himself, whose heart had begun to fail him by the time he was in his mid-twenties, when he suddenly fainted on the street. How much of his physical weakness was he aware of? Certainly, he never spoke of it. Sometimes, rising in the morning, he would feel a velvet press inside his body; it would change to a blade so thin that it was almost translucent, sliding under his skin—and then a sharp stab—quick—gone so fast it might never have happened. Once, he imagined himself as a leaf worn so that only its perfect veins remained, fragile as bridal lace. But there was no diagnosis, ever, for those early episodes. The fainting was attributed to exhaustion after his father's recent death. Nothing was investigated until much later. Too much later. Too late. Though what could have been done, then? Nothing, really. Nothing to help this lover, this dancer. Toward the end of his life, resting in bed (there had been so much damn resting), but now he welcomed it, it was no longer his enemy—he understood that a major purpose of his life had been to push through the membrane that separated him from the deepest love. That he had done that because he met Ruby, because they lost the first baby, a daughter, because Ruby almost died. And because Serena, his jewel, had lived. He had been a loving man with a sweet heart and a true concern for peoples' welfare; it was what had led him to join the Party. He experienced joy. But passion? The kind of volcanic passion and commitment that Ruby had? Her ferocity? No. Not that. Or perhaps only at the beginning of his time with Ruby. And the experience that all of life is a sacred trust? A flash of it, perhaps. He would leave that for Serena.

Ruby was a wild woman. Outspoken, vociferous, shrewd; she was dark topaz, burnt orange, her secrets like nuggets of jet, cached behind dark eyes. She had areas of impenetrable reserve; she was an accomplished pianist, who came from a family of musicians, but she rarely played for anyone but herself and her family; she was knowledgeable about art and spoke proficient French in private. Alexander played the guitar with abandon and some skill, slithered around in French when they went to Paris, improvised what he did not know and painted for the sheer pleasure of it in an unselfconscious way that was beyond Ruby's reach. But she was formidable, always had an active list of people who had offended her, or worse, betrayed her in some complex way that only she understood. "You kill people off," Serena would say as an adolescent, listening to her mother declare someone soon to be among the living dead. "Why not just talk to them?"

"Nothing to talk about any longer," Ruby would answer.

✳ ✲ ✳

Ruby Marks and Alexander Weiss met at a Communist Party meeting, in the roiling 30s when so many were involved with the Party. He was enthusiastic, richly hopeful about the changes that could be made. Ruby was watchful, understood the power structure, was committed, but not enchanted. The moment Ruby saw Alex enter the room, the members watching him, as people always did, acknowledging him, waving, smiling, the women yearning toward him, she knew she would marry him. One of the many chiseled certainties Ruby was to experience. She was a handsome woman, with her thick black hair, lush heavy waves surrounding a high forehead, deep set brown eyes, a wide mouth and a square jaw, altogether brushed with passion, with an indomitable essence that was hidden at first glance, but emerged slowly if someone took the time to notice. She did not advertise herself, felt safer when not much attention was paid her, until she demanded it. And then she was riveting. He was ebullient; she was unapproachable without direct invitation. The next time they were at a meeting together, Alex realized he had been waiting to see if she would be there and at the end of the gathering, asked her out for coffee. There was an explosion between them, something neither had experienced in just that way, passion that tore and soothed again, and fascination and—what? Inevitability? The world torn apart and reconfigured? It did not surprise Ruby, but Alex was in shock. They married in three months, a rabbi officiating and the Weiss family and Ruby's sister, Naomi, present at Marion and Mark's home in their lovely living room, now rocking with this amazing event, this not entirely—to the family—welcome event, not that anyone said. No, not at all. Only an underlying shiver of, "He could do better than that." The Weisses had expected a beauty for their beloved brother, their star. Someone adoring. (Ruby did adore Alex, but not in a way easily recognizable to them.) And they had certain knowledge that no one, not even this formidable family, had the whisper of a chance of taming this woman. Not a whisper. Not a breath.

After the wedding, they travel to Europe, to France—to Paris—Ruby's forever dream and to England. The trip is full of brightness, sliced with the mysterious shadows of the cathedrals and ancient churches, their hovering scented darkness splashed with glorious stained glass, images of still, imploring faces and others that gloried, mouths open to heaven. Sometimes they go to concerts in the churches, sometimes, as they wander and then sit, the organist is practicing, an extraordinary delight. Alex has been to Europe before and immediately dresses the part, making small changes to his wardrobe to mirror the places they visit, an ascot, a beret, a good English umbrella and handsome shoes bought in London. "Last forever," he says. "A lifetime." He loves costumes and wears them elegantly, nonchalantly. Ruby wears whatever clothing she has brought and won't let Alex take her into Parisian shops. She does not feel intimidated by Parisian women (not exactly), but she does not resemble them and does not want to pretend. She does not like costumes. Finally, she does let Alex buy her a deep orange sweater, the wool warm and soft, when they are in London, in a staid harmless looking store—but only because she is cold. (She is often cold, but flourishes in the heat, welcomes it as a lively familiar presence.) Alex is pleased, or maybe relieved. The Weisses are shoppers: clever, devoted, determined, with unfailing taste.

Ruby speaks excellent French, but is almost silent. She does speak clearly to the hotel maid in Paris, assuring her she will pay extra for two fresh towels daily. Daily. Not one small rough towel every few days. The maid is disapproving. No one showers every day. Ruby assures her that she does. Alex sloshes around happily, makes himself understood, gestures gracefully. No one criticizes him; they enjoy his fervor, his pleasure. (The French?) He makes friends everywhere.

At the end of the trip, in London, Alex realizes he has four more days of vacation than he thought, four more days until he is expected at his medical practice, four more days than Ruby, who needs to be back in New York to teach. He is delighted. He thinks he will re-book his passage home, spend the rest of the time in London. He imagines Ruby will be delighted as well. Pleased with his good fortune. He is dismally wrong. It becomes the occasion for their first real fight. They have hardly had disagreements, barely quarreled. Alex is totally unprepared.

They are in their London hotel room on a cloudy late afternoon; they have plans to go out to a real tea. The room is pleasant, spills with rose and green chintz and highly polished, if ordinary, furniture. The rug is a pattern of dark swirls in a color neither of them can quite name. Aubergine? Maroon? When Alex announces his plans, his good fortune, Ruby is still for a moment and when she speaks, her voice is not raised, but slides into an ominous, low range. "How dare you?" she says. "How dare you stay here and enjoy yourself and let me go home alone? Alone." By the second "alone," she is hissing. "I consider this to be a betrayal, a violation. Is this what you think it means to love someone? What do you think love is? I will tell you what it is not. It is not a matter of convenience." The wildness of her hatred is in every part of her body; it is completely focused on Alex. He is stunned. He has never seen anyone in this state before; certainly not in his controlled (and controlling) family, where people "have words," might quarrel or disagree. But nothing like this; not ever. Not ever in the relationships he has had before Ruby and he has had some stormy ones.

"Ruby," he says. "Ruby, please." He tries to reason with her. A mistake. It makes her angrier, which doesn't seem possible. "I thought you would be pleased for me." A ruinous error. Ruby rages for an hour. Sometimes Alex just holds his head in his hands. "Stop," Alex says. "I won't stay. Nothing is worth this."

"Oh, no," Ruby says. "You'll go home and then make me guilty to punish me. You stay. Enjoy every minute. I will go home. Alone. And I will remember this forever." (Which she does. On occasion, she will tell Serena the story and laugh. "He had never seen anything like it," she will say, with some pride.) Ruby recovers, the storm over. Alex is traumatized. Somehow, they enjoy their time together until Ruby leaves for New York. But the ground has shifted.

✳ ✪ ✳

Ruby taught English to adolescent boys who came from poor families, one wave of immigrants after the other and many who had inherited the burdens of slavery and racism. Ruby taught with her whole heart, defended her students: the ones who lost out, were threatened by gang wars, maybe killed—who, later, were sent wholesale to Viet Nam. She gave them strength through her belief in them and they loved her. Sometimes she would sweep a stack of books off her desk to get their attention, but "I always picked them up," she said. They respected her anger, protected her in the hard times of school bombs and anti-Semitism. She was a warrior and took no prisoners.

Alexander and Ruby both wanted to heal a world that they could see was broken, murderous, seemingly unable to free itself from violence. Had he known much about it, Alexander might have taken to Buddhism, to compassion and loving kindness; Ruby had no such plans, at least not in the beginning.

✳ ✪ ✳

On the evening of Serena's birth, Alexander waits amidst the clatter and hiss of hospital sounds, the heavy medicinal smells, the bustle of readying for nighttime as the snow falls heavily and the doctor, their old friend Gerard, rushes in to do what needs to be done.

Serena is born, pulled through a bloody incision in Ruby's womb and abdomen into the glaring light of the operating room, just as the Sun passes through the 22nd Degree of Aquarius, just as the 11th Degree of the sign Virgo ascends, carrying the Moon. Just past full, the Sun and Moon offer a lopsided kiss to each other through the earth's body. Serena is pulled into the world of apparent solidity and the illusion of time, the realm of longing and vulnerability, cruelty and courage and passion. Just after Serena is born, Ruby develops a high fever and is taken away to another place in the hospital. Serena waits and waits in the tall white metal crib; a filament as fine as spider silk connects her to her mother, spins not from the umbilicus, but from her heart to Ruby's. If the room is sunny, you can almost see the minute rainbows glimmering in the silk as it floats through the air, out the door, down corridors of waxy yellowed linoleum, all the way to where Ruby lies, wrapped in a scalding fever that no one can control. Serena senses her guardians around her as she waits, the entities that presided over her gestation and birth, their essences completely empty, infinitely present. Some of them were there even before her conception, teaching her, rocking her in the measure of their wisdom. The guardians. Wise energies, loving configurations not of this earth, but serving all beings on it. Seemingly differentiated, they are truly moving aspects of an eternal tapestry, vast compassion woven into many realms, including the physical. They are present to guide, to protect when possible and to offer unconditional love. Entities, spirits, guardians, power animals; all accepted and integrated in some cultures, but not in the one Serena now enters. In those cultures, reality is composed of multiple dimensions woven together, the earth realm only one of many. And at birth, Serena senses these energies acutely, will continue to experience them throughout her life, sometimes vibrantly, sometimes less so, sometimes barely a shiver of awareness, yet always as an integral part of her larger being. They assured her that she would be born, even as she felt her twisted position in Ruby's womb. Even as she called for help with all her vibrating life force and, losing her awareness of them for a moment, knew human panic in her small, complete body. But they were there, offering comfort and reassurance. They stay with her through the long weeks of Ruby's illness, cradle her in the magnificent iridescence of their invisibility, shepherd her through winter days and bitter nights when the wind howls outside the tall brick hospital building and gulls shrill over the East River, riding on the frigid winds.

"Such a sunny baby," the nurses say repeatedly, slipping the rubber nipple, with its strange pungent scent, between her lips. The entities nod. Serena seems to smile. She is still a new one, so new that she remembers her journey into this world, remembers what she will almost forget and then recall slowly, as the years pass. She feels the enfolded universes in the whorls of her fingerprints, knows she has emerged onto this blue planet as a voyager through many realms. She senses others like her, new ones, scattered over the earth; she feels them laughing or sleeping, sucking on a full breast, or with hungry bellies; some are half a world away, some as close as the next crib. She knows she is in a place where the elements transform. Fire consumes wood into ash. Ice goes to water, then to vapor. Rocks break and break again until they become tiny particles of sand. Winds blow everywhere, some gentle, some ferocious, they flow through her, enliven her as breath. Animals and birds and creatures of all kinds abound here and there are trees and flowers, deserts and oceans. It is a realm of flashing appearances and disappearances, substance that is empty, yet filled with eternal possibilities and the dancing illusion of solidity. Her awareness of this vastness drifts and returns as the hours pass and sometimes Serena is simply her own small body, the home of this new incarnation, warm in the nursery crib. One night, her guardians draw her awareness to the stars, or maybe she finds them herself in the February darkness outside the long windows; their protective ancient light, their cold fire a canopy of blessings. Their timeless nature sooths her. Perhaps it is then that they fall into her heart, mingle with her bloodstream to be discovered later. Of course, she is told when she confides this to her first therapist, a kind woman heavily burdened with arrogance and expertise, that babies cannot even see the stars, let alone remember them, or know any of what Serena is beginning to tap at as she recovers her memories (if, indeed, the therapist said, this was not a ploy on Serena's part to control her world—meditation, astrology!), but the therapist's words never trouble her. Her experiences had been vivid and as the old knowledge was revealed, she knew that it was so.

✳ ❂ ✳

It is not until years have passed and Serena is fifteen that Ruby tells the story Serena has somehow always known in an amorphous way; events hidden behind smoke or wrapped in fog, but palpable since her cells divided, since she was a trace of chance, a whisper of possibility. They are sitting in the living room in the stretching dusk of an April evening, Central Park outside, wide with new green and with embracing spring air.

"There is something I want you to know," Ruby says. "I have waited until I thought you were old enough to understand the complex circumstances." Really, she has waited until she thought Serena could hear about the events without becoming terrified about her body and her own future, hear and understand with as little trauma as possible.

For Serena, hearing the truth will move what has been hidden up into conscious awareness—an awareness that will unfold over the years, bringing ideas that she could never have grasped when Ruby first told her the history of her birth. Then Serena had no real way to realize the layers of yearning followed by loss, her feelings of being punished by grief, of celebration being mangled by death. But Ruby wants Serena to know the truth. This is the moment and this is the way that Ruby begins the tale: she turns on a lamp in the living room as she starts to speak so the shadows roll away into the corners and the falling dark flutters at the windows, curls around the trees across the street. Ruby's voice is unadorned and powerful, without curves or hesitation. This story has been inside her for a long time.

"I had a baby before you," she says. Not, "Alex and I," but neither Serena nor Ruby notice this. "I carried her full term, the pregnancy was easy. And then she should have been delivered by Caesarean section, but they were out of fashion." Ruby pauses, says again, in a familiar and condemning tone, "Out of fashion, you understand. The baby died. She strangled on the umbilical cord. He never forgave himself."

"You had a daughter? There was a daughter before me?" Serena says. Then, "Who never forgave himself?"

"Gerard. Dr. Gerard. He was attending." He is still a family friend, loved. Kind. "Yes, a daughter." Ruby does not mention how the nurses marveled at that child's resemblance to Alex. Striking. Unusual.

"I wanted another baby as soon as possible, so I waited exactly as long as the doctor insisted I wait and not one moment longer. I conceived with no problem and that baby is you."

The cello player next door begins his nightly practice, soft endearing sounds.

"There's more, isn't there?" Serena can sense the story is not complete.

"Yes, there's more. You know some of this already. This part is about your birth itself. When I went into labor with you, your aunt Marion came to the hospital at the beginning of a snowstorm, which turned into a blizzard. Marion called Gerard and told him to come. Told him in no uncertain terms because she was sure I could not deliver you safely. And he came, and you were delivered by Caesarean."

"I know that part," says Serena. Sometimes she looks at Ruby's round belly and, even knowing it was because the muscles had been damaged at her own birth, her fifteen-year-old self feels no mercy. She hates it. She feels wretched about her feelings, and she knows she has them.

"I got very sick," Ruby says. "They took you away from me." She stops, looks out at the dark trees, is quiet for a moment and then resumes. "I almost died. It was before penicillin, you know. I had a very high fever from an infection and it seemed that it would kill me. That is the part you didn't know."

Serena, at that age, in that time, does not understand the impact on her of being separated from her mother for weeks just at birth. But, "Ah." Her cells vibrated. "Ah. The truth. Here is your closeness to death," they say. "Your very early closeness. Your closeness even before Alexander's death. Your closeness at the very beginning."

Serena covers her eyes with her palms. "Oh, Mother. Ruby. How awful. I'm so sorry. And sorry about the one who died." There is so much to say and so little she can find to say. The words seem lost to her, unavailable, nothing much to offer her mother, but she gets up and takes Ruby's hands.

"It has nothing to do with you," Ruby says quickly. "I mean with your body, so there is no reason this should ever happen to you." This is what she wants to convey: that Serena is safe from such events, that she will not have these troubles. But who knows, really?

"I'm not worried about it." This is so; fifteen-year-old Serena is not worried. Maybe about a pouchy belly, since she has already started the maiming relationship to her own flesh by dieting endlessly in an attempt to flatten her curves, pare away her softness, but she has no idea that this is an expression of hatred, is its own kind of craving for harm, for death. In this moment, it is a relief to know the whole story, to rest her flickering questions about some mystery hovering around her birth. A lost sister. Ruby's proximity to death.

Many years later, a careless man from whom Serena is getting some body work, will tell her as she rests against dusty rainbow-colored pillows in his not-very-clean apartment, will tell her, in response to this story, that she was born in a haunted womb. "When a baby dies just before another is born, some say the womb is haunted," he says smugly. "Does that seem right to you?" Hearing him, Serena is furious. This man, who thinks he is so clever—such an ignorant thing to say. She never returns to see him. She does not believe it for a moment; with all her troubles with Ruby, still she knows her mother's womb was sturdy and fine, she is sure of it. Not haunted. Not filled with a ghostly presence that abided with Serena as she grew. When she reaches the street, after the session, she is dizzy. She dismisses the man and his crassness, and goes into the subway. But in spite of actively banishing him, she remembers those words for years.

In the living room where Ruby and Serena now sit, the single lamp leaves most of the room in deep shadow. Serena sits with her mother on the couch, holding her mother's hand. It might seem that they would have hugged, but they do not, it is not their way.

"It had a good ending," Ruby says, feeling her daughter's warm hand. "We had you."

＊ ☉ ＊

After weeks have passed since Serena's birth and hope of Ruby's recovery was fading, an elderly nurse bathes Ruby's lower body in alcohol, an old remedy, out of fashion and rarely used, and this cools her, breaks the fever. When the fever breaks, Serena knows her mother has returned from the hot realm at the edge of never and forever. The silken filament connecting them vibrates, hums. It is now only a matter of time, Alexander says, the worried aunts and uncles say. Time, an element Serena is revisiting, an element essential to her new body and the world she now inhabits. The guardians dissolve their constant watch, retreat politely and return to their realm, leaving Serena safe, their urgent task completed for the moment. But they are never too far away, never out of reach.

By the time Ruby and Alexander take Serena home to the apartment on Central Park West, the daylight has lengthened. It is a day of triumph for the family, a glorious celebration of life emerging where there had been despair. Ruby is thirty-seven and will not have another child. Serena is her one and only. In addition to her age, her doctor, the kindly, misguided and much relieved Gerard, has forbidden her to even try. Her difficulties with the birth, her violent infection, make it impossible. But Ruby, despite her ferocious independence and stubborn will, would not have tried. She would not risk her life and Serena's safety. She suspects Alexander's damaged heart will not last through Serena's childhood, suspects the private rhythms of his heart are precarious, broken.

When she and Alexander had traveled in Mexico, he had had a strange incident: weakness, breathlessness as he emerged from the warm ocean, his big body seeming so sturdy in the sunlight, drops sliding down his skin as, deep in his chest, hidden, his heart struggled in scarlet shadows, wobbled, did not keep its rhythm. He recovered easily and there was no medical diagnosis. Ruby remembered that he said he had also had an episode as a very young man, fainting, collapsing. No diagnosis then, either. But Ruby, with her unsparing, laser awareness, knew there was serious trouble. Oh, she had dreams, powerful and determined as a storm and as implacable; she knew that danger hovered, its edges sharp and certain. Why was there no further investigation? Maybe there was and it was inconclusive. Maybe denial ruled and Ruby, uncharacteristically, participated in the denial.

If, on that day of celebration as fervent as a wild spring river, Ruby feared for her husband's life, she said nothing. If her stitches still ached, if she mourned the milk she would never share from her breasts, she was silent about it. She had planned, against all medical advice, to nurse her baby and trust her instincts rather than the doctors' warnings about the known dangers of breast feeding, the germs. The peasant mentality, although they did not say that, these educated, correct men. Not exactly. "Not modern," they did say. "An old custom, completely outmoded," though they did not say that, these men whose families were recent to America, whose mothers and grandmothers had surely fed children from their breasts. But on the day of their return, Ruby is silent about her fear and her pain. Ruby was a woman who cherished her secrets, not because she was afraid to speak her mind, but because she understood secrets as powerful. They made her autonomous. She did not want opinions.

On the day that Serena and Ruby return to the apartment on Central Park West, the sap is running in the trees and the squirrels are jigging up and down their trunks. Robins have appeared. All the aunts and uncles, the family, are there to greet them with flowers and food and laughter that combines happiness and relief, the knowledge of how close the situation had been to tragedy, its scent potent, invading the hospital room, following them to hover in their own apartments and surround them in its embrace in the wee hours and in the slowly warming daylight.

"The family," is always Alex's family; Ruby's sister and brother-in-law are called by their names. They are not the family. This family is made of people whose parents had escaped to a new country, whose relatives are dying in camps in the old homeland. The gift of this smiling baby, the child of the adored youngest in the family and his courageous (and difficult) wife is astonishing. They did not think in terms of miracles, but if they did, this would have been one. Leah, one of Alex's sisters, went as far as saying it was a miracle, after what we thought—well—we know what we thought. And such a beauty, this baby. All smiles, so perfect.

The group that came is Marion, who saved Serena's life, and Ruby's, her husband, Mark, Leah and Elias, and Lois and Sidney. Alex's sisters and their husbands. His brother Joseph is there, too, and his elegant wife, Margaret. They are all elegant, always. The women wear dark, becoming, suits made for them by a tailor whom Ruby will eventually visit, with Marion, reluctantly, to have some suits made. By that time, Serena will be four and will accompany them, watching the process of measuring and pinning with fascination; watching all those silvery pins in the red tomato cushion bursting with their stiff stems. Rain will splash at the windows as Mr. Stern measures and sighs and measures again. Garb as guardian and protector in the Weisses' world, a world that Serena will, to her sadness, adopt.

During that first family event, Serena reaches her small hands toward them, happy to feel them near her, to hear their voices, lively and a little loud—or anyway, definite—an encompassing group. Strong anchors in a world that will rock violently, relentlessly, in a few short years.

Anna, the Weisses' housekeeper, is at the homecoming, too. She wears her good black dress and a brooch, a starched apron over it. Her hair, silver and streaky yellow, is pulled back and braided, the braid pinned in a bun. In all the years that

Serena will know Anna, she never sees her hair any other way, only the braid down for a minute, to be re-pinned. The guardians have retreated, relaxed their watch for a while and Anna, in her sturdy human form, takes their place. Anna becomes her grandmother, since Serena's grandparents have all died before her birth. No, Anna becomes her safety. She will care for Serena and Ruby and Alexander and the house, be the steadiness and comfort when death does come. She would teach Serena how to be present in an absolute way, to attend to life in the midst of wreckage. She has worked for one of the aunts and she is now going to be one of life's great gifts to Serena. Anna had an innate and absolute authority, no one ever argued with her, not even Ruby. Her values were clear and discerning, but without rigidity. "There's a way to do," she would say. Anna's disapproval was expressed in the reverse of that sentence. "Not a way to do." And she taught Serena, an eager student who yearned to know "how to do," who absorbed Anna's sense of the world and her steady goodness.

Later, Serena would say that she had known several angels in her life and Anna was the first. Anna paid absolute attention to the details of life and respected them. She was Buddhist in her regard for the sacred buried in the ordinary, though it was unlikely that she had ever heard of Buddhism. She was, in fact, a devout Catholic, although she hinted that she didn't think too highly of some of the priests. Maybe Serena's lifelong attachment to cleaning as a sacrament came from Anna: bluing the white wash, adding Clorox to it. Not the machines in the basement, not good enough.

Anna took Serena to her apartment four flights up, in an old building in the East Eighties, with a coal stove for heat and Anna carried the coal. "Watch, Dolly, watch the stove." She was often feeding someone extra, someone from the church down on her luck. (It was always a woman.) "Where would they go?" she said, imparting a sense of social responsibility and a willingness to be generous, as Serena watched carefully. It was the way to do.

✳ ❀ ✳

That first night that Serena is at home, surrounded by her family, by human warmth and lying in her own bassinet, Serena sleeps deeply, forgets about her companions the stars, and has no immediate need of the guardians. For the moment, she is safe.

When Serena is a few months old and spring has come, Ruby wakes with her at five a.m., gives her breakfast and heads out to the park, safe then, even at such an early hour. They walk a circle around different trees, speaking to each one with its just-greening buds or tiny reddish leaves—until they get to a huge tree; how old could it have been, in that park? As old as the park itself, maybe. Ruby holds Serena, whose arms stretch to hug the tree and rests her cheek against it. "Good morning, tree," they say to each one; or Ruby would say it and Serena would make crooning sounds. A woman and her baby, finding ways to touch the earth in the midst of concrete acres, hard ground, morning light. Serena always reaches for the birds. "Up," she would say, as soon as she could talk, which she did at an early age. "Up." Sparrows, pigeons, robins in the warmer weather, geese, as they traveled north in the spring and south in the fall. Later, Alex would show her other birds, bright finches and bluebirds. He explained that New York was a flyway and many birds passed through.

When Serena plays in the park with her friends, when she is older, she will remember both the tree walks and the birds. Sometimes, looking at the trees, she sees vague lights around the branches and the leaves; soft flickers of white or shimmering blue that would vanish if she stared at them directly. They seemed an ordinary part of the world, and she paid no particular attention to them, assuming, as she often would, that everyone was aware of them.

Serena is a sturdy child, affectionate, independent, sometimes willful, imaginative and curious. Her dark brown hair shines, so dark it is often called black, her eyes grey and wide, all of her full of determination. She is also a child who is eager to please and even when she was very young, she understood that about herself. Afterwards, when Serena learns more about her birth, she will wonder how early she developed the need to charm, to appease and whether it started at her birth and perhaps before. Was she soothing Ruby from the womb? It is a habit that grows with her, a necessity beyond her natural ebullience, a force that propels and rules her in a way that she is conscious of, but, for years, unable to change; the pattern, ominous and tyrannical, sitting uneasily with a ferocious independence. Of course, Alexander might have contributed, with his humor and life or death charisma, just as Ruby might have contributed her fierceness and her power to hold an immutable stance. Jumbles of paradoxes in this small child who will experience grief again all too soon, and this time, there will be no rescue.

When she is three, the guardians return to be close to her, although Serena is not quite aware of them. But almost aware, as aware as one might be aware of a scent: mild, intriguing. Also when she is three, Eleanor, who cares for her when Ruby returns to work and Anna is busy with the house, takes her to be tested for her IQ. Eleanor is from Bermuda, a Master's student at Teachers College. She arrives each morning and Serena opens the door and they greet each other, Eleanor saying, "You are as sweet as a tea rose this morning, Serena." Eleanor is tall and dignified and playful in a sedate way. Serena does not know the meeting Eleanor brings her to one afternoon is a test. Why is she being tested at all? Ruby is not for it, but the family urges (and urges); Serena is so intelligent. Why not find out her IQ? Who cares? thinks Ruby, but she agrees reluctantly.

It is a warm spring the year Serena is three and on a day of vibrating sunshine, when the city buildings shine benevolently, she goes with Eleanor to what is a basement office with a series of windows looking up into the street where people's lower legs and feet appear and pass with varying degrees of assurance and speed. This really interests her, but clearly the woman needs her attention. The older woman who "visits" with her is very precise, speaking as though Serena were slightly hard of hearing, or maybe much younger than she is. The woman is wearing a wool plaid skirt made up of reds and greens and blues that fascinate Serena. Neat, alternating rectangles separated by dark blue stripes. Eleanor leaves them together to "visit." Serena, always curious, is interested in the questions the lady asks, though some of them are very strange. "Can you find the door, Serena? Can you open it?" Serena does both and sits down again. Then she asks if Serena can close the door. Serena is too young to know about rolling her eyes, but she does wonder. She considers asking why she didn't ask her to close it when she got up the first time, but for some reason this seems part of the game, the visit, and she refrains. A game with odd rules.

Eleanor picks her up at the end and they have ice cream cones. Serena confides that it was pleasant, but the lady was—what ? "She asked silly questions," Serena says. Serena asked the lady about herself and they chatted, which seemed to amuse the lady. It develops that Serena is unusually bright, in whatever way the test is designed to determine that, and against Ruby's wishes, Serena begins Hunter in the fall; a school for gifted children. The testing center had recommended that they apply. Very high odds against, they said, but Serena was remarkable. When Serena hears that she is going to school, she is thrilled. Serena refers to it as "Hunter Elementary College." How do Alexander and the aunts slip past Ruby's preferences? "It is free," they say. "The most excellent school available and free." Ruby doesn't care about that, but for some reason, she relents. Serena becomes one of the group of fifteen children who are the first three-year-old group and some of the students will know each other more than sixty years later. The guardians nod thoughtfully in their silence. This place will hold her in the years to come.

When Serena is four, she and Ruby and Alexander go to Lake Otsego to stay at an inn near a camp Alexander worked with doing theater when he was young. The lake has a dark scent, liquid full of captivating secrets, shadowy even when light rolls on the surface, something hidden and embracing. The rocks near the shore are a sleek brown and slippery; Serena sits on them and slides a little back and forth, feet in the water. She can't really swim yet, but Alex tows her in a huge black inner tube with its own interesting rubbery scent, hot in the sun. He swims smoothly, assertively, breathing evenly. At the end of the first week, swimming with Serena, he is only days away from the moment when his heart will crash, his breath almost leaving him forever. The guardians hover, their presence a whisper; even softer than that.

On the night of Alexander's heart attack, Serena wakes in the small hours, the waking for her an unusual occurrence. She is in the room she shares with her parents, but, even in the moonless dark, she sees that something is different. Only one person is in her parents' bed and she moves very quietly to see who it is. Not her mother. The sleeping woman is a friend they have at the inn, a bulky, cheerful soul who likes to squeeze Serena's arm affectionately. Serena stands absolutely still and stares through the dark, willing the woman to wake, but nothing happens. She is afraid to touch her and wake her. She is as afraid as she has ever been, stunned and disbelieving and sick to her stomach. Where are her parents? Sometimes her father leaves earlier than expected to go back to the city, though that was not the plan this night, and then Ruby is there, alone in the bed. Ruby almost always awakens if Serena stands near her, even if Serena is silent. In the chilly dark, with its damp lake air, Serena turns and goes back to her bed and gets under the covers, curling as tight as she can. She thinks she is too afraid to sleep, that she will just wait till morning to understand what has happened, but after a few minutes of panic, she falls asleep, a sudden oblivion dropping around her. The guardians circle her, humming soundlessly. It has begun.

The next morning, a clear sunny day, Serena is awake early and the woman, whose name is Arlene, is already dressed and waiting for her. She sits on the edge of Serena's bed.

"I know it's strange to have me here," she begins. Then she stops.

"Where are my parents?"

Clearly Arlene is struggling. "Your father wasn't feeling well and he went to see the doctors at the hospital to help him." It is the best she can do.

This sounds completely crazy. Is this woman crazy? Why at night? Why a hospital? Hospitals are for sick people. Serena's family is full of doctors—her own father is a doctor—and she knows all about hospitals. Her cousin Michael, a heart doctor, is often called away at family gatherings. "Call for you, Doctor." That moment is always solemn and Michael gets his bag and leaves promptly. "That man never gets any real rest," one of the aunts will say, always respectfully.

"Why is my mother there?"

"She went to keep him company." Arlene knows she is floundering badly, that this is a very smart child and she is not fooled at all. "Let's get dressed and have some breakfast," she says. "Maybe we can find out more." She knows this is cowardly, but she is lost; lost in her worry for Alexander, who is cherished by her, as he is by so many people, lost in her inept half-truths.

Serena gets up and dresses, not because she is hungry but because she thinks someone else must have better information than Arlene and she can find out more at breakfast.

But, no, the story is pretty much the same in the yellow dining room full of breakfast smells: cinnamon toast and hot eggs and bacon and coffee, which Serena is allowed a drop of in her milk. "Alexander was sick and the hospital is the only place to find a doctor at night," one woman offers. This sounds a little more plausible, but not much.

"When will they be back?" Serena asks.

"Soon. Mother will be back soon."

"But not my father?"

"We'll see."

There is nothing for Serena to do but move along through her day in a blur of fear mixed with ordinariness. Food, play, the sound of voices. She wades in an atmosphere that is filled with secrets; she floats through their sharp transparent edges, pierced by them and mistrustful of the adults' evasiveness. No one has ever left her without explanation, just disappeared. Except that her first experience of life *was* being left with no possibility of an explanation, since she was an infant, and her body remembers it, if her conscious mind cannot. She is desperate now to know the truth and horrified when she hears it. She goes swimming with Arlene, wearing her much loved blue ruffled suit and holding the inner tube as she floats near the shore; even in the water, the atmosphere of fear is with her. Even when she inhales the scent of the lake warmed by the sun, it is with her. Water plants slither around her legs, stroking her skin.

Serena is on her way back from the lake when an older woman stops her. The woman's face is tanned, red with heat and ripply with wrinkles. She is wearing a heavy black suit, which drips around her as she snaps off her bathing cap. Serena knows she is a doctor. Dr. Bernstein. Hannah. She shakes the cap at Serena as she speaks.

"Your father is a very sick man, little girl. Very sick. He's in the hospital, but who knows? A very sick man," she says again and then strides up the hill toward the inn. Serena stands absolutely still, her heart might be cracking, she thinks; it might split wide with its fast pounding, might fly into separate pieces. If that happened, would she die right there? For a while she simply stands on the grass, the sun striking her back.

That day, many of the guests hover near her, sit with her at meals, watch over her.

"Your mother will be here this evening," says Clara, the inn's owner. "This evening right after dinner." When Ruby arrives, running toward the inn from a strange car, Serena hurls herself against her mother's body and they hold each other fiercely.

"He will be all right," Ruby says. She says it over and over, half crooning. "The doctors are taking good care of him." They walk toward the wide porch together, holding hands. Ruby holds Serena on her lap in a rocking chair. "He was quite sick with his heart; it wasn't working right. They are helping him make it steady."

This is more or less true; it is as much as she can say to a four year old, even if this child is remarkable. Evening wind slides through the open porch, weaving in cool, moist air. Serena does not cry, just rocks slowly with Ruby holding her and waits. She knows there is more coming, Ruby isn't finished saying what she needs to say, all the words have not tipped out yet. The dark rises, bringing stars and the sharp curve of a waxing moon.

"I need to stay with him, near the hospital," Ruby says. Ah. This is the rest of it. "Leah will come tomorrow. She will stay here with you."

Serena nods. "When will you be here?"

"Every other day. The milk truck man will take me." Ruby doesn't drive.

"Can I visit?"

"I don't know, Serena. I'll ask. Sometimes they don't allow children into hospitals."

"Why? I'm quiet. It isn't something catching?"

"No, no it isn't. But sometimes hospitals have rules; usually they do. I know it makes no sense." Ruby hopes Alexander will be well enough to be seen, hopes they will let Serena come. This is not a child who does well with mysteries. (The rule that makes no sense.) She always wants to see, to know.

"Where are you living?"

"At a guest house. A very nice lady."

Actually, the lady seems suspicious and solicitous in a prying way, her too-white face surrounded by thinning gray hair, her light eyes small and eager, but Ruby knows she is not in the best frame of mind to judge character. The place is very clean and near the hospital, so she can walk there easily. Many years later, Ruby tells Serena she had a real paranoid episode about the guesthouse owner, thought she was spying on her. "Only time that ever happened," Ruby will say. "My own fear was so overwhelming." Serena will listen and think that Ruby is always a little paranoid. About a lot of things.

Serena does not ever tend toward paranoia, but in her later forties she will go through a brief—well, not so brief—months, really—of being afraid of things with sharp edges: knives, obviously, and glasses that she fears might break as she touches them, cutting her hands open, causing her to bleed wildly. She comes to imagine that even soft things, the edges of leaves, of certain flower petals, will become razor-like, dangerous. She has no idea, at the time, where these completely new thoughts have come from, though she is surrounded, suddenly, by friends and clients who are dying, their blood tainted with the AIDS virus, their bodies leaking and burning, their minds loosening and vague, their voices shrill and accusatory. Perhaps it was that, perhaps other things. The fears do not involve anxieties about people, their abrupt malice, or their dangerous behavior. No, it is that the physical world, even the world of beloved plants and trees, could become harmful. Serena copes as best she can during this time, holding herself carefully, appreciating moments of calm. Finally, she goes to speak with an old friend and colleague, but by then, that early spring, full of reddish green leaves and warm winds, she is almost well, though her stomach was sore for so long that she lost weight, in desperation ate spoonfuls of peanut butter to get calories, a strange first after years of eating meager meals. When it is over, she has shed some shining layer of her ego, her polish, been humbled in a way that adds to her deep appreciation of fragility and of resilience. The last image she has before the end of these hell visions is of her dear friend Marie, a Buddhist priest and beloved companion, who has died recently. Marie appears in her robes and opens a golden door, ushering Serena through, nodding as she swings the door wide.

"Is it over?" Serena asks. A question and a statement. Marie nods and nods again. Over.

✳ ❁ ✳

Aunt Leah arrives at the inn the next day, dressed for travel in a good dark summer dress. She moves into the room Serena shared with her parents and begins to "settle things down." She makes a plan for Serena's days, meals and swimming and a few walks. They talk seriously about Alexander and what might happen, though Serena is not thinking about death at all, just when he will be home and when she can see him, and certainly Leah does not mention it, does not want to consider it herself. In fact, he is recovering and Leah tells her this again and again, knowing it is true, at least for the moment. She teaches Serena how to tie her shoes, how to set the table, so Serena can help at meals. She is a great believer in the comfort of order, and indeed it is helpful. Serena is an active child, eager to please, eager to contribute something, to be included. Marion replaces Leah; they are going to take care of this situation, watch over Serena, stay close to their beloved brother, the charming handsome restless brother, a magical man. Their darling.

One afternoon, Marion takes Serena to the hospital. They are going to let Serena visit after all, just that day. She dresses Serena in a yellow dress, red sandals, puts her hair in bunches, that glossy dark heavy hair.

I had hair like that once, Marion thinks. Or maybe she says it out loud. They find Alexander sitting sideways on the bed, legs over the side, feet on the floor. His color is good and Serena doesn't know the effort it has taken for him to sit this way. They cannot hug, but Serena holds his legs, rests her cheek against them. "You are getting better? You are?"

"I am. Much better." Flowers fill the room, vases of summer flowers, picked by the young nurses, who all have crushes on Alexander.

Serena holds her father's hands. "I learned to tie my shoes," she says. "I learned to set the table." The hot careless sun shines through the window and onto Alexander's hands and Serena's. "Clara, the lady who owns the inn, says I am growing up very fast." Serena is clearly proud of this.

"You must be," says Alexander, knowing the many implications of Clara's observation.

And then the visit is over and Marion and Serena are back at the inn. Serena gets the tube and Marion takes her swimming, or watches as Serena swims. Marion is not a swimmer. The water whispers against Serena's body as she rocks in the tube. Ripples make small leaps and the light is bright on them. There is so much sun that it seems constant, pleasurable and steady, healing and oblivious; days of cloudless blue, or skies with just feathery wisps, the air moistened by the lake water. The heat lies against the cold layers of her fear; chill drifting forms that have begun to inhabit her. Serena will remember the sad month as a time of warmth on her back, comforting and sure, a time of brightness and formal shadows, an invitation to a moment of sweet coolness. Tall yellow flowers bloomed around the inn, their blossoms opening quickly, just as Alexander went into the hospital. Just that week, there are nodding groups of them, all subtle shades of yellow, with frilled cups. A photograph taken then will remain in Serena's album, still there when she is old. She is standing in front of a group of those flowers, wearing a sunsuit, her hair dark and her mouth trying to smile, to please the photographer, whoever it was. (Not Ruby; Ruby didn't take pictures, ever.) It was already important not to let the grown-ups know her feelings, already a time to be brave and sturdy. The sadness floats in Serena, darker than the deepest part of the nearby lake, making a permanent residence for itself, slick and unfathomable.

August melts and the time to return to the city for school, for both Serena and Ruby approaches. There is some talk of Alexander recovering enough to go with them, but it does not happen that way; he is still too weak, though progress has been made. They pack to go home alone. Serena has never been separated from her father for long, except, of course, just after her birth. They have always been together, these three. Ruby and Serena pack, Serena folding her clothes just so— Anna will be unpacking—and because the neat shapes soothe her. The day before they leave, Serena goes to the hospital again, but this time they will not let her upstairs, for reasons never explained, so she walks in the large garden with one of the nurses, who holds her hand.

"He will be home soon," the nurse says and then, to entertain her, tells Serena the names of the glorious flowers. "Zinnias," she says, pointing to the slender oval petals forming clustered circles in white and orange and even green, their stalks stiff, holding the blooms upright. Phlox (the sweetest fragrance), salmon colored geraniums, golden calendulas, flamboyant crimson roses, petunias in glowing candy stripes and so on through the beds of plantings. The big bush with periwinkle blooms is a hydrangea; their heavy heads pull the stems into a curve and Serena touches one gently. Butterflies are everywhere, wings flashing blue and gold. Serena loves the flowers and pays as close attention as she can, all the while looking up to see if she can spot her father at one of the windows. Finally, the nurse stops and indicates his window, but he is not there.

"Goodbye," Serena says, knowing he cannot hear her.

Ruby and Serena return to the city and the August heat, less than comforting in the city streets. But Serena is happy to be home. Anna holds her close when she comes to ready Serena for school, even though it is a few days early, to check her school clothes with her. The house is already clean and evidence of polish is everywhere; the brass lamps shine, the wood surfaces are fragrant with the paste wax Anna uses. Everything has been done to welcome them in the midst of this terrible sadness that no one quite articulates. Ruby has pooled the energies of her will and her formidable commitment, perhaps drawn other energies to her; the strength of it is contained but vast. If there had been a common understanding of a black hole and its properties that would have been an apt description: pulling in, pulling in, nothing released, ever. Forever. Her will vibrates around the belief that

Alexander will live. Nothing else is possible. Not at all. It is as strong as her will to have Serena be safely born, perhaps stronger. Years later, after Alexander has died, the psychiatrist Ruby and Alexander saw told Ruby that he thought her will had kept Alexander alive longer than anyone had expected and Ruby believed it. She knew it was true. She said so. Her belief had kept him alive.

Serena goes back to school and enters the four-year-old group, her teacher a large-boned woman with a broad, somewhat stooped back and eyes that are bright and aware without being piercing. She walks with a slight sideways turn, one shoulder angled down. She has taught this age group for many years and is skillful and kind. The class rests in her calm, these difficult fours, often uneasy in their edgy development, but balanced and creative in her classroom. She does not draw special attention to Serena, but knows the situation at home and watches carefully for signs of distress, which she expects will emerge. But Serena is genuinely happy to be in school, with her friends; her connections to people interwoven with her well being, lifting her spirits, gladdening her heart. As an adult, she will explore her yearning for connection and wrestle with issues about her needs, but beyond the slippery neurotic threads and biting fears of loss, of being abandoned, which she sees—addresses—sometimes fails to address—and with which she wrestles repeatedly, she always knows that this happiness connects her to the divine. Miss Kowalski, watching, wonders where Serena's feelings about her father are: the sadness, the anger. Not in her play. Not in her drawings. She considers asking to speak with Ruby, but dismisses the idea and simply waits.

Indeed, where are her feelings? Alexander comes and goes, sometimes at home, sometimes in the hospital. He is thinner, but looks surprisingly robust, his skin clear, his hazel eyes lively, even as his heart trembles, unreliable and weary. Serena knows how worried the grown-ups are; does she force herself to seem happy to care for them? Not really. Not consciously, the way she did when he was first ill, when she was in shock and ripped with fear. She is just in her life the way it is; that was how she started, at birth. Somewhere, she remembers that. Even as the months pass, even as Alexander is clearly not going to get better once and for all, will never really recover, Serena doesn't yield to her sadness and certainly not to her anger; truly, they are now beyond her reach. It would be closer to the truth to say that she has no path into them; she cannot yield to them, they are beyond conscious retrieval. When she leaves home at seventeen and goes into therapy—which Ruby had not allowed her to do, saying she was too young—this despite the fact that Ruby herself worked with a psychiatrist—Serena begins to find her tears, lost for so long inside her and by now as frozen as the icy day she was born. When the therapist asks if she is angry, Serena feels blank. Angry? No. She is rarely angry.

Perhaps angry that her mother survived and her father died? Of course not. Ruby has cornered the market on rage. To be overtly angry at Ruby is unthinkable to Serena. Literally.

Is it then a surprise when, at twelve or so, when her hormones begin to change, when her body shifts into curves and softness, when her little girl shape melts and a new one blooms, she launches an attack. Her buried feelings erupt as a merciless war on her own flesh, fed by the cultural poisons she has ingested. And the lurching upward pull of those old emotions now express themselves, as the need to torment herself about her aliveness, her disgusting flesh. Her rage and fears now focus on her body and its treachery in its push toward life. She does not want a peach bosom, or round thighs. She wants hard slender legs and neat delicate breasts. But no, it is not that easy. Not that simple. She gets so much praise for her looks and she loves the praise, but hates herself all the same, and the hatred is active and punishing and aching, a streaming misery. But that is yet to come. At four and then five, Serena is happy in her own body, safe in its health and vitality.

The spring that Serena is five, an unusually bright one, with early green and skies that float with blue, she comes down with chicken pox and is covered with itchy bumps and calamine lotion. Everyone in the house has had it, so there is no danger to them, but they are miserable watching her. It is during one of Alex's stays at home and Serena moves into her parents' room for the day and spends time in her mother's bed; she and Alex keep each other company. They sing Gilbert and Sullivan, and Union songs: "I dreamed I saw Joe Hill last night," they sing, "Alive as you and me." Alex plays his guitar and a warming wind blows through a window, open a bit to let the fresh air in. Anna changes the sheets over and over again, washes Serena, replaces the calamine, feeds everyone soup and mashed potatoes with butter, and Serena and Alex eat Hershey's kisses and dry peppermints sweetly dusted with powdered sugar that Anna always keeps in her pockets.

When summer comes again, Ruby does not want to travel. Alex is too weak—so they stay in the city. Alex's brother Joseph rents an air conditioner for Alex and Ruby's bedroom, this in a time when individual homes do not have air conditioners. Everything is done for Alex's comfort. The family is in and out of the apartment, visiting, the aunts cooking. Ruby is grateful for them and resents them and the implication that she will not do these things correctly: cook delicacies for Alex, be knowledgeable about his comfort. They are right and also completely mistaken. It is Ruby's being that comforts her husband, her sureness, her untamed unfailing purpose.

Serena goes to day camp, which she dislikes, except that she learns to float and paddle in the oily chlorine swells of the camp pool, her feet dipped in cold Clorox solution before each swim. Later, at home, nothing seems to remove the nasty smell. Anna takes her to the playground, where she can play under the sprinkler.

Then camp and the playground are suddenly forbidden. A polio epidemic has struck New York City. Pictures of children in iron lungs appear. It is the first experience Serena has of fear for her own body, save that initial one, that one on the day of her birth in a blizzard. Since camp is now out of the question and even the playground sprinklers are forbidden, Serena then spends summer hours in the tub, under the shower, water spilling onto her through the heat. She longs for the lake, but says nothing, knowing it will upset her parents, which she now wants to avoid at all costs. She is carefully compliant. Though Ruby asks what she needs, is attentive, knows what Serena is doing and why, she cannot help her daughter, even as she sees these patterns forming and worries that they will shape Serena indelibly, which they do. But Serena's determination bursts through and though she wishes to please people and is not defiant, she is resolute and, later, in adolescence, sly when she needs to be. Innocent and crafty, is how she will think of it herself, in a self-punishing way.

In New York, in the hospital again, Serena is not allowed to see her father. He is at Mount Sinai, a serious hospital with no gardens and no children, a bulk of brick and heaviness. Serena repeatedly asks Ruby why she can't visit, as she did when he was hospitalized in the country. "Why? I'm older now. I'm five, that's old enough. I'm not going to catch a disease, it isn't catching, is it?" She is determined to make her point and see her father.

Ruby to Alexander: "Can't they bend the rules a little? Serena would be perfectly quiet, you know that."

"I know it, but the hospital regulations are very rigid."

"Alex, you know so many doctors on the staff. Colleagues. Wouldn't they do you a favor?" Alexander is the kind of man for whom people gladly do favors; they offer them before being asked. But he seems certain that he cannot make this work.

Ruby sighs, almost resigned. "All right, we will do the best we can. But I think it's inhuman." Ordinarily, she would push harder, but she has vowed not to push in any way, Alexander's energy is too precious, conserving it is of primary importance.

"They are very strict," Ruby says miserably, again, to Serena. She knows that Serena will be quiet, make no disturbance. They go over and over this ground, Serena desperate to visit, to be included.

"Everyone goes," she says, sadly. "The whole family. Can't you convince them?" She is unaccustomed to any situation where Ruby holds no power. These doctors are defying her mother?

"I can't, Serena. The hospital makes the rules."

One very cold Saturday morning in the middle of December, Anna takes Serena to her apartment to bake cookies together. Crusty ice is on the streets, remnants of a snowfall, but the sun is warm on the kitchen floor and Anna stirs the coals in the stove and adds new ones.

"Careful, Dolly, remember it's so hot." She takes Serena through the apartment, as she always does. Two bedrooms, one following the other, bedspreads, light green chenille, carefully smoothed. A wooden cross hangs above each bed. The parlor, the front room, with a blue sofa and two plushy chairs edged in dark wood. White sheer curtains at the window, the winter light pressing through, a plum colored carpet with a garland of darker purple flowers in the center. Everything shining within an inch of its life. Then back to the kitchen, where Anna lays out the baking things, carefully lining them up on the table. She drapes a large white apron around Serena to cover her good clothes. Serena stands and watches eagerly. Anna does everything by feel, no recipe, no measuring spoons, but she shows Serena each move.

"This much flour, after it's sifted." She opens her hand, scooping several times. "A little more, if you do it, your hands are smaller than mine." Ruby does not cook, though Alexander does and Anna is determined that Serena will. All of the aunts are excellent cooks, proud of it and quietly mean about Ruby, who has none of these skills, though she tried when she was first married and Alexander laughed. It was gentle laughter, but still. Ruby instantly gave up cooking—permanently.

"This is how it should feel, the dough. Feel it. Just like this, a little spongy, no sticky." The dough rolled thin, they cut magical shapes: crescents and stars and perfect circles. Spades and a bell. Chopped walnuts go on top, and cinnamon. Then onto floured cookie sheets and into the oven. Anna's cookies are prized by anyone who has ever tasted them, light, the sweetness perfect, dissolving. Buttery. Everyone asks for them at holiday time.

"Anna-cookies? Are they here?" This batch is special for Alexander. "Dr. Weiss." Anna never calls Serena's parents by their first names. Last names, or, "Your mama, your papa." Serena and Anna are going to take this box of cookies to the hospital.

It has been planned that Anna will give them to Ruby, who will be waiting. Then Anna and Serena will go to the hospital and stand across the street from it, their backs to Central Park. They will look up at one of the windows and wave.

While they wait for the cookies to bake and cool, Anna makes them lunch. Goulash, already cooked, with cut potatoes that are dark with fragrant gravy and have just enough crispness in the skin to need a firm bite. There is warm bread and butter with canned peaches for dessert, plus a few still-hot cookies carefully lifted off the sheet. The cookies cool quickly though, and by the time Anna has done the dishes, with Serena helping, it is time to bundle up and go to the hospital. The cookies are packed in a red tin with Christmas scenes, wax paper between each layer. Serena carries them carefully as they ride the bus together, through a wind that blows so hard the bus sways slightly. Anna's hand in her black wool glove rests on Serena's hand in her red mittens, but they don't talk.

When they arrive at the hospital where Alexander is, Ruby is waiting in the lobby and Anna gives her the cookies. Ruby hugs Serena and tells Serena and Anna where to stand. "Across the street," she says. "Just there, in front of that bench. Then you can look right up at his window. Third floor. I'll stand there first and wave my orange scarf. And thank you for this, Anna. Also, thanks for the cookies."

"They haven't changed their minds about letting me in?" asks Serena, who has been hoping that someone would relent, there in the heavy stone building with its dark rigid rules.

"No, honey. Nothing has changed."

"Can Dr. Weiss have some?" Anna asks.

"Not really, but I'll slip him one. Not a holiday without your cookies." Or without your love, Ruby thinks. How would she manage without Anna?

Anna and Serena position themselves carefully across the street, their backs to the frozen park. Serena is dressed in her heavy plaid coat and a wool hat, mittens and the dreaded leggings. Nicely dressed little girls do not wear pants in these years. Anna is bundled up, too, her black brimmed hat held by an elastic band under her bun and skewered by a long hatpin for good measure. The wind rattles tree branches, blows beneath their coats and up their sleeves, merciless beneath a gray, solid sky. The light is low, but somehow also sharp in the middle of this winter afternoon. Serena imagines her whole world rocking with the implacable wind; her father unjustly out of reach, clearly ill. Ruby appears at the third floor window, waving her scarf, bringing Serena's attention back. At first, there is no one and, finally, a man appears. They cannot see his face, but he is surely waving. Serena waves and then jumps as high as she can. "Daddy!" she calls, and then louder, to be heard above the wind, "Daddy!" And then he is gone.

"Come, Dolly, it's so cold on you."

"One more minute. One more."

Anna stands behind Serena to break the wind and they wait another minute or so. Finally, they turn down the avenue toward the cross-town bus. Few people are out; they pass only one or two hurrying women, bundled up and moving as quickly as possible. It will be another week before Alexander comes home.

When Alexander does return, his many friends visit, always sitting as close to him as they can in a ladder back chair next to his bed. The whole family visits, though not all at once, so as not to tire him; they bring food and flowers and their sad veiled hopeful love. Appearing strong, assuring themselves and each other that he is looking better, isn't he? Dr. Gerard comes regularly. The visitors cuddle Serena when she allows it, which isn't always. Sometimes she feels stiff, surprises herself by wanting to pull away. When they are alone, she watches her father cut Camels in half and stack the halves neatly in his cigarette case.

"Why are you doing that?" She can see his concentration and his unhappiness.

"To smoke less; it's not good for me."

"Then stop," Serena says, clearly puzzled. She is frightened that he is hurting himself when things are clearly so fragile, when he is already hurting in some way out of his control. She cannot verbalize this, but she knows it with certainty. Her father, whom she trusts, is hurting himself further. This is piercing, a moment that buries itself in Serena's heart and returns for many years; she will feel frantic watching people she loves harming themselves and feel desperate to stop them. More years will pass until she realizes that she cannot.

"I am trying," Alexander says. "I am not too successful here." Rueful, accepting?

At Christmas, there is a big tree; before, Alexander had gotten small ones for Serena and put them on a table in her room—Hanukkah bushes, he says—though the family is in no way religious—but this tree goes to the ceiling and is near one of the windows in the living room. Did Alex order it, and the glorious ornaments? Surely, Ruby did not; it is not something that would occur to her, trees and shiny globes and dripping tinsel. She would not ignore it out of some mean withholding; it simply doesn't reside in her awareness as a possibility. The dry air in the apartment carries the scent of balsam from a faraway forest. Anna puts water in dishes on the radiators and fills up the tree stand. She watches carefully, even though there are no candles on this tree, as there were on the trees of her childhood. Still, careful, careful with dry trees. Ruby plays the piano and they sing carols, their voices joining the thousands of voices singing, celebrating.

On Christmas Eve, Serena is blissful in a long red flannel nightgown, its soft folds falling almost to the floor, a storybook nightgown, this a gift from Marion.

On the afternoon of Christmas Day there is hot coffee and Anna's cookies and friends and family visiting; there is sweet music as Ruby plays carols again and everyone sings. Alexander is up awhile, sitting in the living room with Serena on his lap. People come and go, garlands of loving people. Rebirth of the light.

The days lengthen minutely as Alexander's energy drifts, fails increasingly quickly as he lies in bed on the days after Christmas, winter sun falling on his blanketed legs, the gate of light swinging low in the afternoons. Ruby usually counts the days from the winter solstice until the beginning of spring, but this year, she doesn't even think of it. When Ruby wakes at night and watches him, Alexander's breath seems unsteady, tiny gaps in rhythm as his chest rises and falls in the shadows. The sacrament of breath, wobbling slowly.

The guardians are near Serena when she sleeps; sometimes they appear in her dreams as flowers, swaying blossoms in vivid pink and the palest yellow, delphinium blue and purple streaked with gold. Once, they merge themselves into the form of a large orange cat with soft thick fur and the cat curls around Serena's legs, rests in her lap when she sits with it in a field. The guardians cannot change the situation, but they can nourish Serena.

All through the fall and now, as winter comes, Ruby goes to teach and comes home, or goes to the hospital if Alex is there and sometimes, when she is weary in the deepest, most terrible way, she will allow herself time to look at paintings. She sits with Monet's *Water Lilies*, with Van Gogh's *Starry Night*, with all of Monet's "Cathedrals," in their shifting blue and gold and rose, their capture of light and therefore of time. For a little while, she is comforted. Serena outgrows all her clothes that year; her dresses are too short, her shoes tight. For the first time, she is the fourth in line in school, in the size-places order.

Sometimes Serena wakes in the swimming, three a.m. part of the night; she usually sleeps deeply, dreams unrolling in vivid colors, their themes curious and enchanting. Like Ruby, she values sleep and dreams and they all share dreams, Serena and Ruby and Alexander. But these nights, Serena wakes and sees Alexander standing in her doorway, three dimensional, but diaphanous, wearing his ordinary seersucker robe, blue and white striped. His left elbow rests against the doorjamb. His right arm is straight at his side. She can see his smile in the flickering New York night, as moving traffic stretches lights across the ceiling when the cars move and stop and move again.

"Daddy," she says softly; then more loudly. "Daddy?"

27

There is no answer, which does not bother her; she realizes that in some way he is there and also asleep in his room across the hall. His presence, in this new way, is comforting, rather than odd. There and not there. And no words. Perhaps the guardians are near him, guiding him in his light body, helping him to watch over Serena as he travels in his sleep while his body struggles with its faltering heart; perhaps they split time, open the gateway to multiple dimensions. Serena watches the doorway until Alexander vanishes and then she goes back to sleep. The memory of her father, watching her with love, transparent and vibrantly present, stays with her, a steady treasure.

At the very beginning of January, Marion takes Serena to see the Van Gogh exhibit at the Met. On the way, Serena spots a funeral cortège waiting outside a church on Madison Avenue. One long black car in the front, with a high roof and odd side windows.

"What is that?" she asks Marion. "What is that car? And the others? Why are they all parked there?" She seems intensely curious, focused on the cars and the hearse. Marion is silent for a moment and then she lies. How can she explain this to Serena and why is she so interested?

"It's a church ceremony," she says firmly. "I don't know what it is. We're Jewish."

"I just want to look. Maybe I can ask someone," Serena says, ever curious and persistent.

"No, I think it's private. Come, we're on our way to the museum. We're really close and it's cold." She takes Serena's arm, feeling her reluctance to leave without the information she wants.

The exhibit is a great success and Marion buys Serena a print of a peaceful field of wheat with a hay wagon in it. "I like the one with the black bird," Serena suggests. Marion says no and they get the other one. She frames it and the scene hangs in Serena's room for years. A trophy from that strange day.

The week before Alexander dies, Serena is at home with Anna early in the afternoon; something at school, maybe a teachers' conference. Ruby is still at work. Alexander is in the hospital again. Serena sits on one of the small chairs in her room and weeps, suddenly and relentlessly, rocking herself.

"I want my daddy," she cries. "Please, please. I want my daddy." Anna runs to her, but cannot comfort her. Nothing can stop her sobs. It is the only time Serena sees Anna alarmed, though Anna tries to keep her face calm as she goes to the phone. She calls Ruby's school and says she must talk to Mrs. Weiss and when Ruby is finally on the phone, she says that Serena is crying and crying. Nothing will stop her. Ruby leaves school as fast as possible and takes a taxi home. She holds Serena, who is still crying, and finally the tears stop. Serena's small face is swollen; her belly and chest are quivering. She clings to her mother.

"I'm sorry," she says. "I upset everyone."

"Oh, sweetheart, no. Don't be sorry. You're so sad," Ruby says.

"Cocoa, we will make cocoa," says Anna. "No sorry, Dolly. No. Mama's here."

Why does Serena cry, just that day and no other? Has she dreamt something? Surely, she knows, without being conscious of it. Surely.

Then there is mystery. Until she is a young woman, Serena believes that her father died in the hospital, in that bulky and unyielding brick building; that his last moments were spent there. That he was alone in the room facing Fifth Avenue, the very room he was in when Anna took her and they stood across the street and waved. When she held the box of fragile cookies and hoped, again, to be admitted, to go through the heavy doors. At some point—but how does the discussion come about—Ruby tells her that he died at home, in his bed.

"I thought you knew that," Ruby says. "He was here."

Serena feels relief and then curiosity mingled with distress. She remembers that he went to the hospital shortly after Christmas, but does not remember that he returned home after a brief stay there. The memories must tear apart and reconfigure themselves. That he was not alone is a relief; that he was only behind the closed door to her parents' room, his death so close to her, is shocking. How has she been mistaken? When she remembers all the facts surrounding Alexander's death in light of this new information, she understands that this could have been the only way. And she has always remembered her own version of the events very clearly; they are part of her body as she grows. They are in her cells, present and formidable, with their own rhythm. But she had misplaced this piece—how? Deliberately? The memories she has had are misshapen and she has never noticed the incongruence. How did her father's death really happen? Serena lets the memories jumble and shift, pulling at her as they move, as the mystery releases and invites her in.

Alexander dies at home on a frigid Sunday on the eighth of January. Anna is there that morning and when she goes to check on him, opening the door softly in case he is asleep, she finds him, unmoving, his head turned slightly toward the sunny window. Anna understands immediately that he has died; even without touching him, she was sure. In her early years, most people died at home. She recognizes the emptiness, the seeming weightlessness. But she goes to him and touches his wrist, feels for a pulse, watches the stillness of his chest. She crosses herself and goes to get Ruby.

Serena must have been playing in her room, just across the hall. So near to him. Then her Uncle Mark arrives, dressed in his gray wool overcoat and a darker gray fedora. He is holding his gloves in his hand as he comes into Serena's room, dressed like that, for the outdoors and Ruby is with him. He has come to take Serena to the special children's films at the Trans-Lux. Just enough time if they hurry, a cab is waiting downstairs. Ruby is holding Serena's coat and hat and mittens.

"No leggings," Serena says.

"No. No leggings," Ruby answers.

Serena might have been suspicious; this has never happened before, this hurried departure, her uncle just there, so suddenly, but she is not. Or is not conscious of it, if she is. She puts on her hat and coat and mittens and off they go. To the movies.

What would have happened next? The doctor, the ambulance? The body taken, as Serena sits in the theater, watching cartoons, to which she does not respond. Her uncle has gone "to make some calls," leaving her in the care of the matron, an older woman who supervised what was then called "the children's section." She has never been seated alone at the movies and is conscious of sitting correctly, hoping she is doing the right thing, waiting until the show is over and her uncle returns. The sweet stuffy air falls around her, time stretches, skitters sideways, the images flash on the screen and eventually her Uncle Mark comes to sit with her, just as the show ends. Then they go to his house, to Marion and Mark and her cousin Beth's, to dinner and a story and then to sleep. Ruby is not there, but Serena often stays with her aunt and uncle and to her it is almost as familiar as home. She has no special dreams and night pales into morning.

The next day, the day of the funeral, the family arrives at Marion's, their faces full of broken sorrow, their bodies carrying the torn fragments of their world. They are dressed in dark wools, heavy coats. The beloved youngest. Dead. They do not tell Serena where they are going, what has happened, but they hug her in deep frightened ways, their bodies feeling both stiff and shaky. Ruby and Alexander have consulted with their eminent psychiatrist about whether Serena should go to the funeral, should there be one. The wise man said no. No, she is too young; she should not remember her father that way. It is an informed and terrible decision that will affect Serena into her old age. Sociable and resilient, she should have been included in the circle of family and friends. Should have seen the tears, the many loving faces in their varying degrees of sadness, of trauma. She will be anxious, always, about whether she is included or not. Anxious in small ways, social ways, in deeper ways of needing to be held in a circle of love, not afraid the love will vanish, but that the person will. Especially afraid with men, knowing how easy it would be for them to vanish into death, into gone. Into nowhere at all.

Oddly, on this day she is quiet, doesn't ask about anything; the message, the unspoken demand to be silent is so strong. One aunt holds her and says, "No, darling, no," very softly. But Serena hears her, asks only with her eyes to be told something, anything, but nothing is forthcoming and the grown-ups leave together, to attend a funeral where hundreds of people arrive to pay their respects and say goodbye, to touch each other gently and try to believe that their beloved friend is truly gone. Anna stays at Marion's with Serena and Beth. They pretend they are having a normal day. The sky is silvery, with impenetrable layers of clouds and no sun at all.

The cold rivers cradle the island, ships move on the Hudson, pushing against the icy waves; bare trees rattle along the side street. Some sparrows land on Beth's windowsill, where there is a small bird feeder, and Serena stares at them, wonders how they stay warm in this January wind, wishes she could hold one.

The next day, Ruby comes for lunch. Afterward, a bit later in the afternoon, she takes Serena into Beth's room and closes the door. They sit curled on Beth's bed, on the blue and pink plaid spread. Sun in the windows, so the sparrows must be warmer, thinks Serena gratefully. The mirror on the closet door shines, the maple furniture is glossy, the yellow walls bright. Steam heat sighs and the pipes bang softly. Ruby sighs. Begins.

"Serena, you know your father loves you."

Serena nods, yes, of course, of course. She slides her finger along the soft bedspread, back and forth. She looks at her mother's dark eyes.

"He would never want to leave you or do anything to hurt you, ever."

Serena waits.

"Sometimes things happen that we can't control, that we don't want, that we wish had not happened."

There is more, more story, but later Serena does not remember it exactly. It is in the same vein.

Then, finally, "Your father died, Serena. His body was too sick to go on. He didn't want to leave you, but he had no choice. You understand it was not something deliberate." Ruby is clear, not crying, steady. She does not hug Serena, just talks quietly, with purpose.

"I understand."

"We were at the funeral yesterday."

"Like the one Aunt Marion and I saw?"

Ruby remembers Marion telling her about the cortège in front of the church, half lies, some truth, but Serena must have understood.

"Yes, something like that."

Does Serena ask why she couldn't come? Maybe. Maybe she does not. What she does is get up and wash her hands, which she had forgotten to do before lunch. She stands at the open bathroom door, the water running. She turns the water off carefully. Marion comes and stands with her.

"You can cry, Serena. We all cried, your mother and all the grown-ups."

"I don't want to cry," Serena says. She is a big girl, almost six. Her tears have frozen, their icy body far away where she cannot reach it. Thirteen years will pass before she cries for her father, though she cries for other things.

Alexander, gone into never and forever, his bones resting beneath heavy trees in an old cemetery; his parents and his grandparents are buried there, somewhere on the border between Brooklyn and Queens, a large parcel of land with small rolling hills behind a high black metal fence. It must have looked like country once, when the plots were purchased, when Alexander's parents carefully selected a burial ground for the family. It is roomy between the graves, well kept. It is a place where Ruby never goes, nor does Serena and she will not see her father's grave until she is her twenties. The family visits sometimes, puts stones on the graves, as a remembrance of their visit, but perhaps Serena is never invited? Included. Perhaps Ruby has said she doesn't want Serena there. Alexander lies in his coffin, rolled in the seasons, yet paradoxically separated from their rhythm, isolated.

Serena returns to school after a week at home—a week she resents. She wants to see her friends, to hear their voices and hold her ordinary life. Large baskets arrive at the house in a relentless stream, pale lavender and silver streaked, with tall curved handles; they contain jams and cookies, fancy breads and candies. They are wrapped in different colors of cellophane and Ruby will not touch them, though Serena is fascinated. Anna puts them on top of the piano, then underneath, when they run out of space. They have a somber presence, sentries bearing such sweet contents. No one eats anything from them, Serena taking her cues from Ruby. She just looks at them hopefully, without touching. Piles of letters rest in front of the door every morning. None are opened, though Ruby keeps them, and when she is eight, Serena finds them in a shoebox. She takes the box into the living room and sits alone opening them. Laments fall out, condolences, stories about Alexander, written with love. Ruby has gone back to teach right away. Anna comes every day, steeped in her own way of coping: her church, her memories of light on wide fields and rough stone bridges, the comfort of her family. Perhaps other things entirely.

When Serena does return to school, some of the children are especially solicitous, kind. One small girl with brilliant red curls offers an explanation to a small group gathered around Serena.

"We need to be gentle with Serena because her father died," the child says quietly. Serena is firm in her response.

"I'm fine," she says, time and again and again. She does not want pity; she cannot bear to be different in this way, her longing is to be ordinary, but now that is lost. She is not part of a real family; the magic circle of three has vanished.

One day early in the spring, Serena finds a dead sparrow when the class is at Mother Goose Playground. She lifts it gently and buries it under a tree, scraping the earth away, digging hard with her fingers until the hole is deep enough. She is desperate to understand what happens when the dead are buried. She waits, bides her time. She tells no one. Every day, she reminds herself where the tree is and when autumn comes, she returns with great excitement, an almost prayerful hope. Her friend John wants to see what she is doing but she says solemnly that it is private and something in her voice touches him. He leaves her alone. She digs again at the burial place, digs and digs, deeper than she knows the sparrow was buried, but nothing remains, not even a feather. The hollow bones have gone into the earth.

The grave is empty.

On the way home from the playground, Serena and John hold hands; they pass a tall woman with hair like chrysanthemum fluff, an apricot colored halo. She is slender, walking quickly, holding the leash of a poodle with sculpturally clipped fur that is almost the same color as her hair. The children look at each other and then back at the woman. John tries not to laugh. They both shrug worldly six-year-old shrugs. They pass manicured doorways along Fifth Avenue, polished brass lamps, sleek black grille work on the doors. Several doormen they know from frequent school trips to the playground wave and nod, hats at a smart angle. Leaves fall and whisper on the pavement. Serena gathers her courage.

"What happens when people are buried?" she asks John. He seems a good choice of someone to ask, he loves science—this could be something scientific—and he's a close friend. She does not think he will laugh, or be shocked, and she is right.

"I'm not sure," he says. He is quiet a moment, suspecting that this is about Serena's father. "At my grandma's funeral last month, they said, 'ashes to ashes, dust to dust,' so maybe that's, I don't know, connected?" The words struck him and he had asked his mother about them, but she was sad and too preoccupied to say much. "Could it be dust? It couldn't be ashes, they aren't burning."

"I guess so," Serena says. They reach the school and that is the end of the conversation.

Later, at home, Serena decides to ask Ruby the same question. Dusk is falling from the mysterious place it hides and then appears nightly. Serena knows this is not true, but likes to imagine it that way: concealed darkness that appears rhythmically, earlier and earlier as the weather cools and the year comes to a close. Clouds are deep lavender over Central Park, streaky and layered with gray shadow. She and Ruby are in the living room, reading; just that year, Serena has learned to read a book cover to cover by herself. They often spend time together this way, reading and then talking. Ruby is wearing an old, green wool skirt, but she has taken off her blouse and wears a yellow housecoat on top. Serena changed her clothes when she came home from school because that is what Anna has taught her. School clothes are to be preserved. She wears jeans and a sweater and, because Anna is not there, she is barefoot. "No barefooty," Anna says. "You'll catch cold." But she likes the feeling of the different textures of floor—carpet and smooth wood and linoleum, depending where she is. And she has never caught a cold because her feet were bare.

"Mommy, what happens when people are dead and buried?"

Ruby is startled, puts down her book on Matisse, looks at Serena's bright, hopeful eyes regarding her.

"I think it depends on how they are buried," she says, stalling a little for time. She knows it does depend on the manner of burial, but without thinking about it carefully, she is not sure she knows much more than that.

"I mean my father," Serena says clearly. Her voice is steady, a little louder than normal. "I asked John from school and he said something about ashes and dust. That's what they said at his grandmother's funeral. Does that mean he has turned to dust?"

How much of what she really knows does Ruby want to tell Serena? Does she want to talk about skeletons? She knows bones last a long time and that there are other processes first, before the skeleton emerges. But bones in a casket, the flesh desiccated? What happens when the body is sealed away in a coffin? Who knows? He was embalmed against Ruby's wishes, although she was told it was the law, and the coffin was open, uncommon at Jewish funerals, which infuriated her, made her wild at the thought of the terrible intrusion, her beloved husband exposed in that way, the privacy of his death exposed.

"So many people want to see his face one last time," said the family. And the funeral director agreed.

"That is not his face," Ruby said angrily, but they prevailed. She was too devastated to fight, a rare situation in her life, but she refused to stand at the coffin, refused to look at all. That was part of the reason she did not have Serena come to the funeral, in addition to the advice of her psychiatrist. That open coffin, cradling deadness manicured to look like life. Still life. A still life.

I am going to be cremated, Ruby thinks. Burial in a coffin is ghastly. I am planning to go up in flames. Definitely. I wish I could have a funeral pyre. Not surprising, for Ruby.

Ruby considers what to say. She takes her time.

Elsewhere in the building—a vertical village, Alex called it—mothers are cooking dinner, the heavy food of the 50s for those who could afford it. Plump lamb chops brown, steaks hiss under broilers, roasts rolled and then tied tight with white string turn juicy in ovens. Frozen green beans and bright peas bubble in boiling water. The children drink glasses of cold milk. Ruby imagines their calm lives, their intact families, though she knows this is partly fantasy, everyone has troubles. But it is relative. These mothers are not thinking of skeletons, of the bodily remains of a dead man they adored. Not struggling to explain the nature of her father's decomposition to a six-year-old. She feels completely present and simultaneously as if she is drifting, losing shape, transparent as the edge of a wave. She wishes he had been buried in a forest, where his body would transform, loosen and reveal his bones in rhythm with the rocking of the seasons, the shifting waves of warmth and cool winds and snow; wishes that ferns rested against his grave and soft pads of velvet mosses surrounded it.

Finally, Serena interrupts Ruby's thoughts.

"Is he dust?"

This seems acceptable to Serena, her voice holds the words fairly easily. "Yes, that could be," Ruby says.

"Dust like the dust Anna sweeps?" Those puffed gray balls showing light through them. (Not that Anna leaves many of those around.) Or like the translucent particles that are visible in shafts of sunlight, which land on the shiny surfaces of desks and tables, flickering there, only to be swept away to enter the air again, floating, swimming.

"Maybe more like sand," says Ruby, knowing this must take a very long time. "Do you want us to go to the library together and find out?" How much is Serena asking for a practical explanation? How much information can she simply rest with for a while? Until later.

"No, I don't want to go to the library. I just want to talk to you." She looks at the heavy sycamore across the street, just inside the park. Its branches hold out their arms to her; some are bare; some have leaves turning dark yellow, fluttering against the sky, which is now almost dark. A few tear away and float out into the wind, visible in the light from the street lamp. "He can be sand where he is and I can keep him whole in my heart, can't I?"

"Yes, of course. Yes, you can do that."

Serena remembers her father playing his guitar, sitting right where she is now, the room then full of friends, as it often was—and is no more. She remembers his enthusiasm as he sang and his smile and remembers him holding her in a hug each evening when he came home. She remembers his sad, serious face the time she had chicken pox, was visiting in her parents' room, and he was in bed, sitting at its edge, carefully cutting cigarettes in half. She remembers that when she was very small, he held her up to a Van Gogh in the museum and then hustled her away when she reached out to touch the swirling mounds of paint. They left hurriedly and he took her to a coffee shop and bought her ice cream and laughed with pleasure. She remembers his nightly bedtime stories and remembers him standing in her doorway, a body of light, watching her in the deep middle of the night.

"I am going to hold him in my heart," she says. "I will do that. I am doing it. He is whole right now." And she does keep him in her heart; she sees him and hears his voice. He is alive enough to touch.

As she grows, particularly when many years have passed, people will ask if she remembers him. Well, she was so young . . . The question startles her. Do they imagine she has forgotten her own father?

"I remember him completely," she says with certainty.

And this is so. He is always in her heart. Unharmed. Outrageously alive.

All But Three Are Emeralds

Serena and Rose are in the pool at Hunter College, deep in New York City's east side. They are best friends now and will remain so for the rest of their lives, which turn out to be very long. They are in the eighth grade, but the younger students are allowed—well, required—to swim. It is considered a privilege to use the college pool, as it is a privilege to use their smelly lunchroom. The swimming pool is in a basement space that feels so supremely enclosed that even the water does not suggest nature, but shines, a slippery turquoise, an alien element under a white ceiling. There are no windows anywhere. The wall tiles are creamy, dimpled, immutable and unyielding, and the pool is reached through a series of underground stairs and passageways that turn, heavy institutional doors opening one by one into yet another corridor. The pool is in the new building, connected by a complicated set of tunnels to the old building, where Serena's mother Ruby went to college.

It is the dead of winter and there are all these wet girls. Twenty-five of them. And masses of wet hair, even though they wear the regulation skinny white swim caps, the caps leak, so that every head is soaked. The caps are accompanied by heavy wool swimsuits suits that sag over the girls' loose breasts and reveal tiny spikes of pubic hair pushing through the weave of the fabric. Among them, only Wendy Bernstein looks less than a disaster in these suits, her breasts hard and perfect, dispelling the rumor that she wears falsies. Even Rose, who is trim and flat, simply seems lost, the fabric hanging against her body in saggy ripples. The lights are fluorescent, a shrill blue-white that merges with the echoing room so that light and sound fuse, like the atmosphere in a bad dream.

Some of the girls are seated in bleachers on one side that are enclosed in a small glass booth. They are excused from the class, since, in 1957, you don't swim with your period. Probably no one wears Tampons (the usual whispered fears about virginity) though Serena will struggle with them the following summer, and it is unthinkable to wear the bulky pads and belts, the pads full of blood, in the water. None of the girls can even imagine their blood floating out into the green water. The whole subject is forbidden. Not that the girls mind. It means you can stay on the wooden seats in the observers' gallery and skip the misery of the chlorinated water, always sadistically cold and, Serena thinks, utterly wretched. Well, not real sadism, but a slow pressing meanness.

There is one group of girls, led by the hardy Muffy Banks, who enjoy the water and swim heavily through the chlorine swells, accompanied by hoots of laughter and bouncing dives from the board at the deep end of the pool. Serena, more than Rose, regards Muffy as if she is from another planet, a square, pale redhead who speaks with her friends in a made-up baby voice, lisping. Her group is amused by this and defer to her. Rose thinks she is a bully. Muffy lives outside the city and will soon transfer to a private school. She seems to snub Rose and Serena, yet often looks at Serena with sly hatred. When Serena is elected class president Muffy just smiles as the whole class applauds. People often love Serena and then resent their love, but Muffy simply dislikes her, openly, yet silently. Serena never knows why.

"Jealousy," Rose says, sighing, but patient, over the years about this subject. "They are jealous."

"But of what?" Serena asks repeatedly. "They want me to do something and I do it and then they're whispery and hateful." Serena's response is less innocent than it seems, though this scenario, which will repeat itself, pains her. She likes people to be jealous of her and is sad and ashamed about it. It means she has something precious, even though she knows she is so afraid.

What are they doing in this pool, these girls? They have traveled to school in the early February morning under pewter skies with clouds spread so thinly that they appear seamless. They have moved under their bulky coats, bone beneath flesh, their bones' centers a garden of secrets, a bed of crimson cells and white ones and other elements essential to life. Ordinary sweaters cover their sapphire hearts. Some of them move through the raw cold with scraps of dreams still clinging to them. Serena has dreamed of an old city into which invaders have flung themselves. She has dreamed of terror and mayhem, but she does not remember that, only the city remains in her conscious mind. Rose has dreamed of horses, running and wild.

They have all arrived at the locker room and have undressed because they had to, bared their thighs and breasts, donned the ugly suits and now swim in this great rectangle of disinfected water. But what purpose does this serve (other than the obvious notion that it might save them from drowning one day, which could come in handy, though the topic is never actually discussed). Why must they drill the correct form for each stroke and practice the measured breathing? There is also a lot of emphasis on kicking, a good metaphor, Serena will think later, for the young women of her time. They hold the side of the pool and kick hard. The smelly water rises in plumes.

These lessons are presided over by Amanda Higgenbotham, her name a source of near-hysterical laughter and endless rude puns by the students. She is immensely tall and patrols along the side of the pool watching their progress with small blue eyes, her short tinted hair shines an unlikely greenish blonde (maybe all that chlorine?) and she is the only one allowed her own stylish black suit. Her hands are large and she wears an enormous diamond engagement ring.

"Mmm," says Rose. "Syl would like that one." Syl is Rose's mother.

"My mother says diamonds are vulgar," says Serena. She knows Syl's passion for showy jewels.

"That one is," Rose replies.

This morning Serena sits on the edge of the pool, resting for a moment. She stares down suspiciously at her thighs, now wet and cold in the air, flesh prickly with goose bumps. Her disease has not started yet, but it will. The following summer, a chance remark made by Josephine, the beloved owner of the guest house in the foothills of the White Mountains where she and Ruby spend summers, will uncork the bottle of poison still resting silently within her. They will be eating vanilla ice cream, sitting under a maple tree that Serena and Jo planted when Serena was small. The sun will be very warm. Jo will laugh and say, "You'll get fat eating ice cream." And as suddenly as that, the cork pops. The liquid spills and the poison begins to move everywhere in Serena's psyche. Soon, alarmingly soon, a violent chorus will arrive and comment constantly on her body, her sweet curves. "How fat she is," they will say, "how disgusting." The army will have found territory perfectly prepared for its occupation and they will stay for years. It will be a long war. When it begins, it has no name, this torture, or if it does, no one will acknowledge it. It is not a drive toward starvation, or control, or rage, it is not the hatred of a culture come to invade her, it is just dieting. Just that. Oh, well. And her war, which she will discover she shares with thousands, is far less severe than the onslaught many experience. She seems to do no more than gain and lose the same ten pounds. There is no war, really. Nothing much is happening at all.

Miss Higgenbotham interrupts her rest, shouting from the other end of the pool, her voice reverberating on the cold tile, "Back in, Serena. In. In."

Although she is a very good swimmer—the result of all her summers spent in New Hampshire swimming in a pond considerably colder than this pool—Serena almost fails the course. Her periods, new and wobbly, arrive at twenty-two-day intervals, causing her to miss one too many classes due to the blood prohibition. Miss Higgenbotham is vigilant about attendance. Serena is saved by a miracle so potent that even Hunter can't object: a doctor's note explaining the matter and attesting to her honor. The school suspects that girls lie about their periods in order to skip the class and there's no way to check, is there? (The school is right. They lie.)

Then there is the whole question of dressing and undressing in an open room, no cubicles, with perennially wet cement floors and lockers that jam, making easy access to clothing questionable. How to step in and out of clothes without wetting them? Underpants are the major challenge—and socks. No one wears slacks, it is not permitted, even in bitter weather and skirts can be shimmied over the head. Even more important than comfort is the matter of seeing or being seen, trying to slither in and out of your clothes in small sections, so that no one can see much at any given time. Serena tries to do the whole thing swiftly, making sure her locker is open so that she is not stranded undressed, yanking at it to get her things. She pretends nonchalance and moves quickly. Dressing is made more complicated, because the sticky water is hard to dry with the thin, hard towels that rub, but don't absorb, and being wet for the rest of the day inside your clothes is worse than being seen. It is difficult to picture that there will come a time in the not-too-distant future when many of these same girls will, as young women, lie around together examining their cervixes with great respect and waves of laughter and relief, and share the most intimate details of their orgasms.

At the end of the day, Rose and Serena go to Rose's. The weather is still gray, the clouds unmoving. Patchy ice is in the streets, black lumps and rinds of it pressed against the curbs. In Rose's parents' apartment redecoration is in progress; this a permanent state as Syl has rooms torn apart and remodeled, never satisfied and never finished. Some of the rooms are empty. The house smells of paint. It is a large apartment on upper Park Avenue, not far from where Jake, who years later will be Serena's lover, will one day live. Where Serena will visit him wearing high heels and fancy underwear, full of guilt, and perfumed behind her knees and between her thighs.

But this afternoon they are still schoolgirls, carrying books and hot dogs they have purchased at an ancient deli on Madison. They get Pepsis from the kitchen where May, the Silver's housekeeper, has started dinner preparations. Her hands move quickly under the faucet and two sharp knives rest on the counter, light reflecting off their surface. Rose loads her Pepsi with ice, which she loves, and bites down on a cube with her white perfect teeth. Serena would have preferred hot chocolate—it is so cold out—but decides not to ask.

"You drinkin' that cold stuff give you a belly ache," May says. "Those hot dogs? You bring me one?" May has taken care of Rose since before she was born, when she came to work for Syl. Rose hands her the extra hot dog. They both smile.

Syl does not approve of hot dogs. Not because they lack nutrition, not a general concern in those days, but because she doesn't like the way they smell, though it's hard to smell much of anything through the paint.

The girls go into one of the empty rooms and lie on the floor, eating their hotdogs, dripping sauerkraut onto the elegant parquet. There are no drapes on these windows and a skinny streak of afternoon sun has pushed through the clouds and falls across their outstretched legs. Their bodies are still sticky beneath their clothes and they smell of chlorine. Serena finishes her hot dog, and goes into a guest bathroom to see if she can wash her legs a bit. The room, usually untouched, is damp and steamy from a shower someone has taken recently. Drops streak the tiles. The shower curtain is not quite closed. One heavy towel is slung carelessly on a towel rack. But who would use it? No one is there except May. Curious, she washes her legs and dries them on a clean towel, not choosing the one that has clearly been used.

"Who's here?" she says, returning to the empty room, where Rose is lying looking at the shadows on the ceiling, an oddly quiet occupation, quiet for energetic Rose.

"No one. Well, workmen," she says.

"Does Syl let them shower?"

Rose rolls her eyes. "Are you kidding?"

"Well, the guest bathroom is wet."

Rose shrugs. "One more mystery in this very mysterious house," she says. "Let's go inside."

They begin to wander through the apartment, as they often do. Perhaps the constant renovation creates a kind of restlessness. Some rooms are immaculate, filled with expensive furnishings, art on the walls and heavy rugs, a few with splattered jewel tones, others pale and old. The empty rooms are draped with painters' cloths, though the men are now gone, and the air smells raw, sharp with the odor of paint. The girls look at the odd swaths of color that Sylvia has tried on the walls. Apple green. Dense lemony yellow, and another green with a lot of yellow in it and a grayish undertone. "What is that?" ask Serena, who ordinarily loves color. "That's a terrible shade."

"Avocado," answers Rose. "She thinks it's going to be her signature color." She says it deadpan, but both girls sigh deeply and then groan.

"It's awful," says Serena. "Why does she keep doing this?" The apartment that Serena has grown up in, the one where her father died and she and Ruby still live, is painted by the landlord every two years, all the rooms at once and not much discussion about color, though she did ask to have her bedroom done in powder blue when she was very young, when her father was alive and they were doing things like decorating, an activity that bores and irritates Ruby.

"She's working it through with the decorator," Rose says. "Hard to believe, but true. It's one of Syl's hobbies. My father says it's like a nervous tic, but he pays for it anyway. God knows what she might do if she stopped doing this." Rose squints and then relaxes one eye. "You know, it's out of control."

"Ruby is out of control," Serena says, realizing it for the first time. "When she's angry, she is out of control. I think that's true." The idea is fascinating, just at the edge of a new kind of understanding. Ruby's rages terrify Serena. She feels imprisoned by Ruby's anger and desperate for her love. Serena tries to reason with her mother, terror, like spun glass, in her belly. One rational word after another, pleading for mercy in this useless, measured way. Every once in a while, Serena, too, explodes, screaming, "It isn't my fault! Your life isn't my fault!" when Ruby brandishes her pain like a weapon, cudgeling Serena with the things she has suffered. Ruby, in her rages, is a woman who has swallowed hornets. For a moment, both mothers hover in the room with their separate angers, Ruby's violent, Syl's a poisonous sulk.

The girls continue to wander and then settle into Rose's bedroom, untouched for the moment by the painters, the decorator. "I try not to let her in here much," says Rose. "But she's already done a lot of damage." They stretch out across one of the twin beds, which have frilly canopies, a touch as unlike Rose as anything Serena can imagine.

"What do you think these are for?" Serena asks, looking up at the stretched curve of white fabric.

"I know what they were for," says Rose. "They were to protect you from bits of thatched roof falling on you in your sleep. Syl's decorators do research. It isn't just decorating, it's an educational experience. The ones in the museum that have curtains are for warmth. And probably to keep you safe from the strange vapors of the night, although the decorator didn't say that."

Rose rubs her legs and wiggles her toes. She stares up at the underside of the canopy. "Why do you think Wendy's breasts stay put in that suit?" Her voice, her tone, usually matter-of-fact, is even more so. Conversational, though she doesn't attempt nonchalance. As if this were the kind of thing they discussed regularly, these girls who still seem so tightly woven into the mores of their time as they stay mostly silent and hold their anxious secrets. Serena has wondered the same thing. Probably a full three quarters of the eighth grade have. Serena is as curious about this—about bodies in general—as Rose is, but less forthright than Rose.

"I don't know." She thinks for a moment. "They're pointy? I always thought she wore a bra that made them that way until we took swimming. I don't get dressed near enough to her to see," she says, implying that she might like to. It is not so much sexual as mysterious. Serena struggles with the bras of the day. Stitched in a firm and unyielding conical shape, they are completely different from her anatomy. She pushes her round reluctant breasts into them, always feeling she must be made wrong. In addition to providing speculums, the Women's Movement will liberate breasts of all sizes, but not for long. Before that, Serena will see Indian statues, the women full-breasted, round-hipped, with small waists, everything seeming to undulate, and feel a visceral sense of relief. It is not something wrong with her, then.

"I'm so flat," says Rose, whose breasts are not really flat, but wide-spaced and pressed against her chest. "Syl tries to sneak me padding." She looks disgusted.

"She's decorating you," suggests Serena. They both laugh. "I never fit right," says Serena. "Look." And in a totally surprising gesture, she lifts up her blouse. "They squash out the side."

Rose lifts her sweater. "Mine don't get all the way to the front. The fabric rumples." She pokes her bra where the fabric is loose. "That's where Syl wants to put the fluff."

"The what?"

"The padding. It's fluffy. Like cotton balls, but heavier. Fluffier. That's what she says, 'Just a little extra fluff, right there.' "

They groan and cover their faces.

"Do you wear it?"

"No. Of course not. No."

They look at each other for a moment, really look.

"We're different colors," says Serena. She is pale, her skin lush and fine, though she doesn't think of it this way. Not at all. "Camellia skin," says Ruby, who is vastly approving of Serena's looks. She takes credit for having married such a handsome man and producing this child. Rose always looks as if she has a faint tan, brown skin with a pale red undertone. Serena loves the color of Rose's flesh. Far away in the kitchen, they can hear May opening and closing cupboard doors as she works. They pull their clothes back down, but don't move quickly.

"Syl wears padding sometimes," says Rose. "Come, I'll show you."

They move through the hall and into Syl's bedroom, Syl's and Al's, really, all gold and white with avocado accents.

"This green really is a horrible color," Rose sighs. The pale carpet is very soft and full. The girls are barefoot.

"Fluffy," says Serena pointedly, digging her toes into the wool. They are both a little giddy from inspecting each other's bras, each other's breasts.

A green ceramic bowl—celadon, not avocado—with water and some scent in it rests on the radiator, moistening the air and perfuming it, warring with the paint smell that insinuates itself in all the rooms. There are mirrors seemingly everywhere and a fat crystal chandelier, silver picture frames. Dark, velvet drapes shut out almost everything: the lights along Park Avenue, both cars and streetlights. A thin crack between them reveals snow falling now, in the late afternoon dark, shadowy flakes beyond the windowpanes. It is an interior that is both protected and bright with its own reflections. These large rooms are all designed to be private, shuttered, shaded, draped. Only the ones in the process of redecoration have windows open to the sky. Serena thinks for a moment about the difference between privacy and hiding. She has been reading *The Diary of Anne Frank*, and the question of hiding has been very much on her mind, the plight of all the people caught in that war an anxious subject that she returns to, like a bruise one checks repeatedly to see if it is still there. When she first heard about the Holocaust, Serena wondered why all the Jews didn't convert and secretly stay Jewish. Now, years later, she understands that this was never an option.

Ruby talks about privacy and how important it is, "Crucial," she says emphatically. But it is impossible to hide from Ruby. Alone in their apartment, Serena's dead father a ghostly third, but vivid in his absence, Ruby can intrude relentlessly. Not the way Syl does, going through Rose's bureau drawers, discarding old items, replacing them with what is new and stylish, sending the old things to one of her charities, but emotionally. Syl is checking for fashion and maybe letters, or diaries. Ruby wants emotional flesh. She never touches Serena's things and would not read her diary. She doesn't have to.

Rose's voice brings her back into the moment.

"Let's look in her bureau drawers." She opens one and then another.

"That's a lot of underwear," Serena says.

"Please. Lingerie." There are bras in different colors, mauve and cerise and cream and black, and underpants—no, panties—made of lace. "There they are," Rose lifts out what look like two poufs, which are, as she described, slightly heavier than cotton balls. "This kind goes in the front," she says. "I think she just makes them herself."

She moves her small squarish hands toward the back of the drawer and takes out a plain cardboard box with an old rubber band around it. Opening it quickly, she spills a cluster of rings onto the linen bureau scarf. Serena counts, something she does from time to time. Five women with red hats in the bus. Ten tulips in the bunch. She doesn't do it often enough to be worried about it.

"Eight rings," Rose says, understanding that Serena is counting. Some are in ornate antique settings, some in bold plain ones. Serena tilts her head slightly to get a closer look at the stones. She realizes she is staring intently. Most are shades of green. Green that is dark and has light buried in it. Green that could be a piece torn from a rainbow. Green that is as luscious as candy. Green so deep, its color could have been slipped from a bottomless pond—one ancient, cold and untouched.

"All but three are emeralds," says Rose, breaking the spell.

"I'll show you something else." She closes the box, drops it back into the drawer and then feels under the layers of lacy garments and pulls out an odd round case with a domed lid that looks like a comic book drawing of a spaceship. She smiles slightly and opens it. The case is empty, except for a dusting of powder. Rose's face freezes. "This is weird," she says. She looks really troubled. "The guest bathroom was wet," she looks at Serena, her expression going from closed to fearful to angry, one feeling sliding into another.

"It was," Serena says. "What's the matter, Rose?"

"That box holds a diaphragm. It's for birth control."

"I know," says Serena, "Ruby has one, too. But it's pretty old, I think." She has found it in Ruby's bureau, hers slid under a stack of flannel pajamas. But Ruby has told Serena about birth control and it doesn't seem alarming.

"Well, if it isn't in the box, where is it?" It is not without reason that Rose will choose to study law.

Serena knows something is very wrong and senses, but cannot quite identify, what it is. She doesn't know enough about diaphragms and their pattern of use to quite follow Rose's reasoning. "Rose? What?"

"I'll tell you later," Rose says. She goes to the large bed and sits abruptly on the satiny cover. She stares at the photos of Sylvia and Al on the night table. They are framed in silver that winks in the glittery room.

"Your father looks so young in this one," says Serena. She is making conversation, giving Rose a little time to tell her what she is so upset about.

Rose looks at the picture and then turns away. "He's not really my father," she says.

"What?" Serena is completely astonished. "What do you mean?"

"How many things could I mean?" Rose says, her voice uninflected. Reasonable. "Syl was married before, to my real father."

"Did he die?"

"No, they divorced. I think he left her, but she won't really say."

"But where is he?" Serena is appalled that Rose might have a living father who cares so little for her that he has disappeared from her life. For the moment, this is the only way she can think of it.

"I don't know. We haven't heard from him in years, or at least I haven't. I don't think my mother has either." Rose rarely refers to Syl as her mother.

"When did you see him last?" asks Serena, who feels suddenly desperate to solve this puzzle. Fathers cannot simply disappear unless, like hers, they die.

"I don't remember, Serena. I was a baby. I don't remember him at all." The radiator sighs and hisses.

"Well, they must have divorced, because she married Al."

"I think he divorced her," Rose says. "Maybe in Reno? She won't talk about it."

Serena can imagine Sylvia and her breathy voice, with its sharp undertone. Syl, who talks so much about so little, suddenly just not talking, being tight and silent. He must have left her, Serena thinks. Otherwise she would talk about it endlessly. Syl enjoys stories of being wronged and triumphing, taking charge. This would not have been a triumph.

"Where did she meet Al?" Serena likes to hear how people met. Couples. She thinks this might be a brighter note. Serena searches compulsively for those notes when she sees serious distress, her habit born of attempting to fend off Ruby's rages.

Rose sighs. "Well, there's what she says and what I think, or rather what I heard my grandmother say once and now I think it, too." It is snowing harder and the flakes tap against the window. "My father and Syl were friends with Al and his wife Vivian. 'They did everything together', that's how Syl puts it."

"Well, then Al should know what happened with your Dad."

"I'm sure he does, Serena, and Syl has sworn him to secrecy. He always obeys Sylvia. You know that." Rose smiles deliberately, a schoolteacher admonishing a slow student. She stops smiling and sighs. "This is an awful story. Anyway, Vivian got cancer and died very quickly. Syl was there helping. According to her. Of course. We know how helpful Syl is. And she and Al got so close," mimicking her mother's voice. Rose has always understood the stories about rings and poison, though she knows her mother hasn't poisoned anybody. Not literally, anyway.

"Wait," says Serena. "Where was your father?"

"Oh, gone. Very gone by the time Vivian got sick. That's why Syl had so much time to be helpful, right? I think she just waited for Vivian to die and then trapped Al."

Al, the recent widower, who was enormously wealthy and—maybe?—always a little smitten with pretty Sylvia. Al, whose family made jams and jellies. Al, round and hard, the masses of flesh not so much fat as packed along his body. Smaller than Sylvia would have liked (the decamped husband was tall), he nonetheless had an imposing presence: a large, round, heavy head, big hands and feet, drooping eyelids, thick, almost black, hair, carefully tended. Altogether a bigger man whose growth had mysteriously stopped, leaving the impression that he might suddenly spring higher.

Rose rests her hand against her stomach, as if it might hurt. In the kitchen, May is finishing the chopping and the faint rhythmic sound stops.

"You mean she deliberately waited? It didn't just happen that way?" asks Serena. "Why did your grandmother say that?"

"They were having a fight," recalls Rose. "I was only about eight. And she didn't just wait, Grandma thought she plotted. Syl was complaining about Al. Something about how common he was/is, how he hated the better things, like the concerts Syl dragged him to and the theater. As if she really cared. On and on. Mean. My grandmother called her a spider."

"Spiders eat their mates," says Serena. This fight sounds like something Ruby might get into, if the mood struck her. Serena is all too familiar with its qualities, its power to inflict serious wounds.

"Well, yes, that's the point. And some of them wrap them in silk after they've mauled them. Silk sounds like Syl."

"Even if your grandmother said so, it doesn't mean it's true. That she waited and trapped him." This is the way Serena reasons with Ruby. One logical step at a time, trying to force the logic to dissolve some terrible truth.

"It does, Serena. I didn't really understand it at the time, but the idea stayed with me and I believe it. And you're being naive and missing the point."

"Oh, I get the point. The point is awful." Maybe later, they would say that in a way Syl stalked him, but they don't, not yet. Serena realizes her dismay at the whole situation. She thinks of broken teeth biting into soft flesh, a throat swallowing. She knows spiders don't have teeth in that sense (or maybe they do?), but it's a terrible image. Devouring Al's soul, really.

"They were in the hall outside Syl's and Al's bedroom. Nana was visiting for the afternoon. It was near Thanksgiving and they were planning dinner. So, I rushed in and told Nana to stop it," says Rose wryly. "No. I didn't do anything about the fight. I was eight years old. I didn't hear what started it. I just went back to my room. Quietly."

"Why do you think it's true?" Serena questions this way with Ruby. Maybe the awful things that Ruby suspects, insists are so, are not. Rose, the future attorney, has no objections to this kind of question.

"Oh, Serena. Think about it. It sounds just like her. Besides, Nana doesn't lie. She was angry, but not lying."

How much of this should they know, these girls? Not this much. It is heavy and miserable in the room, with an edge of real grief in Serena, who seems to absorb situations of this kind so that they dig into her skin and press her heart. Many years will pass before she learns how this happens and then almost, almost, learns to stop it. Rose has pushed her feelings so far down she imagines that she doesn't care at all. It is just the way of the world. Of her world. They have still not talked about the diaphragm. Its empty powdery case.

They hear the front door open and Sylvia's voice. Rose closes the drawer. "I'm home," she trills. "I'm back." As if she has been on a long and arduous journey and not just to lunch and shopping or at one of her charity meetings. There is the soft sound of her footsteps on the carpet and then she appears at the bedroom door, a pale fur hooked to her fingers and resting on one shoulder.

"May will give you girls dinner. I'm meeting Dad at the Philharmonic. How are you, Serena?" Syl likes Serena in spite of the lefty mother. Serena is popular and a good friend for Rose to have. Not that Rose isn't popular in her own right. Syl feels strongly about popularity, especially for girls. She thinks—well, she knows—that it increases their options in life.

"I thought Dad was away," says Rose sharply, but something in her face looks relieved. Syl chooses not to notice the tone, though she will often correct Rose's tone when she doesn't like it. And Al's.

"He got back early and went to the office and he's meeting me," Syl says. "Why is that so strange? He can change his clothes there. He has extra." As if the clothes were of any concern to Rose.

Rose is silent.

"It's snowing," says Syl. "Did you see? What a bother."

"We saw," says Serena.

"Well, scoot. I need to change." Syl drops her coat on the bed. She moves toward her bathroom and then inside, leaving the door open. She turns on the shower. The sound of cascading water fills the room.

The girls go toward the kitchen and dinner.

In the kitchen, knives still gleam on the counter surface, carefully laid on a linen towel. May is drying each one and putting them away in the knife rack. Syl, who does not cook, fusses about the kitchen equipment. Light flashes on a thin hard swell of ice that has collected outside the window and flashes on the surface of the knives as well. Serena is afraid of knives, of the switchblades carried by the gangs that proliferate in New York in the 50s.

Ruby's students carry knives. She is unimpressed by them. Not by the harm they can do, but personally unafraid. When she is old, a man in her elevator will tell her he has a knife. He is wearing a rosy pink fedora and is one of the pimps who flourish for a while in that building. "Don't I scare you?" he says to Ruby.

"Don't be ridiculous," she replies. "I taught hundreds of students who carried knives. But now I'm old and might drop dead of a heart attack right here and then where would you be?" He laughs. She laughs and exits the elevator. This is before the stout wires in her brain begin to spark and crack years later, and then fear overtakes her for real.

They have lamb chops for dinner, fat and pink inside and full of juice. May sits with them in the kitchen, apron still on. When May is with Rose and Serena, they eat together. When Syl and May are alone or when Rose is with them, they eat together. When Al is alone, he takes a plate in his study. When Al and Syl are together, or the whole family is eating dinner, May eats in the kitchen and serves them in the dining room, a system that seems hateful to both Rose and Serena. Syl is unbothered by this minuet. "It's the way it is," she says.

"She doesn't think very far," Rose says to Serena.

What May thinks remains a mystery until the 60s, though Rose has asked her about it for years. Serena knows it's wrong because of Ruby and because she herself has strong feelings on the matter. And then, as the 60s unroll, the marches begin in earnest and Serena and Rose and many of their friends march together and see May and her family at them. Serena has been demonstrating forever with Ruby, but it is new to most of her friends.

Before dinner is over, Syl comes in to say goodnight. Rose barely looks up, but Syl doesn't notice. Or appears not to.

After the meal, Serena gets ready to go. As they stand at the front door of the apartment and she puts on her boots, wraps her scarf around her neck, Rose stares at her so intently that Serena feels anxious.

"What?" Serena says. "What is it?"

"The diaphragm," says Rose. "It must be in her. That's where it is."

"Oh," says Serena. "Oh, no."

"Oh, yes," Rose answers. "I'll bet."

Serena stands awkwardly at the door.

"Go ahead," says Rose. "I'll see you tomorrow." She turns away and walks toward her room. Serena leaves and closes the door softly.

Serena feels breathless when she gets to the street. Her heart feels sticky and punctured, the way it sometimes does when Ruby tells her things she doesn't want to know. She stands still for a moment on the corner of Park Avenue. The sky is full of snow. Emptiness swirling with movement. Serena sticks out her tongue—she must be too old for this, she thinks, but doesn't care. The shining flakes drop into her mouth. Nothingness, cold, and then melting droplets as they warm, disappearing. Becoming part of her body. Outside to inside, from the sky into her belly. She starts uptown to the cross-town bus on Ninety-sixth Street, her attention now not on the snow, nor on Rose, nor Syl and Rose's misery, but, strangely, on an experience she had with Ruby that morning when a water main burst, sending water through the asphalt skin of pavement. Serena imagined the web of pipes deep beneath her feet, the crumbling water lines studded with chunks of lacy rust, spilling water underground. She is always curious about what is hidden, though she doesn't necessarily like what she discovers. Maybe that is what brought the conversation to mind, the hidden layers at the Silver's. Secrets leaking underground. Suddenly the cold seems fierce. She stands waiting for the bus, happy to see its round green nose coming toward her, only a block away.

When Serena gets home, Ruby is in a friendly mood, lying on the old plushy couch in the living room, reading a book on art in the ancient world. Ruby truly loves art. And artists. Writers. She loves music and plays the piano well, loves dance and theater. She takes Serena to everything the city has to offer. All the museums, concerts, the ballet, ethnic dancing at the Museum of Natural History in the afternoons. She reads happily in the lamplight. Serena sits quietly with her. She notices that *The Daily Worker*, the Communist newspaper, is on the coffee table and with it, *The Unobstructed Universe*. Both Ruby and Serena have read this book written by a journalist about the communications he received from his late wife, who had been psychic and worked in that capacity under an assumed name to protect herself and her husband from ridicule. They have also read Eileen Garrett's accounts of her life. Garrett, the great medium and healer whose experiments included agreeing to be tested by a variety of scientists.

Serena has memories of what she believes are past lives. They slide like liquid lightning, shining slashes when time splits and fragments of elsewhere swim in the present. She imagines that her guardians, the loving energies that have been with her since her birth and probably before, have helped her recognize some past lives. Even before she and Ruby discuss reincarnation, she feels that some places are familiar, some people already known. She has been drawn to the old Egyptian wing at the Metropolitan Museum since she was quite small, peering up at the cases of jewels and tiny vials, some glimmering, others rough. Staring at the heavy canopic jars where some organs were stored, but not the brain, she learns. The brain was thought to just make mucus. She has sat and looked intensely at the statues of the great Queen Hatshepsut, at the mended cracks from their destruction. Corny, she thinks when she is older and reincarnation is fashionable, in the 60s, And those artifacts were centuries apart, probably. But nevertheless.

Ruby's voice interrupts the quiet. "How was it?" she asks. "How's the mother?" Ruby's voice conveys, with the second question, everything she and Serena have discussed about Sylvia. Syl. Her obsession with decorating, a hobby Ruby considers bourgeois at best and miserably pretentious at worst. The—Ruby thinks and says—terrible marriage to that fool. Syl's controlling involvement with what Rose wears and does. And more. So all of this floats heavily in Ruby's question about the mother. Could Ruby know the story about Syl and Al and how they came to marry? This story that Serena has just heard? Probably. Ruby often mysteriously knows things that Serena has not told her, and she is not friendly with the mothers who meet and talk so she hasn't gotten any information in that way. She is not very friendly, period, though she has kept a few dear friends from high school and college. A few.

"It was okay. Nice. We had dinner with May. Syl and Al were out."

"That's a surprise," Ruby says dryly.

Serena doesn't tell Ruby that they saw Syl go out, dressed in a pale suit, her hair swept up in a froth of curls, wearing spike heels with sharply pointed toes (how will she negotiate the snow?) and a black, black fur. Not seal. Or lamb. Serena knows those. Or mink. Serena hates furs, can almost see the small faces of the animals, feel their warm bodies. (Ruby doesn't like fur either, though she had one when Serena was little. Skunk. She said it smelled when it was wet.) Syl, oblivious, trailed clouds of sweet, sharp scent. She was wearing one of the green rings. Her body seemed circled in deliberate mystery, cunning and patrolled. She tried to press this attitude of careful calculation on Rose, who was matter-of-fact about her own body. Competent and definite, but not absorbed in this way. Serena would have been better prey for Syl.

"How was your day, Mom?"

"Long. I went to the Met after work and had coffee and a Danish and looked at the Vermeers." Serena knows Ruby has been home since late afternoon, maybe had a little chicken for dinner and has been reading all evening. She seems tired but content. Like Syl, but for different reasons, Ruby appreciates that Serena has so many friends.

"I think I'll finish my homework and read a little." Serena wants to go back to the Anne Frank diaries. Lately, she has been dreaming about a young blonde woman who speaks German, though she doesn't exactly hear in dreams, she more understands that it is German. The same young woman appears again and again. She is tall and slender, with a wide angular face and long, hazel eyes. Her fine hair is dark blonde and bundled in back with a clasp, where it fans out. She always wears the same brown shoes with a strap across. Sometimes, Serena just watches. Sometimes, she is in the action of the dream. Sometimes, she is inside the woman. The dream comes in scattered episodes. The woman is in an old city, Serena thinks maybe Vienna, though she isn't sure why. When she talks to Ruby about the dreams, what they look like and the woman and a kind of breathless activity, tense and frightened and excited, Ruby thinks it could be Poland or Austria. The woman's own breath seems tight and fragile. The dreams arrived as Serena started reading the diaries, and don't seem particularly relevant to her own life, though some of them have a sharp, insistent pressure. Some episodes are full and long, others just bits—hallways, staircases, wind—that appear in the midst of other dreams and then vanish.

Serena reads for a while and then sleeps. At first, she dreams of the pool and swim class and losing track of her clothes, then, briefly, of the wet bathroom at Rose's, now, in the dream, painted an odd, dull red. Then, intensely, she is in this dream city and people are screaming, soldiers shouting. A railroad car looms to her left, but it has no windows, just a sliding door, gaping open. Cold wind blows the voices, scatters them. The soldiers are shoving people into the maw of the car and the doors slam. There is no room to sit, only to stand pressed against other bodies. There are screams as the car moves forward. The blonde woman is there. She is trying to comfort another woman, who is old. She holds her and holds her, singing softly amid the din and then her own breath seems to fail. She presses her chest. Serena feels the tightness there, no air. The young woman collapses onto the old woman, though there is no room to fall. In the weak light coming through skinny apertures at the sides of the door, Serena sees a thin gold ring on the blonde woman's finger. It has one small green stone. The stone might be an emerald, but it is too dark to be sure. Her hands are still. Serena understands the woman is dead and half expects her energy to visibly pull away from her body, as in Garrett's descriptions of death, but nothing happens. It feels as if, even in death, she is unwilling to leave the others to their suffering. Serena rides in the rocking car for a while before waking. It is deep in the night. She is still for a moment and then begins to weep. Loose, awful tears stream down her face. She thinks maybe she should go into Ruby's room, but instead goes to the window and looks out at the snow falling on the park across the street. Slowly, her tears stop. When she goes back to bed, she is afraid she will not sleep, but she does, suddenly and deeply. She never dreams of the city again. Nor of the woman.

Inside Out

Ingrid is born on a day in early November that mixes raw wind with sudden blazes of sun. She is born in the Midwest, in Newton, Iowa and grows up there. Newton is near (but not very near) Des Moines. Grasses skim the ring of far horizon and there is an ominous, unshadowed brightness that makes one yearn for dimness and ferny clutter. It is an open place of sky, sun and moon peering down at the planet, God's flashing eye piercing and scouring. His sight and diligence are praised and feared in Ingrid's church.

In the large, yellow house where the Swansons live, everything is polished or scrubbed or both. Order prevails; even the tools in the shed hang with neat precision, each labeled, its place outlined in black. Clothes are in proper drawers, unscented and precisely folded. It is the skinned cleanliness of sadism in a house where the perceived truth, when it is spoken, is used like verbal Clorox, a scraping, poisonous attack that is practiced selectively, punitively or for righteous purposes. It is a place where everything seems continuous, with no beginnings and certainly no changes. A rigorous sameness prevails. What accumulates is removed: dust wiped away, smears buffed out, rips mended and shit flushed promptly. It is a house of secrets; invisible and tangible, they rule absolutely.

The house itself rises up three stories and sinks below the earth into a deep cellar. Heavy, old trees surround it, unusual in this part of the country. Until she is twelve, Ingrid spends a lot of time in the crotch of a tall tree, in the wide, flickering shade. One of her cats is always with her. She is passionate about cats. It would be fitting if Ingrid, who is considered the strange one amongst the three children, were dark, while the rest were fair. But in truth, only Victoria, the baby, is dark. Ingrid is tall with the kind of blond coloring where hair and skin and eyes all shade into each other. Blond hair with dark, soft silver woven into the color, hazel eyes and dense skin with an undertone of the palest, milky coffee. She has long legs and in adolescence develops very large, beautiful breasts that are ignored by everyone in the family and gain, therefore, a determined presence.

Ingrid's mother is Dossie. Dorothy, really, but everyone has forgotten that. She is fair, too, but unlike Ingrid's smoothness, Dossie's skin reddens easily and is often blotchy. Dossie is narrow chested, with long strong arms; below her waist, she is heavy and bulky, legs and buttocks bundled in large swells. "A big gal," her friends say. Big Dossie reads everything very carefully, even the cooking directions for frozen foods, though she has done it thousands of times and understands the principle. Despite her excellent baking, she eats pineapple rings for dessert at lunch, when she is alone. There is a great deal of food at the Swansons, all of it bad tasting except the pies, which are sweet and runny with syrup.

Dossie has a self-effacing smile, humorless and automatic. She is a masterfully controlling woman, her blandness as misleading as the scenery in a TV commercial. Afternoons, still alone until the children return (it would not enter Dossie's mind to have a housekeeper, even now that they are "doing better"), she reads the stock market pages and thinks about economic fluctuations and the bond market. Legs firmly encased in support hose, she ponders her investment possibilities. Her interest is heated, sexual. She can feel the warmth between her legs as she reads and reads. No one is aware that she does this. When she is through reading, she folds the paper neatly. Her interest in money began when her children were away more, with lives of their own. She does not mourn their changes. She will inherit some money of her own (cash, is how she thinks of it) when her father dies and she is going to be ready. It will be the first cash that's actually hers.

Arthur Swanson is a contractor. He started as what Dossie calls a stonemason (he dug ditches) and moved up. He is a slow man in his actions, deliberate and considered. His mind works intuitively, but he doesn't know that, and would scorn the notion. Slow rolls of intuitive understanding inform his business progress and guide him from success to success. Arthur will casually make the right calls, he is friendly and consistent. A thoroughly reliable man. He comes from poor people. He is heavy in flesh and bone, a looming man with a smile; someone who experiences long, silent rages, his anger as deliberate as everything else about him. Ingrid frightens him and the fear makes him angry. Her calm wildness, creamy and totally fixed; ferocity without fire. She is baffling and mysterious and therefore enraging. When he is angry with Ingrid, he beats her buttocks until he begins to get an erection. "You think you're such a queen," he will say as he hits her. "Damn queen. We'll see about that." Then he stops for the moment. The beatings (spankings, is how Arthur thinks of them; good discipline) only take place in the cellar, in that cool dimness. By the time he reaches the staircase to the kitchen, his erection has vanished. Has, in fact, never existed.

Arthur never misses church.

The Swansons live together in ordered, active silence. The silences sometimes sway with heat, balloon in the corners of the clean, awful house.

Ingrid's nature is indeed mysterious, and in some unseen way, she has a streak of violence, although she doesn't seem overtly angry. It is more a suggestion of extreme passions, yet undisclosed. Difficult to identify, especially in that household where introspection is totally unexplored; she also seems to find odd things humorous in a remote, unaccented manner. Without being able to define it, she longs for an environment that will hold her fierceness: an urban life, or one surrounded by hot sun. A desert, perhaps, stark and bleached. Or a very big city. Until she encounters foreign films, the year she is a senior in high school, she cannot quite identify where she belongs. When Godard's film *Breathless* is released (late, in Iowa, in a special film house), she smiles in the dark. The Paris scenes, the misery and danger and half-deliberate posturing, is recognizable to her. The Paris of the screen, the small black and white projection, is more home than the huge fields and solid houses of Newton. She is nowhere reflected in Iowa; she knows she will not stay.

Ingrid is not a girl who dreams. But she does make plans. Once conceived, her plans form a resilient pattern that drops beneath the surface, out of sight unless intentionally revealed. Ingrid does not chatter. Many of her feelings find expression in drawing and later in painting, both of which she loves, though she does not think of what she does as being related to her feelings, exactly. Some of her work is representational, fine and clear. Other pieces are abstracts, though she doesn't call them that until she gets to college and takes art classes. Originally, they have no name to her; they are fields of color, some almost transparent, some filled with heavy strokes, with blackness and places where the thick paint is sharply pierced. She longs for colors that she cannot find, although they exist. The deepest blues. Blacks with purple shimmering inside of them. She uses palette knives as well as brushes. Occasionally, she uses real knives, cutting the canvas so there is a break in the color line. She knows she sometimes feels driven to do the work, sometimes relieved when she is done for the moment, sometimes at the edge of agitation, but always very alive inside herself, though no one would notice an outward change and she communicates these feelings to no one. It is an intensely private world. Occasionally, the active life of the paint, the colors, frighten her.

When she graduates from high school, Ingrid receives a number of honors. She has been accepted to the University of Iowa. She imagined that her family would resist her having a college education, but they are pleased, quite shy about their pleasure, but obviously happy for her. Arthur says the money is no problem. (Unheard of, for Arthur.) None of the Swansons have been to college, or even technical school. Dossie gives Ingrid a string of cultured pearls as a graduation present. Clearly, she imagines a life of dances, of dates and romance. She wants her girl to look right, to be included. Ingrid smiles her thanks, inwardly thinking of the pearls as sad and comical. The year is 1961.

When Ingrid enters the university in late August, a little early because there is an orientation period, she brings four pairs of jeans, two white and two black, sweaters, mostly black, tee shirts—black and white and a ferocious yellow, two dresses and beautiful new boots that she has saved for all summer. And the pearls. Not at all what Dossie has hoped for, but she is only too aware of Ingrid's stubbornness and doesn't even attempt an argument. Ingrid's roommate, Bonnie, is a seemingly bland girl from the far eastern part of Iowa who has somehow acquired an extensive collection of sexy underwear, which she wears daily under her proper plaid skirts and ironed blouses. Ingrid is curious about this dichotomy and watches Bonnie carefully to see which represents her, the underwear or the modest wardrobe and decides it is the latter. Completely different, they become good companions, sharing the room easily. They offer each other snacks, mostly apples on Ingrid's part, and some conversation and begin to delve into their respective courses. Apples scent the room as the leaves turn a showy gold and the cold blows across the campus. Ingrid begins to explore and make friends. There are other students interested in film, in art. Art has become her passion. She is painting and drawing and reading, immersed, soaked in what she is learning. Ingrid's impulses arise from some secret inner landscape where scoured bones lie beneath cold river water, dark and private, the river hidden in the midst of a forest that is inviting, but not comforting. She is not warm, but she is alluring; people are drawn to Ingrid, want to be in her aura, want to get closer to her than she will usually allow. In the second term, Ingrid enrolls in a drama class. She and Bart, who will become her friend, meet in this class.

Bart of the green eyes—flecked like sun-struck water—dappled eyes. He has a boy-face, high color with round, prominent cheekbones and a roundly massed body, but not fat, or even plump. There is no hint, no future-shadow of the body he will one day create: muscled, large and hard, heavy with shape. This new body will be purely sculpted, its roundness lost in muscle, his old yearning for comfort pushed below his daily experiences, a sweet stream banished into a deep hidden channel. As he develops his muscles he will temporarily banish the innocent boy who played baseball, who also loved the garden and the joy of flowers; the boy who learned to sew from his mother, though the old images will still slide to the surface, his feelings twined in them. His helplessness, his tenderness. He is a beloved only child, reared in a religious family; there is love, but affection is rigidly controlled, parceled out self-consciously in a measured way that masks a fear of touch, of moist breath and warm flesh. Only his grandmother escapes this and holds him until even she understands she must stop, he has become too big, although he is only seven when this understanding bears down on her, an insistent push, a command she cannot ignore. The danger of closeness, of holding. Then no one touches him except for his mother, when he is sick.

When Bart and Ingrid meet, he is a religious boy, a churchgoer, active in the community and brighter than most. He attended the Lutheran Church and its summer day camp for years and then became a counselor when he was old enough. He loves the thought of Jesus, of the great eternal love He offers, and he loves the angels, particularly Gabriel, who prepared the way for Jesus and brought the news of His impending birth to Mary. But the angels are problematic. Sometimes Bart's thoughts about them drift to images of resting his head against a bare muscled angelic chest, of being enfolded by great wings. These images arrive in brilliant color, flamboyant glowing hues and they shade toward sexual feelings, sometimes cascade into these feelings, and he cannot stop himself. But the thoughts are only about the angels, never about Him. Not ever. After each bout of these thoughts, Bart is frightened and ordinary things begin to seem dangerous. Washing a glass, he imagines that it might splinter and cut him, or a knife he is using might slip, drawing blood. A car might swerve and hit him. Punishing thoughts, alarming and disorienting and, he feels, deserved. He is in danger. His fear forms a rough rectangle of pain in the center of his heart and then the pain moves to his stomach, sometimes to his gut. He has diarrhea when it gets really bad. He feels disgusted and purged when his bowels heave. Promising not to have the thoughts anymore is pointless, so he prays to be released from all of it. Until he reaches college, Bart's life has demanded a sustained act of deliberate silence. Years and years of silence enforced by terror of his differences, his sweetness, his passion for an angelic chest to rest his head against.

Ingrid has her own fantasies about punishment, but they are not about her punishment. Unlike Bart, who feels pursued by his images, Ingrid's do not distress her; she simply notices that they are there. Her early fantasies do not include active violence on her part. They are provoked by the beatings her father gives her. She imagines an intruder slipping into his room at night as he sleeps beside Dossie, who is always and forever wearing her old nightgown patterned with nasty blue roses, her hair in curlers, covered with a blue net. The intruder carries a knife, which he slips into her father's heart. There is no sound, no blood, her father never wakes. Dossie sleeps on until morning, when she rises to find him dead.

Later, Ingrid has the knife. She is the intruder, but the rest of the scenario is the same. She thinks that very early in her life, when the beatings started, there was no intruder in her fantasies, Arthur was simply dead in his sleep, but this is a blurry memory, she is not sure it was this way at all, ever. Ingrid understands these fantasies represent her rage at her father. They neither satisfy her nor scare her, though she knows she enjoys the idea of his being gone (dead) and she knows why. Until she is grown, she doesn't question why her mother never intervened, but stood in the kitchen cooking when Ingrid returned from the cellar. The beatings were done ritually, in the late afternoon, when Arthur returned from work, so Dossie was at the stove, her station at that hour. Dossie never turned around, just stirred her pots with concentration.

Bart, an only child with a crush on Jesus and the angels, and wild, opaque Ingrid meet in the drama class Ingrid has taken because she's curious and Bart has taken because the muses seem related to the angels and he has a secret wish to become an actor. Ingrid is a terrible actress, but interesting to watch because she does not get flustered, unlike the others who squirm and pose, who are seriously involved with acting. She does not mistake her flat attractive easiness for talent, although the teacher does, at least for a while.

❋ ☸ ❋

Bart and Ingrid sit in her room, listening to the roof dripping and the ice cracking everywhere in the first major spring thaw. The sun is shining and everything is wet and loosening in this late Iowa spring. It is their third year at the university. They are working on a piece together, going over the lines, the intention of each character. The yellow walls glow in this surprising warmth and light. Ingrid wears her usual jeans and heavy wool socks in blazing orange. Bart wears pressed chinos and a light blue shirt, a dark wool scarf draped carefully around his neck, more for effect than anything else. They are sipping espresso that Ingrid has improvised by using a lot of what passes for espresso coffee from a can and very little water. She sips with appreciation. Bart sips as little as possible; he already has a buzz and the taste is vile, though he will certainly not admit it. He has added about four spoons of sugar to the brew. Ingrid watches him fondly.

"You don't have to drink it," she says.

"No, no, I like it." He sips again, trying to look enthusiastic.

They both laugh.

"This is enough work," she says. "We've been diligent for hours. Let's take a walk."

They put jackets on, Ingrid not bothering to close hers, Bart zipping his neatly, and head out onto the campus and then farther into some nearby fields. After walking as far as they can, they stand for a moment at the edge of the field near a black squarish rock that has ice melting on it; the dark surface shines with water in the last of the afternoon light.

"I guess back," says Ingrid.

"Yes. Back."

They turn and begin the walk back to the campus. Then, with no preamble, Bart says, "You know about me, don't you?" He is looking at his boots as he speaks. "You know that I'm different." He stops and looks at Ingrid in silence. He can feel his stomach begin to clench.

Ingrid is not coy. "I know you're homosexual. Different depends on your point of view. Homosexuality has a long tradition. At least back to the ancient Greeks and undoubtedly long before that."

"The Greeks? What Greeks? You mean in mythology?" Bart has read extensively about myths, both Greek and Roman, since childhood. Has he missed something? Some essential clue that would have relieved his misery?

"No. Not myths. In history. Love between men was exalted in Sparta. In fact, it was enforced, although marriage was, as well. For procreation. They believed that lovers made the strongest soldiers because of their loyalty to each other. And let's not forget Sappho and the Isle of Lesbos." Ingrid seems very sure about what she is saying. Ingrid, too, has read widely and investigated topics not part of the general fare in Newton, Iowa at that time. She is not particularly interested in women sexually, but she is always curious. Some of her fantasies involve women and she is simply curious about them.

Bart feels joy and disbelief and the potential of relief so quickly that the feelings run together, like paint colors sliding between each other and mixing rapidly. The possibility that this might be true makes him feel almost faint. He feels like someone underwater, grasping for a root attached to the world above, clinging to its drifting end, a root that will pull him above the surface. "My church doesn't agree with the Greeks," he says. He wonders if his church even knows about this, if it is indeed true.

"No," says Ingrid. "I'm sure they don't. Why do you stay with the church?"

"I don't know." Bart sighs. They begin to walk again. "It's been there my whole life." He is embarrassed to say how much church means to him. He loves the community, even though he knows they would not accept his sexuality, would punish him for it. He can't imagine losing all those voices raised in song, in praise.

The cold increases noticeably as the dark floats around them. Ingrid's coat is still open, her body warm. She stops and turns to Bart and hugs him quickly, holding him tightly. He feels her breasts, her strong back. He is so unused to being hugged. For a moment he imagines relaxing his whole body, resting in her arms. Then the hug is over and she puts her arm through his. "Let's go to New York," she says. "Let's visit there this summer."

"I have to work in the summer," Bart says.

"So do I, but we can get a week off. I have some friends there; one of them will put us up. Let's do it."

"Okay, Ingrid. Let's," Bart agrees, astonished at the sound of his own voice.

✳ ✪ ✳

They arrive in New York City on a blazing day in August of 1964. The tar melts in pockets in the streets, sticking in small clumps to the soles of their sandals. What breeze there is feels cooked and it seems hotter than Iowa ever has, though the temperature may be comparable. They have been invited to stay with Ingrid's friend Sue Ann, who is a year older than they and has been in New York since her graduation. Ingrid and Bart make their way to Eighty-third Street between First and Second Avenues, where Sue Ann has a tiny one-bedroom apartment on the second floor of an old building now "renovated" and faced with spotted white brick, its halls covered in bright, smelly new aqua carpet. She stands waiting for them as they climb the stairs. She is wearing a chrome yellow summer dress and heels (in this weather!), and stockings and lipstick. For a moment Ingrid is stunned by the change. Where is the Sue Ann of torn jeans and loose curls that often smell faintly of marijuana? This is not the person she is expecting. But they all embrace and she is welcoming and happy to see them.

The apartment is the second shock. Ingrid—who visited Sue Ann at school in her messy apartment full of cats, colorful spreads on the old furniture, piles of drama books and scripts, mobiles, a faint, chronic scent of the aforementioned marijuana, along with good cooking smells and rotating boyfriends—expected a New York version of the same kind of place. In fact, the rectangular rooms are sharp with clean corners and everything painted white. The small living room is furnished with two sofas that bulge into the space and are covered in matching beige tweed, bulky animals marooned under the low ceiling, a polished glass coffee table stuck between them; the table holds a heavy glass ashtray and a lanky bouquet of brownish silk flowers. What flowers are brown? thinks Ingrid. Why are there brown flowers? Brown drapes hide what seem to be two sunny windows. A white shag rug squats on the living room floor. In Sue Ann's old place, the floors were bare and cool, slightly gritty if you walked with bare feet; the boards were patched and the whole floor slanted. Sue Ann shows them the bedroom, which is taken up by a double bed swathed in apricot covers and piled with matching pillows. Even the pretty framed photographs of autumn leaves that are hung on one living room wall seem ugly to Ingrid. The kitchen is tiny, no more than an alcove, and there are no smells of cooking. Ingrid is stunned, not so much at the décor, but at the obvious changes in her friend that the décor represents. There has been no hint of this in Sue Ann's letters, unless Ingrid has missed something. Can this be what happens to people in New York? Surely not. Surely? But still, she has midwestern manners and comments on it all with appreciation and real appreciation at the invitation to stay, since they could not have afforded the trip otherwise. During the week of their stay, Ingrid will try to look at the apartment like a Cornell box. In her studies, she has found a lot of artists that fascinate her, and Cornell is one of them. Along with Rothko and, in a completely different way, Georges de La Tour. She tries to look at the rooms as if they were Cornell boxes, squares filled with treasures. But it doesn't work. The rooms remain static and sad.

Bart loves it. Just what he would like to have, he thinks. So clean and pretty. Really pleasing. His appreciation is wholehearted.

Sue Ann is happy to see them, makes no apologies for her changes in taste, dresses every day in a dress, stockings and one of two pairs of expensive heels she owns as she goes to her job as a receptionist in a company that sells fine china. She still reads *Variety,* and tries to go to auditions, but it is hard, she says. Earning a living comes first. At night, they fold out one of the couches for Bart and she and Ingrid share the double bed. They have slept together before, not in a sexual way, but one of friendship and easy closeness. The comfort of another body on a freezing Iowa night when it is very late and you have drunk a little too much wine and home seems too far to attempt. This, apparently, has not changed as a possibility between them. Ingrid is relieved not to have to sleep on the floor, since the second couch does not fold out, and happy to have the physical nearness of her old friend, seemingly so far away in other ways.

✳ ❁ ✳

On their initial full day in New York, Ingrid and Bart head downtown to investigate. Bart wants to go to Greenwich Village first. He knows it is a place where he will find homosexuals. He says the word slowly and deliberately to himself. Other men like him. (He is not thinking of lesbians.) He is quite sure from his reading that they are there. Absolutely sure, really. And he is right. Of course, there are homosexuals at the university, too. A few hang out together, but Bart is not one of their group. Others are loners and still others, he is sure, undisclosed. Like him. No one has talked about being in or out of the closet, and though the phrase is an old one, it is not in general contemporary use. Not yet.

"See," says Ingrid, as they walk through Washington Square Park and then farther west into the Village.

"I knew," says Bart. "This isn't news to me, it's just new emotionally."

"I know," says Ingrid, and then in what is, for her, a very tender voice, says, "I didn't mean to hurt your feelings."

"No, you didn't hurt them." He smiles and links his arm through hers. "I'm glad we're here."

They swim through the stunning heat and find a place for lunch in the West Village. The air conditioning is icy and the food reassuring and plentiful. They have plump salads with rich dressing, and turkey, and tomatoes, and ham, and lots of strong coffee, which Bart has learned to tolerate, if not enjoy. After lunch, they double back and walk to the East Village, the old Lower East Side, which has slid into its new identity, housing hippie intellectuals and drop outs, drugs and brazen music alongside the Ukrainians and a few lingering Jews, not the ones who are hippies, but old families still there from earlier times. Ingrid loves the tilting buildings, some now sprouting window boxes overflowing with bright flowers in purple, red and gold. She loves the Ukrainian stores selling ornate delicate blouses and the butchers selling fresh pork sausage. She loves the clouds of loud music that suddenly emerge and the edgy feeling between the groups trying to live together in this steamy, rickety neighborhood. She realizes that she is unused to loving so many things at once, and smiles to herself. Bart is uncomfortable, but willing. Late in the afternoon, they shop for a snack to take to Tompkins Square Park. They stop on First Avenue at a tiny cheese store. The woman behind the counter is pale, her hair scarce, dark with bad dye; she moves slowly, encased in the milky aura of the store. Ingrid sees the blue numbers tattooed on her arm, stretching out along the wrinkled skin. Bart notices them, knows they mean something and also knows not to ask until they are out on the street, walking toward a bakery for rolls. Ingrid explains to him. They are both silent as they head toward the park with their food. Bart thinks about how many Jews he has known in his life. Not very many, even including his time at the university. He wonders how many Ingrid has known. Probably not that many, either. He thinks about asking her and decides against it.

During the next couple of days, they go to museums, starting with the Museum of Modern Art. Ingrid stands in front of the Rothkos, barely breathing and at the same time wanting to shout or sing or lie down flat on her back and howl. Those huge rectangles, inviting the viewer to passion and mystery, tragedy and redemption. Light that has darkened and taken on breath. Bart looks at them thoughtfully. He doesn't really like abstract art that much. Finally, he says, "They look like they belong in a church. Not a church I've ever seen, but some church."

"They do," says Ingrid. At some time quite close to this conversation, Rothko begins to do work for a chapel in Texas and one day Ingrid will see this work, but that is far in the future. On that first museum day, they look at the Cornell boxes —which are, to Ingrid, both inviting and whimsical and oddly sinister—and at the Hoffmans and Picassos. Bart's feet hurt. Ingrid feels as if her skin is splitting. She is wildly excited by the work and devastated by how little she knows, how unskilled she is. She doesn't feel the devastation as a collapse, but as a great force that will push her forward. By the time they get to the Metropolitan Museum, the next day, and she sees the de La Tours, she is exhausted. Her feet hurt, too, but she barely notices. The paintings seem to inhabit her as she looks at them, the light on the canvases coming from everywhere and nowhere at once, elusive and completely present. She wants to turn the painting of the Magdalene around and see her face. She stares at the candle reflected in the mirror, light on light. *The Fortune Teller* is depicted as sly, grasping and amused. She sees "merde" sketched lightly, almost invisibly, into the lace scarf that one woman wears. Later, the painting's authenticity will be questioned, though the tag at the Met will not change.

Bart doesn't even ask about going on the Staten Island Ferry, or seeing the Statue of Liberty. He doesn't actually care. Not much, anyway.

In the middle of the week they are there, Sue Ann makes dinner and invites her friend Stephen. Since Ingrid and Sue Ann are busy cooking, Bart answers the door. Stephen is tall and slender, with a sculpted face and deep gold hair pulled back into a ponytail. He is wearing old, tight jeans and a turquoise silk shirt that fits him well. On his right forefinger is a lapis ring, the stone worn and pitted slightly. He has slanting eyes, light brown, with long, flat lashes. He is carrying two bottles of wine. Bart stands in the doorway and simply stares. Stephen waits for a few moments and then says, "May I come in?"

Bart blushes and steps back. "Yes, yes, please. Pleased to meet you." He is afraid to extend his hand, afraid to touch this beautiful man. There is no other way to describe it, Bart thinks, Stephen simply glows. Sue Ann moves toward Stephen and they hug.

"Gorgeous woman, glorious woman," Stephen says. Sue Ann introduces Ingrid and she and Stephen regard each other in a friendly, somewhat speculative way.

Sue Ann has cooked a dinner that would be recognized in Iowa, perhaps a bit tongue-in-cheek, but splendid and abundant. Macaroni and cheese, and hamburgers that run with juice and, as a New York touch, a crisp salad with garlicky dressing. They talk easily except for Bart, who touches the wine glass to his lips without drinking and periodically feels his face get hot. He almost forgets to eat. He feels as if thin wires run through him, bright and strong, holding him still, holding him so that he cannot flee. When he does remember to eat, he chews the familiar tasting food, afraid he will not be able to swallow. He can barely look at Stephen, but he does. He tries. He knows Ingrid is aware of his reactions, though she makes no obvious indication of it. He can feel her noticing and feel her kindness toward him. For dessert, Sue Ann has baked (baked! In that tiny kitchen) white cake with coconut frosting. At the end of the evening, Stephen asks Bart out for the following night. "Just to show you around," he says. Bart looks desperately at Ingrid. She raises one eyebrow almost invisibly as a "yes."

"Yes," Bart says. "Certainly. Thank you." But he knew he would say yes, no matter what Ingrid signaled.

The next night, Stephen takes Bart to two bars and a club in the Village. Stephen is wearing an amber colored silk shirt, much like the one he wore at dinner, but in a deep, warm shade, and black jeans that look both worn and expensive. Everything about Stephen looks expensive and Bart still sees him as glowing, radiant. It must be a permanent condition, Bart imagines. (It is not.) Bart is wearing his usual chinos and a plain white shirt he has ironed carefully. And loafers, shined. The night is cloudy, with a warm wind blowing, the air dense. At the bars and club, the only patrons are men. Apart from the men's locker room, Bart has never seen so many men together, without women, in one place. Never seen so many men like him, although he is trying to think of it some other way, trying to shift the accustomed pattern of his thoughts, but uncertain what to shift them to. To some idea that this is normal for some people, for some men. But it is too early and his mind refuses to move much from its habitual stance; maybe moves just enough to both give him hope and make him feel disoriented. As they go from bar to bar and then to the club, they talk about Bart's courses, Stephen's work. He is a designer, working with textiles. He is being very successful, just now, with his plain, elegant fabrics, so different from what is popular, and very much in demand. He is somewhat older than Bart thought at first and, he realizes, without knowing exactly how, that Stephen is wealthy. Which he is. Very. "So what do you make of all this?" Stephen asks, when they are seated at the club. "All of us gay men together?" Bart has never heard the word, but likes the image it presents.

Better than queer, he thinks. Or homo. Or faggot. Or any other word he has heard so far that describes his sexual preferences. He is right at the beginning edge of being able to imagine them that way: his sexual preferences. Not a curse he carries, but a preference. A choice that he has made.

"I feel overwhelmed," Bart says honestly. I feel excited, he thinks, but is not ready to say. The club is luxurious. Soft sofas covered in velvety rose dot the room. The walls are cream and garnet, the lighting flattering, the music loud, which makes it easier not to have to talk too much. Palms and other tropical plants glow green under the flattering lights. Light also comes from candles set around the room and, seemingly, from some other source Bart can't identify. The light plays on the walls so that they seem almost transparent. The men moving around the room seem to swim in light. A lavish bar, bright with bottles and shining glasses is reflected in a large wall mirror.

"I can't interest you in a drink?" Stephen says.

"I really don't drink," Bart says. "I just never have." He doesn't refer to his church, or his upbringing, all the ominous things he has heard about alcohol. Not to mention all the rest of it. The lurid descriptions of hell that have pursued him since he can remember.

"How have you survived at school without drinking?" Stephen asks, only half kidding. "A vodka martini and a club soda," he says to a passing waiter. The waiter makes a small tick on a pad, but no money seems to change hands.

A group of men enter together and are seated at a round table. It is a tight fit and they jostle each other, laughing. Clearly they are friends. "Actors," Stephen says. "They're in some of the biggest hits. *Funny Girl*, and *Oliver!*, and some others." One in particular catches Bart's eye. Black curls spring around his face. His eyes are heavy lidded, his mouth wide and, at the moment, pouting in what seems a teasing way. "Anton Lark," Stephen says. "He's very young, but he's been in a lot of productions. He has a gorgeous voice and he dances." Anton Lark turns his head, sees Stephen and waves.

At the bars and then at the club, Stephen is well known. There are many greetings—small kisses. Hugs. Bart has been the focus of a fair amount of attention, which both puzzles and embarrasses him. Men have asked about him, been interested. Stephen notices his discomfort. "Young and beautiful," he says. He smiles.

"I am? Beautiful?"

"Yes, in your way. All that innocence. Very alluring." Stephen pretends to leer and then stops. "Yes," he says again. "You're surprised?"

"Believe me, it's an unusual experience in my life. Unheard of would be closer. Astonishing." They are sitting on one of the rose colored sofas. The music has stopped and their voices suddenly sound very loud to Bart, even in the midst of all the other noise, all the mingled voices. It is very late for Bart. "I have to go," he says. He looks at his watch. Even later than he thought. "I'll wake everyone as it is."

Stephen stands. "Come, I'll take you home." They leave and walk to the avenue, looking for a cab. Stephen takes Bart's arm, but no more. He looks at him in the city night, which is never really dark. They can see each other quite clearly. "I wouldn't dream of trying to seduce you. Oh well, maybe dream, but that's all. You're safe with me."

Bart listens to Stephen's voice, mingled with the sounds of traffic and their footsteps. Is safe what he wants to be? Yes, he thinks. For the moment.

"When you choose," Stephen continues, "choose carefully." His voice drifts a little in the warm wind, but Bart hears him.

"I will," he says seriously. A cab stops in front of them. "You don't need to ride all the way uptown with me."

"I want to. This is early for me. I'll get you home." They are quiet in the cab and at the end, just as Bart steps out, Stephen says, "Do you want to go to the Statue of Liberty tomorrow? I don't see Ingrid as a sightseeing type."

"I would love to. No, Ingrid isn't really interested. Ingrid is quite vocally not interested." Bart feels daring. He never criticizes Ingrid, even mildly this way. Not that he thinks she would mind. It is just a habit with him, not be critical, ever. Not out loud.

"I'll come by at eleven or so." Stephen closes the cab door and Bart goes upstairs to his sleeping friends and the whispers of a city night.

The cab skims downtown through the grid of streets, now almost empty of traffic. Stephen decides not to go home, but to his lover's. "I want to go to Fifth Avenue and Ninth Street," he says to the cabbie. "Change of destination." He thinks about Bart as the cab rolls through the hot, cloudy night. How he really would like to seduce him. Or not so much seduce him in a purely erotic way, but to lick his skin, to suck him. To have all that milky innocence in his mouth and to touch him wherever he wishes. He regards his thoughts with irony, with his accustomed distance. Would it refresh him? Could he partake of that dewy smoothness and heal himself? He is so tired. Cold and dry inside, everything arid, all the golden heat exploded to the outside, shining in his hair, glowing in his skin. He wants Joseph, his much older lover, to comfort him and he knows Joseph will try and it will fail. He rests his head against the back of the seat and breathes quietly for the rest of the ride.

The next day it is suddenly cooler, with a clear bright sky. Bart sleeps until almost ten, something he has rarely done in his life. Everyone is gone when he wakes and he hasn't heard a thing. There is hot coffee waiting for him in an electric percolator and he drinks a cup, loading it with sugar and milk. He still tries to like it black and doesn't drink much coffee of any kind, but this morning, in the sudden, welcome coolness and with a late night behind him, he swallows it down happily and then rushes to take a shower. A breeze trails through an open window and after his shower he stands for a moment letting the moving air touch his still-wet body. He dresses and sits on the couch, waiting for Stephen, half believing that he will not come at all. But he does. He rings the bell a few minutes after eleven. This time he is wearing an almost sheer cotton shirt in the palest green, sleeves rolled up and some lightweight version of chinos. He and Bart smile at each other, really glad to be together, just spontaneously happy. He declines the offer of coffee and they set out for their day, down to the ferry that will take them to the Statue of Liberty. They walk close together, but Stephen does not take his arm again.

Once at the statue, they climb the steps inside, tight and winding. Bart is frightened of small closed spaces, which Stephen senses, since he is frightened of them himself. He rests his hand on Bart's back as they go higher and higher until they look out the windows of the crown. So many people around them, seemingly from all over the world. Different languages and accents and smells, everyone excited to see the view, the open water spilling wide. Down is worse for Bart than up, but he makes it and then, at the bottom, begins to laugh. He and Stephen laugh together, their mutual relief making them giddy. They go for lunch at the cafeteria that is part of the park and eat awful tuna sandwiches and drink icy lemonade that is not made from anything remotely resembling lemons. Voices curve around them speaking French and German and some languages that Bart can't identify, but Stephen can. "That's Portuguese," he says once. And then, later, "That's Norwegian. My father is in the Navy, quite high up. The family traveled a lot and moved often. Thus my skill in identifying languages. I hated all the moves, always being a stranger, a thin tall blond boy, shy and awkward. Different." Bart listens with absorption. So unlike his own life. Most of his family have never traveled outside of Iowa. Well, maybe the men who were in the army, the wars, but hardly anyone else.

"I can't imagine you were," he says, looking at gleaming Stephen.

"Oh, morbidly shy," Stephen, says. Something he has mentioned to very few people in his current life, though Joseph, his lover, knows. "My father used to beat me to make me more sociable. An excellent technique," he says dryly. "No," he says. "I learned to fake it. I'm an accomplished fake." He seems sad.

Stephen asks him about Ingrid and Bart tells him how close they are, what good friends and how she sort of saved his life by telling him so much about being gay. "You know, the history in Greece and everything." He uses the word "gay" deliberately. He is trying it out. His new identity. Then he says, "Well, our history, really," including Stephen and all the men they saw the previous night and all the men everywhere who are suffering with people's ignorance and cruelty. He can imagine them all, fanning out across the globe. He knows what Hitler did to homosexuals. To gays.

Stephen listens to Bart's earnest voice describing his life and wants to weep. To offer something. "You have suffered so much pain," he says. "The pain isn't unusual, but that doesn't make it any easier." Uncommonly kind, for Stephen, who is so often mocking, in that self-protective amusing way. Oddly, the day continues to cool as they sit and talk, particularly cool here, near the water. Such welcome refreshing air. The sun shifts overhead and Stephen looks at his watch. "I need to go," he says. "I have some work I need to do." This is true, but the work is not pressing. What is pressing is that Stephen has stopped fooling himself about Bart and knows he would very much like to have sex with him, to kiss him and hold him and penetrate him in an exquisite, slow way. The only thing that is going to stop him from pursuing this idea is to flee. Stephen knows himself. He knows he is not trustworthy about sex, about his desires. He understands this would be Bart's first sexual experience and does not want to have an encounter and then abandon him to Iowa. He knows Ingrid and Bart are leaving very soon. Well, he thinks, maybe I am becoming more trustworthy. This idea makes him feel hopeful about himself, his needs. A rare feeling. He cherishes it as it rests inside him. The interior dryness seems moistened by it, if only slightly. "I'll put you on the right train to take you home," he says.

"Great," says Bart. He is pleased to have spent so many hours with Stephen. If he can feel a sexual heat between them, he pretends not to notice it. Maybe it is not there? Surely Stephen is not interested in him? Not possible. He dismisses the idea and they head for the ferry that will take them back to Manhattan. The wind continues to blow, gusting a little as they walk toward the ferry dock.

The day that Bart and Stephen spend at the Statue of Liberty, Ingrid goes to the Frick Collection, which she does not much like, though there are magnificent paintings, Vermeer and Rembrandt and some watery, enveloping Corots. The place itself puts her off and she leaves, thinking she will return to the Met, but as she walks along the park, past the heavy Fifth Avenue buildings, their doormen standing in uniforms and hats, the avenue fairly empty, since it is August and many of the residents of this neighborhood are away, she suddenly wants to see no more art. Cannot ingest any more beauty until what she has already seen has metabolized in some way. And she really wants to get out of this neighborhood, wants to go back to the East Village, still so recently the Lower East Side. She walks to the subway and rides down to Astor Place and spends the rest of her day wandering the streets, looking at blocks she might like to live on when she moves here. Which she knows she will. Appreciating the street life: the rawness and the brilliantly colorful clothes and the wafting smell of food shops and patchouli on warm skin and car exhaust. To her, a peculiarly New York mixture, heady and welcome. She feels as if these sights and smells are mixing with her blood, becoming part of the deepest essence of her bones, totally new, yet familiar in a way that brings a sense of relief, of belonging when she has always been a stranger. Nothing in Iowa looks or smells this way. She knows it will be a while before she can see art like the Frick Collection or the Met again, but she does not regret her choice to leave. This walk has been a mission to imprint herself with her future and be imprinted on it. Ingrid returns to Sue Ann's for their farewell dinner feeling satisfied and determined to return to New York. The city has settled in her body and rests there.

Sue Ann takes Ingrid and Bart to an Indian restaurant in the east twenties for their farewell meal. The neighborhood has a disjointed feeling, seems to have no center, just mismatched buildings, unrelated to each other and of no particular style. There are several Indian restaurants, though Indian food is still fairly unusual, even in New York, and neither Bart nor Ingrid have ever eaten it. "Last Supper," says Bart. "Well, not very original." Sue Ann explains the menu to them, happy to be the expert and to share her urban know-how.

"Vindaloo is very hot and then it's down from there," she says. Bart looks slightly worried. He hasn't eaten much hot food, but seems to remember that it hurts his stomach.

"The korma is mild," Sue Ann says, noticing his discomfort. The restaurant is full of Indians, the women in bright saris, some threaded with gold, shiny black hair parted in the middle. A few wear dark red bindis on their foreheads. Other diners wear jeans, ordinary summer dresses. Outside, it rains lightly in the heat, not relieving it, just wetting everything. They sample the breads—warm parathas, chapatis—and various chutneys and dal, everything so full of taste and texture and scent. They order tandoori chicken and vegetable curries and korma and share all of it. Sharp, dense food. Creamy, sour food. Ingrid particularly savors the heat of the food, thinking how different it is from the bland fare she was raised on and how Iowa is a place curiously without internal heat, in spite of the blasting furnace summer weather. The food burns inside her, merging with the city she has taken into her belly, makes her eyes water where all the works of art she has seen are lying just beneath her eyelids, pressed there, perhaps forever.

The next day, they leave, carrying their bulky bags and sandwiches and cookies that Sue Ann made for them. The gray heat and rain have continued, following them to the bus station so that they are damp as they settle into their seats, which smell of forever, an eternity of tired journeys. The bus motor starts and they begin to roll slowly out of the station. Bart rests his hand on Ingrid's arm.

"Only a week," she says. "It seems longer."

"Well, a week," Bart says. "God made the world in six days." He laughs to detract from what he is saying, what he really thinks.

"I don't really believe in fate," Ingrid says, "But if I did, I would say I was fated to live here." Bart moves his hand and holds hers briefly.

The old Earth spins on its axis, rocks slowly around the sun. Inside their bodies, Ingrid and Bart are digesting the last of the Indian meal. Somewhere, stars are dying and new ones are being born in star nurseries immeasurably far away.

"I know we will," he says. "We will." The bus sounds its horn. One long sad bleat as it moves heavily along the ramp and out into traffic.

❋ ✿ ❋

Ingrid and Bart return to Iowa at sunset on an evening when the sky, now seeming huge, almost unreal after the tight New York skyline, is filled with flamboyant color. Scarlet and purple and gleaming yellow spread in streaks across the immensity of the heavens, so familiar and now new again. Their journey has shaken the accustomed out of its frame. The light is reflected in ponds, on windows, everything saturated with it. A vast display of color, with the wide fields lying beneath it, houses, square and plain, dressed in this glow.

"It was fantastic," this from Bart as he gathers his things.

"It was that," Ingrid says. "I'll call you tomorrow." So much to say, so much more than they even know at the moment. They part with a hug and Bart goes to his dorm room—his still, for this last year. Ingrid heads for her apartment.

When Ingrid reaches home, the colors are fading, but the light is still bright. Her one large plant has thrived in her absence, watered by her friend Sarah. Her cat,

Bistro, who has stayed with Sarah, comes toward her, small striped body trembling with purrs. She picks him up and holds him close, feels the cat pressing against her chest and becomes aware that something feels torn open inside her, the tear both scary and pleasurable. The torn edges shiver. Time has twisted upside down and is whirling, carrying her, invading her heartbeat. A map that she will follow, unrolling silently within her. Still holding the cat, she sits down on the couch and stays there long after darkness has filled the room.

In the dorm, Bart makes himself some cocoa, gets his mail and takes a long shower. The familiar smells of the dorm float around him. He unpacks slowly, considers doing the laundry, then just gets into bed and reads until he falls asleep, quite early. He wants to think about the trip, but there is too much to even begin now. He dreams of Stephen dancing on an icy pond with a man who says he is Merlin, the wizard, and introduces himself quite formally to Bart. Dark trees ring the pond, heavy pines with dense branches that enclose the frozen circle of water, hiding it from outside view.

❋ ✪ ❋

Ingrid and Bart begin their last year at the university. It is a golden autumn, deep golds and bronze and leaves that are shiny and almost the color of mahogany. Sometimes they take long walks across the browning fields and talk about New York and the changes it has wrought inside them. The talk is tentative at first, Ingrid guarded out of habit and perplexed by how to express the experience of tearing open, of time shifting and sliding so that her experience of the present is altered. Bart is simply frightened of what he knows more and more and what he longs for. But they grow closer during these walks, where they mostly look straight ahead, will not face each other. The combination of the rhythm of their walking and not looking directly at each other makes their intimacy easier. Neither of them is yet gifted in intimacy, familiar with its pathways. The sky holds them as surely as the earth beneath their feet. Heavy autumn clouds billow and stretch, blown by the cooling winds, and the days grow shorter.

Ingrid has become interested in the *I Ching* and in Tarot cards, not because oracles intrigue her, but because they deal with alterations in time, the slippery edges of past, present and future, the mystery of what is known, or half intuited, below the rim of daily consciousness. Her interest in synchronicity was provoked by reading John Cage's writing, listening to a lot of his music. She buys the Rider-Waite Tarot Deck with its stylized and, to her, ugly drawings with their bright senseless colors and flattened faces. The images she develops in her mind are more potent to her than the cards. She also finds a French book on the Tarot, *Le Tarot de Marseille,* which she reads with a dictionary near at hand. She buys the Bollingen edition of the *I Ching* and begins to use it, studying the language carefully, both learning and sensing the meanings of the hexagrams.

She imagines the Tarot cards as rooms that contain magical experiences that can, within their landscape, transform what is possible, what can be imagined or revealed. Scenes move, whispers are heard, animals breathe. She wants to build boxes that contain the legends of the Major Arcana—the Empress, the Fool, the Hierophant—but in an oblique way. She imagines that when people see them, they will respond, consciously or not, to the potential for transformation.

She starts with the Empress. In the Empress box, she puts tiny animal bones and glass and torn papers that are covered with her dried menstrual blood. Bits of old cracked mirrors and snips of bright ribbon and old photographs of empresses that she cuts or scars. Shattered pieces of junk jewelry. She wants to break the string of pearls her mother gave her when she started at the university, but she does not. It seems too cruel. She burns part of the Empress card itself and buries it in the box. The cards suggest environments to her as she reads about them and dreams them. One night she dreams about the Empress wearing a heavy gown, hair wild, feet bare, calling to her from a wide and barren field. Ingrid runs toward her, but the Empress vanishes before they can connect, leaving only the imprints of her bare feet on the ground and the sound of her voice in the empty air.

Ingrid has weeks and then months of being with the Empress card, building the box, painting some of the pieces of glass, adding things and then removing them. She puts in dust and sand, things that adhere slightly to other surfaces. Sometimes she breathes into the box, so that it is impregnated with her breath. She would like to use her tears, but she cries infrequently and never when she is conveniently near her work. The irony of the situation is not lost on her. Other times she touches her hands with geranium oil, a scent she loves, so bitter and dense, and holds the pieces she is working with so the scent clings to them, inhabits the work. Why is this the Empress to her? Blood and broken glass and breath and burned images of the Empress card itself and of other real life counterparts? Breath and scent and scorched images. She plans to go on and do the Fool and then the Hierophant. She thinks of the Fool not as an ordinary person, but as wisdom hidden within the ordinary and, in some ways, sees the figure at the edge of a precipice, looking up toward the sky and holding his flower, as the artist, always at risk, maybe oblivious, but maybe trusting. She does not yet know about the Holy Fool, God's juggler, but she will discover these ideas as she works and reads and dreams. She knows very little about the Hierophant, symbol of the esoteric world, but she is strongly attracted to the image and knows she needs to study it a great deal more before she does that piece. She tells no one about the Empress construction, although Bart knows she is studying the cards. She does not show it to her professor, though he suspects her real work is not what he is seeing. Controlled and brilliant, the work she shows him carries no essence, no quality of Ingrid's being within it. This professor is a lanky man, more bones than flesh, with wheat colored hair going thin in back and slanting gray eyes, high cheekbones, raw looking hands. Ingrid devalues him. He knows more than Ingrid imagines, but he doesn't press her; it is clear to him that it would be useless, yet he wonders what she is really doing, so absorbed and focused, so intent. The work he sees is not the product of that kind of intensity. Thus, in her inaccurate judgment, she misses an opportunity to have him reflect on the work with her, to appreciate it, to offer something to her. Much later, in New York, when Ingrid begins to show her work, he comes to see it and is unsurprised at what she has created.

She is simultaneously creating the Empress box and reading about Zen and finds a group on campus to meditate with. They meet in the apartment of one or another of the group members, often doing their Zen sitting meditation amidst dusty furniture and smells of the just-past dinner. The light snores of a resident dog might accompany the chanting and their silence. There is no teacher, no Roshi to guide them, but Ingrid goes regularly and finds that silence is familiar, a relief. A refuge. Behind the silence is a place she can barely enter, a place where time dissolves, where she has no identity and all possibilities seem to exist simultaneously. On the few occasions that her awareness opens to encompass this experience, she feels as though her world has been dismantled and that her perception of ordinary life has torn itself apart. It seems like an extension of the feelings she had just after her return from New York, but more intense. And, in some remembered way, of what she perceived as a little girl, sitting in the great umbrella of the tree, dissolving into the leaves, each a slightly different green, a different shape. For a little while after the perception has vanished and she has returned to a familiar state of awareness, she is afraid that she has lost language, that she will not be able to speak, will not remember the route home and although these events do not occur, she understands that she is changed in ways she cannot explain or communicate.

Gradually, as the winter freezes around them and heavy snows fall, she becomes friends with two people from the group, Jeremy and Beth. Jeremy comes from San Francisco, his father a professor at Berkeley, his mother a pediatrician. A friendly man, whose gaze is humorous and somewhat elusive, a fox man, auburn hair, burnished skin, slinky and sinuous. He is smart, his quiet comments incisive, offered in his soft voice. Beth is wide on the bottom, sturdy legs, flat bosom, cropped brown hair. A woman who looks as if she must live in very clean surroundings, everything scrubbed, laundry folded and put away, though she is ardent and lively, not prim at all. (Nothing like Ingrid's family.) She is clearly crazy about Jeremy, this very sane woman, and he holds his arm around her loosely, not quite touching enough. Beth seems to signal this to Ingrid, to everyone. They go out together after the sittings and talk about Zen, though none of them know much. They talk and speculate and drink gallons of hot tea, sitting in a steamy silvered haze at the café. Happy in their talk, words bouncing between them in that safe, warm retreat, with the cold bitter and relentless outside. One night they bundle up and go out after a sitting to look at the stars in their icy remoteness and flashing presence, staying in the cold as long as they can. Their friendship grows in the dark nights, in the silent sittings, in the shared talk.

Sometimes Bart goes with Ingrid to sit Zazen on those stiff, raised cushions, a little square of quilt under his ankles. He is experimenting in several areas. He has bought a few new things since returning from New York: a pair of jeans that fit more snugly and two new sweaters, one in a soft apricot. He admires the curve of his bottom in the store's mirror on the day he buys the jeans, embarrassed and pleased. He has grown his hair, which, to his surprise, is a lovely nut brown with pale, glinting highlights. Having never had long hair in his life, he had no idea what his hair actually looked like. It had always seemed an essentially colorless brown, thick and soft, but cut so short it had no reality. He touches his hair with love when he combs it in the morning, and rubs his scalp with his fingers. So he sits, in his new clothes and new bright hair, chanting words in an ancient language from a page they all use before and after the meditation. He doesn't really think of it as religion. Ingrid says Buddhism is more of a philosophy. She has assured him this is the case. He still goes to church regularly. One night at the end of the winter, just before the cold gives way and temperatures start to rise, just as the light is really noticeably longer, just as the spring bulbs, buried in the dark frozen earth, begin to move and push those still hidden daffodils and brilliant tulips, Bart accepts a ride home from choir practice from a sweet, plump man who has sung in the church for many years. He is in his thirties, married, with two small daughters. They stop outside Bart's dorm and Stanley suddenly rests his hand on Bart's thigh. Bart is too surprised even to jump. Stanley sighs and leans back against the seat. His eyes are closed. "I just wanted to touch you," he says. "Just to touch."

Bart is absolutely still. He thinks his blood might have stopped flowing.

"This—I don't do this," Stanley says. "I'm sorry." But he leaves his hand on Bart's leg. He is—waiting?

"It's all right," Bart says.

"Of course it isn't," Stanley says. "Now I've frightened you. I'm married. I love Ellen."

The heater pours hot air into the car as moisture collects on the windows. Bart feels as if the space is filled with sharp broken things with edges like splintered seashells. "I know. I'm sure you do." He doesn't know how often he will hear these words, or some form of them. My wife. My girlfriend. My lover. "It's nothing. Let's forget it." He moves his leg and Stanley pulls his hand away. He gets out of the car and smiles, waves. Stanley stares straight ahead and starts the car as soon as the door shuts. Bart hurries into the dorm, his stomach clenched. He hopes his insides are not going to let go and they don't. He thinks of calling Ingrid, but then decides to tell her in person. He doesn't want his words drifting through the phone line, insubstantial. He wants to see Ingrid's face and feel her presence. The songs that the choir rehearsed that evening play in his mind, as he gets ready for bed, for sleep. Waiting beneath the earth, perhaps the bulbs nudge each other, move infinitesimally. This night will be slightly shorter than the one before.

Spring comes in fits and starts. The bulbs bloom, hardy and resilient in the shifting winds that are sometimes mild and other times chill, almost as cold as winter. Leaves unfurl, first pale, with the red undertone of early foliage, then greener, fuller. The air is saturated with the scent of growing life, the creeks run high and fast. Ingrid and Bart are pulling toward the end of their studies, doing papers. Finishing projects and readying for their last exams. Suddenly, at the beginning of May, the sun gets hot, blazing in a clear sky day after day. It is not really warm enough to go swimming, but Ingrid, Bart, Jeremy and some other friends decide to go to a nearby lake. Beth is not there. "Home doing a paper," Jeremy says. "And she hates cold water." They wear suits under their clothes, but no one imagines they will really get into that icy water, no matter how hot the sun. They bring juices and sandwiches. This is not a drinking crowd. The lake facilities are still closed for the winter, the umbrellas put away, the changing rooms locked, along with the bathrooms. They unload their cars, take off shoes and socks and walk gingerly on the half moon of sand, which is surprisingly warm beneath their feet. Spreading out blankets and food, they eat and then lie in the amazing sun, the hard packed sand holding them beneath their blankets. When they are hot enough, Ingrid, Jeremy and a reluctant Bart stand with their feet in the water. The shallow edge is almost warm, inviting. The breeze blows the scent of sun lotion in a small cloud around them. Bart's fair skin is already slightly pink.

"I'm going in," says Ingrid and in her usual extreme way, she plunges forward. No further testing, just her whole body submerged and then swimming fast. "Oh, my God," she says. She heads back toward shore and dives out of the water as fast as she went in. She is shivering and pulls off her suit and wraps herself in towels, rubbing hard. "Almost lost my breath," she says. "So cold." She laughs. "Well, you can't have too many extraneous thoughts in that situation. Maybe an aid to meditating." She dresses and heads toward her car. "I'm going home to a hot shower. Anyone coming?" Everyone decides to leave except for Bart and Jeremy, who have dried their feet and are sitting on a thick blanket. They look at the lake for a while, seeing the dark rocks beneath the greenish water, silent shapes, dark heavy curves. Jeweled water under the sun's light, waiting for the warmth to penetrate its surface.

"Maybe we should have brought brandy," says Jeremy. The light glows on his hair, dark auburn, glinting and bright. They lie down together on their backs and then Jeremy reaches his hand out and touches Bart's arm. Slowly he rolls over and puts his arms around Bart and pulls him close. He begins to kiss him slowly. The sun drops quietly, moving toward the horizon. Bart returns the kisses, his heart beating so hard he thinks it will pop. Their skin is hot from the sun, but the breeze is rising, cooling. Bart starts to shiver. Their faces are wet from kissing. Bart is unused to kissing, to this kind of heat. He has never kissed anyone this way. Or at all, really. Small puckered kisses in spin the bottle early in high school. His body welcomes it, even as he struggles with shame, seeing images that crack open, sharp as lightning and reveal quick, disapproving faces. Faces he knows—his parents, the minister—and faces of strangers, staring. The images flash away as quickly as they came. Bart and Jeremy stroke each other, touching all over. Bart feels Jeremy's long legs; he pulls at his hair, his fingers wrapped in the thick crinkled curls. Jeremy slips his hand under Bart's suit and rubs him. He cradles Bart's balls, rocking. He rocks into Bart's tension. He begins to push gently against the backs of Bart's upper thighs and then kneads his butt.

"No," Bart says. "No, not there." Not anywhere near the place of all those memories, his scalding shaming fear. His accidents. Strangely, he is not worried he will have one now, but he is adamant about not being touched there. Jeremy moves his hand and rubs Bart's abdomen, kneading and then bending to kiss his belly, to suck on the warm skin. He moves to his cock, circles it with his tongue.

"I'm going to touch you here," he says. Jeremy's hand is careful and skilled. He licks Bart's eyelids and they gaze at each other, breathing together. Their breath shifts into sound, wordless. Bart lifts his pelvis. Jeremy strokes him and then stops and then starts again, strokes him until he has an orgasm, saying, "Come, come. It's yours. Take it. Come." Then he presses Bart's hand against his own cock and holds him there. "Squeeze," he says, moving up and down with Bart's rhythm. The wind rises until it is really chilly, but neither of them stops. It is too good. For Bart, his need ancient and forever, soaked in years of loneliness and doomed yearning. After Jeremy comes, they hold each other until it is really too cold to stay. They get up and wipe each other with towels, scrub the sun lotion off. Jeremy wets a towel in the lake and pulls Bart's suit away from his body, carefully washing his cock, his legs. Bart starts to stiffen again at the touch. "More?" Jeremy asks. He leaves his hand on Bart.

"No," Bart says. Jeremy moves his hand and washes himself. Bart is silent.

Jeremy smiles at him. "Are you wondering what happens now?"

Bart is wondering whether the atoms and molecules in his body will conform to their accustomed shape, whether the map of his emotions, now changed forever, will be recognizable. He has not thought any further than that, but he hears something in Jeremy's voice and pulls himself together. He feels like a Victorian maiden gathering her skirts. "Well, yes," he says. "I am wondering. What about Beth? Aren't you together?" Bart's legs are shaking slightly. The leaves, in their new, soft green bodies, move in the wind. The lake sighs and trembles with tiny waves.

"Well, we are and I'm bi. I thought you knew that. I thought everyone knew. I like both. I thought it was general knowledge."

"Not to me. Does 'everyone' include Beth?"

"Oh yes. Sure. She knows I have other lovers."

"Does she?"

Jeremy nods. "She does. She has a girlfriend. Are you shocked?" Jeremy's smile a little rueful. Or maybe hopeful?

"No, I'm confused." And that is certainly the truth, Bart thinks. "Why us and why now?"

"I thought it would be a pleasure for us both. I didn't think I would be as attracted to you as I am, which is going to complicate matters." The clouds blaze above them, suddenly full of color. Scarlet and streaky violet and gauzy cream, pulled out against the shining bowl of sky, their seemingly solid shapes vaporous, constantly changing. "I know we're graduating soon. I'm going to graduate school in California."

"I know," says Bart. "We both chose now. It wasn't just you. It wasn't. I need to go home. We can talk tomorrow." His need to go home is powerful. To be home and alone to pour out this cup of feelings, to ponder the kisses and the excitement. They hug and get into their cars. I need to call Ingrid, Bart thinks, as he turns on the ignition. He notices that Jeremy is sitting in his car, but not yet moving. He rolls out and away from the lake and heads for home.

Even at home, he cannot really calm down. He does not call Ingrid. He tries to eat a little dinner, fails and sits down to meditate, or maybe pray, but he is in a reckless noisy silence, all buzz and static, then blank hot emptiness, then punishing words that move like a freight train. Flashing images again, similar to the ones he had when he was with Jeremy. Angry faces, this time mostly of strangers, staring at him, but making no sounds. He wants to go back to the touches, the kissing, to feel it all again, but he cannot get there. At two a.m., he takes Ingrid's keys and goes to her apartment, knowing that either she will be awake and working or in the deep sleep that is characteristic of her. Or she will be out, he thinks, in which case he will just come back home. For some reason he doesn't call first to find out. He realizes on the way over that he should have called, but it doesn't seem to matter. He knocks on her door before going in. She answers, "Come in," at his knock. It is like Ingrid not to ask who it is. She is in bed reading, not working.

"I thought it was you," she says. "Bart, what is it? What's wrong? You look really frightened." He looks as if he is in shock.

"Ingrid, I…" he stops and takes his light jacket off and sits at the foot of her bed. There is no wind outside. The room holds small sounds: the floor creaking slightly, Ingrid moving to put her book down.

"But what is it?"

He puts his head in his hands. "I spent some time with Jeremy this afternoon." This sounds ridiculous, he thinks. She knows that. He feels panicky about how to continue. Maybe he really should not? Should keep it silent. Secret.

"Yes. I know that. You were there together when we all left." Ingrid is guessing the rest, but waits for Bart to speak. She knows it needs to come from him, that he must speak it himself. She can smell something that is vaguely sweet—Jeremy's scent? And something that is like clay, like earth.

"I, we kissed. We did some other stuff." He feels as if his insides are loosening, but not in the old way. This is like falling. He truly experiences himself falling, though he is sitting upright. He lifts his head and sees that Ingrid has her Tarot deck on the table next to her. The Fool is on top. He almost laughs. "We…" he stops again.

"It's okay," Ingrid says. "I don't need the details." She says it kindly, in a way that invites him to continue if he wants to. "This was the first time?" She asks it as a question, but knows what the answer will be.

"Of course!" He seems shocked. He would have told her. She is his friend, his dear friend. "I'm so frightened. What do I do now?"

"Well, I don't know. It's too soon to know what to do, either internally or externally. You'll see how you feel." These sound like terrible platitudes, even as she says them. She sighs. Jeremy the beauty, the heartbreaker. "But this was inevitable, yes? Not necessarily with Jeremy, but with someone?"

"Well, yes." Bart remembers what Stephen said about choosing carefully. This was part impulse and part choice, although he is quite sure Jeremy would have stopped if he had refused. He had assured Jeremy it was a choice. Almost true. "But knowing it was inevitable and doing it are different." His insides are rolling and shifting in protest. He is too frightened to cry, although he would like to. All the words he has ever heard about sin seem to fly at him at once, birds with razor beaks and violent shining eyes. Whatever simplicity remained in his life has fled, probably forever. The steadfastness of time seems to collapse within him. Its linearity splits and falls in on itself, the way logs burn to embers, dropping inward to become a glowing cone of ash.

"It's late," Ingrid says. "Sleep here." She gets the quilt, some sheets and a pillow for the couch. Bart undresses to his briefs and tee shirt and lies down. Ingrid covers him and brushes his hair back from his brow. His lovely silky hair. "We'll talk more in the morning," she says.

✳ ✿ ✳

Bart and Jeremy make love twice before graduation. Twice before Jeremy leaves with his auburn curls pulled into a ponytail and a group of lovers and other admirers take him to the airport to see him off, Beth holding his arm as they walk. His parents are at the back of the little group, clearly proud of their son, happy that he has so many friends. Bart does not accompany them and thus he is not among the group who wait until the plane lifts off, leaving only a trail of burnt fuel behind.

The first time they meet after the day at the lake, it is in Bart's room at the dorm, Bart so frightened he can scarcely breathe and so excited he is afraid he will make some involuntary sound. The weather is still unseasonably warm, the leaves now brighter green and full, almost still on this windless day.

Jeremy feels Bart's tension and strokes his back gently. "No one's here, it's such a beautiful day. Everyone's out."

"Someone's here. Marshall is playing his drums."

"Well, all the better. That should cover us." Jeremy licks Bart everywhere he can find. "Shh, shh." He is teasing and slow, comfortable in his skin, with his touch.

He stretches out his long legs, freckles like cinnamon spatters. The sheets are wet, the bed a private ocean. Their mouths seems to be the center of this particular universe, their fingers extensions of the wetness, arms branches of a moist sea-soaked tree. They use their mouths on each other. "Is this okay?" from Jeremy.

"I think so, yes."

"Not this?"

"No." The universe of inside. Bart's fears and needs and demons. His shame and wild dreams. But he feels that his private world is drifting out of his pores, perhaps becoming exposed. Visible.

Jeremy looks into his eyes, the deep flecked green mysterious, full of hope. "Ai," he says, half comically. "I wasn't planning this; I wasn't planning love."

Bart doesn't even answer. He is going to wait, he thinks. He can't talk now. He can still barely breathe. But he certainly hears the word and it swims down into the interior, curling and weaving into him.

At the end, they hold hands, listening to Marshall beat a steady rhythm on his drum like an external heartbeat. Bart moves Jeremy's hand up and looks at his softly wrinkled knuckles, a tiny elevated landscape on the smooth, freckled skin. His nails are very white, small crescents at the tip of each finger. Sun presses at the closed yellow curtains, edging them with light. Birds sing loudly in the afternoon air. There are some neat boxes of books already packed.

"Are we talking about love?" Bart asks. "We hardly know each other."

"True, but I know love." Ah, Jeremy. Man of the world.

Bart would have thought he would be eager to hear the word, but instead it puzzles him. "But you're going away."

"That has nothing to do with my feelings, does it? They go with me. I didn't say I thought we could start a serious relationship and be together right now. I know we can't."

"Of course not," Bart says. Thin metal doors seem to open and close in his mind, like poorly hung doors in a shoddy house. Open. Shut. "Then, what?"

"I don't know. We'll stay in touch"

"Oh? Write? Call?"

"Why not? You could visit California."

"California?"

"It's not Tibet."

Jeremy doesn't understand Bart's finances, the counting and saving, always careful.

"My treat," Jeremy says.

"Oh, no."

"Well, we'll see."

They get up; kiss as they make the bed.

"On what basis could you love me?" asks Bart as they tuck the sheets in, smooth them out.

"Just like that."

"Oh. For someone who studies philosophy, there's not much substance there."

Jeremy laughs. "Mystery is hard to explain, though almost everyone tries."

As they talk, Bart waits for the demons, but this time there is only a slight flutter. Very little activity, really.

"Well," Jeremy says, "we aren't going to settle it now."

"Well, there isn't much time now to settle it in." Bart hopes he sounds neutral and not peevish—or frightened.

"People don't disappear when they leave Iowa."

"I suppose they don't, but I don't have any experience of that. Not much experience of people leaving, either, come to think of it. Where I grew up, everyone pretty much stayed put." This seems like the most obvious fact, though he has never given it much thought before, maybe only once, that afternoon in New York with Stephen. "We're going to see each other tomorrow afternoon at the dean's party."

The dean is hosting a big lawn party for the soon-to-be graduates. Bart is not looking forward to seeing Jeremy in public, which he says, somewhat to his own surprise.

"It will be all right. Or it won't and we'll manage," Jeremy says. He is practiced at mixing his lovers together, an ebullient, potent, emotional drink that exhilarates him, uses all his charm and skill. He suddenly realizes the extent of Bart's fears, all the newness he faces, his feeling of exposure. He hugs him. "I won't do anything strange," he says seriously, stroking Bart's shoulder gently. "I will not."

"Okay. I know. It will be fine."

"One kiss before I leave." And they do, holding each other deeply in that last moment before the door closes and Bart is alone.

The day of the party, Bart goes to Ingrid's first. He is dressed in his one pair of new jeans and an apricot colored shirt. He feels daring. When he arrives at her apartment, she is still working, wearing an old, white shirt stained with paint, her hands stained too and a cigarette almost burned out in the ashtray next to her. Her lover, Ethan, a raffish man, competitive and quick, another artist, left early that morning, after trying yet one more time to see the Empress. Fiddling with the sheet that covered it. "Don't touch it." Ingrid said.

"Why is it so private?" he asked. Again.

"Because I say so. I think I like you better inside of me than outside," Ingrid said, not exactly joking. Ethan smiled and took his gear and closed the apartment door, waving genially. Ingrid started to work and had been going since.

"The party," he says, without saying hello. "You have to get dressed." The Tarot deck is open next to her, the Hierophant on top. Bart looks at it, but, unlike the Fool, it has no particular meaning for him. "The room is clean, but you're sort of a mess." Ingrid's room is always scrubbed, her few things put away. Years later, a lover will say to her that she leaves no traces. Even her worktable is organized.

"I'm not a mess. I'm almost dressed." She looks down at herself as if to make sure this is true.

"Really?"

"Yes, I've showered and all I need to do is change into my dress." She holds her hands up. "These are stains; they don't really come out. Everyone will have to bear it. I'm an artist. Artists have stained hands."

She takes off her shirt, wearing only panties underneath, and puts on a tawny silk dress and a shawl. Bart observes her critically. "You're wearing that?"

"Obviously I'm wearing this."

"Did you iron it?"

"What? No. I don't think so. Why?"

"Uh, it needs it. Take it off. I'll do it."

Ingrid looks blank.

"You do have an iron?"

"I'm not sure. Oh, yes." Sometimes she has used it to melt wax for her work. But not recently. She finds it and hands it to Bart.

"Ironing board? No? Just give me a few towels; I'll use the table. Jesus," a new expletive for Bart. "What's on it?"

"Wax."

"Well, I think I can melt it off. Now give me the dress."

Ingrid undresses again and stands in her panties. They have become seemingly casual about dressing and undressing in each other's company. They are intimate in somewhat the way of an old couple, Ingrid thinks. Bart does not think this at all. He is always astonished that they are close in so many ways. Astonished and grateful. Maybe needy, also, but his pleasure outweighs his concerns.

He irons the dress, facing away from her. "Jeremy and I spent some time together yesterday." He imagines he hears the thin metal doors again, swinging open and then closed, a sharp loose bang. Such an odd image and sound he thinks, as it appears, now for the second time. If it were a dream, how would I interpret it?

"How did it go?"

"Oh, it went. I mean, you know."

Ingrid knows quite well. Jeremy, lover of pleasures, so saturated with what he has tasted that it seems as if his skin glows with it.

"I wonder if Jeremy loves pleasure the way that he does as a reaction to his parents." Ingrid has seated herself at the worktable again and is trying to scrape some of the paint off her hands.

"What about them?"

"They are both survivors."

Bart is silent. The steam in the iron hisses.

"They were in the camps. Like the woman we saw in New York, in the cheese store. She had numbers tattooed on her arm."

"I remember," says Bart, a little sharply. "I know what a survivor is, I just didn't know about his parents. Did he tell you?"

"Mmm," says Ingrid. And says no more. "That must be ironed by now." If there is anything implied in Ingrid's tone, or in her vague reply, Bart does not hear it. Or perhaps hears, somewhere, almost, and chooses to ignore it.

"Yes. Here." Bart gives it to her and she slides into it. The silk is sensuous, resting closely against her skin. "Are you considering a bra?"

"No, I wasn't. Should I?"

"Unless you want the entire male population from thirteen to eighty swooning on the dean's perfect lawn."

Ingrid sighs, gets a bra and heads into the bathroom. "An interesting thought, but no. I'm going to pee, while I'm at it."

"You look spectacular," Bart says when she emerges. "And you pee faster than anyone I know."

"Well, that's one accomplishment."

They leave the apartment arm in arm and begin to walk in the hot sun, which has persisted day after day in this unusual spring in Iowa, in these last weeks before their graduation.

The lawn is large and rolling and, on the heavy, perfect grass, undulating with people. Flower beds are planted with individual colors: drifts of pansies, the darkest purple, with soft orange hearts at their center, a white area of frothy petunias, small, compact daisies, and bushy creamy roses. Ingrid starts toward some people she knows and Bart, who loves flowers, bends to look more closely at the beds, noticing that the cream roses warm toward yellow and have a scent, faint and light, that mixes with the odd sweetness of the petunias. He stands and goes to find Ingrid, who has reached the food table and is talking to the tall, thin professor who loves her work and whom she has judged so unfairly. "Trust Midwesterners to try and poison you with mayonnaise in hot weather," she says pleasantly, avoiding the platter of devilled eggs. She scoops up a huge amount of salad and puts it on her plate. "This is probably safe. And bread. You know each other? Bart, this is Professor Bly. Tom Bly." They shake hands, which then begins an endless round of hand shaking with various professors and hugging with the students they know and, as the level of punch in the bowl drops, general hugging. Bart looks up from embracing a small blonde woman whom he is pretty sure he knows and sees Jeremy standing right next to him. Jeremy hugs him and says softly in his ear, "Let's go, all right? Don't you want to get out of here?"

"Yes. I want to. Where are we going?" Bart hasn't had any punch, but he feels high with the excitement of the event, the awareness that he is almost finished, has almost graduated. Jeremy's hair is damp with sweat, his curls loose in the heat. Bart wants nothing more at this moment than to embrace him. The noise of the party has risen to a roar and many of the guests are barefoot, shoes scattered on the lawn, or abandoned on chairs.

"We're going to my house," Jeremy says. "Let's get our cars, if we can find them and actually get out."

"Do we need to say goodbye?" asks Bart.

Jeremy looks at the crowd and laughs. "I don't think so, no. We don't. But you have excellent manners." He comes just close enough to Bart to brush his mouth with a kiss.

They find their cars with no problem, though Jeremy needs to maneuver carefully around a car that has almost boxed him in.

When they reach the house that Jeremy and Beth share, it is relatively cool inside. The ceiling fan spins in the empty living room. Bart has been there before to meditate with the group when Jeremy and Beth have hosted the evenings, but he hasn't been there often. He does remember the room, cared for so tenderly, with its many books and plants and an antique rug that is mostly faded, with only odd patches of rich color left, blues and crimson and a pale, stippled green appearing randomly on the surface. "Nothing's packed," he says. "Aren't you leaving right after graduation?"

"Yes, but Beth is staying here to do graduate work and some of this is hers. And I'm leaving her some things—on loan. I don't want it to be so empty. To leave it so empty."

Bart had a brief moment of hope, bright and then vanished, that Jeremy was not leaving. He doesn't exactly understand the explanation. "Well, are you coming back?"

"No, I'm not coming back. It's a kind of gift, really. Not so much a loan. I have a lot of things in California, I don't need to take everything." He seems embarrassed.

"Oh. Of course. I see," Bart says. Jeremy is very rich, he thinks, like Stephen? Jeremy is very guilty?

Jeremy has taken iced tea from the refrigerator. "Something cold," he says. "No wine. No alcohol. Are you hungry?" He gets out a loaf of bread and some butter and jam without waiting for an answer. They sit at the kitchen table and pour large glasses of tea that frost immediately in the warm air. He cuts some bread. "I don't know how I can eat, but I'm hungry. I have one of those metabolisms. If I don't eat one meal, I start to lose weight."

"Ingrid is like that," Bart says. "She eats much more than I do." They start to drink their tea, suddenly silent. "Who made the bread? It's delicious."

"I did." Jeremy moves his hand and rests it close to Bart's on the table, almost touching.

"Well," Bart says, "then you bake and I sew. My mother taught me."

"What was your life like where you grew up?" Jeremy asks. Moisture rolls down the glasses and onto their hands.

Bart is unused to talking about his childhood, about himself in general. He takes a breath. "Well, quiet. I grew up here in Iowa. Maybe seemingly quiet, is a better way to say it. Contained is a better word. And regular." He laughs. "A real fear of change, of newness, of anything different. Or anyone. People talked a lot about the weather. You know, farmers. Weather means everything to a farm community."

"Is your father a farmer?"

"No. He was a history teacher and then the school principal. He was the first one in his family to go to college. Both my parents. That's where they met."

"And your mother?" The fans turn with a slight whirr. They are talking about these ordinary things and the air between them shimmers and moves, alive and vibrating, a hovering presence.

"My mother took care of me and she sewed. Finally, she started making outfits for the local ladies. I think she was bored. And creative. Maybe artistic, although she would certainly deny that. I loved the sewing and designing, all the colors and trims and buttons, though nothing was very daring. I always wanted one of those church ladies to break down and go for something a little Chanel. Not that that would ever happen."

"How did you find out about Chanel?"

"Oh, I looked at magazines in the library. I would just collect a lot of Sports Illustrated and other sporty publications and slip in a few other things. I loved looking at fashion, though you wouldn't have guessed it to look at me. Still wouldn't. I didn't even feel very guilty about it, it just seemed like an extension of something my mother did, although I knew the librarian wouldn't like it."

"I think that's called rationalizing."

"I guess it must be. I've never talked about this before."

"Not even to Ingrid?" Jeremy looks surprised.

"Not to anyone." Bart stops for a moment and thinks about his mother, May Travis, who prays to Jesus every day of her life and has a private interest in the Holy Mother and the history of women saints, none of who appeared in the Lutheran Church, or were not discussed in the church Bart attended. Well, the Virgin made an entrance at Christmas and again at Easter, a cameo role. But May had told Bart about these women and he read her books, shared her secrets. May, who dresses plainly, but in lovely fabrics, soft wools, linens, so that no one notices her indulgences, her round, pretty body carefully covered, rendered almost, but not quite, invisible. He can see his mother, her long, smooth hair pulled straight back, held in a clip she seems to have had forever. He sees her with Ian, his father, a tall man with a wide build and strong muscles; he thinks of their polite and loving relationship, of his father's love of storms and turbulent weather (like Ingrid, he realizes) and his passion for baseball. There is something his parents have between them that Bart cannot define, something more secret than May's explorations into the lives of the women saints. It suddenly occurs to him that their secret is probably sex, and he is right. Their fiery sexual attraction is something they never mention to anyone and barely acknowledge to each other, although they occasionally allow themselves to laugh, to delight together in what so mysteriously and unexpectedly belongs to them.

"You got very quiet."

"Yes. I think I just figured something out about my parents," Bart says, and then lapses back into silence, his thoughts connected to his childhood with cobwebby threads, ethereal and strong.

"How did your parents feel about your interests?"

"Oh, they were surprisingly accepting. They thought of me as artistic. I was pretty good at sports—well, at baseball—and that helped, I guess. I liked baseball. I still do. I was different, but I never did anything obviously weird. I certainly didn't tell my parents about my fantasies. I didn't tell anyone, but of course no one ever talked about sexual fantasies, hardly ever about sex, except locker room jokes. There were some girls I was friends with and dated. Sort of." Bart remembers these sweet girls, one who still writes to him, and how repelled he was by them sexually. "I think it all passed as good manners. Iowa in the 50s."

"Then what frightened you so badly?" Jeremy asks.

"Do I seem so frightened?" Bart feels exposed and ashamed. He swirls his tea in the glass.

"Yes. Some combination of frightened and hopeful."

"Well, it's a big question and I don't really know the answer. Or answers. Certainly the culture I grew up in, the culture in America was hostile to who I was. Am. My church was no help. They're pretty clear about which sexual identity is acceptable. And they are not forgiving, or liberal, or any of those things. It was Ingrid who told me about the Greeks. I didn't know there was any culture that accepted homosexuals. A guy in the choir tried to feel me up once. I think it frightened him more than it did me. He barely spoke to me afterwards, not that anything happened, or that I wanted it to. These fears are really old." And probably stubborn, he thinks. And located in my guts, alive in all that heaving. "I knew something was strange about me when I was very young. I just didn't know what it was, exactly." Bart looks down at his glass. "The ice has melted and this is a very hard conversation. Tell me about you."

"Oh. Okay. We can change the subject, but not that much." He gets up from his chair and kisses Bart for a long time. "Now I'll tell you about me. My parents are both survivors, but you probably know that."

"Ingrid told me."

"Yeah, it's usually the first thing anyone ever says about me. They grew up in Amsterdam; their families had been there forever, or anyway forever relative to the history of most Jews, and they didn't get out in time." Jeremy pours more tea. "You know, the rabbinical records say that there were Jews in Utrecht as far back as the Roman Empire. Anyway, my parents knew each other growing up. They were interned in Westerbork and then they were both transported to Bergen-Belsen and survived. They were lucky and got to America quickly and married." He is quiet for a long moment. "I notice that I always tell this story in a certain way. It sounds pat and contained. There doesn't seem to be a path for me to express the real misery. Well, I guess this is how it is for now." He drinks some more tea, feeling the cool wet of the glass beneath his hand. "They came to California and went to school. They're both very active in Jewish causes—they talk to people about the camps, about the Holocaust. My father is a philosophy professor who invested in real estate when it was still available and inexpensive. My mother is a pediatrician. I had a twin sister who died at birth and then no siblings for twelve years. My mother had a breast cancer scare, but she was fine, nothing malignant, and then they had my little sister, Vivian. I grew up in California, sped through school. I guess we're doing our histories." He slides his chair over and takes Bart's hand.

Light shifts in the room and shadows appear; a small breeze blows in, cooler than it has been in days. They both notice the cooler air. They have been so focused on each other that the world outside seems lost, everything beyond the room temporarily vanished. The filaments of their words spin out, the gift of each history twined with other strands, an offering of feelings weaving them together in this pleasant room where they balance at the beckoning edge of change. "What will you do after graduation?"

"I have a job assisting in the theater department. I'd like to be an actor, but I don't think that's likely to happen. I'm talented, but my personality's wrong, somehow. Do you see me as Hamlet, or Othello or Lear? Or even Puck? I'm a great stage manager, though."

"What roles have you played? I don't think you ever talked about them."

"Oh, no productions that you saw. You like Beckett, that kind of thing. I like it too, but they wouldn't cast me for it. I was in *Oklahoma!* as a farmer. Big surprise. And *Carousel.*"

"Playing . . . ?"

"Mr. Snow." They both laugh. "And you're getting your master's in Philosophy. Probably your doctorate."

"I am."

"Well, leading the life you do, philosophy is probably a good place to start."

"Is that hostile?'

"No. Just honest." Bart rolls the tea glass between his hands. "Jeremy, where's Beth?"

Jeremy gets up and starts to rub Bart's back. "Out. Or, at the party and then out. I'm not setting any of us up for an unhappy surprise. Let's go inside."

The bedroom is painted white on three walls. The white has a shadowy violet undertone. The fourth wall is a translucent blue, the color of the sky just after the sun has set, when the edges of things merge in space, tremble at the rim of reality before night falls and the solidity of the dark descends. Like the rug in the living room, the one in the bedroom is faded and old. Some ancient tale seems to be unfolding on its surface, figures in motion, scenes with houses and gardens, now just barely visible. The colors are gold, rubbed through to a faded gleam, with beige and tendrils of terra cotta that have survived the years of wear. The curtains are a deep chocolate, velvety and dense, pushed apart so that the remaining light outside can still be seen. Like Bart, Jeremy has packed most of his books in this room and the cartons stand against one wall. There is a white, patchwork comforter on the bed and piles of white pillows resting against the headboard.

Jeremy enters the room and walks toward the bed, but Bart goes in and then hesitates. "Is this the bedroom you and Beth share?"

"No. Beth has her own bedroom. Why?"

"I feel like an intruder."

"We make love here sometimes, but I don't think the bedroom is really the point. I make love to her with my body, no matter which room it is, or what place. Isn't sharing my body with her really the issue?"

Bart is silent for a moment. "That's true, but a shared bedroom is so private."

"More private than a body? I think that's a displacement, although maybe not entirely. Come here, let me rub your back. I understand what you're saying. I don't mean to be difficult."

Bart sits at the bottom of the bed.

"Lie down on your stomach. I give a great back rub."

Bart lies down, cradling his head on his arms, listening to the sounds of the bedclothes beneath him, feeling the welcoming surface of the bed.

Jeremy comes close to him and almost whispers, "This might work better magic if we got undressed first." He turns Bart over and starts to undress him. Bart looks as if he might refuse, but then he opens his arms laughing and says, "Oh. Yes. Okay. Do it."

When they are both undressed, Jeremy rubs Bart's back and then all the way down his legs. He rubs the soles of Bart's feet.

"I've never had a backrub. I don't think ever. Maybe when I was little. My mother rubbed my back when I was sick."

"How is it?"

"Luxurious."

Jeremy looks at the round shapes of Bart's back and limbs; even his joints are gently curved. His skin is rosy, like a mild blush, as if the blood is running very close to the surface. Jeremy feels as if his own blood is deep down, flowing near his bones, hidden and dark red. If Bart scratched him in their lovemaking, reached into those depths, would the blood of the old rabbi who lived in Utrecht rise to the surface, stain the sheets? He lies down on top of Bart's back, his own body longer, smooth, but with his flesh pressed hard along his bones. He starts to kiss Bart's shoulders and massage him more deeply. He pushes down against him and slides his hand around to Bart's belly, still rubbing. Bart can feel Jeremy's erection against his butt and starts to speak.

"No," says Jeremy. "I won't. But what frightens you about having me inside you?"

"I . . . " Bart's voice is muffled through the pillows. Jeremy moves and Bart turns onto his side. "I don't know. It just terrifies me."

"It feels really good."

"Not if I'm terrified."

"No. I'm not trying to convince you. I'm asking."

"I don't know, Jeremy." Bart feels suddenly miserable, drowning in his own foolishness, in his fears. It is true. He does not know.

"Okay. Let's do what's good." They both sit up, legs apart and slide forward as close as they can. Bart kisses Jeremy and rubs his nipples. Jeremy pinches gently at the top of Bart's inner thighs. They rub and suck and come, collapsing against each other onto the pile of pillows. "Can you stay?" Jeremy asks.

"Yes."

"Good."

Bart is almost asleep when he says, "You know, there's nothing you can do about the night. Did you ever think about that? Nothing, no lights, no amount of money, nothing in the world can make a dark night shorter. Or change the length of a day, I suppose. But I was thinking about the night." He falls asleep almost as soon as he stops speaking and Jeremy holds him, and then sleeps himself.

In the morning, the first day in weeks with flying, dark clouds and a damp wind, they shower and eat breakfast. Jeremy slices pink new potatoes very thin and sautés them quickly in butter, adding a sprinkle of salt at the end. He makes mounds of scrambled eggs and toast. There is sweet butter and tart strawberry jam. "This is a feast," Bart says. He usually has cold cereal and a cup of tea for breakfast. In the winter, he eats oatmeal in the school dining hall. Occasionally, he goes out for breakfast. He looks at Jeremy across the table. He imagines for a moment that they are not graduating. That Jeremy can stay and that they will truly become lovers. "This is our goodbye," he says. "I don't want to say goodbye at graduation, with a lot of people around, with our families there."

"I'll call you. I'll visit."

Bart laughs. "You'll visit Iowa? Why?"

"To see you." Jeremy goes around to Bart and bends down, his face close enough to look into Bart's eyes, to see the green and brown flecks and the tiny gold ones. He looks at the silvery creases on Bart's eyelids and touches his lips with his index finger. "I will."

Bart does not really believe him, but time proves Jeremy to be as good as his word. He will call and write and sometimes he will visit. When Bart and Ingrid move to New York, he will visit there. Their relationship will unfold and endure through the time when many of their friends are dying. It will last until the worst of the epidemic in America passes, until there are drugs that hold the disease at bay for the lucky ones who can afford to get them. It will continue until Bart's hair is threaded with silver and Jeremy's blazing copper curls have paled to a reddish brown. It will last even longer than that. They will sometimes be lovers, but they will always be friends. The long duration of their love begins with this first goodbye.

Finally, it is graduation day. Bart's, Ingrid's, and Jeremy's families gather on the lawn before the ceremony begins. The Swansons and the Travis family have met on occasion, but the Levys know no one. All the fathers wear suits and ties, Aaron Levy's suit a fawn colored cotton weave, lightweight, Ian Travis in dark summer wool and Arthur Swanson in plaid polyester something. It rumples on his big body. Ingrid thinks maybe the fabric squeaks. She observes her father, sweating in his new suit. May Travis and Rachel Levy have both chosen beige linen and low heels, with one good piece of jewelry: Rachel's an antique pin, intricately swirled with garnets, May's a string of pearls, heavier, but not unlike the ones Dossie gave to Ingrid on that summer day four years ago. Rachel drove into town early that morning and bought a drift of colorful sun hats for the women. Dossie is wearing light blue spattered with rosy flowers of some unknown origin and black flats. She is wearing small gold earrings, but she thinks one of them is loose and sliding off her earlobe. She can feel her feet swelling against the sides of the shoes even this early in the day. Her plan is to slip out of them during the ceremony. "I can't wear heels," she said plaintively to Arthur, when they were packing. "I'll be dead by the end of the day."

"No one will be looking at your feet, Dossie. For God's sake. Wear what's comfortable." Arthur himself is a little nervous going to this fancy place, but he brushes it aside and storms around, aggressively making sure that everyone is ready. All packed before they need to go. He doesn't supervise the packing, but keeps repeating, "Just make sure you're ready, that's all I ask." Victoria, Ingrid's younger sister, just smiles at her father. They have some sort of silent agreement that they amuse and love each other, find each other appealing. Michael, Ingrid's older brother, pays no attention to his father and simply does what he needs to do, mostly in silence.

For all the families, the trip has entailed motel reservations and car rentals for some. And of course, the Levys flew in from California. Rachel is still frightened of trains, has memories that overtake her of the transport cars, but she loves planes. Aaron Levy likes travel of any kind.

Just before the graduates-to-be leave their families and gather in a line to march formally to their seats, Ingrid looks carefully at her father. He stands in the sun, sweating in his new suit, uncomfortable in his tie. There is no trace of memory on his face; his clear blue eyes reflect the sky. There is nothing at all to indicate that he remembers his violence toward her. He is her proud father and that is all his expression reveals. Ingrid touches the pearls that she is wearing, wears often, as an ironic private statement. She wears them, braless, clad only in an old pair of men's bikini briefs, when she is working. She wears them when she makes love and in the shower. She takes them off when she sleeps because she has a tenacious, irrational fear that they might take on a life of their own and choke her, but she knows this is foolish. Once she loaned them to Bart for a while. Now she drops her hand to her side and joins the others to begin the ceremony.

The ceremony is held in a wide outdoor arena on yet another hot day with the sky bright and almost cloudless. There are grateful comments about the good fortune that it is sunny, rain would have been awful, but the heat! Well. The comments repeat over and over again, in one form or another. The farmers are already anxious about the weather, the long spell without more than a brief shower. The trees around the campus, their leaves darker, but still not full grown, are suffering, their roots plunged into earth that is too dry. The ceremony unfolds as it should. Endless speeches and then one short one by a member of Johnson's cabinet. (How did they get him?) At the end, the graduates stand to get their diplomas, wanting it to last and impatient to have it over. Ingrid and Jeremy have won awards in art and philosophy, respectively. Bart, quite unexpectedly, won a special award for the outstanding help he has given the drama department. And then it *is* over. Each graduate has been called. Tassels are shifted, hats thrown in the air.

Families gather again to take more pictures and then go out to eat and celebrate. Jeremy and Bart wave cordially, but do not speak to each other. They have said their goodbyes. The Levys need to catch their plane and Jeremy will go with them. The Travises and Swansons go out together and then leave to go home. Ingrid and Bart stay.

The next day, Bart will move into an apartment in the house where Ingrid lives. They have both gotten minor positions at the university. They go to Ingrid's place, too tired even to eat. Night is dropping from a plush, rosy sky. They talk about New York, their longing to be there and the wisdom of saving some money first, Bart because he feels it is practical and Ingrid because the risks she takes are calculated. Finally, they go to bed, Bart on the familiar couch. Ingrid goes into her bedroom, leaving the door partially open. Bart knows she will be asleep in minutes. The moon has risen, dancing its ritual minuet, stepping from darkness into a whisper of light, blooming fully, hovering and then fading, disappearing once again, ancient and absent. For a long time, Bart looks at the full moon, far above the thirsty trees. Then he sleeps, surrounded by Ingrid's work, the shrouded Empress construction, her paintings and drawings. Finally, he dreams of New York City, of the streets, and the wide, curving Hudson. In the dream, he is looking down at the river, sitting high on one of the hills that rise at its banks, wooded and green as it was long ago. Ingrid sits near him and he feels her presence, though he doesn't quite see her. They are both silent, watching the river unwind, catching its scent, river water mixed with the brine of an ocean neither of them has ever seen.

It will be two years before time unlocks them from Iowa, like a combination of tumblers finally spinning to release. The earth will make a sufficient number of revolutions, the seasons will swing, rising into golden heat, dropping into bitter cold, Bart and Ingrid will breathe a particular number of inhalations and exhalations. Work will be done. Money carefully counted. And then the catch will unfasten, the basket of days will tip and they will be free to go, to enter the mad concrete embrace of the city they have waited for.

Crossing

It is early October and in New York the weather is at its finest, with sun-filled light that is almost blue, light that makes clear, inviting shadows, skims the turning leaves so that yellow glows in the ancient, fan-shaped ginkgos and even the sycamores, their green fading, their edges crinkling, look appealing.

Serena is wearing jeans and a white, frilly Mexican shirt with a scoop neck and delicate silky ties that gather it in the center. Her bare feet are in sandals, all of her still faintly tan from a summer in California. Her heavy, dark hair is twisted and pinned up, her eyes, which sometimes seem blue and sometimes gray, are large, the lashes carefully brushed with mascara, even on this quiet Sunday morning. She is sitting on the worn sandstone steps of a building on East Twelfth Street, waiting for Matt to bring the Volkswagen bus around. They are picking up their friends, Rose and Hal, to go apple picking and hiking upstate. She feels her belly a little tight under her jeans and goes over what she has eaten in the last few days. Loose clothes are good (reflect her goodness, her strength?) and tight clothes mean trouble. She had black coffee and nothing for breakfast, which is not unusual. Matt had a huge, blueberry muffin and mugs of creamy coffee with lots of sugar. He offered her bites of the muffin, as he always does, and she refused. He says he was a skinny kid, but he is not skinny now, just slender; he has wide shoulders, a flat butt and long legs, his upper body strong. A tall man, but not one who is easy in the world. He does not eat well, but he doesn't worry about it, either.

Serena is a woman with powerful intuitions, a strong will and ferocious, clustered fears about her body. She is small, with bones that are long for her size. She has never been fat, but still her weight torments her. This is before anyone talks about distorted body images, about the dynamics of intentional starvation. She feels as if she is scraping at the day with these thoughts. The sunny surface, the brightness, scarred until it bleeds a clear liquid, wounded. Lost. She sits quietly in the sun and breathes into her healthy lungs, touches her soft cheeks and wishes she were thin. Thinner. Even thinner than that. She often wonders if she wants to disappear.

Serena began to be frightened of her body—of her own flesh—a while after her breasts developed. She felt proud of her breasts, of her body moving in time to its ordained rhythm. The movement was slight, then faster until there were two small, soft, half-moon curves above her first bra. She would look at herself, amazed and admiring, turning this way and that, seeing all possible views in that long mirror with its flecks of darkness where it was a little worn underneath. She was completely satisfied. Happy.

No, it didn't start then. Although she had earlier fears (of illness, of polio when there was an epidemic), her body was mostly an ally, a trusted friend. The trouble began as her hips and thighs changed and rounded, responding to the same body music that swelled her breasts. It was then that the poison erupted, as if from nowhere at all. She had no way to understand that she had been sipping the poison for years. Tiny sips. Then larger ones. No one had ever mentioned this particular change; she was unprepared, sad and surprised. Hips and thighs, her straight, little girl's legs gone forever, shaped in this hated new way. Just fat. Just awful.

The street is almost empty, save for a man in the briefest shorts who passes her, walking his dog. The mutt bounds forward on the warm pavement. The man nods at her and smiles. She nods in return.

Serena has explored the subject of the insubstantial, the invisible, the concept of emptiness, in a variety of ways not connected to her woes about her body. Until she was twelve, she was fine with her body. Lived in it then as a beloved home.

Sitting in the sun that morning, she reflects on her past, particularly on her father's death, not sure what has reminded her of him. Perhaps the memory surfaces because it is near the time of year of his first serious illness. Her handsome charismatic father, gone and gone forever. This left Serena with Ruby, her mother. Smart angry Ruby, with her wicked humor, her unconventional ideas, with the grief and loss that will last the rest of her very long life. Ruby developed an interest in life after death, in Zen Buddhism and reincarnation and yoga. By the time Serena was ten, she was reading about all these subjects; reading Eileen Garrett, the great twentieth century intuitive, reading Evelyn Underhill's work on mysticism, reading *The Unobstructed Universe,* a treatise on the after-death state of consciousness. She will wonder later how much she could possibly have understood, but she will also remember a feeling of familiarity with the subject matter, quite beyond the comfort it offered. She has, over the years, read extensively about the astral realms and etheric bodies. She has meditated and absorbed herself in learning about the way consciousness slides into the physical world, manifesting itself visibly, and she has grappled with the Buddhist teachings on impermanence. The illusory world of the senses. Impermanence—well, none of this helps her much with her feelings about her own flesh, however. She does not know about anorexia, about the addiction to perfection, a wretched hunt for another intangible and, in this case, wholly unreachable state. She had been captured by an impossibility. Her entry into this arena of body-misery both harnesses her willfulness and exacerbates her feelings of helplessness. It bypasses her real independence, which is gritty, stubborn—wild and sharp and electric. Her mismatched inner pieces remind her of the crazy quilt that Matt bought for her somewhere in Ohio, on their way back from California. It has pieces of dark green velvet and thin black silk; pieces of calico worn to a whisper and snippets of red wool. There are embroidered designs of a musical note in gold thread, a spider in dark brown with a silvery web and the wing of a butterfly in blues. It is old and torn in places, the backing shredded. It reminds her so strongly of herself, all the inner pieces stitched together, unique, a little ragged, keeping odd company with each other. Her crazy quilt search for Spirit, for meaning. For relief.

Some of this is on her mind as she waits for Matt, who seems to be taking a long time. She scratches her fingernail along the seam of her jeans. She thinks about empty and full, about empty as full of possibilities, about empty as lonely and bereft. She sits among her private paradoxes, waiting in the rich October warmth.

The night before, she and Matt had been awake in the middle of the night, talking. Lying on the big bed with its terrible hollow middle, holding each other gently, washed by a cool breeze and accompanied by Bill, Matt's dog, a mutt with floppy, folded ears and happy eyes that are always full of hope, waiting for the next flashing moment. She watched Matt in the half-light of the city night. She could just barely see his coloring. She and her friend Rose call him the Golden Man and it is true. Everything about his body is all gold and red gold, glossy in places, rough in others. Narrow deep-set eyes behind thick lashes and heavy brows, eyes that are unexpectedly dark, the pupils almost as dark as the irises, making his gaze seem somewhat hidden. Some time later, Serena will meet a man named Stephen with similar coloring (who turns out to be Matt's cousin).

Serena is fascinated by Matt, this intelligent, restless man full of words that gather tightly in his mouth, are spoken in bursts, without much breath and often punctuated by a small smile, a slight tilt of his head. A laugh. He holds himself very carefully inside all that glow, is anxious beneath his genial manner. A little lost behind his laughter. A handsome man, who is dismissive about his looks, has no vanity about them.

They talked, deep in the night, about his fears as a child, fears he still feels when he wakes in the dark. Matt talked about memories of his father, who would come into Matt's room in the middle of the night, with his body loose under his striped pajamas, parts of him half out. "His cock would fall out," Matt said. "His damn cock would fall out and he would cry and try to hold me. He smelled of liquor. He stank." Serena has heard this story before, but not often.

Matt has also told her about when his older brother died, seemingly accidentally, on a holiday trip to the mountains in Colorado. A fall into a deep gully, his skull smashed, no one seemed very interested. An accident, tragic, but not unexpected when climbing. (But he was not really climbing when he fell?) The rangers came, and the medics, and they got him to the nearest hospital. They found he was carrying a gun. The night the family arrived in Colorado, Matt's father took him and his mother and his younger brother to a grimy bar, where they listened to old country music on the jukebox and his father drank cheap scotch. They watched men play pool, bathed in the rackety music while Luke, his brother, struggled for life in the hospital room where he then died. Alone. Luke was nineteen, Matt seventeen. His mother was forty-five and although physically present had been emotionally missing in action for a long time.

"Your mother didn't just take you and go to the hospital?" Serena asks. "She didn't just go?" She is incredulous, thinking of Ruby. Ruby the warrior, Ruby the valiant.

"No, it's not the way my family works. They just don't. It seems incredible, but that's the way it happened in my illustrious family."

It is an illustrious family. Several senators. One cabinet member. All accomplished mountain climbers. All crack shots.

"Why did your brother have a gun? Why would he travel with one? Why would he climb with one?"

"Well, we all had guns. My father grew up in Montana. Everyone had guns," Matt said. "Why Luke was traveling with one is another question. He was depressed. But he didn't shoot himself, Serena, he fell. There was no evidence of a gunshot wound. I get depressed too, but I'm on medication. You know that. I'm sure my father drinks because he's depressed and God knows about my mother."

Serena does know. She has given it considerable thought. Matt doesn't seem depressed, but perhaps it is the medication? Or perhaps it is just that he doesn't talk much about his inner life. His feelings. But she certainly knows what depression looks like. Her mother was frequently depressed. Depressed and then angry. Matt almost never gets angry, or at any rate, seems angry. Serena feels that Matt's life has been tragic in a soundless, hidden way. Living on naval bases, rootless, enduring his father's sexual abuse and ensuing daytime coldness and his mother's ceaseless tears, all of it witnessed and then closed tight as a trunk lid.

If she wakens when Matt does, he will sometimes let her comfort him. Other times he just turns away. It is a relationship of tenderness and friendliness, but not much heat. But some. Mostly enough—a small steady blossom of warmth. This past night, she held him until they both slept on the half-broken bed under the open window in Matt's very messy apartment, enfolded in the warmth they do share.

Finally, Matt pulls up in the blue bus in which they have traveled to California and back. It is amazingly intact, given Matt's impatience as a driver.

"What took so long?" Serena asks, opening the bus door. Then she smells the coffee and sees the brown bags, probably filled with bagels and cinnamon rolls. Bill, always anticipating the best, has his nose pressed against one bag.

"Snacks for the road," he says and smiles. "Hop in."

At about the time that Serena is sitting and waiting for Matt, farther east and two blocks down, on Tenth Street, a man named Leo is asleep in the bed where, earlier in the night, he made love to Lou Lou, who is really Louise, from Great Neck? Or maybe Woodmere? Somewhere. Leo has never gotten it quite straight. And it was more sex than love; really, only sex. Although the several times they have been together she has mentioned love and performed extravagantly, embarrassing Leo who was sadly aware of the performance. She is an intelligent woman, seven years younger than his twenty-seven and a Barnard student. They met at a poetry reading and she obviously knew more about poetry than he did, although he has read quite a lot if it. But there was something about the insistence of her yearning that put him off, though he is certainly attracted to her. Her legs are soft and round, her belly slightly curved, her eyes light brown under brows so pale they are just hinted at. Her loose, blonde curls, long, fall over small breasts with heavy, dark-rose nipples, slightly upturned. "My breasts are funny," she said to Leo, the first time, clearly pleased with them. She is pretending to be a hippie in her very black clothes over a garden of peach underwear, silky and quickly discarded. But she is innocent and desperate, yearning for his love, for someone's love, for love itself. Leo cannot feel her when they touch. It is like moss growing on glass, impossible, defeating. She knows she cannot claim his love, it will not ever belong to her, it will not be offered.

Leo is a tall man whose large hands always touch her tenderly, his hazel eyes looking into hers. He is an architect, a musician who does not play rock music. His loft smells of rosemary in pots lined up against the window wall. His hands, pressed against her, try to reach something beneath her skin and he fails. Even inside her, he feels disconnected from her. (Maybe especially then.) She feels her own impermeability, her sadness. Her anger. In the wee hours she gets up and dresses. Standing near his bureau, in the street light coming through the window, she sees a gold ring resting in a china cup. She looks at it as closely as she can. It has a rough, oval stone, probably blue. She tries the ring on and it fits. She takes it off. It is obviously a woman's ring. Maybe Leo has stolen it from some woman. But no, that is not really what she thinks. She is angry with him, but he is clearly not a thief. She finishes dressing and, just before she leaves, grabs the ring, wears it out the door, which she shuts with a slight bang. Leo does not wake. He continues to sleep deeply until what is, for him, quite late in the morning. When he awakens in the sweet October light, Lou Lou is gone. He assures himself he will not spend time with her again. It demeans them both. Odd thoughts for a healthy young man in the late 1960s, that time when a gateway opened into violence, into shattered bodies and pools of blood, misery and cries for justice and for peace. And in the midst of it all, very, very available sex.

As Leo dresses, he notices the ring is missing, the cup empty. It is a thin, delicate china cup with a tight curved handle and a faded, blue design of roses. It was his grandmother's, the last of a few remaining pieces from a set that came from Ireland, the place of her birth. And the ring was old—had been hers and perhaps her mother's before her. Leo had once given it to his first love. He simply stares at the cup, not wanting to believe the ring is not there. He looks for it under the bureau and around the rest of the loft, but he knows he is looking in vain and it is truly gone. Payment for my greed, he thinks, in some old moralistic way that is more like his grandmother than his parents. He knows this is foolish. Mostly knows. He holds the cup gently and washes it. When his coffee is made, he pours it into the cup and drinks it black. He decides he will not have this kind of sex again; his thoughts come as he sips the strong, bitter coffee. The erotic pleasure seems mixed with something hateful. Always? No, no. But it isn't worth it. Later that day, his father will come and plant spring bulbs with him in the scrap of garden behind his loft. The garden always rescues him. That and his love of form: building, restoring. And music, with its own forms. Respite. Love.

Also, at about that time of the morning and also on Tenth Street, just off Third Avenue, a woman named Frieda stares carefully and critically at her reflection in the bathroom mirror. She has a small dish of reddish henna balanced on the edge of the sink and is touching the roots of her hair with a henna-covered toothbrush. She notices the flesh on her upraised arms is softening. She is fifty years old. Well, just a little past. Maybe a little more than a little. She moves very carefully, squinting slightly through her glasses. Frieda is not her given name, but it is the name she has used for many years. As she works on her hair, she talks softly to herself in a combination of Russian and French. Scriabin plays on her phonograph. In the street, a passerby sings about Lucy and the sky and diamonds. Like Serena, Frieda is half thinking about emptiness and form and what she wants to teach to her group the next evening. She teaches small groups. Teaches them . . .

what? Mindfulness, meditation, compassion. Astrology from a symbolic viewpoint, Jungian, characterological, not predictive. Tarot. She is not technically a Buddhist, has not taken vows, but she has studied Buddhism in its various forms, as well as other spiritual teachings, for a good deal of her life. She met Gurdjieff in Paris, during the Second World War and worked with him briefly, but she was suspicious of him and it was rumored that he was Rudolf Hess's teacher. She feels, long before it is proven in physics, that information of all kinds is shared across time and space, that there are slivers of openings, sometimes whole portals, that usher the mind into a different realm, unbound by time. She feels connected not only to people she has known, but to complete strangers, someone she might sit next to on a bus, or pass on the street, sharing a glance, some mysterious hum of connection. Sometimes the beloved dead inhabit her rooms. Some are restless, unsanctified at death, demanding a blessing. Others are peaceful, moving like pale, sweet fog, kissing the physical world one more time and then evaporating. Frieda knows a lot; enough to understand that much of what she knows is not what she thinks it is and that much of it may be worthless.

But at that moment she is mostly concentrating on her hair and on the wobbling flesh on her arms. Ordinary life in its march toward disintegration, she thinks. "All things are impermanent," she says aloud, in English, and laughs. She goes to sit in her living room, letting her body rock slightly in the sunlight. The room has full cushiony couches and two wing chairs, a rocker, a chest with red zinnias on it in a copper vase. Walls of books. Both sofas and one chair have afghans resting on their backs. One paisley, soft and old, the colors bled together, and two fluffy white ones that a student made for her. One of the many fears that remain with her from the war is of being cold, although she is sturdy and does not feel the cold acutely in her present life. Another fear Frieda has is of breaking a bone. She has a jar of heavy skin cream that she makes herself and she begins to rub it into her legs, imagining it going deep into her bones. During the war she developed a horror of her bones breaking, especially a bone in her leg. More than capture, more than dying, the thought of her bones breaking terrified her. She saw many people running on the streets of Paris, pursued, falling and having a bone crack as the Nazi soldier caught up and much more terrible things began. She knows it must have masked other fears—doubtless it still did—yet it seemed dreadful and always present. It haunts her now. She pushes the cream into her skin, kneading her bones. She massages herself daily. Healing, healing. She opens her Tarot pack at random and the Lovers falls face up. The phone rings, Serge on the other end. Her companion of many years. She smiles. "Frieda," he says. "My beautiful Frieda." He has a slight accent, a touch of French, just a whisper. But they never speak French with each other. Almost never. "A concert tonight at Tompkins Square Park. Drumming. Would you come? Maybe I could come over earlier and we could eat? I am eager to see you, Frieda."

Frieda touches the still damp henna. "Come at six or so. I'll make something." She wants to say she is eager to see him, she is working at saying this kind of thing, but it does not come. She is courting emotional generosity, the capacity to yield into giving until she is overcome, until her defenses break open and bounty pours out. She is so far from this that she would consider it comical, were it not something that made her so sad. She does look forward to his company. To their dinner and the concert. But eager? Maybe not that. But maybe. She sighs.

"Good. Till then."

She walks into her kitchen and opens the refrigerator, looking at the bin of vegetables and fruits, lush colors, life-giving leaves and fruits. The seasons collected in the unfurled greens, the ruby stems, the dusty potatoes. So beyond her reach for years in her childhood, then in the war and the time that followed. Frieda's cupboards are always full. Her refrigerator stocked with all this produce and cheeses under a glass bell. Breads wrapped in cloths. Jars of grains line her kitchen shelves. She is not hungry, she just looks, appreciating. She feeds everyone she can. Her students, her friends, cats on the street. It is an unbearable urge and one that she can satisfy momentarily, but the urge reasserts itself. She savors the entire process, including the yearning and the giving. This kind of giving is easy for her.

By the time Serge comes for an early dinner at Frieda's, Serena and Matt are back at his apartment, slicing apples for sauce. Golden fruit. Red fruit. Streaks of one color in the other. A cloud of scent breathes itself into the air of the small rooms. Their feet are bare and Matt has taken off his shirt. Bill sits happily in the kitchen. He doesn't like apples, but he likes the atmosphere. Matt kisses Serena's neck, holding the knife, wet with apple juice, aloft. "Good day," he says.

"Yes. Good," she answers. The apples are already cooking, sweet and hot.

Leo falls asleep early, before dinner. Lou Lou has exhausted him. Not the sex, but his sad feelings. What would ordinarily be slippery and moist inside him feels dry as bark. He and his father have been planting bulbs for the spring. Rounded forms covered with papery skin. Some hold the possibility of green fire and rosy cups, others of fragile stems, early white blooms that emerge through cold and dirty New York snow, tiny fragrant stars. He told his father a little about Lou Lou. Not much, but his father got the idea clearly. "Well, Leo. Men and women. Men. You have to live with your integrity for your whole life." Leo thinks that his father is one of the few people he knows who can say that and not be maudlin. Or trite.

"I know. I know." They continue to dig and to plant, patting the earth over each bulb.

✳ ☸ ✳

On the Friday following this same Sunday morning, Bart and Ingrid are packing for New York, for their life there. They are leaving Iowa, have left their jobs and have only one more night in their respective apartments, just across the hall from each other in the arms of the drafty house surprisingly full of sun and saturated with memories. Bart does not have much to pack, just his books, some clothes and a few photos; one of his sometimes lover, the auburn-haired Jeremy; Jeremy, the man of pleasures as deep as the green lake they were at the first time they made love on a strangely hot spring day.

Ingrid has packed her white paintings, rolling them carefully. Unimaginable shades of white, she has worked with these paintings, as well as drawings, as if she had discovered the color herself, given birth to its gray and lavender shadows, its rose undertones. White that is almost golden. Or pale blue. Or green. She knows the colors don't belong to her in any personal way and she would never admit her feelings, but there they are. The undertones seem violently etched, each a flamboyant world of color floating in the whiteness. Inescapable. Each shift in color seems bold. Some of the surfaces seem prickly, others have a smooth grain. Still others are velvety, alluring. She has tracked whiteness, looking at snow in sunlight, moonlight, starlight and under the long gray Iowa winter skies. Looking at white sunlight skimming water and the flashing transparent white of rain on wet fields. And she has photographed a lot of it, learning to use a camera in the process. Her collage boxes, made from her interpretations of some of the Major Arcana of the Tarot, are packed as well, each in a larger box with special padding. She has done three: the Empress, the Fool and the Hierophant, and she sees each one as a realm that can be entered imaginally. Can be absorbed consciously and unconsciously. She wants to take them on the plane with her, they are her secret family, but they are too bulky. She will have to trust the movers and the care with which she has packed them. The company will store their things until they find a place to live. Like Bart, she doesn't have many clothes. White jeans, black sweaters, a heavy orange sweater, old now, but beloved, and three silk dresses: one amber, one deep green and one a gold washed so often that it has become almost white. A few pairs of shoes, including one pair of spike- heeled sandals that she almost never wears, but will not throw away. She thinks they may become part of a piece. They are wicked and sculptural and miserably uncomfortable.

Ingrid and Bart have done well in their just-postgraduate years in Iowa. Ingrid has taught as an adjunct in the university's art department and Bart has worked with production for the theater department doing stage management, as he predicted he would. Bart has had several professional jobs, which he hopes will boost him forward in New York. He already has a job as an assistant manager at a very small theater in New York. His friend Stephen, whom he met on his first and only visit to the city, has arranged it. Ingrid has also had a small show of her white drawings—the drawings only—organized for her by the professor she had judged so harshly in her undergraduate years. The professor, long an admirer of Ingrid's, would have liked something more with her, but he didn't press. This same professor has recommended her for a job in New York, in photo research. His cousin owns the business and they have hired Ingrid, sight unseen.

It was an extremely successful exhibit, which Ingrid pretended to take in stride, but she was anxious about it. She had not prepared herself for the vulnerability, the skinned exposure of having strangers look at her work and—worse—talk about it, some within earshot. She only admits this to Bart and even with him, is cautious about what she says. She felt so shaky; badly off-center. Strangers with sticky eyes and stretched mouths, smiling, maybe later not smiling. But she does not have to pack the white drawings, because they are gone. Well, sold. She confronted her resistance to letting the drawings go, but she has not coped with it, it sits with her, as a longing and occasionally a fantasy of going to the owners (owners?) and grabbing them back, tossing money behind her.

Then Ingrid and Bart are finished packing and decide to go out for dinner. Their friends have already given them a party on a blustery, late September night full of stretched rushing clouds and the scent of grasses soon to bear the cold. At the end of their last evening they hug and Bart goes over all the flight arrangements, assures himself that Ingrid has her ticket and that they will have breakfast and then leave for the airport. Early. Once safely on the plane, Bart thinks about how soon he might visit home. Thanksgiving, maybe? Ingrid thinks that, with any luck, she will never go back to Iowa at all.

* ☸ *

They arrive in New York in the afternoon, on an unseasonably cool day. Bright shadows and a brisk wind in the big open spaces at the airport. But how different from their first trip, several years ago, when it was broiling and they staggered off the bus after their long, uncomfortable ride. How luxurious to arrive by plane, to be somewhat familiar with the city. Not complete strangers. And this time, they have come to stay. They have been invited, as they were when they visited, to stay with Sue Ann. She has been in touch, if not regularly, and they know she has married a man named Richard Parkhurst, a stockbroker who is a bit older than she. Well, older. Fifteen years, or maybe it is sixteen. Sue Ann invited them to the wedding, a formal one, reported in the *Times,* but in those days young people did not ordinarily travel to weddings and anyway, the cost was beyond them. In addition, neither of them wanted to go. Not at all. Sue Ann has been married for a year and a half. She and Richard live on 101st Street and Fifth Avenue. Ingrid remembers fleeing Fifth Avenue that summer she and Bart visited. Fled the ranks of apartments with drawn shades, the occupants elsewhere during the hot season. Fled the doormen, languid, watchful, sweltering in their uniforms. Neither Ingrid nor Bart know the strict social and geographical rules that govern Manhattan. So they do not know that, no matter how vast the apartment, the street is too far north to be quite fashionable, up there beyond the great divide at Ninety-sixth. She doesn't think that Bart knows much about Fifth Avenue in general and she isn't going to mention anything. She would rather leave people to their own experiences, especially first impressions. She is always curious about how it will turn out, what the spontaneous reaction will be. Anyway, they are going to find apartments quickly, not stay with Sue Ann and this new husband for long. Ingrid has not liked the sound of him in Sue Ann's letters and the few calls they have had, but she knows she is probably—well, definitely—prejudiced. A broker and a Republican. What could be good? she thinks. Even her terrible father, Arthur, is a Democrat.

They ring Sue Ann's bell and wait. The door opens and a young woman dressed in what Bart thinks of as stage costume greets them. The costume of a maid. (They have a maid?) No one in real life—in his real life—employs someone and dresses her like this. Even people who serve at big parties in Iowa just wear black pants and a white shirt. Ingrid is not puzzled by the maid, but it does not auger well. She feels her body tense with dislike, not for the woman, but for the situation. The young woman is fair-skinned with a narrow, tight forehead that gives her the look of having perpetual pain around her eyes. She speaks with a slight accent. Maybe Polish. She stands quietly as they enter and says, "Mrs. Parkhurst will be with you in a moment. I may show you to your rooms." (Rooms?) Bart looks at Ingrid and smiles a slightly sardonic smile. Rare for him.

"Do you imagine that Sue Ann is Mrs. Parkhurst, or just someone dressed up to look like her?" he says quietly, as the maid turns and they follow her. Ingrid remembers their first visit, when they were still students. She remembers Sue Ann at the top of the staircase in the reclaimed tenement and how she looked in her yellow city dress. Her eagerness. Her pleasure. Ingrid breathes in sharply.

On the way to their rooms they move from the black and white tiles of the foyer to carpets whose thickness seems to render them animate, so you feel you are walking on something alive and not quite pleasant. Intricately designed rugs rest over some of the carpets. Vines crawl through them and fringes sprout from their edges like silky growth. They go down halls and through a suite of rooms. Some walls are elaborately papered; others finely painted, with colored trim. There is a glass chandelier anchored above them in the hall where they stop, just outside the rooms they will stay in. Meant to be festive, or elegant, it looks moody, as if the whole thing might pull free in a restless fit of bad will. Everything is artificial, contrived. Down at the end of this hall, there is a large, open room with bare wood floors, dark and polished. The sun shines in deep oblongs on the floor like a voice calling from afar, from some lost world. They have not yet seen the entire apartment and already the décor makes a statement, both confusing and demanding, about the wealth of the apartment's occupants. (Look! No, don't notice. This is all to be expected. Taken for granted. Of course.) Sometimes Richard, who considers himself quite sexually inventive, fucks Sue Ann on one of the heavy rugs, after carefully spreading a sheet beneath them.

Ingrid and Bart have just put their valises in their respective rooms and come out to look for her, when Sue Ann calls from somewhere in the apartment. She appears in the hall and rushes toward them, arms outstretched. "Hugs," she says. "Hugs." Her voice is warm with an undertone of something else. Desperation? Fear? Her usually clear skin is slightly blotchy, looks slightly rumpled. The even, light tan she always had is gone. Her eyes have odd lavender circles under them. They do hug and then she pulls them back down the hall toward the kitchen. "Only place you can really talk," she says. She nods at the maid, who retreats. The maid has not been introduced.

The kitchen is a small universe of shining surfaces: polished granite, stainless steel. A stove, also shiny, hulks against one wall. Gadgets are lined up on the counters, armies of implements, sprouting dollar signs and unknown possibilities. There is a counter and an antique wooden table, heavy and waxed, but looking more human than the rest of the room. It is not a safe haven, but a monument to excess. It is sad and terrible, that large bright room that seems unrelated to food in any discernible way. Sue Ann sits at the table and Ingrid and Bart follow. "There's coffee?" she says hopefully. As if she is asking a question.

"Good. Coffee sounds great." Ingrid and Bart both nod, agreeably. Like the maid, Bart thinks. Characters in a play they were not expecting. They settle with the coffee, cream. No one takes sugar. The mugs are mammoth, swirled with a nasty green glaze.

"Well," Ingrid says. She gestures around her. "Tell us. There must be quite a lot to tell. You never mentioned any of this." What, she thinks, is the secret? Because there must be one. At least one. This lavish horror. How did Sue Ann arrive here?

"Well, I met Richard at a fund-raiser," she starts. "A gala. My boss invited me and I borrowed a fancy dress and got new shoes and had my hair done. I don't know why. I wasn't even that interested in going." She has clearly told this story many times, both to other people and to herself. Over and over to herself, trying to puzzle out the trajectory, unexpected and extreme, that led her to be here at this table, living in this house with him. With Richard. "I was there awhile, and thought maybe I would go, and then Richard came over to me. He just descended on me, really. This big man, bearing down through the fancy crowd and the clouds of perfume and pinched feet." She is talking to them, but also, in part, to herself. "Perfume and alcohol. You remember I don't drink much. He introduced himself and said he was so pleased to meet me, I looked so natural among all the others, so appealing." There was something hidden and avid, she remembers, although she couldn't have named it then. "I thought, oh, the farm girl look. He's one of those. Maybe he'll ask to look at my teeth. No, only joking. You know there seems to be a whole group of sophisticated New York men who rush to women like me out of —I don't know—some fantasy. Some strange need. This wasn't the first time." And then he pursued her with determination, with his money and his success and with his big square body. Being with him was like visiting a foreign country and, initially, as intriguing. Then there was the sex, she thinks, but does not say. Not yet. Something has gone terribly wrong there.

Ingrid tries to imagine this happening to her, this certain kind of man being suddenly, absolutely attracted to her. She did not grow up on a farm, but her grandparents were farmers and she certainly spent her life, before college, in the country. But it is unimaginable. It would not happen to her, she is too taut, too angry. She is not what these men are after, thank God. And she is right. But really, why had he chosen Sue Ann, with her Midwestern expansiveness, as revealing as the huge windows in Holland, land of her ancestors, with their wide un-curtained windows, aggressively demonstrating propriety? A woman of apparently little guile, little need for it. Sue Ann had left her family's farm, gone to college, studied acting (maybe that was where the guile flourished, if there was any) and arrived in New York—to get the usual tiny parts.

She did not succeed in the theater, but, practical and wanting to stay in the city, she found a job and a boss. Who took her to this gala, this celebration of some worthy cause.

They talk until twilight slides into the room. Sue Ann turns on the lights. A cook prepares dinner, oblivious to them. She is not introduced to Ingrid and Bart, and Sue Ann merely smiles at her. "That's what Richard says is 'appropriate' with staff," she says in a low voice. "Not to be too friendly."

"Well," says Ingrid, "you are succeeding admirably. Does Richard have a lot of instructions?"

"I do talk to them when we're alone." Sue Ann is clearly embarrassed. "And yes, he does. Lots." There is a bit of silence. "I still go to church," she says.

"Still," says Ingrid. "When did you go to church?"

"When I was growing up," Sue Ann says. "I mean I go again. I go now."

This is clearly related to something as yet unspoken. Maybe one of the secrets?

"I go," says Bart. "I'm going to find one here. Where do you go?" He looks sideways at Ingrid. "I am," he says. He thinks it is much more likely that he will find a church in New York that accepts gays. Almost certain.

"I know," says Ingrid. "I know you will."

A man's voice is heard, far away, at the end of a hall. There are several halls, but the sound comes from the one leading to the front door. "Richard," says Sue Ann. "We are in here," she raises her voice. "In here, with our guests." "Guests" sounds like a reminder.

Richard reaches the kitchen and stands at the door. For a moment, they all stop and just watch him. He is a big man, large everywhere. His face, which looks as if it should be square, is oval and slightly heavy. Heavy, opaque skin. Dark blue eyes with thick lids. At first his stance seems vigilant, as if he is guarding an elite world with the needy clamoring to enter. He will guard it forever. Longer than that. Looking more carefully, the impression shifts. He holds himself stiffly, as if something inside him might cave in, making him alert to any possible movement. As if there is an interior wound full of violence and of pain. Even though he stands quite still, he has a restless quality, like someone who will become easily bored. His suit is expensive and repellant, but his tie is a radiant blue, appealing and smooth. Maybe that is the part that Sue Ann likes, Ingrid thinks. The part that chose that tie. Unless, of course, Sue Ann chose it. "Hello," he says. "Welcome, welcome." He looks at Bart sideways, just a flicker of those dark blue eyes, and Bart knows what he is seeing in Richard and he doesn't like it. Richard smiles.

Ingrid holds out her hand without moving anything else. "Richard," she says. A shocking, conservative man, she is thinking. She is genuinely shocked. Bart is speechless. But they have just met him, they signal to each other with their eyes.

Let's hold off for a while.

They eat an elaborate dinner in the formal dining room. Wet sticky food, too many sauces that are white or pale. The maid that greeted them serves, along with a still younger woman with a plump rear and heavy ankles. This time, Richard introduces them with a brief nod. "This is Lise," he says. A slight pause. A whisper of empty space. "This is Dolores." A warning in his voice, thinks Ingrid. But his face is unrevealing.

Another chandelier hovers above the table. Like the one in the hall, it looks uneasily anchored, as if it might mutiny. A lot of china and glasses. Wine. Bart takes a little of it. It is too complicated to explain that he doesn't drink. Richard asks about their plans and Ingrid realizes later, when she and Bart are sitting curled together on her bed in her flowery, painfully decorated room, that a lot of the talk revolved around reassuring Richard that they were not staying long as guests. Were going out the next morning to find a place. Were going early. Very. Sue Ann is practically silent throughout the meal.

In the morning, Ingrid and Bart rise early and meet in the kitchen, intending to go out for breakfast then down to the East Village, which is where they want to live. Plan to live, no question. They have the Sunday real estate section from the *Times,* which Sue Ann gave them the night before, and the *Village Voice,* possible apartments already circled in red. It is one week after the Sunday that Serena and Matt and their two friends picked apples, that Leo regretted his sexual encounter with Lou Lou and the loss of his grandmother's blue ring, gone forever, and Frieda hennaed her hair, pressed herself to be more emotionally generous and went to a concert with Serge. It is a gray day with thin, high clouds that cover the sky completely, only a faint spot of light where the sun is. A small wind tugs at leaves that rustle against the emptying tree branches. They are neatly dressed, Bart in chinos and a pink shirt and polished loafers, Ingrid in slacks (well, no, not a skirt. She doesn't own one) and a topaz colored shirt that sets off her hair, the ashy, shining surface of it. This is in case they meet landlords and need to make a fine impression. They do not know enough about the city yet to understand that they will meet superintendents—if they are lucky. Landlords will be later.

Just as they are about to leave, Sue Ann comes into the kitchen wearing a yellow silk robe and not much underneath it. Her eyes are tired, her lips dry. "Could we talk a minute before you go?" she says. Her voice is beyond hopeful. Almost pleading.

Ah, here it is, thinks Ingrid, who is about to ask if they could talk later, when they return.

"Of course," says Bart, always softhearted. "Yes, of course." He sits down at the table.

Ingrid sits down as well. She just sits quietly, without any show of reluctance, although all she wants to do is get out—maybe run out—and start looking for apartments.

"Well, I . . ." Sue Ann stops, seems as if she might cry and then does not. "It's about Richard. About our marriage."

Why, thinks Ingrid, is this not a surprise? She can feel her resistance to the story that is coming, but she simply sits still and waits. She thinks of her meditation training. Of abiding patiently. But these are just thoughts. She doesn't feel either patient or abiding. "Where is Richard?" she asks.

"Oh, out. He goes out every Sunday to play squash. Or something. Anyway, he's out." She gets up, begins to make coffee and begins the story. Her robe sways open as she moves around the kitchen, gathering mugs, spoons, cream. She remembers that no one takes sugar. Her long legs are strong, muscled and spattered with freckles. "When we were first going out, he was so charming. We went to the theater, to good restaurants, to museums and concerts. He was eager, but somewhat formal at first and then it got warmer—you know."

"You mean the feelings got warmer, or you had sex?" asks Ingrid. The smell of coffee is rich in the air. The kitchen gleams ominously even in the weak light of this sunless morning. Ingrid thinks the whole apartment is hostile to human presence.

"Well, both. And the sex was, you know, really good. Good chemistry. Once we got started, he was very sexual. Very, uh, well—maybe demanding. Sometimes." Sue Ann brings the coffee to the table and pulls her robe across her legs, looking as if she suddenly feels too exposed. "I knew we had very different opinions about the world, about politics. Probably about most things, except maybe the theater, but even there. He loves opera."

"Sue Ann," Bart says. "What's wrong?"

"He asked me to marry him about six months after we started seeing each other. And I said yes, but I think I was uncomfortable about it even then, although I didn't know why, exactly. I had heard a few things about him. Rumors."

"What rumors?" asks Bart. But he thinks he knows.

"That he hadn't been kind to his old girlfriends. That he had been cruel to them, talked behind their backs, badmouthed people who didn't agree with him."

This is not what Bart thought she would say. He was waiting to hear about rumors having to do with boys. Men. No, boys. His intuitions on this subject have gotten very sharp. He looks at Ingrid, whose face is closed. A blank expression she sometimes gets, as if she has withdrawn from her skin. It is like looking into the eyes of a blind person. No help there.

"We had this big wedding, you know, I invited you. Very fancy. My folks were overwhelmed and not pleased, really. And then we got this huge apartment and it had to be decorated by a professional, everything the way he wanted it." Sue Ann pauses. "But I'm not getting to the point. He started to be mean to me. Little things at first. Criticisms. He began to hint at trying some S&M. Just for fun. Not my idea of fun." She stops. "And then he started to become obsessed about having a baby. A son. His son. He knew I didn't want children yet. We had agreed to wait. He got really crazy around it. Wouldn't let me use a diaphragm, stopped using condoms, said he knew when it was safe. Which he didn't and of course he didn't care."

"Wait," says Ingrid, "what do you mean he 'wouldn't let you' use something? How did he get to be in so much control?"

"I don't know. I don't know what happened to me. I just fell apart. He frightened me."

"You must be very frightened," says Bart. "Frightened enough not to be able to fight back."

"Oh, no," Sue Ann says. "You don't fight Richard. You have to find some other way."

"Leaving," says Ingrid. "That's a way."

"I know, but I feel paralyzed. I do know. I have been thinking that I need to leave for a long time. Knowing I need to. And the last few nights—well, not last night because you were here—he pulled me over onto my belly and started to pinch me and smack my butt. It seemed like he was in a trance. He kept saying, 'We are going to have a baby. You're going to carry my son.' I've never heard him sound that way. I've never heard anyone sound that way." Then he had his fingers inside her and was rubbing her cervix, but she can't say this. "Right here," he had said. "It's going right here." She stops for a moment. "I got a prescription for pills a few days ago," she says. "It's at the drugstore now. It's ready. I just hope I'm not pregnant." I am ready to bolt, she thinks. Maybe I was waiting for Ingrid and Bart to come. Especially Ingrid, with her ferocious courage and her own shadowy violence. She would be a strong protector.

As she listens to Sue Ann, Ingrid experiences the room of shining equipment and impermeable surfaces as vaporous, with fixed objects sliding sideways. The stored fire in the stove seems appealing. Appealing to burn something. Pain pierces her throat like a safety pin snapping open inside, a sharp digging, quick and unexpected. The safety unpinned, she thinks. My safety. Ingrid is not prone to anxiety, yet Sue Ann's story pulls her memories out of storage. Her father and the cellar, the floor cold even in summer. His belt. His rage. The dead silence after. All of this flashes in a second but she has lost what Sue Ann is saying. I have to leave, she thinks. Has Bart just said this? That they need to go? Ingrid breathes into her belly, feels her feet on the floor. Bart has, indeed, just said something. Then she is saying, "This sounds like rape. It sounds crazy. You have to get out of here."

"I know, but I have nowhere to go."

"No friends?" asks Bart. "You've been in New York a while. No one?"

Sweetheart, Ingrid thinks. Bart's sweet heart. He will always be a good Christian. Well, this is my new life and I am not taking care of Sue Ann. Sue Ann has to get the pills. But she knows she will do what she can to help Sue Ann.

"Not that kind of friend. No," says Sue Ann.

They are all quiet.

Ingrid is afraid of what Bart is going to say, that he is going to say Sue Ann can live with him. But, miraculously, he doesn't.

"We'll find a way to help you," is what he does say. "First we need to find a place." That is as far as he goes. Ingrid understands that they need to leave the apartment before he offers anything else.

"Well," Ingrid says a little too loudly, "We need to start our search. Get the prescription tomorrow. Today, if the drugstore is open. Take it. Hide it." She hugs Sue Ann. She hopes this is where some of Sue Ann's guile is. That she can conceal her plans from Richard. "We'll see you later."

"Is this okay?" Sue Ann says. "That I told you?"

"Yes," Bart says. "You need help. We're friends. We are your good friends."

They gather themselves to leave. The newspaper is neatly folded in Ingrid's bag. Ingrid can barely stop herself from fleeing, but she walks slowly toward the front door. She can hear Bart reassuring Sue Ann again. Then he catches up with her and they ride down in the paneled elevator. The man running it greets them, his voice pleasant. The elevator smells of aftershave, strong and astringent. The smell of limes. The apartment recedes behind them, its sticky, furnished deadness sealed behind the heavy front door. The street is orderly and composed in the morning light. The leaves in the park are scarlet, dark glowing caramel, fading green.

Ingrid and Bart walk east along Twelfth Street, passing the building where Matt lives. Ingrid is tall, with long, strong legs and ashy curls caught up in a comb; she moves through space with a sense of purpose, the air parting in front of her, covering a lot of ground as she walks, yet she does not seem to be in a hurry. Her secrets rest inside her as she moves, invisible, though there is something carefully contained about her. No loose edges. Bart walks close to Ingrid, a breeze floating through his soft hair, his large green eyes look hopeful and eager. Ingrid has given him the paper, with its red circles around likely apartments. Ingrid looks upward for telltale signs of empty windows. Clearly they are friends. Clearly they are looking for a home. The bell they ring on Twelfth Street doesn't answer and they go down to Tenth Street, which is lined with trees. They go past buildings of purple-brown sandstone, sparkles embedded deep in the worn stone, past buildings that are cream brick, veiled in soot to a shadowy transparency. Some doorways arch with curlicues and have windows with rounded garlands that sprout carved leaves. Other doors are black painted steel, battered, with chicken wire sunk into the glass panes. The houses lean in all directions, some toward each other, resting tired sides, one against the next. Some tip slightly forward, others seem to slump down. They pass Frieda's house, with its large uneven windows and heavy banisters. Walking east, they find the second house on their list. It is an indeterminate gray. "See super," the ad says. Ingrid looks up to see if there are any obviously vacant windows. None she can see. The super's bell doesn't answer, but as they ring a lanky man with a cigarette in his mouth approaches them. His blue pants are washed to a color of near invisibility, as is his yellow shirt. His ears are large and wide, seeming to occupy an unusually large area of his head. He is wearing glasses with clear plastic frames. Behind them, one brown eye squints to avoid the curling cigarette smoke. He is probably no more than forty, but looks considerably older.

"You looking for the super?" he asks.

"Yes, we'd like to see the apartment? The apartment." Bart corrects his questioning tone.

"Super's out for the day, but I can show you the place."

They follow him into the tiled hallway. Bart holds his breath slightly, afraid the hall might smell, and it does, but mostly of industrial strength disinfectant. The stained, yellow tiles quiver with the chemical scent.

"I'm Mike. I help Dom out. The super. He's away for the day with his family. It's up," he says and starts up the stairs. Up it is. Five flights. "Top floor," he says. "That next staircase is to the roof. There's some laundry lines up there, but a lot of people use it to, you know, sunbathe." Neither of them has ever been on the roof of a building like this, so they do not imagine the scorched tarry surface and bodies slippery with suntan oil stretched out on towels, radios playing. They merely nod.

The apartment is in the rear. Mike opens the door with a sweep and they step into the kitchen which houses a bathtub covered with an enamel lid, as well as a narrow stove and a white refrigerator with its door painted yellow. The walls are beige, their surface uneven. Beyond, the living room windows face south. Bare, they are full of sun. The room is bright with it. Rooftops are visible. There is a small toilet off the kitchen. A wooden box with a chain to flush is hung above it. Neither Ingrid nor Bart has ever seen one like it.

"Window in there," Mike points out, as they look at the set-up. "Bedroom in the rear. You from out of town?"

"Not any more," Ingrid says.

They follow him into the bedroom, which has a west-facing window with panes that have recently been cleaned. The room is so small that the three of them cannot stand in it comfortably. Mike moves back into the kitchen. The floors are wood, badly scarred. Splintery.

"Whole family lived here," Mike says. "Nice people. Polish."

Ingrid goes back to the living room and looks out at the rooftops and water towers. Sun lands on the sadness of the floor. Bart goes and carefully flushes the toilet, pulling the chain so that water rushes heavily from the wooden box above. He tries the sink, which abuts the tub. A trickle appears, then a brownish gush.

"Well, how much is the rent?" Ingrid asks, though she is not considering this place. Not at all. No place for her to paint and too big a stretch for Bart, she guesses. (Correctly.)

"Seventy-five," Mike says, though his tone indicates that it is negotiable.

"Well," Bart says, "We'll—uh—think about it. We need to talk." As if he and Ingrid were a couple, were considering sharing this apartment, its very walls worn to exhaustion.

"Right," Mike says. "Well, the number's in the paper." They can see he knows it's no and that he will continue go up and down the stairs on this cool Sunday.

They retrace their steps and stand on the street, leaves rattling in the gutter as the wind picks up. A large cat whose gray fur is not unlike the color of the building itself bounds up from the cellar. His feet are huge, with white spats and a fat, extra toe pointed delicately outward. He purrs around Mike's legs.

"Buster," Mike says. "Good ratter," he adds, unaware that this might reflect badly on the building. "Always hungry." Mike pulls some kibble out of his pocket and gives it to Buster. They say their goodbyes.

"Well, we have a lot of places," Ingrid says. "That one was too small and too expensive."

"Absolutely," Bart looks distressed. ""Can we get some coffee?"

"Already? Sure. Are you tired?"

"No, but the Sue Ann thing is worrying me. And that apartment was really marginal." A moment of silence. "Wasn't it?"

"Marginal is polite."

The next address is farther east, so they cross First Avenue and head toward Avenue A, where they find a coffee shop. It is full and some of the diners are speaking Polish, or that is what they think as they hear it. "I don't know," says Bart. "Could be Russian or Polish, I guess." He has never heard either language. The light inside is custardy after the hovering gray of the day.

"I think the name of the place is Ukrainian," Ingrid says, "I'm not sure, though." They find a table toward the back and a heavyset waitress in a see-through pink blouse appears almost instantly and sets menus down for them. "Coffee?" she asks, in a slight accent.

"No," from Bart.

"Yes, please," from Ingrid.

They look at the menus and at what other people are eating. Some have just eggs and toast, heaps of home fries. Others have plates of small dumplings and still others have crisp plump cakes of something that has been fried.

"What are the dumplings?" Bart asks.

"Pierogi? I think that's how you say it. Pierogi? They must be on the menu."

"I'm having those."

"I don't want that much food, I'll just have eggs, but can I try yours?"

"Sure."

"Well," Ingrid says, "we need to talk about Sue Ann. Were you going to invite her to live with you?"

"No. I have no place to offer her."

"That's not the answer I was looking for. We can't take care of her; can't hide her."

"I wasn't imagining that. Not exactly."

"What, exactly? Richard would find her. She needs to work this out carefully if she's going to leave. She needs a lawyer. Richard is nasty. He's dangerous."

Bart has a flicker of memory, his thought when Richard looked at him a little too long. Little boys. "He's probably worse than you imagine," he says, uncharacteristically. "But she could visit."

"Yes, of course." Then Ingrid, who is usually blunt, hesitates. There is an uncomfortable silence between them, the emptiness filled by the din of people talking in the restaurant.

"When we looked at the first apartment you made it sound as if we were a couple."

Bart puts his hands over his eyes. "I did?"

"Yes, you did. When we talked with the guy."

"Yes, you're right. I did. Maybe I'm still hoping . . ."

"That we're a couple?"

Bart laughs. "No. Ingrid, of course not."

She looks at his flecked green eyes, at the rounded lids that seem carved in the way that Egyptian statues' eyes were carved, though surely Bart has no ancestors from that part of the world. She looks at his forearm resting on the table. It, too, is rounded, the muscles curved. His kindness is everywhere in the sweet form of his body, in his eyes and in his actions. "Luscious," she will say to him, when she wants to tease him. "You are so luscious." He is always embarrassed when she says it. He always likes it. Now she is going to hurt him. Again. "I need space to paint. Literal space. And I need privacy."

"I would give you those things. We lived in the same house. It was wonderful."

"We lived in different apartments. And it was wonderful." It had been. The closeness they shared. Neither one shares intimacy easily. Ingrid takes the last pierogi from his plate. She doesn't want to harden against his yearning and she still needs to say no. One more time. Ingrid feels the solitary aspect of her nature like a vein of minerals running inside her, or a cold aquifer, or a black night sparked by ferocious lightning. Primitive, private, non-negotiable. "And what about lovers? You'll want to find someone."

"And we know you will," Bart smiles.

"I will. We don't want to hear each other."

"No. No, we don't."

"We'll find places close to each other. It's all the same neighborhood. How far away could we be?"

Bart takes her hand. He manages to hold back a sigh. "Okay." He looks at his plate. "You ate the last pierogi. Let's get the check."

The day passes, getting chillier as it goes. It is late afternoon and Ingrid and Bart have found yet another Ukrainian (or maybe Polish?) coffee shop, this one on Second Avenue and Ninth Street. They are drinking hot tea and sharing a muffin. They have seen one apartment that has potential, and there are two left to go.

"Are you discouraged?" asks Ingrid. Bart looks a little weary.

"No, no. I know we'll be guided to find the right place. I'm sure of it."

"Are we scraping the bottom of the Jesus barrel, here?"

"No," Bart says with dignity. "And I can separate my faith in Christ from the political body of the church, for your information." One of Bart's struggles; to maintain his faith while dealing with an organization that hates his sexual preferences, that has tormented him about his feelings.

"Oh, good. That's certainly a relief. I think I'll go for spaciousness and non-attachment as a path. Except that I am attached. We need somewhere to live and we certainly need to get out of Sue Ann's. The tendrils of attachment are twined around me."

"Okay. We have a two-pronged approach, no pun intended. There are two more places left. Let's look on Seventh Street first, it's closer."

The building on Seventh Street turns out to be red brick, with dark brown painted trim. It has a little walkway in front of the door and a patch of grass with a fat rose bush in front. Most of its leaves have fallen and lie in a small, ruffled circle around the base of the trunk. The building looks as if it could have been transported from some quiet side street in Brooklyn, but since neither of them has ever been to Brooklyn, they have no thoughts about it, other than it looks very appealing and tidy. "It says, 'Ring Dereszewska,'" Bart says, fumbling with the name.

They do and a woman of about sixty appears at the front door. She is wearing a brown tweed suit and lace-up brown shoes. Her eyeglasses have tortoise frames; her hair is pulled into a long braid and wrapped at the back of her neck in a bun. She has substantial shoulders. "Yes?" she says. Her tone is friendly, if not cordial.

"We've come about the apartment," Ingrid says. "We'd like to see it. How are you today?" Her Iowa manners are still intact.

"Very good," she says. "I'm Mrs. Dereszewska. Mary. My husband and I own the building and we live here. Come, it's on the third floor." (So, they are meeting a landlord. Landlady.) She opens the apartment door with a slight flourish. It has polished parquet floors, a square living room with a galley kitchen on the far wall, an ample bedroom and a pink tiled bathroom. The windows face south and light fills the room, even on this gray day. Even empty, it is inviting. It embraces them.

Ingrid looks at Bart. He has stars in his eyes. "It's wonderful," he says. And then says it again. "Wonderful." The rent is listed as seventy dollars.

"Are you a couple?" asks Mrs. Derezewska.

"No, no," says Bart. "Friends. Very good friends."

"Where are you from?"

What, thinks Ingrid. Are we wearing signs? "From Iowa. We went to the university there. We are moving here permanently. Have moved here." She would like to impress this woman with their respectability. She knows Bart wants this place, absolutely. And it is for him. Not enough room for her to paint anyway. He looks at her and she nods slightly.

"I'll take it," says Bart, as Ingrid's nod finishes. Not a split second longer. "I mean, I know I have to apply and all."

"Well, just come downstairs to our apartment and I'll give you the forms. I imagine everything will be fine." In this neighborhood of hippies and tie-dye and unwed couples (she has noticed they have no rings), these two look like an answered prayer to Mary. She and her husband worked hard to buy this little building in the neighborhood of their butcher store and their church. She only wants a certain kind in here. Well, she has prayed, as a matter of fact. She smiles as they go downstairs.

"I will check with your employer," she says to Bart. "Would you like to leave a deposit?"

Ingrid thinks Mrs. Dereszewska is as eager as Bart.

"Yes. Just tell me how much." He takes out his neat checkbook. "How shall I make it out?" He is prepared. They have saved money for two years for this day.

"You know," says Mrs. Dereszewska, "everyone calls me Mrs. D." She takes the check and the form. "I don't foresee a problem. I will call you as soon as I speak with your employers, past and present. Probably tomorrow."

Not Mary, Ingrid notices. Not that cozy.

"If you want another place nearby, you should look across the street. That small building with big windows. He has a place to rent. He owns the building, too." And is an artist and seems to know a lot of women, she thinks, but that is not her problem.

"Good," says Ingrid. "We'll go look." They bid each other goodbye.

"This is fabulous," says Bart. "It is perfect. I know just what I want to do with it." He is perspiring slightly. "I wonder if Stephen will help me with the colors." Stephen, whom they met on their first visit. Shining Stephen. Stephen who was not his lover, but would have liked to be, Bart knows now. Knew then, but it was too early.

"Oh, no doubt," says Ingrid. She takes his arm as they cross the street to the building Mrs. D has pointed out. It is small, only three stories, with large windows and a dark metal door. There is only one bell and it says, "Jacobs." They ring and wait. Ring again. Then the door opens suddenly and a man with dark eyes and broad shoulders is standing in front of them. "What?" he says. "You aren't the plumbers?"

"No. We wanted to look at the apartment? Mrs. D. said you have space for rent," says Ingrid.

"Space? Oh, the third floor." It sounds as if he has just then remembered it. "Mmm. Mrs. D. The mayor of Seventh Street." He is wearing jeans with several colors of paint on them. He seems intense, the space around his body coiled. "You don't know anything about plumbing, do you?"

Ingrid, who grew up in the country, in a house where her father fixed a lot of things himself, actually does know a little about plumbing. "I might," she says cautiously.

He leads them inside. "Something is leaking under my sink. Quite a pool of water. Plumber said he'd come today. He lives around the corner."

"Do you have a shut off valve?" asks Ingrid.

"I don't know. A what? There must be one, don't you think? Let me show you."

He brings them into his studio. A large, industrial sink has a widening pool around it.

"Let me look," says Ingrid. She ducks under the cupboard surrounding the sink and finds the valve. It turns easily. "Off," she says. "Can we see the place?"

"Oh, great. Sure, yes. Thank you." He focuses on Ingrid for the first time. Her long legs and her butt and her long, almost gold eyes. And her breasts. Astonishing, he thinks. And she knows something about plumbing. More than he does, at any rate. "Come, it's the top floor. It isn't very fancy."

Indeed, it is not. It is an empty space, save for a tiny cubicle with a shower. A door with a pebbled glass panel says, *"Men,"* and leads to another tiny room with a sink and toilet. The large windows in the space go all around; the side windows face other buildings, but the ones front and back face the street and the rear courtyards, respectively. There is no stove or kitchen sink. There is no refrigerator. The floors are sturdy, wood halfway and the back half concrete. Everything is dusty. It is sooty, in the usual New York way, but there is also a fine gray dust on the windowsills and around the doorjambs. And it is the entire floor.

"What was here?" asks Ingrid. The dust is puzzling.

"This was a small factory," says Dan Jacobs. "Long gone. I think they manufactured paper products on this floor. My father owned the building originally. We had a tenant here, but he moved out a year ago."

"How did he cook?" And did he ever clean? Bart is trying to keep his face neutral. No reason to show that he is appalled.

"Oh, I don't know. Maybe he didn't. I can get you a stove and a fridge. And a sink. No problem. There's gas in the building. What do you do?" He is looking at Ingrid.

"I'm an artist," she says succinctly. She doesn't like announcing this to people, but there doesn't seem to be much choice and it would explain why she wants to live here. Surely not too many would. "This would be a good place for me. And I do need a stove and a refrigerator. And a kitchen sink. I like to cook. I also need to cook. I'm not going to eat out all the time."

"I'm an artist, too," Dan says. He has long, black eyelashes and hasn't shaved in a day or so.

"Yes," says Ingrid, "I noticed." But she was careful in his studio not to look at his work. "How much is the place?"

Dan looks at her seriously. How did this woman land on his doorstep? "It's sixty," he says. "I'll get the kitchen stuff for you. Maybe paint?"

"No," Ingrid says. "Thanks. I'll paint."

"We'll paint," says Bart.

"Okay. Great." But this guy is not her boyfriend, Dan thinks. He is definitely not. "When do you want to move in?"

There don't seem to be any papers to sign. Ingrid proceeds along smoothly. "As soon as possible. When can you get the appliances?" They are having two conversations at once, she notices. He clearly hasn't given any thought to renting the place and she knows he is attracted to her. Too bad for him.

"Do you want a deposit?" asks Bart. It is clear to him what the transaction is, but he wants something solid to change hands. Like a check.

"Sure," says Dan. "Of course. I should have that. I live here," he adds. " In addition to having my studio here. I'm the other two floors. The heat's good. Solid building." Is there something else he should say as a landlord? Ask if she has a job? He is sure she does. This is a serious woman. He doesn't ask.

"I have a job," Ingrid says.

"I believe you. I don't need to check. I can get the appliances in a couple of days. I know everyone in the neighborhood. Only way to get things done. Just leave a number where I can reach you."

Ingrid gives him Sue Ann's number. He looks at the piece of paper. Upper East Side exchange. "You staying with people?" he asks.

"Only for a couple of days," says Ingrid. "Till the stuff gets here."

"I'll call you, then." A bell rings. "Ah. That must be the plumber."

They all head downstairs. "I'll let you know tomorrow," Dan says.

"Good. Thanks. Really. Thank you."

"Oh, you're welcome. Really." He puts out his hand and Ingrid shakes it and then Bart does.

Dan opens the door to a man with a huge belly and a flat butt. The plumber.

Then they are out on the street. Bart is wildly happy. Ingrid sits down on the curbstone. Her body is shaking.

"Are you crying?" asks Bart. He doesn't think he has ever seen Ingrid cry. He is sure he has not. She looks at him, not covering her face or wiping her eyes.

"I certainly am."

He sits down next to her.

By the time Ingrid and Bart leave to return uptown, Frieda is preparing for her Monday night group comprised of two women who are professors of French at NYU, one chef-owner of a downtown restaurant that is becoming popular, a retired detective from the New York police force, and a young man who plays oboe in the Philharmonic. They come to study meditation and Buddhism with her. They have been working with non-attachment, the nature of clinging. With emptiness as filled with possibilities. Subjects that are virtually endless. Frieda's preparations are not focused on her teaching. She is preparing a rich lentil soup for after the meditation. Monday promises to be chilly.

Serena and Matt are at a movie, holding hands.

Leo is having an early dinner with an architect from Venice. Halfway through the delicious meal, in a room garlanded with candlelight, woven with spicy aromas, Leo understands that Luca is interested in him sexually. He manages to convey the impossibility of this idea without either of them ever mentioning anything.

✳ ✪ ✳

When Ingrid and Bart return to Sue Ann's, the apartment is dark, but music is playing.

"Sue Ann," Bart calls. "Are you here?"

They find her asleep on the couch in the living room. Their footsteps inaudible on the heavy carpet, they walk into the room and stand close to her. Sue Ann's hair is pulled back, her face red, as if she has scrubbed it harshly. She is wearing worn sweat pants and an old gray sweater. The music, insistent and rich, is Coltrane. Coltrane, thinks Ingrid. Since when does Sue Ann like Coltrane? The room is full of gray: the velvet upholstery, the smoky shadows of the rug, the silvery silk drapes mingling with the cloudy early evening, merging with the outside and simultaneously holding it at bay. In the midst of this smoothness, Sue Ann looks rumpled. Bart and Ingrid observe her quietly and then Ingrid touches her shoulder. "Sue Ann?"

She opens her eyes without moving her body. "Hi. You're here. I'm so glad to see you." She reaches her hand under one of the soft cushions. "I got them." She rattles a round, plastic vial. "Got the pills. Took one. I don't think I followed the directions exactly, but I've started." She smiles. "I'm on my way. What happened with your search?"

"We got apartments," Ingrid says.

"Both of you?"

"Both. We find out tomorrow, we hope. Then we can send for our stuff."

"Then we are all on our way. Where are they?" Sue Ann gets up suddenly. "I'm starved. Let's eat and talk." They all move toward the kitchen. No one turns on any lights. Coltrane continues to play, the music inviting, impossible.

"When did you start listening to him?" Ingrid asks.

"Oh, last year maybe." They reach the kitchen and Sue Ann turns on one lamp. "He's good company."

Sue Ann makes melted cheese sandwiches with tomato slices and bacon on heavy bread, dense with flavor. She lights a lamp. The kitchen is friendlier in shadow. "This bread is very expensive," she says, when they are at the table with the sandwiches and warm cokes. She laughs, spitting a little tomato. "From a very fancy bakery. Richard's favorite."

"We're on Seventh Street," says Bart, continuing the conversation about their new potential places. He is quite sure they will get approval. "Across the street from each other. Not, you know, in the same apartment."

"Looks like the bread at the Ukrainian bakery," says Ingrid. "Maybe they import it from Ninth Street. These are great sandwiches." Everyone is chewing appreciatively. The ominous sterile kitchen and its angry objects and shining knives recede as they eat.

The plastic circle of pills is on the table. Sue Ann rattles them from time to time. "Happy music," she says. "Almost as good as Coltrane."

By the end of the meal, Ingrid and Bart have described the apartments they found in some detail.

"Why don't you move downtown when you leave?" says Bart.

"I might. I have a plan. I've been putting money away for about six months. Just putting it in my own account. He always gives me more than I need. It didn't start out as a plan."

"Not a conscious one," says Ingrid. "He doesn't check it?"

"No. Yes, not conscious. I'm going to contact my old bosses, get a job and leave. They'll be happy to have me back. They wanted me to stay in the first place. Just like that. In the meantime, I'll look for a place."

They go to bed early and sleep on the expensive linens, dreaming maps of the future and, in Ingrid's case, about her paintings arriving to find that they are red, not white, when she opens them. Her dream self stares in disbelief. She begins to laugh.

* ☼ *

Frieda and Serge sleep at Frieda's; the cats surround them on the bed.

Serena sleeps at her own apartment with Rose. Hal has gone back upstate.

Matt and Leo sleep alone.

The moon comes up, winks at the violent, loving, paradoxical city and departs behind rough heaps of clouds.

When the sun rises in persimmon shimmers it is another Monday. Bart and Ingrid get word of the approval for their apartments in the afternoon and start downtown for keys and to look at paint and buy cleaning supplies. They plan to move in by the end of the week at the latest.

Bart does contact Stephen, who is happy to hear from Bart, perhaps a little surprised that he made it to New York—but then he remembers Ingrid and is not surprised anymore. Bart asks, somewhat hesitantly, if Stephen would advise him about his new apartment. Stephen smiles into the phone and says yes—where should they meet?

"I'm down here now," says Bart. He is in a phone booth. He gives him the address. Stephen takes an hour or so to arrive and when he steps inside the apartment, they embrace briefly. He looks the same, thinks Bart; and then, looking more closely, no. He looks older, as if something is sinking underneath.

"Oh," Stephen says, "it is truly great to see you. You look marvelous."

"And you," says Bart gallantly.

"No," says Stephen. "I don't. But I'm still here." He moves around the apartment, looking at everything carefully. "This is a nice place for you. So much sun. You couldn't come from all that open space and live in a dark apartment."

"Ingrid is right across the street," says Bart.

Yes, thinks Stephen. Of course she is. Ingrid scares him a little. Maybe more than that—though he barely knows her. "Good," he says.

"What do you think about peach?" asks Bart. "And yellow."

"No," Stephen says. "It will look like a fruit cocktail exploded. No pun intended."

Bart is hurt for a moment and then laughs. "What, then?"

"Colors that complement your skin, that bathe you in light and turn to velvet in shadow."

"I look okay in peach."

"No, no. My friend will paint. No cost to you; consider it a housewarming present." Stephen knows everyone, has everything Bart needs.

"Do I get to see the colors first?"

"I'll bring samples."

123

"This is just a three room apartment." Bart thinks of Sue Ann's awful place and feels a pinch of wariness.

"Which means it should be ugly? Some darker tones. A little mystery. Nothing too bold."

"Jesus. Ingrid is painting everything white, except the floor. The floor is black."

What a surprise, thinks Stephen. "But you're not Ingrid."

Stephen steps close to him and strokes his cheek, outlines Bart's lips with one finger. "Just listen to me, all right?" He pauses. Closes his eyes briefly. "A lot has changed, hasn't it?"

"Yes." Bart pictures Jeremy and hopes his eyes will not fill with tears.

"But still no?"

"No. For now."

Stephen looks more closely at Bart. "This was serious, wasn't it?"

"It was and he is in California and is going to stay there. I don't know what can happen, really. Nothing much seems possible. I want to go and look at St. Mark's. Do you want to walk up with me?"

"To the church?"

"Yes. The very same. I want to see when their services are." Bart is planning to pursue his faith, to see what Jesus is like in New York City. And this is a very liberal church, he has heard. Of course, the Episcopal Church is not the one he grew up in, but this is a choice he wants to make. The Lutherans in New York are not going to be that different, is his opinion.

"I have a cousin who lives near here," Stephen says as they walk. "Matt. I hardly ever see him, but I think we're right near his place. Maybe I'll call him, since I'll probably be in the neighborhood more often."

"You probably will." Bart smiles.

As they are walking, Ingrid is deep in the process of cleaning her loft. If there is one thing she knows how to do, it is clean, she thinks. Dossie didn't bring me up for nothing. Although she associates her mother's cleaning with hopelessness and fear and habit, Ingrid is enjoying this as a ritual, making a home for herself and her work, a spare, cleansed place. A sacred place, she thinks, with some humor. Mythic cleansing. She imagines the walls and floors moaning with relief as years of grime are lifted. She has chemicals to scrub the walls and other ones to peel the debris off the floors. She cleans from early in the morning till dark and when Dan comes to say hello and bring coffee and maybe help out, she hands him rags and says thank you. An unusual gesture of acceptance for Ingrid, who is inclined to be suspicious of help and to refuse it automatically. They talk as they work, the new refrigerator keeping them company, looking like a large, single tooth, shining and white in the mostly empty room. It was delivered earlier than expected. By the time they have finished, at almost midnight, it is chilly and Dan says the room hasn't been so clean since the day the building was finished.

"Where do you sleep?" asks Dan, looking at the room as he is leaving and seeing no evidence of a bed.

"On the floor," Ingrid says, "in the sleeping bag. You aren't going to ask further, are you?"

"I'm not," Dan answers. He is just curious, not anywhere near hopeful.

They touch hands when he leaves and Ingrid goes to take a very hot shower, scrubbing herself as clean as the room.

The next day the furniture arrives for both Ingrid and Bart. They buy food and move right in.

＊ ☸ ＊

A few blocks away, Frieda has been experimenting with her vulnerability; opening to Serge, her trusted friend. He holds her tightly at night and kisses her soft eyelids before they fall asleep. He tells her how much this means to him and she is embarrassed and sometimes angry, but she persists. Her fears about her bones breaking lessen, just slightly. Leo is buried in work and often alone. Serena and Matt are meditating together, at Serena's suggestion. Bill sits with them and snuffles. Matt closes his eyes and pretends. Sue Ann has gotten her old job back, but will not start right away; she finds an apartment on Sixteenth Street, near Fifth Avenue. She is still living a secret life. At the end of the month, she lies and says she thinks she might have been pregnant and miscarried. Richard is reassuring that they will keep trying, but seems less frustrated than he has been.

Leaves fall and the cold drifts in. Bouquets of autumn sunsets flame and the days get shorter.

Part II

It is toward the end of November that Richard and Sue Ann separate. Richard is strange; gravely comforting, assuring Sue Ann that it is no one's fault, reassuring her that he will take care of her, his voice low and soft, a kind of hypnotic crooning. He wants everything to be as easy as possible and, it seems, as fast. Listening to him, Sue Ann feels slivers of worry. His comforting words slide in and out of the sound of rain; it is a November of great dense rains slapping at the windows as she packs her things.

A movie company is filming on the street in front of their building and at night huge, backlit flutes of light press against the wet glass, eerie and demanding. There is very little she wants from the apartment, just one rug she particularly likes and her dresser, and one small painting. Her clothes, although she doesn't see that she will have much use for formal evening wear. Never mind, she is taking it anyway. She has heavy wool slacks lined with some silky material and sweaters in every color she loves: canary, cerulean, rose. She has expensive, soft leather boots and raingear and glamorous underwear. The underwear, bought for Richard's particular taste, she considers leaving and then reconsiders. Her midwestern thrift; it is perfectly good. Usable. She can give the evening wear to the Salvation Army. She would like to know what Richard is up to, exactly—but she is certainly not going to ask. It is puzzling and not at all what she expected. He wants a quick divorce. The quickest. She moves into the spacious apartment on Sixteenth Street between Fifth and Sixth. It is in a brownstone that has been carved up, but the rooms are large and there is good light, sunny. Her rear windows look out on a garden, just now splattered with dark leaves and puddles, but it is nice to see trees. She is near enough to Bart and Ingrid, but not in the same neighborhood. Hers is an odd neighborhood, belonging neither to the Village nor Chelsea. Sue Ann likes the vague anonymity after living in the cradle of the Upper East Side. Very upper, but still. She never felt really at home there, or in the heavy grip of the mercilessly decorated apartment.

Sue Ann is describing the situation to Ingrid when she is visiting on a day that is dry—the first in weeks, it seems—and very windy. Leaves spin everywhere in whirlpools of dust and grit. The sky is pale gray and tight. It is a day when the city looks stripped down, abraded. Ingrid has made coffee and they are eating cheese and the same delicious dark bread they ate at Sue Ann's the night of the celebration of the pills. They sit on Ingrid's daybed, which is covered now in heavy, Indian cotton in a blazing orange. The spread will last until Ingrid is sixty, even longer than that, though it will sprout a few holes. It is the single burst of color in this severe room. Ingrid's work is covered, as always. After a while the sky brightens and a map of sunlight flickers on the black floor. Ingrid listens to Sue Ann's story without comment. She has heard it before, but not in such detail. "What the fuck?" Sue Ann says. "This has been so hard on me? That's what he says. Who's writing his material? What is he talking about? Of course, it has been hard on me, but not in the way that he means." When Sue Ann is finished, Ingrid looks out into space, her tawny eyes moving slightly, as if she is watching something.

"Ah," she says. "I've got it. He wants you to go. You're not giving him the baby; he wants the baby more than he wants you."

"What? Is Richard that calculating?" Sue Ann sounds truly startled, although she has thought this herself. What else could explain his behavior? "Could he be that obvious? Yes, I'll bet you're right. And he is obvious; he's always been obvious, at least superficially. With all that mess and cruelty rolling around underneath." Sue Ann takes another sip of coffee, Ingrid's standard stunning brew. Her stomach heaves from this now certain awareness, as if small stones were shifting in her belly. For a moment she thinks she is going to be sick. She feels a broken tornado of fury and then relief. It passes and she makes a sound somewhere between a sigh and a hiss. "What an incredible thing. That shit. But it means I'm really free." They both whoop. "Free! It seems impossible, but it's true," Sue Ann says. "I will be gracious and appreciative," she says. "I will be disgusting."

The week after Sue Ann moves out, she sees Richard. It is late in the afternoon and raining again; she is passing a small restaurant in the Village, the windows full of amber light glowing through the wet. He is with a woman who looks alarmingly like Sue Ann, tall and blonde, with broad shoulders, big bones. They are just at the end of their meal and she stands, his hand helping her gently. When she is standing, she touches her belly briefly and in that gesture, Sue Ann knows the woman is pregnant and feels much worse than she imagines she would have. Of course. All those sudden trips to Boston and emergency meetings. Beyond trite. And what had he planned to do with her? No wonder he was thrilled that she was leaving—and so generous. It went further than even Ingrid had imagined. Her legs feel as if they will drop her to the concrete; she has read about this feeling, but never experienced it. Then she straightens and has an almost overwhelming impulse to run into the restaurant screaming. Shrieking. She does neither. Moving away from the restaurant so they will not bump into her, she thinks of all the women who are divorcing, fleeing violence, alone and poor, possibly with children to care for. She feels misery for them all, including herself, in her much cushier position. She raises her hand to hail a cab; she is one of the lucky ones. A privileged loser.

* ☸ *

It is early December, the very end of autumn, when Ingrid, Bart and Sue Ann begin to go to poetry readings in the East Village. These readings include some of the poets who will ride the waves of history well into the next century, who will be included in anthologies, who will produce books of their own and read their poetry in many places in the world. Others will read and be forgotten, mostly or entirely.

Ingrid and Bart love poetry for somewhat different reasons. Ingrid likes the architecture of sound, the color and shapes of words. The breath held, measured and released, the rhythm of the poems as they unfold. Bart likes them as theater; the way poetry evokes entire scenes, times in history, flamboyant love. Sue Ann knows nothing about poetry beyond the anthologies she has read in school, but she is delighted to be included. The first reading they attend is on a cold night with wind skimming over puddles left from yet another downpour. The temperature hints that soon ice will hover on the dark water, that molecules will quiver and slow and the cold will settle in, no longer drifting, but solid and confronting. The faces at the reading seem a bit familiar, perhaps people who live in their new neighborhood. The room is warm and they gradually unwrap their scarves and jackets; they have come from an Italian restaurant that has been in the neighborhood for generations and a light aroma of garlic clings to them. "I think I smell of garlic," Bart says, sniffing his hand discreetly.

"Oh, yes," Ingrid says. "I think so. We all do." The pasta is satisfying in their bellies.

Bart recognizes one familiar face, a man who goes to his church. He remembers the church discussion he and Ingrid had the first week they moved downtown. "I've chosen St. Mark's," Bart said, as Ingrid helped him unpack his new sheets and towels. The sheets are the yellow of dandelions, the towels a soft purple, to go with the pink bathroom tiles. Stephen definitely will not approve of any of them. "It's an art church, you know. They have concerts and poetry readings." He sounded prissy and defensive, even to himself. It is also an Episcopal Church, all that kneeling and a font of holy water at the entrance, but he likes it; it's where he wants to be, where he wants to pray.

"I know what St. Mark's is," Ingrid said. "Good choice." There was silence as the unpacking continued. Ingrid looked up. "Did you think I was going to argue with you about it? The church; its brutal history and hypocrisy, not to mention the fear it instilled in you. No, I wasn't going to mention it. I know it's important to you." The towels were folded; the sheets ready to go on the bed. Everything was new and clean.

Bart brings his attention back into the room, now full of the gray transparency of cigarette smoke, full of voices and greetings. A slender man with black hair almost to his shoulders bends over a tape recorder and checks microphones. His face is one of sorrow mended into wisdom and an alert curiosity in his dark eyes, bright behind black glasses with heavy square frames. He has a wide brow and his nose flares out sharply at the base. He has a small moustache and beard. People move around him and he smiles, lifts a hand in acknowledgement; he moves carefully, with determination and focus. This man seems integral to the event, his presence in some way essential, woven into the nature of the evening. When finished with his tasks, the group settles and the reading begins.

Matt is at this reading, without Serena. Frieda is there, her hennaed hair curling out from under a black knit hat; Serge is next to her. They are holding hands. Leo is at a lecture about restoring ancient churches; he had been enthusiastic about it, but the speaker is dull, the room cold and he leaves early.

The second reading Ingrid, Bart and Sue Ann attend is at St. Mark's; it is almost Christmas. The church is decorated with wreaths and balsam garlands and pots of red poinsettias. "It looks so pretty," Bart says. Sue Ann nods appreciatively. They both love Christmas. Ingrid sighs, making a point of not saying anything rude and trying to stay focused on the decorations as essentially pagan. The room is very full, though fortunately there is no one smoking, it is not permitted in the church, but refreshments are promised for later. The same man with dark hair and black glasses is working with the tape recorder. When he is finished, but before the reading starts, he moves toward the three friends. Bart is sure he is going toward Ingrid, but he says hello to all of them, says he has seen them before, and then turns slightly toward Sue Ann and asks, in his clear, light voice, if she would like to have some wine with him later. After the reading. "I'm Theo." Sue Ann is too startled to answer. She looks around, as if he might be speaking to someone else. Bart clears his throat.

"Yes," she says. "I'm Sue Ann. This is Bart and Ingrid."

"Well, good. I'm often the last one out. Is that okay?"

"Sure. Thanks; I'd like to." Where has she to go? Her presence is not urgently required anywhere and she is really delighted. "That was a surprise," she says. Ingrid and Bart both smile.

"Why? He's terrific and talented. Extraordinary," says Bart, who enjoyed Theo's poetry at the last reading and bought one of his books.

"That's the surprise," she says dryly. "Why me? I feel so downtrodden. My face is splotchy from the hormones; my breasts are swollen and aching. I am not the picture of allure."

"No one knows all that," Bart says. "Clearly you are alluring." He likes the word. "Alluring," he says again, positively. "You're an actress, you have presence." He is inventing.

"You're inventing," says Sue Ann. "However, I will do my best."

A man with a light brown ponytail bends toward Theo and says something brief before sitting near the front of the room; he has the kind of face that is at first pleasant and then emerges as increasingly handsome if you keep observing. When

Bart looks around, he sees two men with bright, almost golden hair sitting together. They have perfect square chins; one is wearing a rough, dark fisherman's sweater, the other a sweater in chocolate cashmere. "Oh," he says. "There's Stephen. That must be his cousin, Matt." He waves and Stephen waves back. He feels so pleased. He is starting to know people already. The reading begins.

Frieda and Serge are at a holiday party, which Frieda has resisted. "Call it a solstice celebration," Serge urges. Serena is at home alone, reading Anaïs Nin. The church is scented with the balsam and steam heat. The poets' words weave around the brilliant flowers and the heavy, white candles. It is indeed, very near the winter solstice and the light is about to return. Almost the end of the year: the new one will also be a year scarred with violence, with murder.

Sue Ann and Theo leave together, walking east in the now biting cold. In her flat boots, they are almost the same height. Sue Ann is freezing in just the few blocks to his apartment. Theo notices immediately. "You look frozen."

"Aren't you cold?"

"No. I grew up in Montreal. This is nothing."

Sue Ann knows they are headed toward his apartment. The thought of being approached sexually frightens her and she is aware of the disparity between her feelings and her actions. But that isn't necessarily what he's up to, she thinks. The cold slips under her coat and skims her bones, rests in the torn places inside her. Even if it is, I can say no. I would certainly say no. Memories of Richard's crazy rage mixed with sex is lodged in her nervous system, she can feel them there, vibrating and fierce.

Theo's building is typical of the neighborhood: old, the stairway listing slightly, the doors sporting two and three locks. When he opens his door, they are in the kitchen. A square room with shiny, black painted floors, a round, maple table with three blue chairs around it, a narrow stove, and a surprisingly new looking refrigerator, its bright white face shiny. Against one wall is a very large claw-foot tub with an enamel lid. The windows are tall, one windowsill built out to accommodate a collection of seashells and three ivy plants. Two small, black cats are curled around the shells and plants. When they see Theo, they stretch smoothly and jump down. Theo sees Sue Ann looking at the tub. "Yes. It's a tub."

"I've never seen one like that. It looks magnificently large." Even Ingrid has a wonky shower stall sitting in a small enclosure.

"Sit down," Theo says. "I'll get us wine."

Sue Ann sits at the table; the apartment is very warm, but she feels chilled and tense. "Could I have tea instead? I'm still cold. I think maybe the cold is interior, you know?"

"Sure." He puts the kettle on. "I do know. It's the worst kind of cold."

Sue Ann is looking at the drawings and photographs of birds pinned to the walls. She remembers birds appearing as symbols in his poems. There are also photos of the ocean and of hillsides bearing gnarled trees; the grass on the hills is sparse, the land rocky. "Where are these from?" She doesn't think it is anywhere in America.

"They're from Spain. I lived there for a while."

"I've never been anywhere much. It's embarrassing. Ingrid and Bart and I, all from Iowa, from families that never travel. Maybe in the service, some of the men did. I didn't see the ocean till I came here. My husband was going to take us to Europe, but it didn't work out. The understatement of the year," she says more softly.

"Mmm," he says, aware of her sadness as it pulls at her eyes and sighs in her voice. "Would you like to take a hot bath? It would warm you. Water's comforting."

"No. Oh no. Listen, I'm in this odd situation, you know. I don't want to have sex with anyone yet. Not anyone. I just left my husband a month or so ago. It was very bad. Bad hardly covers it." She feels stupid, getting herself into this. Just foolish.

"I wasn't offering sex. Just a hot bath. I have had some recent troubles of my own with a lady."

She considers the oddity of this moment. He seems sincere, simply quiet and caring.

He moves some neatly arranged papers from the tub lid and lifts it off. Steam hisses under the windows and his cats rub against Sue Ann's ankles. She has a sense of peace, like a low, sweet sound, one she realizes has been missing for months and tears hover in her eyes, loosening the sadness, singing it. "Well, okay. I've never tried this before. Like traveling." She looks inside the tub, which has been scrubbed so often the bottom surface is patchy.

"This tub is ancient and venerable," Theo says. He turns the water on and it streams out with surprising force, rising. It is the palest green and translucent, rocking and alive over the white enamel.

Sue Ann undresses slowly and Theo puts her clothes near the radiator to warm. He gets a soft maroon robe and gives it to her to wear while the tub fills. He gets the kettle for tea, his body graceful, holding a shimmer of fire. Sue Ann watches him and realizes that though she feels peaceful here, he is not a peaceful man. But he is a kind one. She gets into the tub and Theo brings her tea and pulls out a small, low table to rest it on. "I have birthday cake," he says. "Just had a birthday and there's some left over. Yes?" She nods. He takes a plate out of the fridge and uncovers the remains of a dark chocolate cake; he cuts her a slice and brings it on a blue plate with a gold rim. She doesn't feel very different undressed than she did dressed. He looks at her appreciatively, as one might appreciate a landscape, her peachy skin and full curves. He doesn't comment, but smiles a little.

"What happened to the lady?" Warm water cradles her; she can feel her muscles relax and she breathes into her belly, which has been sore since she left Richard. The bellyful of him that still hurts.

"To my wife. She was the lady. Is. It turned to broken stones and then we started throwing them at each other to express our mutual unhappiness and frustration. Her unmet needs, my inability to be intimate, except sexually. She claimed I sexualized everything, though tonight would certainly prove that she was not entirely correct in that assessment." He looks at Sue Ann and light catches on the lenses of his glasses, so she cannot really see his eyes. "Do you want soap?"

"Sure."

He brings her a small dish holding a cake of lavender soap. She washes her handsome feet carefully. "I left my husband because he was brutal and wanted to bully me into having a baby. A son, specifically," Sue Ann says as the water cools. Wind comes out of the blackness and knocks at the windows; a draft slides under the front door. "I got birth control pills secretly, got my old job back and left. He was more than magnanimous about my departure. Couldn't give me enough—an interesting phrase. He's very wealthy. Rich is a better way of saying it. He is a mean rich man. The week after I left, I saw him in a restaurant with a woman and she was pregnant. The most shocking thing was how upset I was. No, not upset, enraged. What was he planning to do with me? He had guns. For a while I imagined he was going to shoot me." She breaks off. "This sounds really crazy. I didn't think he would kill me; I fantasized it. Does that sound less crazy? I haven't said this to anyone, not even Ingrid, though it would be hard to shock Ingrid."

"Maybe you would like to kill him," Theo says. "I was so angry with my wife I wanted to kill her—or wanted her dead. Betrayal has very powerful effects. It's always shocking." He hands her a large, white towel, with spots worn almost through with age, and she steps out of the tub, wrapping herself carefully. Theo gives Sue Ann her clothes, now warm from the radiator, and she dresses. He takes the stopper out and the water drains noisily. When he replaces the tub lid, he replaces the papers that had been there. Sue Ann notices them.

"Are you doing some accounting?" she asks, half playfully. "Those look like bank statements."

"They are. The lady of the house did the banking and she took a good chunk of money with her. Not that we had that much. I'm not very skillful with this; I was trying to figure out what I have left and where it goes . . ." He seems embarrassed.

"I can help you with that. I do a little bookkeeping at my job. A little of everything, really. Let me help."

He hesitates, but not for long. "That would be great; I'm sure I can learn. I feel foolish to be so helpless." She has finished dressing. "Let me take you home. It's so late."

"No, I'm okay. I'll get a cab. Thanks for—just thanks. When can I give you the banking lesson?"

Theo pushes his glasses up on his nose. "Oh, soon. The sooner the better. This Monday, here, at two?"

"Sure. My hours at work are flexible."

"Do you know the address?"

"No."

He writes it down for her. Particles of cosmic dust float in the soft light; strands of connection spun out from eternity nestle on the dark floor of the room; having brought these two unlikely people together, they rest. "Let me at least get you into the cab." They walk downstairs together, Sue Ann holding his arm. The night is sleek with cold. He waits with her and they hug.

"Goodbye," she says.

"Goodbye, I'll see you next week."

It is very late. Everyone is asleep except Frieda, who often wakes in the wee hours and reads, sipping a cup of chamomile tea.

Part III

Ingrid is working as a photo researcher in a building in the West Thirties, mostly occupied by companies in the garment industry. "The rag trade," is the expression she learns that people there use. The building is well constructed, with high ceilings and large rooms and heavy walls; it is cared for, the brass elevator doors polished, the floors waxed. There is something comforting about the structure itself; it seems enduring. Clothing in colors and styles two seasons away racket into the large elevators, pushed on garment racks. Tall thin women carrying portfolios and fishing tackle boxes filled with makeup often appear at mid-morning.

Ingrid imagined that she would not like her work much, but she took the job to pay her bills. She is practical in that way, unromantic about the fact of earning a living to support her art—or until her art can support her, is the way she prefers to think about it. She does not wish to be a waitress, though she has often been told that it is the fastest way to earn good money. No, she wants a schedule with regular hours and good benefits. She needs to know when she is free to do her own work and that she can plan on it. To her surprise, she enjoys the research and the satisfaction of solving small mysteries: which photo is the exact one needed? A sepia print of New York at the turn of the century? A gap-toothed girl, her hair blowing in the wind, standing at the door of a one room schoolhouse at the top of a grassy hill? An apple orchard wild with pink spring blossoms? As she looks at the photos, it occurs to her that she would like to use some of them in her own work, particularly the girl. She would like to make a collage, photographing the photograph, using snips cut from a petticoat, painting a hair ribbon with layers of color, using fingers of woolen gloves, making the background heavy, sandy, bright blue, including objects that might belong to the life of a child, or to her future life. This is an unexpected bonus—finding images that inspire her, urge themselves into her work. She asks Allen, her boss, about the legality of using the images. He is a small man, delicate, quick, with a good sense of humor and not a lot of patience. "What for?" he asks. She tells him it is to use in a collage, that she is an artist, though she is always reluctant to mention this to anyone. She does not want to hear their ideas, be entangled with their thoughts and opinions about art, about her, about her and art. But all he does is wave his hand dismissively. "Oh. Sure. Just nothing for commercial purposes. But check with me first." Oh, it could be commercial eventually, she thinks, but says nothing. She thanks him.

She sees the same groups of people coming and going in the elevators, the halls. She notices one man in particular. He is tall, with large features, big hands, a wide back. It is not the ominous largeness of her father, or of terrible Richard, blocky and threatening. It seems to express a vitality of spirit that has taken this form. His walk is both determined and easy, someone who is sure of his direction, relaxed with his choices. He wears a heavy, tweed coat in this already relentless winter cold and an extravagant patterned scarf in crimson and purple. Ingrid imagines it might be from India. He carries a caramel-colored briefcase and worn leather gloves of the same color. His dark curls are split with silvery gray and he is hatless, even on the coldest days. Sometimes he has a camera; sometimes he cradles a cone of flowers from a florist. They seem to eat lunch at the same time—later than most of the people in the building. Often, Ingrid brings food from home, but when she is very busy, she splurges and gets her lunch from one of the local delis. On those days, they frequently meet in the elevator, both carrying aromatic brown bags smelling of coffee and dill pickles and freshly cut bread. Hers is always the larger of the two. On one of the days, he gestures to her bag and says, "You have a healthy appetite. My mother would approve." His voice is deep. A manicured New York voice. "I'm Max," he says.

"Ingrid. I'm Ingrid. I have an extremely high metabolism. If I don't eat regularly —and a fairly substantial amount—I lose weight. My mother used to have the family doctor check me periodically. She thought I had worms. But no, just a gross feeder."

He looks puzzled. Ingrid realizes he doesn't understand "gross feeder," and it must sound very strange indeed.

"Those are plants that need a lot of nourishment," she says. "I grew up in Iowa." She imagines him eating a superb dinner that his wife has prepared. She imagines them at an elegant table. "You don't eat much. You must eat later."

"You mean for someone my size?"

"For anyone. That's a pretty small bag."

Later that day, they leave the building at the same time. "May I offer you a lift home?" It never seems to him that Ingrid is wearing heavy enough clothes. And yes, she intrigues him.

"I live downtown," she says. "I don't think it's your neighborhood."

"No, it isn't. And the offer is still good."

"Sure," she says.

It develops into a pattern. Max stops by when he has the time and drives her home. She learns that he has two daughters in college—a year apart. "Irish twins," he says and laughs. She tells him about Iowa, a little about her family. She doesn't mention her art, but he is sure she does something besides photo research. She doesn't think he is Irish. She never invites him up and he doesn't ask.

It is February 9th, another day of impossible cold, and it has been snowing all day. The predictions are for a massive snowfall and offices are closing early. Max thinks of Ingrid's thin boots and generally inadequate clothing and stops at her office to offer her a ride home. By this time, they have been riding downtown together on and off for about a month, all of it cold, much of it snowy. "Yes," she says, "that would be welcome." He watches as she gathers her things. He imagines her as a bronze sunset falling on dark water, layers of bronze sun, shading to amber light, then fading to the palest gold and disappearing into the watery shadows. He is accustomed to looking at colors, at rare objects and their fragile yet enduring beauty, their ephemeral consuming riveting magic. But Ingrid is not an object, could not be owned or possessed in any way. He does not want to possess another human being. He does not want to possess objects, either, though his wife said otherwise. He wants to admire, yet the longing is not for possession, but something less tangible and never quite satisfied. All this, while Ingrid puts on her coat, her scarf, a black wool watch cap and says goodbye to the remaining people in her office.

Max has not thought of asking Ingrid to go for a drink until he hears his voice moving through the warm air of the car; he feels self-conscious halfway through the sentence. They are headed downtown in the slow traffic; snow everywhere, piled against cars, spinning under streetlights. People at the crossings are bundled into anonymity. Hats, scarves, boots. In this weather, even New Yorkers bow to the elements. The snow seems to come from some ancient frozen store, a bottomless reservoir of whiteness tumbling around them, covering the city. They are heading into what will become an historic blizzard, but they don't know that yet.

"Would you like to go for a drink?" There it is, between them. But Ingrid does not seem surprised.

"Sure. Even better than a ride. A ride and a drink."

"Good. There's a nice bar on lower Fifth, if the traffic ever moves." Which it does, but slowly. The dark is almost purple at the edges, laced with swirling flakes. Ingrid seems peaceful with the snow, the slowness. With the warm hollow of the interior of this heavy, black car.

"Does it snow a lot in Iowa?" He stops and laughs. "Silly question."

"No, not silly. It probably snows less than upstate New York. It does snow, though, and gets cold. Not much protection from the howling winds. But the sunny days in winter are stunning." She remembers the huge brightness of the sun shining on snow, sometimes on ice, flashing and alive, the wide sky absolutely blue. Of the demon embrace of the cold. (But New York is colder than she had thought it would be. Much.) Ingrid likes extremes of weather, likes weather in general, and seasons. She does not think she would like California, the sameness of it. "Have you ever been to Iowa?"

"No, never."

"To the Midwest?'

"Chicago, does that count?"

"Umm, almost. No, not really. Newton, Iowa is nothing like Chicago. Less than nothing like."

They have reached lower Fifth Avenue and Max turns into a garage. The bar, which turns out to be in a hotel, is just around the corner. By the time they get inside, snow has collected on their shoulders, on Max's hair and Ingrid's black wool hat. The air is sweet inside the bar, that sharp sweetness of alcohol that pinches the nose. They check their coats. The waiter nods to Max and shows them to a table. The bar is quite empty, its velvety chairs shadowed in the low light.

"A lot of folks went home early," the waiter says. "Such bad weather. They say it's a real blizzard." He is tall and pear shaped, with heavy, sloping eyes. He and Max seem to know each other.

They both order scotch, no ice (ice!) and slowly begin to talk about their lives. Their conversations in the car have been circumspect, nothing much revealed on either side. Just casual words floating in the soft interior of the car. Sometimes they played the radio.

"Did you start out as a dress designer?" Ingrid asks. She imagines he works with his father's firm, which designs and sells dresses. His office and his father's are next to each other, with different doors.

"No. As a historian." He considers whether he will say that he attended Harvard and decides against it. It gives an impression of him that he dislikes, although the school itself, in those strange heated days of the early war, was an amazing place. "I graduated in June of '43; I skipped a grade, so I was a little young. Then I went into the army. I was in Europe." He says this carefully, his voice not flat, but controlled. He is not ready to talk about that. About those years when the membrane of his awareness ripped open and hell rushed in. He doesn't speak of it often at all. Almost never.

She hears this in his voice—the carefulness. She would not have asked further and understands that this part of him is closed, at least for now. She wonders about the "for now" which came to her spontaneously. Does she imagine there will be a "later?" Arthur was in the war. Her Father. He was in the Pacific. He still meets with old Navy buddies, this man who sailed heavy seas, who hailed from a family of landlocked people, this violent man who must have killed other men, but has always been silent about it. Even though Ingrid is a woman who likes secrets, she would not ask about this. Some secrets she keeps are inconsequential, others ragged and painful. Some are secrets about what she finds beautiful. They reside within her, potent, sharp, inviting and inaccessible to others, although their energy is often tangible. Max and Ingrid sit quietly, letting some emotional space spread out around them.

Meanwhile, the bar is filling with groups of people looking bewildered, angry. People who have not managed to get out early. "Can't get out. This storm has everyone locked in. Rooms? Are there any rooms?" Some of them leave their coats on the velvet chairs and head for the desk, ordering drinks on the way. Ingrid knows Max lives on the Upper West Side. She is genuinely concerned for him, which surprises her somewhat. He has been generous with her, driving her through the cold these last weeks. She thinks she could walk home, but she is wrong. The weather has closed in.

Max laughs. "This is going to sound planned, but it wasn't. I have a sort of permanent, small suite in this hotel. My family has had it for years. My father stays here when it's too late to go back to the Island. Sometimes he and my mother use it after the theater. Clients stay here, though not that often. May I invite you upstairs? I'll order dinner before we go up and I can sleep on the couch if I can't drive you home." The bar has gotten crowded and noisy. Ingrid would like to be somewhere quiet where she can watch the snow. Also, she is curious. She has not been to many hotels, just for family weddings sometimes, for the receptions, if they are especially fancy. She has never had the occasion to be in a room in a hotel like this one. What assortment of furniture and objects would have made their way into this suite? What ambience, what gathering of fabrics in the draperies, the bedspread? What might be contained in the room and what does it signify, if anything? In some ways, to her, rooms are like her boxes, all of them filled with potential inspiration.

Max waits while this goes through Ingrid's mind. He sips his scotch. He is as curious about her reply as she is about the room.

"Good," she says decisively. "How lucky that we're here." And suddenly she feels lucky. Happy to be with Max and to be taken care of, a rare pleasure and one she —mostly—refuses to allow. He takes their drinks and gets their coats and walks toward the elevator. More people gather. Their voices sound excited, a sense of adventure mixed with anxiety.

Max opens the door to the suite and switches on some antique brass lamps; the living room is larger than Ingrid expected—square, with high ceilings. The walls are painted a flushed rose and the two armchairs upholstered in tapestry designs. The silk drapes are a muted version of the walls and the carpet is blue, with vines and flowers faintly marked. Beyond is a bedroom and against one wall are shuttered doors, which must lead to a kitchen. He takes her things and hangs them in the coat closet. Ingrid is aware of a fragrance like parched flowers and sees a bowl of dried petals on a small table. "It doesn't look like my idea of a hotel, not that I have a lot of experience. Or any, really."

"My mother brought some of her things. She likes rooms to look a certain way."

"Let's turn out the lights and watch the snow," Ingrid says.

Max turns the lamps off and they both move to the windows. The snow is magnificent, unrelenting, sparkling in the streetlights and broken by the occasional slow-moving car. "There are colors hidden in the whiteness," Ingrid says. "You can't see them in the city; there's so much pink from the lights."

"There are," Max answers. "White is always full of color."

"I've painted a lot with whites." She does not elaborate about her passionate study of all the whites she could see, all that she could find. How the undertones moved almost behind her sight, how she struggled to paint both their delicacy and their force. They stand near the window, feeling the cold drift through.

"This is a major storm," Max says. "We're going to be here all night. I'm going around the corner to the deli. I'll get food for tomorrow before the store runs out. I hope he's still open."

"Ah," says Ingrid. "A man who provides. Admirable."

"Are you teasing me?"

"No, no. It's a rare quality." Arthur provided for his family, every cent given with a mean tug, as if he was giving it and pulling it back simultaneously. Ingrid worked as soon as she could, eager to avoid these interchanges and be free of her father's grim hold.

"Okay. I'll be back as quickly as I can. There are blankets and bedding in the cupboard; I can sleep on the couch."

"Okay. You mentioned that earlier." She considers saying something else and then stays silent.

When Max leaves, Ingrid explores the rooms. There is an armoire made of various woods, polished, shining softly. A bookshelf holds some classics, large books on Middle Eastern designs and a small collection of mysteries. The bedroom is ample; the bed covered in a plum-colored quilt, with porcelain lamps on each bed table, their shades fluted silk in dusty blue. An inviting place, sweet and welcoming. How much of it might she use for a new box? What would she add? Sharp edges, worn cheap things, half broken. She doesn't look in the kitchen. As she explores, she asks herself if Max is too old to be sexy. For her to find him sexy. But she knows it is a false question and understands that she wants to touch him, wants him to touch her with all that warmth and generous vitality. As she waits, she is aware of a sensation pulling low in her abdomen, a fallen red moon turning in a slow tide beneath her pelvis, a full, heavy feeling she has had before, and associates with particular experiences. It often comes just at the moment when she realizes an idea for a new piece and when the change of seasons first becomes visible, a scarlet spot on a leaf, a whisper of ice covering a puddle, passing over the edge from one season to the next. It is a feeling she had when she first came to New York: danger and embrace, paradoxical desire, both flamboyant and elusive.

She goes to the window again and opens it a few inches, dipping her fingers in the deceptive lightness of the snow; she holds them there until the cold enters her fingertips and then she hears the door open and Max has returned. He is carrying a very large bag. The waiter with their dinner cart is right behind him and he wheels it into the room. Max hands him some bills. They nod at each other.

"How much did you buy?" Ingrid is laughing. She appreciates the bag. Max is not cheap and tight like Arthur and Big Dossie, her mother, who shopped so carefully, studiously, even after Arthur was making good money. Ingrid herself buys the food she wants. Mangos in winter, puréed chestnuts (a new find), the darkest, most bitter chocolate. She buys these things in small quantities and the choices give her great pleasure and a feeling of power. He comes out of the kitchen and stands next to her. His face is wet, his coat still on, snow on his shoulders. Ingrid turns and kisses him, rubs his lips with her cold hand, slips her fingers into his mouth. To her astonishment, he carries her to the large soft armchair and puts her on his lap. She rests there, surprised and as comfortable as she was on the great tree outside her parents' house, where she sat for hours among the branches and the green. She rests against him and releases a sigh that has been hidden so far inside her that she has lost any awareness of it. The red moon floating in her belly turns fiery.

"Ingrid, this is—isn't what I planned. It isn't even what I imagined."

And then they are lost and don't speak for a while. He holds her in his lap, their arms around each other and he begins to rub her back. She moves the side of her hip against his pelvis and rocks slightly. He says gently into her ear, "This is a decision point. Do we want to go further?"

No one has ever mentioned deciding in this way. Ingrid's sexual encounters have just moved along, from one thing to the next, though Ingrid was choosy, if not exactly careful. She has had a number of lovers (but not as many as Bart teases her about) and one fairly serious relationship with a man getting his Ph.D. in geology. A man who played the harpsichord and basketball and tutored children. They had the edge of something, the borders of connection, a small commitment. But they had separated before she left Iowa and she had no longing for anyone new.

"I have decided," she says. She can feel his erection, but does not put her hand on him there. "My body has decided."

"I want to choose to make love," Max says. He lifts her onto her feet and holds out his hand to her.

She takes his hand and says, "I am choosing." They walk into the bedroom and Max takes the spread off the bed. They undress slowly, watching each other, putting their clothes neatly on a chair. Naked, they embrace and then they are on the bed. Max rubs Ingrid's belly where the red moon is flaring. He holds her beautiful breasts. He kisses her everywhere and then rubs the soles of her feet. She hasn't known there were so many places to be touched, so many ways to embrace. She feels as if she is moving through a scrim into a room that has been mostly unreachable and then past that, into a realm unknown to her. It is slow and engulfing and alarming and transforming. She touches him in return. She cannot stop kissing him for long. Tasting him. He tastes like pears. He puts his fingers inside her and moves deliberately. Once she suddenly draws back in fear and Max holds her until the feeling passes. He twists her long hair and pulls it softly. "Do you use pills, Ingrid?" One serious question before he enters her. No one has ever asked her that either.

"No, no pills. A diaphragm. I have one with me." She knows this sounds odd. "I was going to visit someone. Not—a friend. Sometimes we have sex." Ingrid, so rarely awkward, feels clumsy.

"Bring it here. We can put it in."

"We?" This is truly shocking. "I'll do it."

"Okay."

When she has come back to the bedroom, Max has turned one lamp off and left one burning. He holds his arms out to her. He enters her, and they seem to Ingrid to be inside each other, beyond the realities of time; their pleasures rise, fall away and rise again. When, for a while, they are not joined, Max says he needs to make a call. "Your wife," Ingrid says as a statement rather than a question. She has always assumed he was married.

"I have no wife, I'm divorced. Her name is Evelyn and she is in California. No, to my daughters. I don't want them to worry."

"I should call Bart. My friend. No, not that friend."

They make their calls. Ingrid reflects on her assumption that Max was married and wonders about other women in his life now. Surely there must be one—or several. He is a desirable man, she imagines women must pursue him and she is right.

Max has had various lovers and one affair since he and Evelyn separated, all with intelligent, stylish women. He has not loved any of them; he didn't even wish that he would love them. What he feels for Ingrid is entirely new; like her, it is a world he has never entered. He feels disoriented and willing to be so, curious about where the edges are, amazed at his own heat and his sense of strange, slow patience.

The night passes and they sleep and wake to touch each other as the snow outside continues and covers the hard shapes of the city, rendering it almost silent on this very cold night in February.

The next day, Max makes a huge breakfast, including an omelet with the vegetables left from the previous night and, on the side, some cold, sliced lamb. They hadn't eaten dinner at all. He makes piles of buttered toast and asks Ingrid about coffee. "Do you like coffee in the morning?"

"I like it all the time. Black. Strong." She looks out at the street. "Do you think the Met is open today?" Ingrid has been planning to go to the Met and look at as many different kinds of green she can find, starting with Egyptian ceramics and glass, moving on to Greek and Roman art, Medieval painting and as far forward from there as she can get. She wants to know all the shades and highlights and secrets of the color. She is planning to use it in her work; not the way she used whites, which embraced everything. But as parts of paintings. In corners of drawings, in the rooms she makes, sometimes using it boldly, sometimes in an almost hidden way. Green, the color of the mythic garden, where she has most unexpectedly found herself. She moves from the window and stands in back of Max, holding him.

"We could call. Yes, and then we really have to get dressed . . ."

The museum is open, though the phone rings for a long time before someone picks up. They dress and make their way to the subway uptown and then to Fifth Avenue. Max has given Ingrid extra socks from the small store of clothing kept in the suite—he is worried about those thin boots, but she is happy walking and holding his hand, not minding the cold. They walk down the center of the almost deserted streets.

At the end of the day, they walk down Eighty-second Street to a coffee shop on the corner and order macaroni and cheese. They pass the private school where Serena once worked, but it is closed and they have not yet met Serena.

Before they leave the museum, they sit on a formal wooden bench. There are no other people near them. Max takes her hand. "It will be tomorrow soon and then the day after that. It only seems as if time has stopped."

"Of course. Yes, I realize that."

"I would like to continue, Ingrid. I would like to be your lover and your friend."

"Yes," she says without hesitation. Ingrid, who is so guarded about intimacy, treating it as a dangerous landscape that she must enter with utmost caution, a place of capture and remorse. Such a ready answer; so heartfelt. "Surely, we will continue."

✳ ✦ ✳

Where was everyone else the night before, when the snow fell relentlessly, seeming to have no end? A night that arranged new bedmates, if not sexual partners, during that majestic paralyzing outrageous storm.

Leo missed it all; he was in Arizona, studying ancient structures, climbing narrow ladders to second story rooms. But he thought of the snow covering his small garden, nourishing the bulbs he planted with his father that day in October when Lou Lou stole his blue ring.

Serena was at home with Rose, in the apartment they shared, rapidly developing what would amount to a life-changing flu. Matt hadn't come home the night before and Serena had left his house early in the morning.

Matt was falling into a snow bank with a redhead from his Eliade class. By the time he got up and helped her up, he knew he was in love.

Sue Ann and Theo were at her apartment, going through yet another stack of bank statements and talking about poetry. They did sleep together, chastely, holding each other.

Bart was at Stephen's, looking at a mirror Stephen had bought for Bart's approval. Stephen often bought things for Bart. Bart liked the mirror, but balked at the gift and stayed over in Stephen's guest room, the soft creamy drapes and carpets an interesting note in the midst of the whiteness of the snow, whirling in darkness, still unyielding.

Frieda and Serge were visiting in Bucks County; an old friend named Sarah from Paris and the war had a house there. They stayed several days beyond what they had planned and Frieda made five loaves of bread for them all, the snow having triggered her fears about starvation. The others were pleased, they shared her history, and ate bread with homemade strawberry jam and thick slabs of butter the whole time they were there.

Who knows what else happened? Who were the children conceived that night, what stars collapsed, went suddenly dark, what music was written, what quarrels healed as the snow shifted people's awareness, forged new circumstances?

Part IV

Serena is mourning Matt, the Golden Man; though the mourning is not dreadful, but etched with what has always been known between them, an awareness that began at the start of the relationship—that this was not forever. They met the previous April, or re-connected. They had been acquainted with each other. Serena had gone to see if Matt lived in the same place and as she was checking his name on the bell, he came down the street. The blue air was full of the sweetness of new leaves and warming earth. Serena had always been attracted to Matt, her heart was filled with bright longing, as well as with the shadows and yearning that were her companions. Her prickly shows of independence and her unexpected willfulness were not, for the moment, on display. How extraordinary that he should suddenly appear. Perhaps not that extraordinary. It was where he lived, but she has walked down this block many times and never met him, or even seen him passing in the neighborhood. Matt's heart had its own mysteries: it was full of myths, of philosophy and, deeply covered, of his wrecked, brazen family. At the moment he saw Serena, he was thinking of Eliade and also *Morning of the Magicians,* which he was reading. They went for a cup of coffee, clearly delighted to see each other, and made a date for the coming Thursday. At the end of their very first evening together, they arrive at Matt's to hear the news that Martin Luther King Jr. has been shot. A romance's tender opening on a night of exploding misery and violence. They had been aware of a rumble in the streets, something rolling through as they walked, but had paid no attention. Serena is blind with sadness and they both weep with shock and at the fragility of it all, the tattered social membrane tearing yet again. Do they wonder at the synchronicity of these events? Such violence at their beginning? No, not really. And indeed it does not portend anything personal. It is clear fairly soon that this will be a tender friendship, sexual, but not passionate. She does not feel him pulling at her heart, disturbing its center of gravity. They do not feel fire, leaping and consuming. At the quick end, he writes Serena a letter expressing respect and friendship. The flu that started the night of the storm erupts and she gets very sick.

During her sickness, Serena reads a book on macrobiotics called *You Are All Sanpaku.* It has a shiny, orange cover and a black, plastic, spiral binding. It is not a food plan, but a philosophical and universal understanding of Yin and Yang, the balance of forces, correctness and purity, including the extreme importance of the choice and preparation of certain foods. *Sanpaku,* the name of a condition where the whites of the eyes are visible above the lower lashes and the irises drift upward, is a sign of danger and impending doom. The book lists famous figures who have died violently whose eyes exhibited this characteristic. (It does not mention the thousands, perhaps millions, whose eyes rest this way and who live long lives.) The whole scheme was made for Serena—a rigid tent of rules that would lead to harmony—even though the warning about eyes frightens her and she stares at her own large and beautiful eyes, wiggling the mirror to ascertain whether she might have an incipient case of *sanpaku.*

As her fever waxes and then subsides, she is physically weak and emotionally sore from Matt's rejection (respect or no). She has inhaled every word of the book. She is contemplating an existence wherein she can create a perfect, lightly swaying balance, a control that is both humble and majestic. And everyone she has ever known who was macrobiotic got very, very thin. They also tended to smell wetly of aduki beans, but Serena is sure she and Rose can avoid that. Maybe a matter of bathing? As soon as she is strong enough to move, she and Rose go shopping for the proper foods. Rose is skeptical, but willing. A local delicatessen, aware of the rising interest in these particular organic foods, has started to stock them. Sam Greenberg, not himself a believer, now carries huge hairy carrots stored in a small, refrigerated room; he also has daikon, a kind of white radish, and other acceptable vegetables. Rose and Serena cruise the icy room and make their selections. They buy brown rice and dried seaweed and tamari. Aduki beans and sesame seeds and tahini. They buy the required iron skillet. Serena stops drinking water, a forbidden substance, and coffee. They begin to cook. Part of the philosophy is to cook everything slowly; one week into the regime they realize that slow is the only possibility, as it takes all weekend to prepare what they will need for the week, but never mind. This is a spiritual journey that will also provide glowing health and peace of mind. The apartment begins to smell of sesame and the dreaded aduki beans. Serena scrubs everything and opens the windows to the still-frigid air. The book mentions dire symptoms of failed femininity, such as hair on the limbs. Serena stares darkly at the soft fluff on her arms and legs. No one seems to realize the philosophy comes from Japan where women do not have fluff-covered limbs. It is another worry for Serena, another unacceptable way her body is expressing itself. Rose doesn't pay much attention to that part, but they do cook and eat the food and patronize a local macro restaurant, where the kitchen is less than clean and mishaps occur; the occasional piece of glass lands in the food, not to mention hair. Rose's boyfriend Hal eats with them sometimes, as a sign of support. Serena has not gone out with a man in a month or more, probably her personal record. She has been reading Anaïs Nin, along with the macro book; Nin describes the necessity to detach from men in order to find inner strength. (This is Nin? What?) Maybe there is one sentence that implies this is desirable, but it flashes out at Serena. It does not match the macro philosophy of vital femininity and the relationship between the sexes, but Serena is, as she sometimes can be, oblivious when it seems necessary. In between Nin and macrobiotics, she is working with the Tarot. She is familiar with the cards and has used them, but she is not skillful with them, as she is with astrology. She has never entered their mystery, gone through the transparent corridor into that particular reality.

March begins, but nothing seems to melt; dirty ice clings to the curbstones and the daffodils are reluctant, as is the sun.

Theo is weary; the woman from whom he is separated is more in his life than ever, always bitter, full of hurtful words, or well-bred cruelty. Had she always been so? Theo is no longer sure. In the midst of her incursions, he is doing new work and exploring many kinds of symbols. The Tarot has always interested him and he knows Frieda teaches Tarot classes; they are old friends and have spent a great deal of time together over the years reading poetry and discussing Buddhism. And eating. They both love food in a sensual way.

One afternoon when the sun has finally appeared and rides on Theo's newly cleaned windows bringing an almost audible hope, he calls Frieda.

"Is there a bitch in the cards?"

"Theo?"

"Yes. Who else?"

"In which cards?"

"In the Tarot. I'm reading about them and I can't find one. A bitch."

"Well, not exactly, no. Are you in need of one? Is this conversation about something else? Are you hungry? I just made fresh soup."

"Oh, always. Hungry. Not always in need of a bitch."

"Well, come over and we can eat soup and discuss the Tarot. Maybe I can help with your bitch problem."

People are out on Second Avenue, dressed in fewer layers of clothing than anyone has dared for months. Theo watches the shadows made by the sun—so welcome, the shifting patterns, stretching and colliding. He watches his salt-scuffed boots as he walks toward Frieda's. He passes a blond couple coming out of Gem Spa eating strawberry cones and stops inside the store to buy Frieda some ice cream. When he arrives, Frieda greets him with her strong hug.

"Come in, come in. Sun at last. What a beautiful day to be preoccupied with a bitch." Theo laughs. "Come, sit. I'll get the soup."

He puts his coat on one of the wooden pegs in the hall. The pegs are full of winter coats and jackets and one black raincoat, heavy and worn. End of winter; by summer the pegs will be all but empty. He thinks of them filling slowly in the fall, escalating through winter as the light changes and darkens, emptying again in spring. A dance of garments, shifting with the rhythms of light. He is standing still in the hall.

"Theo, where are you?" Frieda comes out of the kitchen carrying a thick, white china tureen of soup. "There's bread. And bring some butter. And the cheese."

The table is near a sunny window and is set with a blue cloth and red bowls. They sit down and smile at each other, happy in that bright moment. "You look too thin. Eat." Frieda is ladling out the soup. "Now, what is this important question about bitches? You are having bad troubles with Emily?"

"Bad, yes. Grim. I feel carved. It should be possible to separate without this hatred. She was the one who wanted it to begin with."

"I don't believe only one person can want a separation, although I grant you it often seems that way. And couples often separate in a way that mirrors their relationship."

"Ah. Wisdom. Do they? Have we? Yes, I suppose that's true. This pulling apart is so slow, every fiber is tearing. I want it to be over." He is cutting wedges of cheese and has started on the soup. Hot, full of the fragrance of tomatoes and the sweetness of plump rice. Theo knows Frieda buys these tomatoes in the summer and freezes batches of soup. He knows about her feelings regarding food. He is grateful for the plenty. No one has fed him in what feels like a long time.

"Your appetite seems healthy."

"Must be your influence. I am thinner; my substance is being sucked away by hatred."

"Yours or hers?"

"Both. You're right. One could not exist without the other. You have never married?" In all the years they have known each other and despite the intimacy of many of their conversations, Theo has never asked this question. Frieda has a way of silently and forcefully indicating the kinds of questions she will and will not answer. But he has always been curious and the moment seems to invite him forward.

"How do you know I was never married?"

"I don't. I'm asking."

"Ai. Yes, I was married twice. Once very young, to a man who died in the war. A man. Not much more than a boy. But no," she stops for a moment, "he was a man. The second time was in America, to help—you know—with the immigration. It wasn't a real marriage, but after the divorce, we remained friends. He died a few years ago. He lived in California, near grapes somewhere. I still speak to his children. Now, do you know anything about me that you didn't know before?"

Theo takes some more soup. "No, I don't know how you felt about them, I only know a few facts. But even the facts are revealing—a little."

"Why are we talking about this?"

He takes his glasses off and rubs his eyes. "I don't know. Maybe I was hoping for a sad story about your marriages so that we could commiserate. I'm sorry. This is a clumsy conversation."

"Ah, Theo, I don't require grace and I have plenty of sad stories, as you know. They just aren't about my marriages ending with acrimony. One ended tragically, the other peacefully."

They eat for a while in silence. The radiator sighs. The hot soup relaxes Theo's stomach; he feels his heart unclench. The sweet tomato taste reminds him of the south of France, tomatoes warm from the sun, the sea's rolling edges meeting the sand, rubbing it, pulling it forward and back like lovers in ancient, unceasing play. With these memories he feels Emily's arms around him, her strong muscles and elegant bones fed by decades of wealth and somewhere, beneath her sexiness, her body chill and defiant, cold at the center. They are standing at the water's edge, gulls shrieking above them like angry crones. A grasping sound of acquisitive and permanently unsatisfied yearning.

"Theo?"

"Yes. Lost in memory here. France. Emily. It's so comfortable here, Frieda," he says. "Your apartment always seems more 'inside' than mine, more protected from the elements. A substantial home. Maybe we could go back to the Tarot and bitches."

"As I said, there is no bitch. The cards are too complex for that. I don't know what card Emily is, but right now in your life there seems to be a strong Falling Tower, a significator of disaster, the death of the ego and possible rising of kundalini. Now I have said more than I wanted to. And been inaccurate. It is not possible to isolate the cards this way." Frieda sounds distressed.

"I'm sorry. I'm pushing."

"No, no. I am allowing it."

"Well, this is a good reason to teach a Tarot class—so I can really learn."

"It isn't easy to teach Tarot properly," Frieda says.

"But is it rewarding? Might you do it?"

Frieda is silent. The soup bowls are empty. She shifts in her chair, and then leans forward. "Yes. I will do it. It's a good idea for spring. This new class."

"Thank you. Really. I already know people who want to come."

"Oh, people. That is never a problem." She laughs. "I sound so vain, yes?"

"Just confident," Theo says. He gets up and starts to clear the table. Then he puts the dishes back down and lifts Frieda from her chair and hugs her. Indeed, people will come. Theo will tell Sue Ann, Sue Ann will tell Ingrid and Bart, and Serena will hear about it when she is shopping for hairy carrots. Frieda herself tells her old friend Sept, in the course of another conversation they are having.

Serena plans on focusing on the Tarot during the week before the class begins, but it is also the week that Rose officially moves in with Serena. (The date chosen months ago.) The sunny day when Theo visited Frieda is followed by days of dark rain, drenching the trees until their branches are wet and sleek; the hardy sycamores on Ninth Street shine with water. And then, just before the move, the sun is out again; buds appear and swell, though the air is cold. Serena and Rose track around the apartment deciding where Rose's things will go and it is clear that they don't have enough space. There is only one tiny wardrobe, built into the wall in the front room. It has two deep drawers beneath it.

"You're sure you need more space?" asks Serena.

"Of course I do. I have clothes and shoes and books. It isn't more space. It's *any space.*"

They look for a good buy in a small newspaper that lists cheap items for sale. They find a likely candidate in the far reaches of the Bronx and buy it, lashing the tacky wardrobe to the roof of Rose's VW. Rose drives home slowly. When they put it in the small room next to the kitchen, Serena is shocked. It is ugly, cheap wood. It hadn't looked that bad when they bought it. Actually, Serena is shocked that Rose needs space. "Another control issue illuminated," she says to Rose.

They decide to paint the wardrobe French blue and do so the next day, covering themselves with paint in the process. Finished, it looks quite handsome, but smells for days. Finally, Rose stores her things there.

Serena and Rose have known each other since just before adolescence and have developed easy ways of being together, so Serena is able to focus on the Tarot, even as Rose gets settled.

Serena is excited about the class for several reasons. She has started to practice as an astrologer, incorporating archetypes into her interpretations, describing the chart and its overt meaning, as well as its shadow face and mystical importance. She wants to add the symbols of the Tarot to her work, since they are intimately woven into astrology, and has already done some explorations of the deck. Her practice is going well and she has been asked to teach, which she would like to do. She is eager to experience Frieda's methods. She has heard of Frieda from friends and has seen her quoted in Tarot books and books on meditation. Though they have never met, Serena and Frieda are going through an almost parallel process that week before the class. Serena is looking at her dreams to see if the figures or symbols from the deck appear there. She is attentive to her peripheral vision to catch sight of people who might represent the Tarot and she is bringing the mystery of the cards into her meditations, asking for guidance about how to approach her studies.

Frieda, too, has begun to focus on the coming group about a week before their first meeting. As is her habit, she contemplates her dreams, looking for signs about her teaching, about the group itself, about her particular role in this circle, which will be different from any other circle. Even though she follows the dreams and is curious about what they offer, she is open to the surprises of the path. Open to not-knowing.

The Tarot class begins on an April night with an icy sky, the quarter moon's curve sharp, a brilliant edge around it. Theo comes first to help make coffee, cut bread, put out cheeses for later, and stir the vegetable soup, a thick mixture that is almost a stew. It is inconceivable to Frieda to have people in her home without feeding them. "Something warm," she will say, in weather like this cold spring. Or, in summer heat, "Something to cool you." Together, they move the living room chairs to form a circle and put the fat, kilim cushions on the floor.

The group arrives almost together. Frieda has positioned herself near the door to greet them and to watch as they enter. She can observe them without appearing to. How is each person clothed? How do they move in the space? What do they say? She considers this to be the beginning of their relationship to the cards, the first layer of the group's evolution, and her initial perceptions are part of her greater awareness about them. She is watching the deck open through them, their costumes, their choices.

As they climb the stairs, Serena is noticing the people coming up with her, as she has noticed her dreams. She and Rose are wearing leather boots to their knees; they have splurged on them this winter; they are wrapped in bright scarves and almost identical coats, Serena's gray, Rose's beige, a triumphant coup from a big sale at Klein's. Their skirts are short, their legs bare between coat and boot. "Are you going to Frieda's?" Bart calls up from behind them on the stairs.

"Yes. Yes," they answer.

Ingrid's coat is long and black, over black jeans; she is wearing a watchman's cap and her curls spill out beneath it. Bart has on an old pea jacket that has seen him through many winters and an azure cashmere scarf, a gift from Stephen, who loves to dress him and will bestow as many presents upon him as Bart will allow. A moment after they arrive, Sue Ann rings the bell, taking off her rich amber tweed coat as she enters. A coat from her days with Richard. She is slightly embarrassed by it, but it is warm and useful.

"Welcome," Frieda says. As soon as Serena sees her, she understands that Frieda is watching in much the same way that she herself is. "There is coffee in the kitchen and ginger tea with honey. More food later. Help yourselves." She continues to observe as they move to the kitchen, choose mugs, pour their beverages and go to sit in the living room. She is most interested in the way a group arranges itself. The deck is unfurling through them, a moving dream, its symbols ancient and forever and always new. Serena and Rose squeeze together on one of the large chairs. They look comfortable and happy. Ingrid takes a cushion. Bart looks around and then takes one next to her. Sue Ann sits on the couch, carefully not taking up too much room. Theo watches Frieda watching. He knows she often does this. He is not aware of Serena's gaze.

"I am taking coffee," he says, in a voice slightly louder than normal. "Black. And I am going to sit on the couch." He smiles at Frieda and almost winks.

The last to ring the bell is a rangy man with deep, soft lines around his mouth and hair gone silver. When he arrives, Frieda hugs him fiercely. "Sept, my dear." A very old connection between these two, the refugee from a war and years of terror and courage, and a man who grew up in the racist south, who is only too familiar with terrors of many kinds, as well as with courage. He was a detective in the New York police department, just now retired. She takes his coat and puts it on the last empty peg. "I'll get your coffee," Frieda says. History glows between them. Respect and intimacy of some kind.

He goes into the living room and waves at Theo, nods hello to the others. "Good evening." He too, sits on the couch.

Frieda takes the rocking chair and looks around the room. "All of you, too," she says, gesturing, as the group watches her. "Look around the circle, notice who is here, what the room is like, let yourself be aware of your perceptions and your judgments. You know, at the beginning of a new situation, most people are afraid to really look, to openly observe. It isn't considered polite." She laughs. "No need for that here. Here we are deliberate. The judgments have plenty of room, but perhaps not a lot of weight. Be curious about your mind so that, eventually, you learn discernment. Having looked, now close your eyes and sense what is in the room for you without your sight. Let the judgments keep going, so that you are aware of them. Of the stories they tell." The group closes their eyes, their bodies shifting slightly as they do. Frieda reviews some of what she has become aware of so far. There is the small woman with blue-gray eyes and the blackest lashes, her gaze full of tenderness, but scratched with a lightning scar of sorrow. She is sitting next to a woman with an air of competence and humor, their closeness evident. There is the tall, dignified woman carrying imploded vitality that probably pushes her through the world with an intense focus, and the man she came with, his face full of hope, some devilish conflict an old companion. He has the face of a young priest, Frieda thinks. And Theo's friend of the banking skills, the one to whom he is teaching poetry; the one he does not have sex with (not that Frieda completely believes this), a woman both lost and determined, bearing her confusion with grace. Frieda observes her own judgments, the stories she is already creating about these people seated earnestly in her living room. They are the deck, revealing itself through them, displaying its intricate, moving symbols and interactions. One the Emperor, perhaps, whose steady power hides his vulnerable interior, which might be the Fool, half-wise, but not really the figure the Beatles sing about, though Frieda likes the song. And the other cards, in varying combinations, all sitting, eyes closed on this spring evening.

"So," Frieda says. "Open your eyes and look around again. Notice if this room and the people in it seem the same or different. Or if you feel the same. Or different. Notice what has passed through your thoughts."

When they open their eyes, Ingrid notices that when Frieda spoke, she began wondering what "same" and "different" meant. She believes that the world, seemingly stable, is shifting all the time, yet to an amazing extent, forms appear to maintain themselves. The room seems neither different nor the same, but simply what it is at that moment. She is curious and eager to know more about the cards she has used in her art; the cards that already have particular meaning to her.

Theo knows that he has been seeing Emily behind his closed eyes, visiting her body, her consistent withholding made physical in her shape. At one sudden moment, he feels his longing to have a child, to make one, and knows a seed would not root in Emily's wrecked coldness. When he opens his eyes, he looks immediately at Sue Ann, who now seems to take up a larger space in the room, in his vision. Her sunflower face glows. His experience of longing was so vivid; he hopes he will not get an erection. (He does not.) What the hell card would that be?

Sue Ann was conscious of how hungry she was, and, aware of the scent of Frieda's soup, she was remembering they were going to eat at the end of class. Since she left Richard, she has lost a great deal of weight, is not often really hungry, so the sensations are welcome. A little celebration.

Rose was following her breath, steady and quiet and at the end, thinks of a kitten she wants to adopt, so she is smiling when the short meditation is over.

To Bart, the room looks increasingly inviting, the company he will have on this journey appealing. While his eyes were closed, he thought about his delight in learning the cards, his interest in the symbols, their swaying magic. The exploration feels bold and he is hugely grateful that he has joined St. Mark's, a church that would applaud his curiosity. He knows there is a devil in the deck. He is unmoved by it.

Sept has been following the long line of his relationship with Frieda, which had its beginning on a summer day in Central Park before he had silver in his hair and when hers was its original auburn; her accent stronger then. He, with his two small children in tow, had run to catch the scarf that had blown away from her. When they stood and talked, there was something he recognized in her voice: terrible fear, overcome, if not vanquished. He is accustomed to listening carefully to the tone of people's voices. Bravery mustered again and again in her life, he imagined. He was dazzled, he with the little boys and his wife dead just a year. Nothing much had reached him in that time, living under the broken rainbow of his marriage, trying to care for his children so that, somehow, they could grow in the arms of his comfort, without their mother. He wanted to hold Frieda, to feel her push against him; her breasts round under the white linen shirt. He was alarmed, jubilant. All they did that day was talk. That first day.

Serena opens her eyes and immediately sips her tea. She has been focused on sensing the room and how that was different from seeing it. Her hands are cold, still, from her walk to Frieda's. People do seem different now—softer, maybe. The edges between them less noticeable. A web of connection has begun to weave the group together. She is aware that her stomach has relaxed. A pewter vase full of daffodils and rosy tulips catches her attention. She looks at Frieda, who now seems older than she did when they came in; her hands veined. As she watches, Frieda lifts her index finger. Then she begins to speak again.

"People do not come to study in this way by accident. Perhaps there are no accidents, which seems like another subject, but is not, and the cards you choose are not accidental. Perhaps all of you in this room have been crossing and crisscrossing for many months, or years. Or many lifetimes. Who can say? But in this moment, we are here, at the beginning of this spring, in a time of radical change. Discover this as we work. Sept, of course, I know you already, and Theo. But every time is new." She smiles. "The rest of you are still mysteries to me. When you enter the realms that the cards represent, you have the chance to find an intimacy with symbolic energies. You encounter both the order and the wildness of your life experience reflected in the cards. This journey may be familiar, but may also be at the outer rim of familiarity and beyond. Please allow yourselves to be intuitively aware and perceptive as well as confused." As Frieda speaks, she feels the arteries of her own history: violent, complex, magnificent and humbling. Whatever wisdom she has, or can create access to, is what she wants to make available to the people gathered in her living room. Even in the face of realizing the emptiness of all form, she thinks, aware of the irony, these are her strong feelings. The reason that she teaches. She takes boxes of Tarot decks from a basket near her chair and passes them around.

"Open the boxes and take out the decks and look through them. Notice any cards that appeal to you and any that repel you. Also notice if you feel any particular sensations as you hold the cards. It is just something to be attentive to; it might have meaning and it might not. In the weeks of this class—this teaching— you will step into the vast and paradoxical world of symbols, which are not only in the cards, but also around you always." Pluto, Frieda's large marmalade cat, strolls into the room and jumps into Sept's lap. The group laughs and Pluto preens in a dignified way. "At their most potent level, symbols are not static, but are constantly in process, interacting with each other, transforming themselves. You will become increasingly intimate with each other, because you must open your hearts to find the vibrant life that is in the Tarot. All of life is filled with interacting layers of reality and as your perceptions grow, this becomes apparent. It may also become apparent that this earth realm is one of myriad realms, woven together, but functioning at different frequencies. But this is to go too far ahead." Pluto purrs audibly as Sept strokes him.

Ingrid thinks she has no major plans to open her heart in this way. Then she remembers Max, and lets the thought loosen its grip. Serena and Bart look enthusiastic and hopeful, Rose seems curious, if a bit skeptical. Theo and Sue Ann feel their hearts badly scraped, but are pulled toward Frieda's words. Sept looks at Frieda and continues to pet the cat.

"So, please shuffle your deck three times and then cut it three times. Focus on what this moment is for you and choose one card. Look at it and then let yourself move with your breath, rather than your thoughts, and see what emerges." They regard the cards in silence for several minutes. "I will look at three of them and talk about them," Frieda says. "Sue Ann, what is yours?" Sue Ann shows her the Ace of Cups. "Look at the table on the card. It holds food, so the card is connected to nourishment. It is a water card, so it is connected to feeling and the water is spilling over. Abundance. Fertility."

Theo looks at nothing in particular in the card and then settles his gaze on the apples in the fruit bowl. He smiles to himself at his choice. Already in the world of symbols, he thinks, appreciating the redness and full curves of the fruit. Frieda continues, "It is a card of stability, of blessing and enthusiasm." Sue Ann looks pleased, if not convinced.

Sept shows her his card. "Strength," says Frieda. "When certain feelings are conquered—the passions that are unruly—we have made allies of them. Passion is mastered. Fortitude and constancy emerge. Life's obstacles can be tolerated, used as a doorway to knowledge. I know this is old-fashioned language, but bear with it," she adds. "Passions that begin as hard to control, or are controlling you, become your teachers. Or, as I said, your allies. This is the strength of union." Sept nods. It is not exactly the story of his life, but he aspires to it.

"And one more? Bart? You have chosen the Magician. It is a fire card, the card of Aries, so it represents beginnings and potency. Power that is present, but not yet developed. This is indicated by the raised right hand. Action available, but not yet taken. He has all the elements on his table—fire, earth, air and water—and that is another indication of power and connection to many forces. The infinity sign floats above his head, the serpent around his waist. His gifts are eternal." Bart is surprised by the card. He does not think of himself in this way—potent, with power available—but it is a direction he wants to pursue, so he is encouraged. It is a path Ingrid is always suggesting for him. And Stephen, in his way. They show each other the cards they have chosen and speak a bit of what they imagine their meaning might be.

"The cards reflect the mystery of events and circumstances, their many possible meanings and how people come to cross paths, become close, or do not. The Tarot describes these events and people, what and who they are to you. The experiment cannot be separated from the experimenter. This is modern physics, too, yes? So, let us get the soup and relax. During the week, please reflect on what brought you here and also how you met the people you may already know."

Sue Ann gets up immediately and walks with Frieda to the kitchen. Food is always her element. When it is brought out and put on the table on trays, along with the fresh bread and several cheeses, Serena notices that it is vegetable soup and she can eat it. Jubilation. She is hungry. The group eats, talks more about their cards; they describe how they got to the class, whom they know already. And then it is time to go. Sue Ann and Bart start to clear the bowls and mugs.

"No," Frieda says. "I will do it. It is part of my own ritual." But Sept says he will stay to help. The rest of the group retrieves their coats and scarves and hats and go out into the cold night. The moon is hidden now, the stars veiled by the city lights, which shine on them, revealing the contours of their bodies, but keeping their faces streaked with shadow. The street is fairly empty. Mostly people with dogs, hurrying along.

Bart expects that he and Ingrid will walk home together, but she touches his shoulder and says she is going uptown. She has told him about Max—told him early on. Bart is too dear to her, their commitment to honesty too precious and rare for her to want to hide this vast change in her life. "Oh, yes," he says. "Of course. Okay. Enjoy. See you tomorrow."

In fact, Max has offered to pick her up after class. If he can see her one moment earlier he will. Also, he worries that she will be cold and maybe hungry. (Hungry in Frieda's house turns out not to be an issue.) He knows he is being irrational and he enjoys it immensely.

"No," Ingrid said, to the proffered invitation. "No, thank you." She is working on being consistently appreciative. "I'll just get on the subway."

"It's a subway and the cross-town," Max says. "Or the shuttle. Take a cab." This exchange was in the afternoon, standing in his office. She kissed him for a long time, his hands on her breasts.

"Yes," she says. "A cab would be nice." He will have hot tea waiting for her and a fire lit and they will undress in the foyer and wrap up in robes.

Rose and Serena go home together to their apartment, which is mysteriously warm and comfortable. Rose has made friends with the oil company man, whose office is on the ground floor of their building. "Cold," she said that morning, when she left for work.

"I'll fix it, Rosa." He has taken a real liking to this competent girl; and his mother's name was Rosa, may she rest in peace. Why should this beautiful child be cold because of the stingy landlord? Or the old ladies in the building, either, though they never complain. He says he will fix the heat and he does.

Theo and Sue Ann go to her place; it has become a pleasant habit, their sleepovers that started the night of the snowstorm. Cozy and chaste. Well, maybe not always.

Sept stays and he and Frieda wash the dishes and put them away. "Do you see me as Strength?" he asks, half joking. He hugs her and nuzzles her neck for a moment.

"I do, exactly," she says, smoothing her hands through his curls. They separate easily and finish the clearing up.

Before Frieda goes to sleep, she rubs the heavy skin cream she makes into her legs, pushing deeply toward her bones. She is pleased with the class. A good beginning. She calls Serge to say goodnight.

Alone in his loft, Leo eats some toast and concentrates on a drawing. He knew about the class, knows Frieda a bit, but felt he had too much work to do and could not attend. He dreams of a river in a dark forest; the water is rising.

❋ ✸ ❋

The classes continue as the temperature slowly rises; buds appear, and then trembling leaves, their light vivid green skimmed by ruby shadows along their surfaces. The city unfolds its particular kind of spring, each splash of green a celebration amidst the brick and concrete. Trees of Heaven, wedged between the tenements and flourishing in empty lots, sport vigorous growth and the hard-packed earth in Tompkins Square Park softens slightly; some semblance of grass emerges there. The students have their own decks now. Serena's is wrapped in a piece of old soft violet silk and tied with a worn blue ribbon. Ingrid's is tied in a large black linen handkerchief that she has taken from Max's drawer. ("What is this?" "A handkerchief." "In black? Why?" "Maybe it's a napkin." "In your underwear drawer?" "I don't know, then." "May I use it for the cards?" "Sure.") Sue Ann has made a little case for hers from a small basket that ties on the side. The others keep them in their original boxes. They learn the card meanings, begin to find creative interpretations, ask each other questions with increasing ease in an intimacy that begins tentatively and then blooms. The walls of Frieda's apartment absorb more secrets, waves of yearning are revealed with shyness and courage; confessions of despair and early tragedies are offered truthfully. Splinters of the interior emerge, are lifted out so the pain can heal. The Tarot draws them together, the symbols vital, confusing, alluring. Frieda observes the group carefully, watchful of the pace at which hearts may open with relative safety, of how much can be tolerated at the perimeter of growth. The cards hum and offer themselves; they flatten and are immobile. Unreadable. They reach and pull and whisper.

In late April, Serena's cards repeatedly show the Lovers. "Mmm," says Frieda, who moves among them as she teaches, going from pair to pair as they work together. "Mmm. Second time. Lover. A young man. Gallant. Maybe musical."

"Where do you see gallant and musical?" asks Serena. " I don't see it. Is this a real man? Not my animus?"

"Your animus could be a real man," says Frieda. "The musical part is just my feeling. It isn't really in the card."

"I thought we weren't doing predictions."

"We are not. Mostly." Frieda puts a hand on Serena's shoulder and moves on.

Serena looks at Theo, who is her partner for the evening. "What do you see? I feel crass. I just want to know."

"I would take Frieda's word for it," says Theo. "That's twice for the Lovers."

"Been a long time," Serena says. By this she means three months.

Theo wants to smile, but sees her eyes are brimming, so he holds still. This tender, ferocious woman with pliancy covering a formidable will. She would be a handful, he thinks. And worth every minute. It is a mercy that he is not attracted to her. Almost not at all.

It is May; the sun embraces the city generously. Max and Ingrid are at the Met and run into Sue Ann and Theo in the hall that once housed the huge Etruscan warrior, later identified as a fake. Important Greek vases and pieces of broken statuary repose under the white skinned light. Ingrid is wearing a soft, green, woolen shawl. Max's arm is around her. Max, who grew up in the city, remembers the statue with fondness as he describes it to the others. Theo wonders if Max is the Emperor who keeps appearing in Ingrid's cards. Sue Ann looks at Max and Ingrid together and wants to hug Ingrid. This substantial man, love evident in his expression. So different from the men Ingrid has been with, who were mostly streamlined, ever poised for flight. But that was what Ingrid wanted, then. Even the sweet one she was with for a while was nothing like this. The group decides, after some awkwardness, to have a snack in the museum's strange, echoing café, with its turquoise central pool filled with hopeful pennies and the occasional nickel or quarter.

The symbols have taken on fullness, have started to move and interact, as Frieda said they would.

Serena has been cautiously adding her new knowledge of the Tarot to her astrological skills. Sometimes, she will see the cards interacting as she looks at an arrangement of planets in a chart. She is developing new ideas about the planets, particularly the Moon (called a planet in the Tarot and in astrology) which as a Tarot card always has a shadowy underside, an element of potential ill will; not her usual understanding of the intrinsic essence of the Mother in an astrological chart. There, it is the significator of emotions. Though certainly in its relationship to other planets, there can be shadows, intricacies that are difficult to navigate, hidden and potentially sabotaging qualities.

Inspired by the class, Ingrid is working with a new box. She breaks the spike heels that she has had for so many years and splashes them with greens—yellowish green and green like ancient bronze and green that is almost gray. She adds small, violent patches of orange. Debauched flame that is cut into the fabric of the shoes with a razor. The box is the Devil and the Devil is a woman. It has open safety pins on its floor and images of infants' faces very near them. Some of the faces are photographs; some Ingrid has painted on neat squares of heavy paper, their faces cherubic. In one corner of the box is a pile of broken lipsticks, smeared and bloody, their cases dented. A small, haggard Christ looks on from the side, he seems aghast, but so remote that he is useless. No savior.

Bart has started to accept the devil as a principle, rather than the real and menacing force that has long been his understanding and his fear. More than a force; a person. The incarnation of evil. He knows it is naïve, but it has been a desolate and terrifying reality for most of his life. He and Ingrid have had numerous conversations about this. About evil and renewal and autonomy and the gift of chaos. He can feel the old ideas losing their grip; he thinks maybe he is at what Frieda calls the outer edge of new growth, and mentions this in class.

Bart and Sue Ann go to church together. Ingrid stays with the Zen group and meditates with them weekly. They have a real teacher, a roshi from Japan. Sometimes Bart goes with her and she is trying to convince Max to try it.

Symbols become evident in the world, in daily life. Synchronicities abound. Words are said on the radio just as Theo writes the same word in a draft of a new poem. Sue Ann notices women with babies everywhere and realizes that Richard and his new wife's baby must be about to be born. Sept sees rainbows painted on trucks and party napkins and calendars. He wonders if he, like Serena, might have a lover in the offing. The Lovers card features a rainbow stretched above the two figures.

Sue Ann, who has mostly been alone in her apartment, except for Theo, decides she would like to invite the women in the class for dinner. She has not made a dinner for guests since she left Richard, though she and Theo cook together. This is a small dinner party, she thinks. Not like the ones she made as Richard's wife. My edge of growth, like Bart's new understanding of the devil. My experience of the pleasure of autonomy; I am choosing this party for pleasure. She is excited to be connecting with Rose and Serena outside the class and to have Ingrid, her old friend, there as well. The entertaining she did with Richard was studied, manipulative, formal, wretched and haunted by her chronic fears of failure. The only thing that prevented those evenings from being boring was her terror. She was too frightened to be bored, though as she thinks of it now, chronic fear can be boring: repetitive, crushing, claustrophobic. Not ever any possibility of creativity. This evening she is planning will be a joy. And she loves to cook. The women are enthusiastic in their response.

They arrive together on the designated Saturday evening, wet from a downpour, warm rain gushing onto the spring earth, making the wind visible as it sways the watery gusts and shakes the leaves.

"Water," Serena says as they come in the door. "Your first card. The Ace of Cups. Blessings." She gives Sue Ann a huge bunch of peonies, soaked through the paper, wildly fragrant. "These are from Rose and me." Ingrid has brought white wine, very dry. She hugs Sue Ann.

"Can we do anything?" they ask.

"No, everything's done. Do you want towels?"

"No," says Ingrid.

"Yes," says Serena. "The furniture will get wet." She is looking around at the apartment. Her endless curiosity about other people's houses, left over from her childhood, she thinks. Her aunts' thoughtfully organized, lovely homes and Ruby's obvious disdain for interior decoration (though her own home is still well cared for by Anna, Serena's adopted grandmother and their longtime housekeeper). That, plus grooming would surely save her, Serena believed as a child. It would pull her back into the family circle of acceptance, of being cherished, after her father's death. The curiosity makes her sad, but sadness does not diminish its existence and now, at least, it shares psychological territory with genuine interest. Sue Ann has painted the walls an off-white that has the faintest, almost invisible blush of peach. The rug in the living room is faded amber with blue scrolls and edges. The two couches are covered in natural linen; only the armchair is bright. A dense, orange velvet, inviting and a bit humorous. On a side wall, Serena notices a small oil of a full-blown rose, its cream petals tinged with lavender edges, some so dark that they are brown, a whisper of death. "Is that what I think it is?" she asks. "It is, isn't it?" Sue Ann nods.

"It is. It's a Renoir. Last gasp of my utterly brutal failed marriage." Serena knows all about Richard. By now they all know a great deal about each other. Fleeing from her marriage, Sue Ann has managed to take a few things from the apartment as part of the divorce settlement. The rug, the Renoir, two ceramic vases that are luminous blue-green, almost black, are among them. They seem to hold the complex secrets of the oceans near their ancient home.

Ingrid looks around and remembers Sue Ann's first place in New York, filled with browns and nubbly, beige polyester. She also remembers her apartment with Richard. The house of horrors. She dries her jeans as best she can and sits on the floor. On the towel. Serena has made her vaguely self-conscious, no easy feat. Serena, the small queen, quite capable of tyranny. She likes Serena. Maybe she will put her in a box.

Sue Ann has made brown rice and, from Serena and Rose's recipe, tahini sauce. There are vegetables and a bright salad with lemon dressing and, for her and Ingrid, broiled chicken with rosemary. "Oh, I eat chicken," says Rose. "Serena's the purist."

The dinner is filled with conversation about their lives, now so revealed through the Tarot, about lovers, about art. About their bodies. The women's movement has not caught up with them yet, but it is coming. Oh yes. It is coming very soon. Ingrid doesn't give her body much thought, though how she accomplishes this, given the amount of attention she attracts, is a mystery. Denial, thinks Serena. Something's up with that. Rose likes her body and always has. Serena has been troubled for so many years, her body a coveted enemy and Sue Ann is not far behind. Richard did not help much.

They discuss their understanding of what Frieda has taught, that a symbol will shift intuitions into new awareness only when the symbol's meaning remains fluid. If it becomes definite, it becomes merely an alphabet. "But alphabets are powerful, too. They create languages," says Rose.

"Yes and the words are symbols, often with paradoxical meanings," says Ingrid.

"I believe it is the fluidity aspect that Frieda wants to convey. And the relationships that transform the card's meaning as it makes new patterns with other cards," says Serena.

"The walls of concepts break and reveal a greater truth," Sue Ann adds, taking a last bite of salad. "Maybe the way the taste of the same salad changes depending on what it is paired with. I am always back to food," she sighs. "My constant metaphor."

They end late, with many thanks, and leave in the still heavy rain. There is one more class, but this evening has produced connections beyond the class that will flourish over many years.

At the last class, Frieda announces a party. "Next week," she says. "At our class time. I will make you all dinner."

"No," they answer, almost in unison. "We will bring the food. We will make you dinner. Potluck. A Tarot dinner." Various suggestions follow: an Empress casserole, the Lover's salad. Fool's punch. A Devil's food cake for Bart.

Frieda is silent. For a moment, she looks as if she might disapprove and then she nods, laughs, claps her hands sharply with pleasure. The cats, cruising the room for love and possible snacks (Sept sometimes keeps spare kibbles in his pocket), jump slightly at the sudden sound.

"We will figure it out," Sue Ann says. "You relax." There are general smiles at this last suggestion.

"Invite your friends," Frieda says. "Guests." The group agrees. Thus Max is invited and Frieda asks Serge to come. Rose invites Hal and, at the last minute, Bart invites Stephen. Stephen has badgered Bart about the class, has asked Bart to read his cards. Bart has refused.

"I don't know anything yet, Stephen."

"So? Practice on me."

"No."

Max, who knows a bit about the Tarot and, to Ingrid's surprise, has a beautiful edition of *Le Tarot de Marseille*, never asks. Wisely.

The party is a grand success. Everyone who was invited attends, bearing Tarot gifts. Ace of Cups wine, a deep red from Max's considerable collection. A rich Devil's food cake that Stephen and Bart made together. Serge brings a Lover's salad and Hal an assortment of cheeses to be cut with the sword of the Knight of Swords. There is an Empress casserole and a batch of Hermit cookies. More food than they could eat in two dinners. Frieda wears a long light dress in forest green linen, her hair freshly combed, rich with henna, and small diamond earrings. Not her mother's—nothing is left from then—but a pair she bought herself that resemble the lost treasure of her family. She feels her heart break open at her students' kindness. The others wear summery clothes, bright colors of the 60s. Ingrid brings out her amber silk for the occasion, last worn when she and Bart graduated from college. Theo carefully ironed a white peasant shirt he bought in Spain. Serena is in the softest purple cotton, a white rose behind one ear and Rose wears a strapless blue sundress. Max is elegant in a perfect, worn, cream jacket and dark slacks; he tries not to touch Ingrid at every opportunity and partially succeeds.

Theo and Max discover a mutual interest in Middle Eastern art. Serge, who loves to cook, shares recipes with Stephen, who is lately developing some cooking skills himself. Hal and Ingrid talk about horses. People move around the room, mingling happily as they eat the summer feast.

"Ingesting the mysteries you are beginning to discover," Frieda says, as part of her toast. "Now they are part of your body."

Theo, raised as a Catholic, looks at her with a hint of an ironic smile. She raises her glass to him, and to all of them. The secrets they have shared over these two months float soundlessly in the room, now so full of happiness. Other, older secrets blend with them. At the end of the evening, Serena overhears Sept ask Sue Ann if she would like to have dinner and go to the theater with him. Sue Ann answers yes. Before they leave, they plan a time to resume their studies with Frieda. There are hugs and more hugs and then the room empties, leaving Frieda and Serge, who sit down on the couch and hold hands silently.

Where is Leo? During the party he has been sitting in his garden on Tenth Street, just east of where the party is. He is not with the partygoers, but he is nearby. Almost touching.

Hooks and Stars

When Serena and Leo meet, it is as if a gentle breeze pressed them lightly to each other and they had mysteriously joined by the time it passed. The movement was so subtle, that they were barely aware that anything happened, nothing more than a wisp of June air trembling in the garden where they stood. It was a party at an exquisitely renovated townhouse in the East Eighties. Leo had not been involved in the renovation, but had been invited by the architect, who was a colleague, to play the cello. (Clarice, the hostess, mentioned to Serena that there would be "musical architects" entertaining.) Leo played for pleasure and because he loved music. Another kind of form, he felt, if an ephemeral one.

Serena had just started her practice as an astrologer and the hosts were among her new clients. She hoped to meet more potential clients at this gathering. She knew if she just wandered around and smiled, people would be attracted to her and she knew it gave her no real power, but was a sad convenience. A few of the guests had already spoken to her about appointments for charts, the hosts having talked about her.

"What?" her uncles responded, when she said she was starting a private astrology practice. (They were too polite to raise their voices, but the implication of shock was there, if muted.) "A what?" Those good lawyers and doctors. "You're doing what?" Unable even to hear the word. Serena was barely flustered by the uncles, the aunts and cousins who sighed deeply and tried to smile, standing bravely on their lush carpets, sipping good wine, their eyes slightly frozen. But Ruby, her mother, was supportive, even admiring. She appreciated Ruby's support and had expected it, since she and Ruby had been reading books on Hinduism, Buddhism and mysticism for years and shared these topics with interest and love. A sweet part of their relationship.

The garden was large for New York, with more sun than is usual. It shone on fat drifts of perfect roses in peach and cream and what is called pewter, which is really lavender as pale as a cloud at the rim of a clear summer dawn. There was only one group of red blooms, scarlet and crimson mixed, planted together at the edge of the bed. Light touched petals and leaves and caught the edges of a few heavy thorns, which were mostly hidden. There were lavish white peonies flecked with cerise drops and floods of pansies in a purple so dark it was almost black. Ferns moved slightly as guests brushed past them. The earth in the flowerbeds smelled moist, like night and warm rain. In the shady corners, mosses were banked in plush careful pillows.

"Millions," said Leo, who saw Serena looking carefully at the flowers. He had noticed her while he was playing. She stood very still, listening to the music, the bright afternoon dropping onto her dark hair. Leo was studying her bones as he played; Leo liked bones, probably for some of the same reasons that he was an architect. Hers were surprisingly visible, lying under what looked like soft skin. High cheekbones, prominent nose, big hands for a woman who could not have been more than five feet and a couple of inches. She wore a ring with a heavy creamy stone on her left index finger. Her ankles were clearly defined, her knees smooth, the hem of her pale blue dress well above them. All this while he played correctly, making lovely heartfelt sounds, if not brilliant ones.

"The garden. It was expensive."

Serena smiles and nods.

"I'm Leo," he says. "Leo Heffernan." He is much taller than Serena and bends just slightly to look into her gray eyes. He offers his hand and she extends hers. Maybe that was when that little breeze blew, a slight flutter in the warm afternoon.

"Serena Weiss," she says.

"Would you like some food?" he asks.

"Ah, food. Yes, yes of course." Serena, who had been macrobiotic since that January, had already worried about the tables spread with a fashionably ample display of food. Probably nothing she could eat. Well, one afternoon. It was a party. She was already interested in Leo, if concerned about the food.

They move toward the food, Leo guiding Serena, his arm not quite touching her back. They are surrounded by other guests in their 60s clothes, colors that explode like sounds, a great deal of bare flesh and swaying jewelry. Lots of long hair. Loud laughter in the enclosed, very expensive garden. The slightest hint of marijuana, somewhere?

Serena eyes the food carefully. She picks up a plate and selects a tiny piece of salmon, which she does not plan to eat, and some cold, cooked vegetables. Leo thought he heard her sigh. He takes quite a lot of everything, but not so much that his well-mannered mother would have been embarrassed had she been there in any form other than the one of her he carried inside himself. They take their plates and walk toward the shady corner near the mosses so they can eat and talk. As they walk, Clarice catches up with them. "Serena, we're so glad you came. And Leo." She stands quite close to him, looking as if she wants to touch him, but does not. "You make beautiful music." She smiles, teeth tiny and even, hair so pale it looks more like the concept of blonde than a color. Then she turns quickly and walks away, pulling sharply as if they had been attempting to hold her there, saying, "Well. Enjoy." Serena simply shifts her eyes to Leo as they continue to walk.

"What?" says Leo, watching her eyes.

"You tell me," Serena says.

"Nothing, it's nothing."

Serena thinks of saying, It doesn't matter to me, but does not.

When Serena saw Leo playing, she realized that she had seen him before, several weeks ago. She and Rose, who has been her friend since they were twelve—abandoning macrobiotics for the night—and Ingrid, who was not macrobiotic anyway, had gotten slightly stoned. Not very. Just enough. Well, hardly at all. Rose, because she disliked the feeling, Serena because she didn't want to eat a lot and Ingrid because she never got very high. It didn't seem to take with her. But they were hungry and decided coffee ice cream was a good idea. The best. So they walked into the warm dark, up a block from Serena and Rose's apartment up to Tenth Street to The Nite Owl, a deli that was always crowded at these late hours. First Avenue streamed with traffic and with people walking in the soft June air. The drums from Tompkins Square Park were clearly audible. The old bricks of the buildings exhaled, whispering their night secrets. The women got their ice cream and, after some debate, some ginger cookies to go with it and stood in line. The man just in front of them was holding two containers of strawberry yogurt and a modest Sara Lee cheesecake. He waited patiently for the heavy woman at the cash register to take his money. When the man in front of them finished paying and turned to go, he smiled slightly at them. He was tall, with brown hair tucked behind his ears; he had a wide brow and hazel eyes and that was all they saw of the front of him before he was out the door. He was wearing a denim vest with what looked like parts of old churches embroidered on the back. The women had been studying the vest carefully from their slightly stoned perspective. Nice vest, they signaled with their eyes. Very nice altogether. They paid for their food and started back to the apartment. By the time they got to the avenue, the man was gone.

* ❂ *

Leo and Serena reach the shade and stand with their plates balanced, the question of Clarice still skipping around in the air between them. Serena decides to tell Leo that she has seen him once before. She pushes the salmon around on her plate and eats a few mouthfuls of vegetables, then starts, obliquely, "I think maybe you live in my neighborhood."

"This is delicious," says Leo. "Is that all you want?" And then, "Why do you think so?"

"Because I saw you the other night at The Nite Owl. My friends Rose and Ingrid and I were there getting a little snack."

Leo smiles. "Oh. Post midnight snack. Little snack. What was I doing?"

"You were getting two containers of strawberry yogurt and a cheesecake. Small cheesecake. Was that your snack?"

Leo laughs. "Not that kind, but yes, in a general sense. I was working on something and it got late and I was hungry. And I know something about you. You're Clarice and Dan's astrologer."

"I am. How did you know that?" Clarice must have told him, Serena thinks. And then, she told him in bed? Dan and I have this astrologer . . .

"Clarice told me when I got here. She mentioned some of the guests and said you were among them."

Serena does not ask when he was born. She knows the question about birthdate implies an answer that involves astrology and can be received in a number of ways: some curious, some arrogant, some hostile. She doesn't really want to engage that way with Leo at the moment. Airplanes fly far above in the seamless blue. Some routine questions about astrology are: Why do you? Is it serious? Are you serious? Are you kidding? None come. Astrology isn't really that unusual in these circles in 1969.

"I'm a Sag," Leo says cheerfully, then looks down with surprise, or maybe regret, at his empty plate. More guests have arrived. He looks at the food table where dessert and coffee have appeared, along with lavish pitchers of iced tea, lemon wedges. Sprays of mint.

"Dessert?" he asks, already starting toward the table. Serena follows, watching his long legs move in front of her. Leo regards the possibilities thoughtfully and then chooses a fat wedge of chocolate cake, around which he carefully arranges strawberries, with one on top. Serena takes a very thin slice of the cake and then, equally thoughtful, another even smaller one.

"Wouldn't it be easier to take one piece?" says Leo, looking at her curiously.

"Yes," she says. "I suppose it would." She slides the pieces close together on her plate and smiles.

This time they move toward a flowering cherry tree and stand beneath it. One or two blossoms fall around them. Serena begins to eat the cake very slowly. "I'm macrobiotic," she says. "Since January."

"My condolences," Leo says. "Is it more macrobiotic if you eat very slowly?"

"Well, there's this thing about chewing slowly and digesting in your mouth, but no, not really. This cake isn't macrobiotic by any stretch of the imagination."

"You don't look macro," he says. "It seems to me they're all emaciated and smell of wet beans."

"Well, I'm glad I'm not advertising, either by the way I look or smell." She sniffs her wrist, which is warm from the sun.

"Do you want me to check further?" Leo says.

"No. Thanks for the offer." They both smile.

"Are berries okay?"

"Not exactly, but I'll have one anyway. Strawberries are the best because the seeds are on the outside."

"Okay," Leo says. "It's arcane. That might make it more interesting, though I doubt it."

"How did you get interested in architecture? Clarice mentioned you are an architect." Serena says, steering the subject away from food.

"Astrology," Leo says, not answering her question. "There's a composer who is an astrologer. Oh yes. Rudhyar. Dane Rudhyar. I have a friend who plays his music."

"Yes," Serena says. "He's an extraordinary astrologer. What is his music like?"

"Rhapsodic. I think he describes it as the music of speech. When he wrote it, he was breaking the rules. Now it sounds like something from the 20s. Dense and opulent, but not romantic. Maybe if I understood it in the context of astrology it would be better."

"Not great?"

"Well, I don't know it that well. Not well at all, really." There is something evanescent about Serena, Leo thinks. She also seems to shimmer slightly. The way a butterfly quivers or the wing of a hummingbird shines. He is not surprised that she fell in love with the bright patterns of the stars.

Their plates are empty. Serena has no watch, but seems aware of the time. Leo sees her shift slightly. "Do you need to leave?" he asks.

"I do." She has a dinner date with Rose. They share the apartment on Ninth Street. It is often hard to explain to a man that you need to stop what you are doing with him to meet an old friend, who is a woman, for dinner. The last time she tried, the man in question seemed interested in whether she was a lesbian, or maybe bisexual?

"I need to go, too," Leo says. "I'll walk you."

"You don't know where I'm going," Serena says.

"It doesn't matter," he answers.

They say their goodbyes to the hosts and leave the garden, walking through the pale colors of the living room, past the Oldenburg piece and a wall of smoky mirrors, incongruous in the space. People stand in loose groups, drinking coffee and wine and the lovely iced tea. This time Clarice does touch Leo, very softly, on his arm. Serena thinks she looks less than happy watching them leave together.

They get to the street. "Where are you going?" Leo asks.

"Downtown. Ninth Street. I think I'll go down Fifth, even though it's a little out of my way. What's the deal with Clarice?"

"No deal," Leo says.

As they start toward Fifth Avenue, a light rain begins suddenly, delicate as petticoat frills, falling through sunlight and thin gray clouds. They do not stop, but keep walking, letting the drops cling to their hair and dampen their clothes. When it stops as quickly as it began, Serena says, "Could there be a rainbow? I've never seen one in the city. Never in my life."

"The light is at the wrong angle, or maybe we are at the wrong angle," Leo says. "But we have them."

"Have you ever seen one here?"

"At the beach, once."

They reach the avenue. "I'm going to cross," Serena says, pointing at the bus stop. She thinks of the long rattling ride down, of the fat, now moist greenery of Central Park and the tour of all the different neighborhoods, which she loves. "I have a date with my friend Rose for dinner. We've been friends since seventh grade. We share the apartment." Leo neither looks startled, nor makes veiled inquiries about her sexual preferences.

"I have a date with my mother and grandmother," Leo says. "On West Eighty-third Street. The old neighborhood. Theirs, not mine. I grew up in Queens."

They stand at the edge of the curb, waiting for the light to change. Serena rests one blue patent leather sandal at the stone rim and wiggles her foot gently.

"Could we have dinner? I mean, not tonight, but another time?" Leo asks.

"Yes. Yes, I'd like to." Leo has a small notebook in his hand before she can ask if he has a pen and paper. She gives him her number and he outlines it carefully with scallops. Pigeons lift in a dusty cloud from a pool of crumbs someone has left them. The trees exhale moisture. Leo puts the notebook away.

"I'll call you," he says. He turns and starts uptown toward the crosstown bus. Then he turns again. "I will," he says.

✳ ✪ ✳

Leo takes Serena to Chinatown, to a restaurant he has visited many times. She suggested the Paradox, a local macrobiotic place, but Leo sounded so appalled that even Serena relented. Once there, Leo goes into a conference with one of the waiters; he seems to know them all. Periodically, he asks Serena if she can eat this or that. Mostly she nods. She doesn't exactly know what they are talking about, but she hears the word "vegetables" several times and that seems safe enough. The first dish that arrives is green fish and then plates appear heaped with vegetables. Finally, an entire fish, its eye appearing cool beneath the fragrant steam.

The restaurant is bright and ugly. Sharp green paint on the walls, metal tables with Formica tops. The menus are written in Chinese and on long pieces of paper and are pinned to the walls. Large streaky windows face the street, East Broadway. She has imagined him touching her hand gently in a shadowy restaurant at a secluded table, not in this bright place with Chinese families eating delicious food and talking loudly. At the beginning of the meal, it is mostly about the food.

"Here," says Leo. "Taste this. And this." He holds his chopsticks toward her, offering morsels clothed in spicy sauce. Others that are slippery and bitter. He is not the first person who wants to feed Serena. Serena has eaten a lot of Chinese food, but none quite like this. She looks at the shapes and notices the different textures. Leo eats slowly, chewing with concentration and appreciation. He sees that she is watching him.

"Think of all it took for this food to be here," he says. "Years of evolution for the fish to become this particular fish, its whole life under water, then caught and touched by how many hands to bring it here. And trucks and ice. And the vegetables and their life under the sun and stars. The cooks. The china it's served on." He smiles at her and at the food.

"Are you a Buddhist?" asks Serena.

"No. No, but I have read a good deal about it. I'm a very lapsed Catholic who was never much interested anyway, with a Jewish father."

"Heffernan is a Jewish name?"

"There are Irish Jews," says Leo. "Robert Briscoe, Lord Mayor of Dublin was Jewish."

"Your mother is Catholic?"

"Technically. She doesn't go to church much, though she would probably ask for a priest if she were dying. God forbid," he adds.

Serena laughs. "That's the Jewish part, that expression."

"Yes. My mother considers herself a citizen of the world. My whole name is Leopold."

Leo looks at Serena's plate, which has tiny pieces of everything.

"Is that like the chocolate cake?" he asks.

"Yes. It is. I don't eat a lot." She knows she started to hate her body at a particular time, but she does not understand what it means: how she has absorbed the cultural hatred for women's flesh. All the hatred mixed with desire. She has no context for her emotions. They seem normal. All women diet. But Serena knows this is a crazy dark part of herself, her hatred of her body and its menacing tendency toward roundness. The lengths she will go to stay slender. The way she stares at her flesh with loathing. Her poor, lovely body. Sometimes, ravenous, she stands at the open refrigerator and pulls pieces from an apple crisp, or a heavy bread, eating it piece by piece until the broken shape looks gnawed. Women have just begun to talk about this collective hatred, about raw, bloody secrets and starvation and vomiting, but she doesn't know any of these women when she and Leo sit eating this luscious dinner. Soon. Soon, she will meet them.

They move toward the end of their meal. The room is packed and noisy with the rising and falling inflections of Chinese, flying wedges of sound, and the slap of the swinging kitchen doors.

"How did you become an architect? I mean, what drew you to it? Ho. No pun. I don't know many architects. Maybe not any," she says. She asked him at the party, but he hadn't answered.

"I love shapes," he says. "I love the idea of what holds things together. Not so much building new structures, but saving old ones. Rescuing crumbling arches, healing the underpinnings. Mucking around inside the walls. Saving old fruit."

"What? What's the part about fruit?"

"Old buildings often have stone fruits and leaves and stems and flowers. Sometimes vegetables. Old churches do. More the ones in Europe than here. I love old churches," says Leo.

Serena remembers the vest, embroidered with pieces of old churches, that night in the little grocery store. "Oh," she says, "the vest. Who did the embroidery?"

"I did."

"Really? Never met an architect and never met a man who could embroider. Is your father an architect? No, never mind. Silly question."

"No," says Leo. "He was a longshoreman. Then a union organizer. Was and still is."

They tell each other some of their stories. He has two sisters, one a teacher working with emotionally disturbed children and one studying to become an orchestra conductor. "She won't ever get work," Leo says, "but she loves it. She is a passionate musician." Leo is the middle child, but he thinks his mother miscarried just before he was conceived.

"You think, but you don't know?" asks Serena.

"No, I do know. I don't officially know."

"Ah," she says. "Secrets." She tells him that she is an only child and that her mother lost a baby a year before Serena's birth. She tells him that her father died when she was five. She doesn't say that Ruby almost died when Serena was born.

She does not talk about Ruby's rages, about her constant fear as a child that her mother would one day leave her, free herself from the terrible burden of raising a child alone. Or about Ruby screaming, "You don't know how to love! You don't know how!" The scent of the food drifts through their tales, rich and comforting, even in the midst of her difficult feelings.

The plates are cleared and the table spotty, but empty of dishes. Serena's hand is resting on the shiny table surface and Leo covers it with his own. When he touches her, it is as though her whole history falls into her lap. Her yearning, the loves she has had. Her father's death so early in her life. The feelings pile on top of each other, invisible and vastly present. She looks at him and wonders about what energies draw people together. Forces that move silently, perhaps glimpsed in dreams or at odd moments. Energies that tug us, even as we think we are making plans.

Leo pays the check, not even a mention of splitting it, and the waiters bid them a cordial goodbye. One smiles and pats Leo's shoulder quickly as they leave.

"There's a great coffee shop around the corner," Leo says. Even as they walk, Serena feels her memories clinging to her and sighs. She keeps her face neutral, she hopes. Her longing embarrasses her. In the street, the heat seems to lean against the old buildings. It rises along Serena's bare legs and the wind blows it through her hair.

"I love the summer," Leo says. He walks close to her, but they do not touch.

The coffee shop is almost as noisy as the restaurant. The have milky coffee and sticky moon cakes. Napkins litter the floor, and Serena notices that people finish their coffee and then toss the napkins down. Leo notices her watching. She is aware of how carefully and easily he observes her.

"I think it's an old custom to do that," he says. "It's to give someone a job as sweeper." And then a very thin man appears with a push broom and begins to clear the napkins away. "You ate the whole bun," Leo says, looking pleased. "Well, almost." She nods. People are often pleased when she eats and their pleasure often distresses her, but with Leo, it simply feels kind.

"Did your mother not like you to leave food?" Serena asks.

"No, she didn't mention it. It almost never happened. Do you want to walk back uptown?"

"Yes. Let's walk."

They start the walk uptown, the light still bright at this time of year so close to the summer solstice. Going east on Canal Street they pass a construction site, its gate half open and a huge shadowy hole in the earth visible. They stop and look inside at the torn earth, yellowish and uneven as it slopes down. "It's good earth," Leo says. "Sometimes I've asked the construction crews for a bucket for my plants. You have to add fertilizer and a little peat, but it grows things surprisingly well."

"You garden, too?" Serena smiles. She has a houseful of plants.

"I do," he says and takes her hand as they continue toward her apartment.

By the time they reach Ninth Street, the dark has trickled down, hovering, lavender and smoky. They sit on the steps of Serena's building, just holding hands. Cats prowl, quick and sinuous. "Do you want to come up?" Serena asks.

"Not this time," he answers.

"Okay."

"Let's just sit for a while," Leo says.

People pass by. A short man dressed in orange pants and a bright green tee shirt drags an upholstered chair along the street, the chair clearly a refugee from a group of furniture left near the curb for people to take. It is the way of the times, to leave things as offerings. Serena knows the sanitation department's furniture pick up days in different neighborhoods. Serena and Leo are quiet, just looking at him. Then Leo turns to her and kisses her softly, just on the lips. A completely tender kiss. "I'll call you tomorrow, Serena." She touches his hair and then starts to go upstairs, opening the heavy front door. She thanks him for dinner.

"Isn't that door locked?" Leo asks.

"No."

"That's not good."

"No." She shrugs and disappears inside.

When Serena reaches the top of the stairs and puts her key in the lock, Rose shouts from inside, "Are you alone? I'm in the tub." The tub is in the kitchen, within open view of the hall. It is an ancient tub, claw-footed and now painted bright blue on the outside. The inside has stains so old that not even Serena's determined scrubbing can remove them.

"Alone," Serena answers. Entering the room, she finds Rose up to her neck in water, applying ice to her forehead. Serena smiles. Rose has had a long love affair with ice and staying cool. She perceives anything above sixty-eight degrees as too warm. Rose turns in the tub, sloshing a little water onto the floor.

"Where is he?" she asks.

"Went home. We sat on the steps for a while and talked."

"Did he invite you to go with him?"

"No. I invited him up, though. I guess it's just as well."

Rose laughs. "I would have hopped out and even wrapped up in a towel."

"No. It's too soon," Serena says. "He thinks it's too soon."

"Is that what he said?"

"Well, in actions, if not in words. I guess it is. I don't like having sex on a first date. Not really. I feel a little rejected, though."

Rose sighs. "Not too many guys who've made that choice. Not since 1959 or so."

"No." Serena smiles. "Be interesting to wait. And to see how long. Are you staying in there forever?"

"I'm getting out now. Get some iced tea." Ice is not part of the macrobiotic regime, but they drink it anyway because, of course, Rose loves ice. "We'll talk. There's some tea in the fridge." Serena starts to undress. Her feet are a little sore from the heat and the long walk. She puts on an old white cotton shift, loose and cool, and gets up on the curved lip of the tub, dangling her feet in the water as it drains. Rose puts on a tee shirt and shorts without drying off. Her long hair is twisted up and dripping. She calls it instant air conditioning.

"So, what was dinner like?"

"It was intense," Serena says, "but in a soft way. Or maybe a smooth way. Not smooth like operating, just—I don't know. As if he's trying to see something about me without being intrusive. He's very aware. Watchful, but without that hyper-alert thing. But I think he isn't as relaxed as he seems." She realizes as she talks that she is hurt he didn't pursue anything sexual. Hurt and intrigued, since he clearly found her attractive and was affectionate.

The 50s changed to the 60s without benefit of any profound shift in the deep strata of Serena's consciousness—that fertile underground of sun-patched ferny growth and sudden stones, ancient and sullen, that attempted to protect her virtue, watch over her reputation until the groundswell of what appeared to be change demanded new behavior. Serena will never be nonchalant about either sex or love, will often confuse the two. But she has tried nonchalance in these past years. She has taught herself. She can approximate it, though she will understand later that she has paid a mean price for this attitude. In saying goodnight in the way that Leo did, he has both insulted her and appeased her. There are parts of this awareness that are hidden, but she is conscious of some of it. The insulted part hooks into her fears of rejection. The appeased parts are relieved. She and Leo will have some room to explore each other first. When she has sex too quickly, the buried stones grumble and low, break their silence, beg that she protect herself. She knows their sound vibrating beneath her when her clothes are off and she is betraying herself and smiling.

Rose gets the tea and they sit on the green sloping floor, drinking it slowly. They have been talking like this since childhood, stretched out on one floor or another.

Rose takes one of the marbles they have in a bowl and lets it roll down the down the slope of the floor, where it disappears under the tub. Serena retrieves it. "They collect under there." Rose nods and shrugs.

"It's as though he's lost something," Serena says, thinking of Leo. "Or someone. And now he's being careful. Not that he said that, or anything like it."

"Is he sad?"

"No. Thoughtful. Careful," she says again.

Rose laughs. "Yeah."

"No, not that way, though I guess that way too. More as if by being with him, I was in his care."

When the tea is finished, they begin to make the sofa into a high-rise bed, the modern version of a trundle bed.

"Did you see Hal?" Serena asks. Hal Morris is Rose's boyfriend, her love. He is a large-animal veterinarian whom Rose met at a friend's house near Woodstock. She had gone to visit and to ride and Hal had come to treat one of the ailing horses. A compact man, with brown curls and dark eyes and a passion for animals. He had grown up in the city and moved to the country to practice. His parents, good liberal New Yorkers, were surprised at his choice of profession, but supportive.

Syl, Rose's mother, was apoplectic. Syl, of the smoothly kept skin, the endless furs, the heavy jewelry. The sharp pointy shoes and expensive silk in flamboyant colors. She is especially fond of French silk. When Hal and Rose began to see each other and Rose finally told her mother, Syl was, for one historic moment, speechless. And then the tirade began, continuing ceaselessly during the year or so Rose and Hal have been together. "A horse doctor!" she screamed. "A man who puts his hand up cows' you-know-what? Are you doing this to torture me?" It was hard for Syl to imagine choices that were not directly aligned with her own preferences, one way or another. Rose's step-father, Al, liked him, mostly silently. Opposing Syl is pointless. Rose refused to argue with Syl. She had always refused and this time was no exception.

"No," says Rose as they finish making the bed. "I see him tomorrow." They stretch out and Rose closes her eyes, someone who sleeps instantly and deeply under almost all circumstances. Serena reaches for a book of Paul Blackburn's poetry and reads for a while. Then she turns out the light and meditates for a while. Sometimes when she meditates, she senses her guardians, non-physical energies that have been with her all her life—perhaps before that. Serena experiences them as protective, loving yet not personal. On this night, they feel close to her as she falls asleep.

Serena dreams of Leo. Flies into him, against his skin, his bones. She is moving quickly, but gently, under a huge sky with endless edges that ripple and unfold. She swoops up to meet him where he is floating in the blue air and he is startled by her touch, yet stays with her. "A lake of tears," someone says and they look below at transparent water far beneath them. Then the dream shifts and she is in a red, empty cabin high on a mountain. She is alone. Late in the night, she dreams of the peonies in the garden where she and Leo officially met. The flowers burst, petals drifting, then settling in soft piles, their colors varied. They land in corners and on the surface of tables. Some land on the bed where Serena sleeps. Though they have burst, the blooms somehow remain intact, both dispersed and whole, living twice. It is hot until almost four o'clock and then the wind cools and Serena pulls up the sheets, ruffling the petals. When she wakes to a pale sun, Rose is still sleeping. The room is empty of petals, but perhaps smells sweet. She considers the dream and wonders when Leo will call.

Rose leaves early in the morning and Serena goes into the little room off the kitchen where she meditates. She has learned to meditate from reading books on the subject and a little from friends. She sits almost every morning and evening in this odd small room that holds the grumbling refrigerator, a round table made by an unreliable boyfriend (both he and the table were short term, though the table outlasts the relationship) and a delicate old desk she found in the street, fumigated and painted a pale marigold. She sits on a cushion on the floor facing east toward the window, sometimes imagining the footprints of people long dead resting beneath the green paint, their tread hidden but still present. This is a very old building. Many people have walked through these rooms. She breathes softly. Her blood seems to settle. In winter, the steam pipe hisses and shrieks as she sits. In summer, noises from the street collide around her. Often, at night, she can hear the drums in Tompkins Square Park. Vigorous, repetitive, they accompany her. As she breathes she watches her thoughts roam, random and sometimes as insistent as the drums. What is in her bottom cupboard drawer? The red wool winter socks she cannot find, maybe? She remembers the cold river in her childhood summers in New Hampshire. Wonders if Rose misunderstood a comment she had made? On and on, drifting by, or catching her so that she is lost in that icy green mountain river, or suddenly back at her mother's house, hearing the hissing, ominous tone of Ruby's voice when she was enraged. She longs for the quiet mind she has read about and she is staunch and determined in her efforts, not yet learning surrender. Dusty skeletal memories rise unbidden. The old red music room in elementary school and the day that Norman, the boy sitting next to her, suddenly looked at her arms and pointed out, loudly, how much hair there was on them. Her arms were downy, pretty. But she remembered his words so well that the first time she went to a formal dance in high school and wore a strapless dress, she shaved them bare.

Every once in a while there is a little open space in her meditation. Melting. The edges of her body feel connected to everything, even the inner edges, her heart and belly and the sweet moving form of her blood trembling beyond their boundaries, fanning out into vastness and union. Sometimes there are dark flashes—so dark they shine—and sometimes just her breath, rising and falling. When Serena reads more about Buddhism and the practice of meditation, she is sure she is not doing it right, yet dropping into what feels infinite is so healing, so touches the aloneness secretly tucked everywhere into her. A friend has taken her to meet Trungpa Rinpoche, the Tibetan teacher, and she knows people study formally with him, but she isn't drawn to do so, so she stumbles along, her determination her companion.

At the end of this particular meditation, she stretches out on her back and simply listens to all the sounds in the room; she rests her eyes on the ceiling. She thinks of Leo, of sweetness so delicately held in his manner, and his concentrated happiness playing the cello, combined with his eager, easy movement toward the food (which makes her smile) and the direct way he asked her to have dinner. In a way she cannot explain, he seems a man of happy surprises.

Later, in the first weeks after she and Leo meet and are dating—in this time when no one Serena knows dates—Leo will buy her two large cartons of strawberries. Washed, in a white bowl on the tub top in her kitchen, she will smell them as she meditates—melt into them and their plump redness, tiny sharp seeds flung from the center to rest on the outer skin.

When Serena gets up from her cushion, she takes a bath in the shiny blue tub. The phone rings and it is Leo.

"How are you? You survived the journey up the stairs I take it."

Serena laughs, both with delight at his voice and his concern for her. "I did. And slept well and meditated."

"Oh," he answers. "I meditate sometimes. I don't think I do it right."

"That's just what I was thinking about myself," she says. "But I like it and I do it anyway."

"I'm going to a performance tonight," he says. "Would you like to come?"

"I would. Yes. Sure. What kind of performance?"

"It's New Music. At Judson Church. My friend Charlotte invited me. She plays the cello."

Serena has read about New Music, a little about John Cage, but that's about all. "I've never heard the music performed," she says, "and I'm interested." Her friend Ingrid is a John Cage fan and has been to performances and happenings of all kinds. "My friend Ingrid is a big Cage fan," she says.

"Invite her," Leo says.

"Oh. Well, I—okay. I might ask her if she can make it." Serena has no intention of sharing Leo on this second date. "What time?"

"I can't have dinner, but I'll pick you up at seven. Is that okay?"

"It's fine." She pauses. "I had a dream about you last night."

"What kind of dream?"

"Mmm. I'll tell you later."

"All right. You might have to participate tonight," Leo adds

"In what?"

"In the performance."

"How?" she asks. She had thought that "participate" might be an odd way of mentioning sex. But, no, it wasn't that. "I can't play anything," she answers.

"No, no. You don't have to. You'll see."

It is not an area where Serena imagines she will feel adventurous, though she is soon to get better at it and, eventually, love it.

"Just let it be a mystery," Leo laughs. "Until it isn't." His voice softens.

"Mmm," she says again.

"See you later. I'll come up and get you. What apartment?"

"Sixteen. To escort me down the stairs safely?"

"Yes," Leo says. "Bye."

"Bye."

If Leo is coming up, she should clean the already spotless apartment. Rose would laugh, but Rose isn't there, so Serena gets out the vacuum and the mop. As she cleans, she does something she thinks of as floating, feeling herself move through the past and present simultaneously. The June day drifts through the open windows, its breezes moving against her skin. She goes through the rooms in her present self, feeling the earlier ones moving with her as well. Her younger selves seem to share flecks of their wisdom with the current Serena. She senses all the ages she has ever been. Sometimes she wonders if she could slide forward and meet her future selves. She has had experiences of what she thinks are past selves and other lives, and entered them fully, unsurprised. As she floats, the vacuum cleaner roars. She pokes its nozzles into all the corners.

Leo arrives a little before seven and knocks on the ancient, lumpy metal of the door.

"Sorry," he says. "I'm always early. You look beautiful." He is relaxed with compliments, seems to take real pleasure in offering them.

Serena looks down at herself briefly, as if she has forgotten for a moment what she is wearing. It's an off-white linen shift, loose and quite short. She has on long turquoise earrings and her hair is pinned up, a few tendrils loose on each side of her face. The earrings make her eyes more blue than gray. Leo is wearing old, very soft jeans and an embroidered Mexican shirt.

"No Ingrid?" he says.

"No, she's away. No, she—I didn't ask her. I'm embarrassed. I wanted you all to myself."

Leo laughs and hugs her briefly. "That's a good sign for me, I guess. Are you a jealous woman, Serena?"

"No," she says. "Not really," knowing this is a complete lie. She is jealous and ferociously competitive. Ruthless, she sometimes thinks, with regret about herself and these hard, explosive feelings. "Yes," she says. "I am. I would rather not be." Something about Leo inspires honesty in this area that is so complex, so full of contradictions and shame.

"Mmm," he says. "You were pretty quick on the uptake about Clarice."

"That was really more intuition. I didn't know you. I wouldn't have any reason to be jealous." This is not true either. "Well," she says, "maybe."

"Is it okay to look around?" His long frame is leaning toward the doorway leading to the next room. There are no halls in this apartment. He was clearly curious.

"Of course. I'll give you the tour. It's very short." She is happy to change the subject.

Serena is extremely pleased that she has cleaned, though it is unlikely that anyone but she would have noticed the difference between before and after. But she loves the scent of polish in the house, and the bouquet of yellow daisies bought just that afternoon, and the bright new wax on the floors. She takes him through the rooms, starting with the one facing south, out to the gardens in back of the buildings on St. Mark's Place. The room is painted white, with a floor almost the color of her dress, an ivory paint that never quite dries and peels easily, but looks lovely, even with the few patchy spots. Serena has hung white linen curtains at the windows and there is a row of plants: a bright croton, a palm, a fig tree, an avocado. A tall bookshelf is against one wall; an oblong pine table holds books as well. Light seems everywhere in the room, though the sky is cloudy and rain has loomed all day. Leo inspects each plant carefully.

"I love plants," he says. "The avocado could use a little water. And obviously you like white."

"I never met a man who loved plants, and yes, it could. Use water. I can't seem to get its water quite right. Everyone teases me about all the white. But I like colors, too. That's three things about you that are unique to me. Never met an architect or a man who could embroider, or one who loves plants."

He takes her hand and they go through the other three rooms. She feels as if the whole house shifts to accommodate them together, their newness, their touch. Now he is here, his footsteps crisscrossing with all the others and he will always have been here, she thinks. He is here forever. They move to the center room, where Rose and Serena sleep, which has a blue Indian throw on the couch and a small mahogany chest that was Ruby's, on top of which Serena has placed the daisies in a dark, almost black pitcher. This room also has a Spanish style dresser that Serena will still have when she is in her sixties. Then the kitchen with its green floor; at these windows, green and white checked curtains that Serena made, and last, the odd little room with the refrigerator, desk and table, the room where she meditates. Leo lets go of her hand and turns to hold her, rubbing her back slowly. She is on tiptoe. After about ten seconds she feels his erection.

"Concert," she says pressing a little more against him, looking up at his face.

"Concert," he agrees. They leave the apartment, Serena carefully locking the police lock behind her. "You have a beautiful eye," he says.

"Eyes?" She is ahead of him on the stairs.

"That, too. No, I meant an eye for putting things together."

"From an architect a great compliment," Serena says and smiles. She is very proud of her house. She gives serious thought and enormous care to wherever she lives. This will be true all her life, sometimes a pleasure and sometimes a burden.

When they reach the street, the warm, damp air enfolds them and though it is heavy with moisture, there is no rain predicted. They hold hands as they walk toward Judson Church, at the south end of Washington Square Park. Inside the park, people wander or sit at the chess tables or gather to sing; a few ask if they are "buying," or "looking." Their inquiring voices are pitched only slightly lower than normal. Serena and Leo shake their heads no, just a small shake. Life as usual in this park, not to mention in the neighborhood where they both live. The old trees sigh, moisture hovering around them.

"Do you smoke?" asks Serena.

"Not very often," Leo says. "I don't really like being high."

"No, I don't either. Once in a while I smoke a little. That night I saw you at the deli we had." And anyway, Serena thinks, it makes me hungry and I'm odd enough

179

as it is, all the things I sense and dream.

When they reach the church, it is filling rapidly, more and more people until the room is full, the audience dressed in bright clothes, long skirts on the women, or very short ones, just a faint hint of skirt and then bare legs. Breasts loose under tee shirts full of tie-dyed stars and swirls. Serena thinks her breasts are too full to go without a bra, though she will try it for a while, feeling horribly undressed when she does. (It also turns out to be uncomfortable when she runs.) The men in the audience are wearing jeans or loose, cotton Indian pants, tied at the waist. One very tall, very blond man with the lightest eyes Serena has ever seen wears what looks like a medieval jacket, plum velvet, with full sleeves, the front completely unbuttoned and his chest bare. He and Leo nod and wave. Leo is saying hello to a lot of people, introducing Serena to some, or just nodding across the wide, accommodating space. It is getting hotter and hotter, this big, friendly and un-air-conditioned space, but no one seems to mind. Without any warning—the lights don't even dim at first—a woman begins to play a cello. She is topless, her breasts substantial. Her dark brown hair falls across her shoulders. She holds the cello with complete attention. A few people move around her, sweeping up bits of broken things, it is not clear what unless you happen to be standing very close to the sweepers. They bend with absorption. Some of the audience take seats, some stand. Serena sees Ingrid across the room just as the lights go down a bit. She smiles to herself, her greediness to be alone with Leo foiled.

When the cellist, who turns out to be Leo's friend Charlotte, finishes, a piece played on a kettledrum begins. After it is over, a tall woman with large, confident hands makes a salad in the drum and serves it to the audience. Serena expects the salad to be warm, as if playing the drum would have warmed it, but it isn't. Even in the hot room, the leaves are cool and oily, some bitter ones mixed with sweet, with sharp watercress and runny tomatoes. Then, as if at some secret signal, a few people begin to walk around the room, tapping on things, or rubbing them. Striking them softly. They touch the heavy walls, listening as they tap; they flutter their fingers on the edges of chairs and on the legs of other people. They rattle jewelry and make soft singing and hissing noises. Occasionally someone wails. Leo joins them. Serena sits frozen, her throat tight. Oh. The participation. This is it. She lifts herself from her chair, moves to an empty space on one wall and rubs her palms across it. She feels ridiculous, but is determined to include herself. The sounds mingle and rise, textural, organic. A long undulating voice. She begins to enjoy it just a bit and finds other things to make sound with. She knocks her feet together, listening as her shoes touch. All of this goes on for quite some time and toward the end, Serena realizes that she has seen Leo once before she and Ingrid and Rose stood behind him at the Nite Owl. Something confident and graceful about the way he occupies space in the room, perhaps? She isn't quite sure.

❋ ✪ ❋

The war in Vietnam was the background for many people's lives in the 60s. It was very much in Serena's thoughts; always present somewhere, either as shadow or overt terror and helplessness. The war burning orange, scorching bodies, exploding villages, ravaging forests. The roaring heat and mud; the endless lies. She and Rose watch the news on their ancient black and white television set, gray static snow falling through the boiling images of destruction. The war tears through Serena's dreams. She and all her friends marched and marched and it was on a peace march the previous April that she remembers she saw a man who must have been Leo.

This particular peace march was on an April day chill with gray mist and rain that got colder as the hours passed. Serena went with Rose and Mike, the slightly sadistic, short-term boyfriend who made the table that sat in the room where she meditated. Making love, he had stared straight at her and said, "Tell me you hate this. Tell me." It happened only once and was her first and only experience of such a request. It was the last she saw of him, though he did call her once after to tell her he had head lice and she should check. She did have them and she and Rose spent a week washing their long hair in ghastly, poisonous shampoo and sending everything they owned to be either cleaned or washed. But the march was early in their relationship, before the slight sadism and the lice, and she and Rose met him in Central Park, joining a large group of friends who often marched together.

They held the cold, hollow stems of daffodils, their frilled yellow cups alight, moving in the grayness as people began to sing and then started to march in great waves down Fifth Avenue, holding banners aloft and chanting. Serena tried to keep her mind focused on peace instead of shouting, "Hey, hey LBJ, how many kids did you kill today?" But there was something satisfying about chanting with everyone, voicing their outrage, venting their feelings of hopelessness in the righteous noise. Serena had forgotten her gloves and ended up walking with an affable man who put her right hand in his pocket and gave her his left glove.

At the end of the march she and Rose and Mike went to a theater on Second Avenue in the East Village to hear a concert given as a benefit for the anti-war effort. One group was just packing up when they arrived, among them a tall man with a cello. She noticed his competence and grace and his air of being right where he needed to be. After the concert, they visited friends of Mike's who lived nearby in a large, dirty apartment where they ate hot, delectable bread, scooped red jam from heavy pottery jars and slathered the bread with the jam and hunks of rumpled looking butter. Someone deposited a baby with a full diaper on Serena's lap. There were knives on the table and the low counter and small children were wandering through the gathering. One reached for the handle of a knife and Serena started to move quickly to grab it, but the child's mother and father, who, it turned out, were their hosts, assured Serena that they left knives out all the time. That the children knew they were dangerous and that indigenous people taught their children to exercise care in this natural way. Serena, who thought they lived in unbelievable dirt and now seemed a little crazy on top of it, simply nodded and gobbled her bread, too tired to protest.

✳ ✣ ✳

Serena realizes that the tapping piece has stopped and she has been lost in this memory, all the while tapping and rubbing and singing. She wonders suddenly if Leo knows Mike, and hopes he does not. She takes her seat and Leo joins her, reaching for her hand. She thinks maybe the concert is over, but she is a novice in the avant garde. There are still many pieces to come.

At what is truly the end of the performance, though Serena is not absolutely sure it is, and looks around to check, she sees Ingrid is coming toward them. She is wearing worn, white jeans and a skinny, black shirt with a strand of pearls at her throat. Ingrid's idea of a joke. A splashy, orange scarf is the only touch of color. She hugs Serena tapping on her back, as the audience and performers tapped in the piece.

"Your first experience participating?" she says, smiling at Serena.

Leo offers his hand. "Leo. I'm Leo." He is looking at Ingrid very directly. "You look familiar."

"Concerts?" suggests Ingrid. "I go to a lot of performances."

"Are you a musician?"

"No," Ingrid answers. "I'm not." She does not elaborate.

Serena is watching them. She thinks they are built something alike: tall, with wide shoulders, both with limbs that are long and muscular, slender below the waist, with high round butts. She notices herself watching, aware of her vigilance in the most innocent situations. It feels prickly and sour. But Ingrid and Leo are not alike in other ways, she imagines, though she barely knows Leo at all, really. Ingrid, with her dark interior maps, parts in shadow, parts completely hidden, but palpable, and her brusque generosity. Ingrid, who likes the edges where things change: spring, autumn, the last biting slice of winter. Who likes standing at the rim of a subway platform or the last possible place she could put her feet on a rooftop. Serena has seen her stand this way, her tall body pressing out into nothingness. Leo seems a much softer soul.

"Going to Fanelli's," she hears Ingrid say. "Would you like to join us?" She points to a group of people gathering at the door.

No, no, Serena thinks.

"Absolutely," says Leo. "Okay, Serena?" He is genuinely asking. Not just for form.

"Sure," she answers, hating the idea. Being compliant? Serena knows she is only compliant at the beginning of a relationship. Is that true? Almost true. But she is a good negotiator when her willfulness surfaces. Fair, she thinks. I'm fair. She sighs.

Fanelli's is dark and smoky, which seems like a permanent state, as if it will still be that way when it is closed and empty and the dawn peers through the windows. Leo introduces her around as the waiters pull two long tables together and people slide into seats. Serena ends up next to John Cage who says, in his distinctive soft voice, that he wants to stop smoking, it's so bad for him. He laughs and lights some terrible cigarette. Menthol. "Why do you suppose people do things that are bad for them?" he asks Serena. He looks at her seriously. "It doesn't make very much sense, does it?"

"I think we do destructive things for a lot of different reasons," Serena answers. "Your reasons will be different from someone else's, though I suppose there are general similarities among some people."

"Leo says you're an astrologer, but another friend mentioned you before he told me. I think I should come and see you, don't you?"

"Oh yes," Serena says, startled. "Yes. Come. I'll give you my number."

"I have it," he says and then begins to discuss the concert with the others at the table, carefully keeping her in the circle of talk. The tall woman who made the salad in the drum is there and next to her, the percussionist himself, also tall, with a broad forehead, curving eyeglasses and heavy hard leather boots with laces, even in this heat. He is introduced as Mark and he has his arm around Ingrid, who appears not to notice.

A lot of wine appears and some good food. Salads, a huge platter of antipasto. Names Serena has never heard float by. "Feldman's latest work," someone says. "Going to see Vostell in Germany." They are friendly and loud and inclusive. And then it is very late.

"I'll take you home in a cab," Leo says as they leave. They find one right away, the seats moist and warm and sticky on this still, hot night. He gets out with her. "I need to go home, I have an early meeting, but we could go to the beach on

Wednesday. Could you?"

"Yes. I could." They go upstairs and once inside her apartment they kiss, plastered against each other. They have gotten about an inch inside the door. Leo rubs her back and presses his hands against her thighs.

"This is not a good prelude to leaving right away because you have an early meeting," Serena says.

"I know," he says. "I know." He separates himself and strokes her hair. "Wednesday," he says. "We'll start early. My parents belong to a beach club. Little club, nothing fancy. I'll pick you up at nine."

"Goodbye," Serena says. "Thank you for the evening."

"You never told me the dream," he says as he opens the door. The hallway smells of old marble and dust, the scent colliding with the sweet herbs Serena keeps in bowls.

"Wednesday," she says. "I'll tell you then." The apartment is empty, except for Bella, who looks at Serena hopefully. Serena picks her up and strokes her, holding her close. She sits on the little loveseat, just holding the cat before rising to slide the extra mattress out from under the daybed. A nightly chore. The leaves in the gardens in back of the house are still. Behind the clouds, light shines down from stars that have died long ago and from new ones, resting in their glorious beginning.

Wednesday is clear and hot with a surprising cool wind that is even cooler at the beach. They drive out in Leo's old gray Saab, with its clean, worn seats. He has brought cups of coffee that slosh onto Serena's fingers as he drives and she holds them. She hasn't had any coffee in months, since it, like so many things, is not part of the macrobiotic diet. She wonders if it will make her giddy. She has brought a bright yellow bag with towels and suntan lotion, in these times before it was generally known that the ozone layer was torn and the sun dangerous. She has her bathing suit on under her clothes, hoping to avoid the damp and inevitably moldy cabanas at small beach clubs. They listen to the radio as the miles pass and they move toward Long Island. The Beatles are playing. The Stones.

"What was your dream?" asks Leo.

"First, at the beginning of the dream, I heard someone say, 'A lake of tears,' I think meaning that the tears were in you, but maybe not. Then there was a red cabin on a mountain. I think of mountains as symbolizing wisdom; the lonely climb to wisdom. I was alone on the mountain. The red was vivid—life energy. I saw the peonies in the garden where we met and then they seemed to burst and be in the room." She wonders what he will make of the last part and whether to mention it, but she does.

"The peonies were in the room for real?"

"Yes. For real. But they were gone in the morning."

The cars hum around them. Trees appear, blowing in this odd, cool wind. Leo's long legs move slightly as he shifts gears.

"Has that ever happened before? That something moves from a dream into the physical world?" Leo asks.

"No. Not that way."

"What way? I mean what other way?"

"I've dreamt things that then happened in the world."

"Like what?" He sounds curious, but not skeptical.

"Oh, people I dream about and then meet. Sometimes the faces are close, but not exact. Sometimes the whole situation comes about just the way I dreamt it. Places I've never seen that appear later in my life. Also, funny nonsense things, like how much my shoes will cost to repair, or how much the laundry will be." Serena likes talking about these experiences, but feels slightly defensive. She wants it to seem inviting—which embarrasses her—to use these experiences to draw Leo in. Her calling card. I am a unique and mysterious person. And she doesn't want to seem strange. Added to that, she truly wants someone to understand. People often nod wisely in recognition, but she never knows if they realize this is serious to her. Has happened all her life. Different realms and times that slide in and out of each other this way.

"I think I have had dreams that contain fragments of the future." He sighs. "Not always happy fragments. The 'lake of tears' is interesting." He doesn't say any more and then they are there, turning into the club, passing into the parking lot.

"We have a spot with a cabana," he says, taking her hand as they walk toward the sand.

"Ah, the cabana. I have my suit on under my clothes."

"Well, after. You'll be wet."

"Mmm," says Serena, hoping she will not be wet, will have dried so that she can dress without ever entering the cabana.

Various people greet them as they go toward the family's spot.

"Oh, Leo. How are you?" A big boned man with a broad chest covered in wiry gray curls. "Kathleen, it's Mary's boy." He gestures to his wife, plump and very pink from the sun, her face happy and shiny under the fruit smell of the sun lotion. A small holy medal sticks to the lotion on her wide bosom.

"Leo, sit down a minute. Who is this?" She gestures toward Serena and Leo introduces her politely.

"My friend, Serena Weiss. Kathleen and Tom Brady. Old friends of our family. No, we'll go on, but thanks. Good to see you. Maybe later."

Their walk is peppered with similar stops. "I warned you," he says. Finally, they get to a relatively open space and Leo goes to get beach chairs. The water is dark and choppy from the wind, though the sun is hot and the sand close to scorching. When they are settled, Leo says, "No. I don't think it's odd. The dream. Well, odd, but not bad. Just interesting." They are lathering on sun lotion. They do each other's backs with great care. "Do you want to swim?"

"Yes, but I don't really swim in the ocean. I learned in fresh water. I want to go in, though."

Suddenly Leo picks her up, holding her in his arms and carries her to the water. "I'll take you in," he says and he does, cradling her in the cold, blue splash, her arms around his neck. He holds her that way for a while, the water slapping at them, leaping at their bodies and then he puts her down gently. "Just stay near the shore," he says. "I'm going to swim." Which he does, going quite far out, beyond the breakers.

Serena stays near the shore, experimenting with the waves. One catches her in the abdomen and spills her over, so that her head is upside down under the water, sand everywhere. In her eyes, her hair. Up her suit. In her mouth, sharp against her teeth. When she rights herself, she returns to their chairs, drying off, a little shaky and dizzy. Leo is making his way back to shore, much to her relief. They eat the sandwiches he has brought and watch the sun wrinkle on the surface of the waves. They hold hands and are quiet.

"Time to go," Leo says.

"Is that a question?"

"Yes and no. I have some work to do, but we could stay a bit longer."

"Let's go," Serena says. "I don't want to burn."

Leo starts toward the cabana. "Shower?"

"I'm okay." She walks with him though. The little buildings are painted blue that has weathered in streaks, with wooden lace trim in white. At the door he pulls her in, gently.

"Are these for men or women?" proper Serena.

"No. This is my family's little palace." He closes the door behind them and kisses her. Sand is under foot. They kiss in the sticky mess of hot sun lotion and gritty sand.

"Shower," he says. "I'll leave."

"Okay." She is reminded of the horrible changing room at her junior high school. At least this is private. The tiny shower has a concrete floor, pitted and dark. She thinks of the cabins closed for winter, of cold sand drifting under the door and of snow. Of the icy darkness left somewhere in the walls, now so hot. She dries quickly, still sandy, and smells the baby powder resting in a large can on the shelf. She decides against using it. She braids her long hair, a wet, drippy plait down her back.

"Your turn."

Leo showers even more quickly than she and they leave. Most of the family friends have gone, so it is a much faster walk to the car.

On the ride home, Leo asks, "How is this going?"

"Which part of the 'this' are you asking about?" The buildings rise as they near Manhattan.

"Well, seeing each other. Not having sex?"

"I like seeing each other and we are having sex, we just aren't making love. Officially." She thinks of saying "fucking," but she dislikes the word in this context. "I like talking to you and touching you and learning about music where the piece is composed of tapping." Serena pauses. "Do you explore this way with all the ladies?"

"No, no." Leo laughs and then his face shifts. "Only with one other and that was a long time ago." The sky whitens above them as they near the city.

He leaves her at her door. "Can we have dinner on Friday?"

"Sure. Is seven good?"

"I'll see you then." And he is gone. Sun has reduced patches of asphalt to gooey softness that sticks to the soles of her sandals. The late afternoon street is busy with children riding bikes and adults smoking various substances and drinking cool beverages. Serena goes upstairs. On her way, the elderly Ukrainian woman who is the super is mopping the old tile floor, wearing a starched, ironed housedress. "Tch," she says at Serena's sticky feet. Serena apologizes and tries to tiptoe. Once upstairs, she runs a bath. The cat balances on the rim of the tub as she washes.

When Rose returns from work, Serena is still in the water. Rose has graduated from law school, passed the bar and is working with civil liberties, much to Syl's disgust. "You choose a profession where you can make good money and then you don't," Syl has said. "Just like you."

"It is like me, mother," said Rose. "It is me."

Serena is looking down at the tub, at the surface between her legs and at their wavy shape seen through the water. "Can you get sand up your vagina?" are her opening words.

"Is there sand there?"

"Yes. Little pile of it coming out. A wave up-ended me."

"Then I guess the answer is yes," Rose replies. She begins to take her work clothes off. "I'm next. How is Leo? I assume you didn't have intercourse on the beach."

"Not this time," says Serena. They both smile. "We're having dinner on Friday."

＊ ☼ ＊

June passes into July. On the Fourth of July, Serena and Leo and Rose and Hal and Ingrid gather on Serena and Rose's roof to watch the fireworks. The night is strangely cool for July, with a wind full of the salty smell of the rivers that cradle the island and they all wear long sleeves and eat corn on the cob and drink red wine that Leo has brought. The lights flash and bloom in the sky, melting into shining petals and sparks before disappearing. Around them, on other rooftops, people are clapping and calling out as the sky shimmers. Along the street, the windows form a random pattern of bright and dark. Leo holds Serena tightly as the brilliant colors of the fireworks rise and fall away. He kisses the top of her head.

"Here we are," says Rose, "celebrating the birth of a nation that committed genocide, held slaves and is currently engaged in this horrifying war."

"Well," Leo says, "to peace everywhere." They raise their glasses.

"And to inconsistency and paradox," says Ingrid, who has now stepped to the edge of the roof and is leaning quite far over.

＊ ☼ ＊

Three nights later, Serena and Rose are at home, making the ghastly, inevitable pot of seaweed, when Serena starts to scream.

"What?" yells Rose. "What is it?"

"Water bug! There! Huge! Huge!" Serena has run across the tiny kitchen, still screaming. She is deathly afraid of these bugs.

Rose, who isn't that frightened of them, catches Serena's mood. "Get the spray," she says.

"You get it!" Serena shrieks. The can is under the tub. They have organic bug spray that they have used against the roaches. There are no roaches left in the apartment. If Serena sees the slightest suspicious movement she lunges toward it. She is not afraid of roaches, they are relatively small and wily, but these bugs seem monstrous. Rose gets the can and starts to spray madly, but the bug lumbers into the next room and goes under the bed.

"Call Ingrid," says Serena. "She'll whack it."

"Ingrid is out. She's at a concert."

Serena is silent for a moment. "I'll call Leo. He's home working."

"It's late," says Rose. "After ten."

"Oh, he works late. Anyway, it's not that late."

So, Serena does call Leo, who comes over and hunts up the poor dreadful bug and dispatches it. Then they look at each other for what to do next.

"I'm not sleeping here," says Rose. "The stink is awful. I'll go to Ingrid's. I have her keys."

"Come to my house, Serena," offers Leo.

"Aren't you working?"

"I'm just about finished."

Serena has never stayed at Leo's. They have not actually made love yet. Not technically. She looks at his eyes and his smile, tries to remember what underwear she has on, feels embarrassed at having thought about it, and agrees. "I just need to collect some stuff," she says.

Rose is already gathering underwear and an old tee shirt and Ingrid's keys. "See you tomorrow," she says. She smiles and is out the door.

Serena gathers her own things more slowly, but not too slowly. The smell of the spray is really awful, hanging in the summer heat.

Serena has been to Leo's only a few times before and then very briefly. This time she will be able to really look around. She is deeply curious about other people's living spaces. It is a curiosity that seems embarrassing to her. She is not only curious about the décor, what they have chosen to live with. She knows the curiosity extends to opening medicine cabinets, looking inside cupboards, but doesn't understand exactly what she is trying to find, having the doors to closed areas open, revealing their contents. Serena can see the obvious, that there may be secrets suddenly displayed, that she might come upon some starkly revealing item, but it doesn't seem so much that, as looking at their things to see if hers are normal. Some lingering way she felt that she and Ruby were never normal, never all right. If she can see inside the closets and the cabinets and behind all those closed doors, she will finally unlock how she should be and be able to right herself. She feels voracious when she does this. Sly and ashamed. Maybe she will just ask Leo if she can open the closets and the cupboards and the medicine cabinets and see what he says. She thinks all of this as they climb one flight of very clean stairs and he opens the door to the apartment. The building looks as if it once contained light industry of some kind. Leo has said he thought they manufactured table linens. When he was renovating his floor, he found bundles of old napkins and faded yards of tablecloths, soft whites skimmed with age and some blue and white checked material, made into napkins. The windows go almost all the way from the ceiling to the floor and the hot night rests against the panes, blurry with streetlights mixed into the darkness.

Serena sniffs her clothes. "I still smell," she says. Leo closes the door and heads for the bathroom. He has a real bathroom with a tub and shower that he installed. She hears the water rush.

"Not a moment to waste," he says. "I think I can smell you from here."

Serena washes with his lavender soap and shampoo and then just stands under the water, scrubbed and happy. Leo knocks at the doorjamb. "Is it all right if I join you?"

Serena smiles. "Yes."

He comes into the bathroom carrying a glass of red wine and into the shower holding it, one hand covering the mouth of the glass. He tips her head back slightly and slides his fingers apart so she can drink. Then he drinks some. She looks at his body, at the long, tanned legs, which are quite slender, and at his arms, which are muscled. She touches one arm lightly, stroking the curve of muscle.

"Yes," he says. "It's from hauling things mostly. Or I inherited them from my father's early life as a longshoreman."

She looks all the way down and laughs. "You're a redhead." Leo's pubic hair is deep auburn.

"I am half Irish," he says.

"Yes, I can see," says Serena, "and this is the half."

"Not entirely," he replies, taking another drink of wine. "I have a red beard." He puts the wine down outside of the shower and begins to soap his body and touch her alternately. They have not been undressed this way until now. They hold each other under the falling water. Eventually, they climb carefully out of the tub.

Leo wraps her in a huge white towel and then dries himself. He gives her a shirt of his to wear, which is more like a dress on her small body. He picks up the wine. "Let me show you the garden," he says. She follows him to the back of the loft and they go up three stairs, out the door and then down a flight of stairs, these made of metal slats, like the stairs on a fire escape. Then their feet are on grass. There are drifts of low-growing white flowers, their scalloped petals touching, just barely visible even in the half-lit city night. They float around a small tree. "Impatiens," Leo says.

"What? Impatient?" Well, Serena thinks, after two weeks, they must both be impatient, though Leo has never seemed so.

" 'Impatiens.' It's the name of the flower. Appropriate?"

"Oh," says Serena. "I guess it must be. Well, are we?"

Leo takes her hand. "Yes. But enjoying it. Those are hosta." He points to heavy leaves striped with pale lines. "I had tulips earlier in the spring, but they're over."

"Hostile?" Serena asks.

"No. 'Hosta.' Those are the leaves. They haven't bloomed yet. This is like a bad joke. Let's sit and I'll dry your hair." They sit on the metal steps and he takes the towel from around his shoulders and starts to dry her long hair, alternately kissing her and drying. They finish the wine and rest the glass on the ground. "When I moved in, this was a junkyard. Someone had paved it over and then just thrown things out here when they wanted to get rid of them. My father helped me make the garden. We brought the earth in."

"You didn't lift it from a construction site?" Serena asks, remembering their first date.

"No, not this. Dry enough," he says and lifts her up, carrying her back into the loft and shutting the door behind him. He lays her down upon the bed.

She looks up at him. "No fruit in the garden."

"There is," he says. "The little tree is an apple tree." They both smile.

Leo lights one large, white candle and turns off the light. Serena notices that there are red roses in a vase on the night table. They are not long stemmed with a single bloom, but clusters of blooms, deep in color, with trailing leaves that spill over the vase. Leo sees her eyes move toward them. "They're from my mother's garden. They're climbers."

The leaves in the park across the street rustle in a sudden strong wind. Serena thinks of some old movie she saw as a child, where the windows blew open and a high wind ripped at the curtains to indicate sex. Leo begins to massage her feet. Serena's sturdy feet. Then he moves up her body, kissing her, rubbing against her. They are both still slightly wet, lying on the cool sheets, smooth with age, and repeated washing. Leo's words are very soft. "You are so beautiful, Serena. You are desireable and beautiful." Serena thinks that after these weeks, they will make love quickly, but Leo is slow and concentrated. He is not really patient, thinks Serena, he has a kind of restlessness that he contains and focuses and it seems like patience. But he is surely determined, a combination of resilient and insistent. He sucks on various parts of her, pressing his hands against her, stroking her. She kisses him everywhere she can find: his back and chest and arms and legs. She licks his nipples, which are pale creamy brown. Periodically, they stop to look at each other in the wavy candlelight, both half-seeing and sharply present. Eyes open, he enters her and she rests her fingers around the base of his cock. It feels as much like her sliding over him as being entered. It feels like joining each other. "I'm going to stay still," he says. "I'm just going to rest here." For a moment, Serena sees a color as dark as the stunning black satin cupped in the heart of some tulips. The color fragments and glitters. It melts into fireworks, bursts of light vanishing into wind and time. They are both still, feeling the connection and then they are moving and rocking, coming so fast, everything gone. They start to laugh, as helpless in the laughter as in the sex. And then Serena begins to cry.

"Serena, what? What's wrong? What is it?" Leo gathers her to him.

She shakes her head, too immersed in the sudden tears to speak, completely surprised. She feels as if something has loosened in her belly, something that she was unaware of, a cord that holds things together, keeps them aligned in some familiar way. Her crying comes from a place as deep as the caves that shelter fish with blind white eyes, eyes never touched by the sun's light. Leo simply holds her and finally the tears stop. "I don't know," she says. "An old sorrow boiling to the surface? But why now? I don't know, Leo." She breathes quietly for a while and then Serena touches Leo's heart and rests her lips against his chest. "It feels as if there's sorrow in you, too. Is that okay to say?"

"Yes, it is okay to say. It's true. How much do you want to hear?"

"I want to hear whatever you're ready to tell me," Serena says. She settles into the crook of his arm, curious, wondering what he will say. Beyond what she intuited when they first met, there have been no clues.

Leo begins slowly. He is entering the skeletal door of the past cautiously, wary of its splintery bones. "I knew Katherine all my life, or almost. We met when she was four and I was six and her family moved into our neighborhood. Our parents were already friends, although they had a lot of differences." He laughs, just a little. "The McNairs were very devout and my mother almost never went to church and didn't have anything good to say about Catholicism and my father never converted. Well, anyway, Katherine and I played together and I think I fell in love with her then. I was the older man."

"And then she was always your girlfriend?" Serena can feel her own heart pulling, her fears of displacement and abandonment already there, looming, sticking her with their sharp, familiar worries. God, she thinks, we're only one paragraph into this story and I'm anxious already.

"No. Not at all. Perhaps a little. When you send those valentines? I always sent her one. We would kiss sometimes, when we were older, just on the cheek. And hold hands. We went to different schools and two years is a big age difference for children. Then we grew up and I went to Columbia and when I was a junior she came to a dance and that was it." Leo turns a little and looks at Serena. "I didn't even try to resist."

"Do you usually? Resist?"

"I'm not sure," Leo says. "Maybe when I'm not that interested, I'm just not. That's not really resistance."

It is if you express resistance as avoidance, by just not being interested, thinks Serena, but she doesn't pursue it.

Leo sighs and gets up to find an ancient pack of cigarettes. He comes back with one lit, coughing slightly.

"Do you smoke? I've never seen you with a cigarette."

"No, not really. Just now," says Leo. "God, these must be two years old. They're awful." The smoke mixes with smells of Leo's house. Oranges in a bowl on the table. Bread. Something Serena can't quite identify; paper, maybe, and ink. And, just now, with the smells of this new part of their life together. Sex and perfume and sweat. He lies down beside her again. When he speaks, his voice is clear and steady, but what he says seems as if it has been long unspoken. It does not have the smoothness, the careful pauses and accustomed rhythms of a story that has been told repeatedly. "We were together all through the rest of my college years and then through graduate school." He pauses. For a split second, it seems as if nothing moves, not even the smoke. "We were going to get married the year after I finished grad school." He is quiet again. "And then she died." He says it very plainly. "It was a freak accident. We had just said goodbye and were going to meet later for a movie. She was running to get a bus and she tripped and fell and hit her head on the edge of a stone step. The ambulance came and took her to the hospital, but she never recovered. She was diabetic, maybe that made it harder, I don't know. Though, no one really said that." It feels to Serena as if the seams of the walls might crumple and open, edges sagging apart, revealing the street as they fall. But they remain intact. She tries to find a place to hold on to this information.

"Oh, Leo, how awful. I'm so sorry." Serena knows that nothing she can say will feel adequate. Now the air seems to break, everything around them breaking, solid forms flying apart with Leo's words, the innate flimsiness of familiar shapes rising to the surface, demanding to be noticed, more powerful than the accustomed agreement of order. Death entering so casually, tragedy intruding, exploding soundlessly, changing everything forever. Serena's heart is pounding. She is silent, watching Leo.

"I thought I would love her forever," he says.

Serena can feel his broken heart. He takes her hand. His rawness feels totally exposed, though his face is calm. He rolls over and holds her. "Such a sad thing to tell you on the first night we make love."

She strokes his back. "I knew there was something," she says. She imagines different kinds of weather rolling through the room. Tides and storms of ice, a burning sun. Summer rain. "Let's just hold each other and sleep. All of this is part of you. I want to know all the aspects, all the facets. As many as you can reveal." Serena's heart, often so embarrassingly full, opens toward him, tipping at the confines of her body. She presses against him as if to hold the fullness back.

Leo sighs and touches her hair. "All right. Sleep, beautiful Serena. I loved making love with you."

There is one part that Leo does not tell Serena. It happened in the hospital, just after Katherine had died. He was sitting on a blue plastic chair, apart from the immediate family and the conversation they were having with the doctor. He sat still, tears running down his face, but he was listening to the doctor's voice. "Pregnant?" the doctor asked tentatively. This was a Catholic hospital. "Might she have been?"

And then Katherine's mother saying vehemently, "No. No. Absolutely not," her body shaking with feeling. Mrs. McNair in her navy silk dress and her navy pumps, a small cross at her throat, her pale hair silky and straight at the scalp and then torturously permed at the ends. Mr. McNair echoing her, his voice quieter, issuing from deep within his broad body, his girth asserting itself, as if to protect himself and his wife from all that was happening and certainly from this added, awful thought.

But Leo's thoughts were the same. No. Not possible. How could she have been? And how would the doctor know? Surely, they didn't do a pelvic exam on a woman dying from an injury. If she had been, she would have told him. When they first had sex, she was so guilty. The teachings of Catholicism were vibrating in her cells, dragging her into misery as sharp as splintered ice. She was almost frozen with it. But her strong body prevailed, and their love, and they grew to relish each other. They were careful. Always so careful. Beyond that, he had said that if anything happened, if there was to be a baby, they would marry immediately. They were going to anyway.

The McNairs never spoke of it. He didn't ask. There was such profound grief to cope with. Such violent, commanding sadness. Nothing would have been gained by asking. Sometimes, Leo wonders whether he imagined it. Whether he misunderstood the doctor's words. Ultimately, did it matter? Katherine was dead. But, if it was true, it did make a difference. He will never know.

He says nothing to Serena that night. The knowledge stings his memory as he speaks about Katherine, but the sensation is quick and then it all sinks down again, into the resinous dark of his unconscious.

Before Serena falls asleep, she thinks about what Leo has said. A dead woman. A lost love. A ghost. Serena is very familiar with the presence of ghosts. Her father's death created such fierce longing. His absence was fierce. Ruby was never free of it and perhaps Serena was not free, either. She closes her eyes. focusing on an image of the night sky, paying attention to the emptiness that holds the stars and moon. It is a practice from her early days of meditation and it calms her breath and quiets her heart. She sleeps and dreams of an endless meadow. Looking down at her feet, she sees a daddy longlegs with a jeweled head watching her. Somewhere in the meadow, she thinks she hears a baby cry.

✳ ✿ ✳

Serena and Leo begin, in the days and weeks following this night, to build a life, to consider each other in their plans. To do this is to recklessly imagine a future. They shop for food that Leo cooks and he teaches her how to make bread, or really, he makes it and she watches, knowing she will not ever do this herself. One afternoon, they lie on Leo's living room floor, stretched out on their backs, the soles of their feet touching, waiting for the bread dough to rise and listening to Baroque music. The ceiling fan turns slowly and they breathe softly together. They let themselves touch and this time, do not make love. But they make love often. Slow love and quick hard love and everything in between.

They visit with friends, sharing the people they know with each other. It turns out that Mark, the tall percussionist Serena met at Fanelli's, the man who wore the heavy boots and had his arm around Ingrid, lives on a boat. The boat is moored in the Hudson River, at the Seventy-ninth Street Boat Basin. Leo and Serena join a small group, including some of the people from that same dinner, for a trip up the Hudson on a sunny day that has a strong, hot wind blowing through the cloudless sky. Greasy smoke trails behind them in the choppy water. Ingrid stands at the edge of the boat and, as usual, leans over as far as she can go. Food is passed around. Leo holds Serena on his lap and strokes her hair as the boat bumps. He is an openly affectionate man. Generous and welcoming. At one point in the bumping, she can feel him getting an erection. She pushes harder against him and they both laugh. The others on the boat are all artists of one kind or another. They are friendly and talkative, slapping along in the old boat as webs of light break and shift on the surface of the water. There is a river smell, deep and old, with salt mixed in.

Some days, Leo takes Serena to his favorite restaurants, which are scattered all over the city. They eat cold octopus salad in a small Cuban-Chinese place that will still be in the same location thirty years later and apricot ice in a Middle Eastern restaurant in Brooklyn. Once, they eat at the Paradox, the local macrobiotic restaurant. Leo is aghast.

"This is such terrible food," he says, somewhat wonderingly. "Why does anyone eat it? I think the real paradox is calling it food." Why Serena eats it is a long, tangled story, having to do with her endless misery about food and with the idea that she must always be thinner than she is. Her heart sinks a bit at his question. There is so much to explain. Macrobiotics combines the promise that she will be thin (everyone on this regime gets thin) with a complex set of ideas about purity. And, strangely, this diet does not make her thinner, just sleepy and full of cravings for things she doesn't generally like. Coffee ice cream heads the list.

It is the perfect vehicle for her, always deeply certain that she is stained somewhere, the product of years of Ruby's screaming at her. "There is something wrong with you!" her mother would shout. Or sometimes hiss. The sense of the wrongness lives in Serena's cells. She will struggle with it for years.

"Oh," she says to Leo. "Oh, it's supposed to be healthy. Well, no, there are other reasons, but I don't want to talk about them all now. I'll tell you. I will." And eventually she does.

As July unrolls, Leo plays the cello and works long hours on a potential project to restore part of a church in Venice. Serena sees her clients, talks about solar eclipses and the nodes of the Moon, digs into the spinning mysteries of the planets and their relationship to each other.

"The church must be very old," says Serena one evening when she is watching Leo work, watching his beautiful hands move as he draws. He looks periodically at a photograph of the church as he works. She wants him to have the project and cannot bear the thought of separation. Already, she thinks. I am having this trouble already. Well, I always have it, I'll cope. These thoughts about coping come in the moments she feels brave. Other times she feels her neediness and her fears, sticky and miserable, inhabiting her belly and her heart, dark with pleading. Even her bones ache with it. All of this hidden, more or less, under her soft skin, her quick independence, her competence.

"All Venetian churches are old," Leo says. "The question is, how old?" He does not ask how she feels about his leaving for a month. He knows without asking. He can feel what she is only partially revealing, unwilling, in this early time, to let him see what she judges to be the primitive mess of her longing.

✳ ❂ ✳

Some nights, Serena goes home to her apartment. One night when she is home, scrubbing the green kitchen floor, Rose says, "This is getting serious with Leo." She regards the floor. "The floor's pretty clean, Serena."

"I know and yes, it is serious." Serena looks critically at the sloping floor, with its odd metal patches.

"Are you both serious?" Practical Rose.

"Yes, we both are." Serena looks up slowly from the soapy floor. It is so hot in the room, the heat of the water in her cleaning pail adding to it. "I hope he is." She rinses the floor carefully. Rinses the rag. "He might get that Venice project. I think he probably will. I'm always so afraid. He'll go away. He'll disappear. He'll die. One night when Leo was late I got as far as imagining his funeral and my outfit. Nothing fucking helps. I'm in therapy. This is supposed to change."

"I thought Leo was always early."

"He is. The train was stuck."

None of this is news to Rose. They have known each other for so long. Many years later, in another round of therapy, Serena's therapist will say, in his British accent, "It's the old brain that gets activated. The reptilian brain. When it's engaged, you can't reason. Have some wine. Take a bath." A baath. "Wait for it to pass." It is probably the best suggestion anyone will ever make. Through years of therapy and meditation and transformational work, this stubborn issue remains, always a stumbling block. Or, in a Buddhist sense, something interesting to be explored, but this attitude is not constant, by any means.

Serena finishes the floor. "I'm going to take a quick bath. Then let's go for a walk."

✳ ✿ ✳

It is Sunday, July 20, the day astronauts Neil Armstrong and Buzz Aldrin are set to walk on the moon. Even in the East Village, bastion of cool, people are excited. Serena and Rose and Ingrid and other friends are set to watch the landing at Leo's, since he has the most space and the best television set. Serena has been thinking about all this in symbolic terms. The Moon, guardian of the night and the seas; the Moon as mother and nurturer, as feeling and intuition, as belly and breasts. Milky or dark or sharply bright, changing rapidly, it's reflected light playing on the surface of the earth in regular rhythms, pulling the tides with its steady force. Her teacher has said it might mean a greater awareness of the feminine in the collective consciousness, but Serena feels it more as an intrusion. Leo is interested in all the science involved. The massive computers. The daring. In the afternoon, they make a huge fruit salad, blueberries and mounds of cantaloupe. Wedges of rosy watermelon. Fistfuls of green grapes. Leo shreds coconut on top of it all and adds a little Marsala. "Let's let it steep," he says. They filch some and eat it and then undress each other and make slippery sweet love.

It is after they make love, when Serena is lying half on top of Leo, the sheets damp and both of them sweaty, that the phone rings. Leo answers it. "Oh, Arne. Hi." Arne is his boss, the owner of the small architecture firm Leo works for. They are fairly good friends, though with some slight, formal distance. He listens for a few minutes, and then says, "Great. That's wonderful news. This is terrific." He is smiling widely, sharing his pleasure with Serena. "Really? That soon? Okay. Yes, I have one already. Yes. Well, you can give me the other details tomorrow. I'll start to get ready. You too. Thanks for calling right away." He puts the phone down. Serena watches him carefully, not quite able to smile yet. "We got the Venice project," Leo says. "They want me to go."

"That's wonderful," Serena says. "It is a wonderful thing for you." She feels as if her body is emptying, hollowness replacing her bones, her organs. As if her blood is turning white. No, she thinks. I don't want to feel this way. I can't. But it is too late. The ritual fear inhabits her far faster than she can stop it. It has a ceremonial presence, majestic and commanding. She does smile, finally, but she is not fooling Leo.

"Oh, Serena," he says. "I'll be back. It isn't very long." She does not cry, but looks as if she might.

"No," she says, both aloud and to herself. "I am not going to do this. This is a burden for you. This is my craziness."

"It isn't a burden. I just . . . I don't know. I don't know what. I don't want to say, 'Don't be sad,' because you already are."

"I'm more frightened," she says. "And somewhere, angry. I'm always angry when someone I care about leaves." She feels totally exposed, her shadow-self torn open and exposed to light. She can imagine him making love to an Italian woman, gorgeous in her nakedness, imagine them lying in a room with high ceilings and grainy, ochre walls. Serena has never been to Italy, but this doesn't stop her from careening forward into the heat and pain of her flamboyant imagination. She can see his plane dropping into the ocean, flames rising. "Oh God," she says. "I'm sorry."

"No," Leo gathers her to himself and holds her. "No sorry. This is just here with us, we'll deal with it."

"I am happy for you," Serena says. "I can extend myself that far. Really. All this stuff coexists. I know you'll be back." But this is not exactly true, or not true enough for her to feel it, only to understand it in some logical and emotionally meaningless way. "When will you be back?"

"I don't know, exactly. End of August. No later than that."

"Well," Serena says, "that's not so long." Thinking that it seems too long even to contemplate.

Leo just holds her and strokes her back.

"It sounds like you're leaving soon." Serena suddenly remembers the morning her father died, in the bedroom of her family's old apartment. The door to the bedroom was closed, which was unusual. It was a frigid Sunday in January. Shining ice everywhere. She was not taken to the funeral. She remembers the day after the funeral when Ruby told her that Alex had died. An obsidian needle, icy and swift, lodged in her heart. It penetrated so quickly she was not aware that it had entered her. It froze her tears. Deeply buried, the needle rested in place for years. During the time of Serena's first work with Nick, her therapist, it began to warm and move. She could feel its sharp presence and her pain awakened, along with panic and sadness. And then rage. Serena had never been able to say goodbye to her father.

"Serena? Where are you?" Leo asks.

"Remembering," she says. "Remembering."

"What are you remembering?"

"I am remembering my father's death and it's too long a story for now. I will tell you some other time." She draws her attention back to the room and the moment and Leo.

Leo continues to hold her and the astronauts pull closer and closer to the surface of the mother moon. Finally, Serena and Leo wash and dress. Serena manages to ask details about the project. She shakes herself back into the present as best she can. The guests will arrive soon.

Everyone gathers at Leo's house at nine that evening. They drink white wine and eat the fruit salad; some of the musicians have brought instruments and they play. Leo holds the cello firmly and pulls lovely sounds from it as they improvise. People tap on things in the room and Serena joins in, this time undaunted. The television is on in the background. Finally, they stop playing and just watch. At 10:56 p.m. Neil Armstrong steps onto the Moon's surface. They cheer and can hear people shouting in the street and up and down the block. Aldrin joins him about twenty minutes later and they collect samples and then move around, almost bounding forward, dusting up the surface, planting a stiff flag, getting a message from President Nixon. Old, empty, silent Moon, with two men walking on her. The party breaks up very late. Leo and Serena clean up together, and then look at the heavens from the garden. Serena feels as if the Moon is now tied to Earth and all her creatures with a floating umbilicus, new and tender and strange.

She and Leo sleep very late the next day. When they wake, they do not make love and after breakfast, he starts to pack. He will leave the following evening. He irons his clothes and packs everything very carefully. He and Serena are tender with each other. "I'll write to you regularly," Leo says. "Letters, postcards. You'll get tired of hearing from me."

Serena smiles. "No. I wouldn't get tired of it. Actually, Rose and I had planned a trip to Canada before—well, you know, before we met. So, we'll go."

"Would you not have gone if I were here?"

"I don't know. Yes. Probably. Probably we would not have. That isn't the right answer, but it's true."

"Well, then you'll have a stack of mail when you get back. How long will you be gone?"

"Why?" asks Serena. "Are you anxious?" She hugs him for a moment.

"No. Just curious."

"We'll be home the fifteenth of August. You don't know, do you? When you'll be back?" She hopes she doesn't look as miserable as she feels. Miserable and what she thinks of as weak.

"Not exactly, but I will as the work goes along. Not later than the end of August," Leo says.

Serena leaves in the afternoon the day of Leo's departure and goes home; she cannot bear to see him leave. His flight is in the early evening. They hold each other for a long time and then she goes, closing the door firmly behind her. As soon as she gets to the street, tears pour down her face. "Someone done you wrong," a young man jibes, but not unkindly, as she walks toward her apartment.

"No," she says. "No, not really."

※ ❂ ※

Serena and Rose pack on the same evening that Leo begins his flight to Italy. They pack clothes and all their macrobiotic paraphernalia and their iron skillet, the skillet being the only approved way to cook vegetables in macrobiotics.

Serena packs her mascara. "Are you wearing mascara in the wilds of Canada?" asks Rose. Serena nods. They leave early on a calm, gray morning, passing miles of dark pine trees as they move north, sometimes driving on an almost empty road. Rose's old VW Bug is packed full. When they reach the Canadian border the immigration inspector asks them to open the car. Rose opens the front of the Bug and the tall man peers down at their sacks of food. His bristly blond hair gleams with hair cream. His shoes shine. He is standing quite close to Serena. He is probably not much older than they are. She thinks he smells faintly of potatoes.

"Please open the sacks," he says. They do. Rice is revealed, then dark aduki beans and seaweed. He regards the seaweed carefully. There is a bottle of sesame oil wrapped in brown paper and, of course, the skillet. He looks at the neatly dressed women, at Serena's long, thick hair and Rose's composed face. "What is this?" he asks, half perplexed and half suspicious. They don't really look like hippies. They are too clean, is what he thinks.

"It's food," smiles Serena. She barely misses breathing into her chest to highlight her breasts. She will not do that and she does not. "It's healthy food. We are on a special diet."

"Oh," the inspector says. Diets. Women are always on diets. His wife is on one this minute, trying to lose weight after the birth of their son. But hers does not involve these odd things. Thank God. "Okay," he says. "Enjoy Canada." Rose closes the trunk gently. They drive off. They stay overnight near the border, and then continue on to Prince Edward Island, their destination. Rose liked the way it sounded in the brochures, and as a child Serena read all of the *Anne of Green Gables* books, weeping her way through each one. They rent a cottage near the water, one that has a kitchen, since they need to cook. The water is inviting and, on fine days, the sun is vigorous. Serena lies beneath it, eyes closed. The heat rests on her body and she practices self-hypnosis, which she and Rose have studied the previous year. In these hot trances, smelling sun lotion and the scent of the cool water, she imagines Leo and their eventual marriage. She is always careful to release the image at the end, so that it is not intended as a manipulation. Of course not. Spiritually, she knows that manipulating in these fluid realms is improper. She is simply exploring the possibility in this tranced meditative state. She finds she has mixed feelings about it, about marriage itself, that she had not realized were there. She and Rose both read a lot and swim. One night, on the way to a movie, which is sixty miles from their cabin, they stop and buy raisin pie. Neither of them has heard of raisin pie. It is horribly sweet and runny and delicious. Rose teaches Serena to drive the Bug and they cruise down to the very end of the island, the edge where its final rocks disappear into the water. They turn at the end of the point, at the church in Tignish. "You have to go into fourth," Rose says.

"I like third. It feels as if I have more control," Serena replies. "Fourth feels too loose."

"You do have more control in third, but you can't drive that way."

"Okay," Serena says. The sun sets in pale gold swaths, thin violet trails. The wind is fresh and strong. "What do you think Leo is doing?" Serena says one night as they are finishing their drive.

"Sleeping, now," says Rose.

"Sleeping alone, I hope," says Serena.

As a matter of fact, Leo is not sleeping alone. Not exactly. There is an Italian designer working on the restoration project with his company. She is quite tall, with sturdy, long legs, broad shoulders and deep red hair that curls wildly and is worn caught up at the nape of her neck. She wears formal black suits that fit her body closely and white shirts, open far down in the front. She has dark eyes with a twist of magic in them. Her name is Angela and she has taken an immediate liking to Leo, which she expresses openly. The men on the project laugh gently, pointedly. "She is something, that Angela. She likes you, Leo." Leo shakes his head. "You are not married," says one, looking at Leo's bare hands. No ring.

"No," he says. "I'm involved."

"Oh, involved. Everyone is involved, no?"

One afternoon, Angela invites Leo to her apartment, to see some of her other work. He agrees and meets her in a building with dark stairs and an ancient door that she has left open for him. He is more than half aware of what he is doing. The door leads into a large room with high ceilings and pale, yellow walls stippled with light from the canal below. Light is everywhere. The very room seems to float in slender waving streams of light. She pours glasses of cold, white wine and they begin to look at her work, which is very precise and organized. Angela stands close to Leo and then, after a while, puts her hand firmly on his butt. "Angela," Leo says. "you are beautiful and I am involved with someone."

"Oh, involved," she says, in somewhat the same tone as their colleague had used earlier. "You are engaged?"

"No," says Leo. "No, I'm not. No."

"Well, what is the harm? Your pleasure won't hurt anyone."

"It will," he says, but she is starting to rub his back and then his legs and then she turns him around and kisses him. Angela, who is really something. Serena is lying in Canada with the sun on her eyes during the long August days. Venice is shimmering in its glorious wet, home of the doges under their gold umbrellas. Home of famous courtesans and fabulous stolen wealth. Leo kisses Angela back and she unbuttons whatever buttons are not already undone on her bright white shirt. She puts her hand under his balls and laughs. Then they are undressed and on her old, wide mattress, held in a smooth wooden frame. The sheets are pale yellow, like the walls. A small ceramic image of the Virgin hangs above the bed. She is garlanded with fruit and flowers. The hem of her blue gown is chipped. They make love on the bed and, later, on one of the couches. Leo does not stay the night.

In the morning, the men in the office nudge each other and smile at Leo. How could they know? Is he wearing a sign? Angela and Leo continue for a few days, and then, on a trip to Murano, watching the boiling mass as the glass blower spins it into a vase, into a solid shape, Leo says, "Angela, we can't make love anymore." But it is very noisy in the shop. "Come," he says and they walk out into the street, go along an almost empty side street, where cats prowl and cry. "I can't make love with you. I do have someone at home." He has wondered, almost non-stop, why he has done it at all. For years, he was faithful to Katherine. Faithful. Full of faith. In some odd way, Angela reminds him physically of Katherine, who was also a redhead, also sturdy looking, with strong, muscled legs. But she was not bold in the ways that Angela is. Determined and brave, but not bold.

Angela reaches up and touches his face. "*Cara*," she says. "Then we will stop. We will just admire each other. What a loss," she sighs. "Why give up such pleasure? And you are such a wonderful lover. But if you must, you must. We will be friends. Very good friends." She takes his hand. "I promise."

Leo feels his stomach relax for the first time since he and Angela became lovers. He knows that he and Serena have not made any promises, no agreements, really, but it is all implicit in the way they were together. And he suspects that Serena can be ferocious about pursuing what she wants. About protecting it. The ferocity doesn't scare him, in fact he finds it attractive in some way, that she will fight, but he truly does not want to act in a manner that will hurt her, hurt them both, whether he keeps this a secret or not.

✳ ✵ ✳

As intuitive as Serena is, and as anxious, she does not actually imagine that anything has happened, that Leo has had a lover, however briefly. Even in her dream life, there is only the vaguest hint, a dream where she sees a woman's shoulder, a sheet dropped away from it and half in shadow, a halo of long auburn curls. She does remember the dream, but thinks she might have dreamt of Katherine. Leo once mentioned that she had red hair.

When their time in Canada ends, Serena and Rose pack, the baggage lighter by all that food they have eaten. They are quite tan. They take an old, peeling ferry back to the mainland and on board, Serena drinks a weak cup of coffee, which affects her like a drug after this time of consuming almost no caffeine. She is high and chatty. They head back to New York, again driving along the miles of road bordered by heavy, dark pines. Serena begins to feel unaccountably sad, suddenly afraid that Leo will not call her, will indeed be lost to her. The skies are overcast and pale the whole way home, the sun and moon lost behind the pale, uniform gray. She and Rose are quiet during the long hours of the trip. They listen to the radio, to classical music, to the Beatles and Dylan. Dylan is singing about a lady laying across his big brass bed, his voice raw and inviting and somehow rejecting.

Everything is in order when they get to their apartment. Bella is thrilled to see them, though Ingrid reports that Bella enjoyed staying with her. The cat purrs and purrs, her thick, striped fur soft against Serena's legs. There are piles of letters from Leo, but none say when he will return, exactly. The project has gone well, better even than expected. They will probably go back to Italy. "Great," Serena says to Rose when she reads that particular letter. The days bloom and close into night. The weather is hot and gray or hot and sunny, but no rain. The city needs rain so badly. Everything seems harsh and too dry. Serena calls Leo, but there is no answer. She walks past his apartment one night and the shades are drawn, only darkness behind them. By Labor Day, she is sad, a miserable, heavy sadness that does not ever seem to yield for long. And she is angry with herself for letting him affect her life this deeply. She feels this kind of sadness steals something from her, diminishes her life force.

On the day after Labor Day, Serena is coming up the stairs late on one more cloudy, dry afternoon, when she hears the phone ringing. It stops just as she enters the apartment. She waits a moment, and then calls Leo, but there is no answer. She stretches out on the small couch, just lying quietly in the empty room. About ten minutes later, she hears someone's footsteps on the stairs and then a strong knock on the door, repeated immediately by another, equally strong. "Who," she says loudly, running to the door, "who is it?" But she knows.

"It's Leo," the voice replies as she opens the door. They do not touch at all at first, but stand still, just looking at one another. Then he steps inside and holds her and they kiss. They kiss each other's faces all over and then stop and breathe and then kiss deeply. "Oh God," Serena says. "It was so long. I didn't know when you were coming."

"No," Leo says. "No. I wrote you the date." But he has spent a few weeks in Italy. "Oh," he says, understanding. "The mail. The famous Italian postal service. You never got the letter. Or you haven't yet."

"Never mind. Now you're here." Serena presses against him, her arms around his chest.

Leo moves away slightly. He is holding a small brown paper bag. "Open it," he says, handing it to her.

Inside are apples. "They're from my tree," he says. At the bottom is a small stone apple. Serena removes it carefully. It is old, with a chip on the side that looks almost like a bite. "From the church," Leo says. "Unrestored."

Serena smiles. "It's perfect."

"Serena," Leo says. He stops, starts again. The room gets darker. The clouds are gathering beyond the window. "Serena, could we live together? I mean, would you like to live together? I would like that. I missed you so much."

Serena holds the stone apple, rubbing her fingers lightly across the chip. "Yes, Leo," she says. "Yes. I would like it too."

There is a clap of thunder and the heavens open. The rain begins, heavy and commanding.

Bedside Manners

Their story becomes one about balance and losing the center. It is about leaning and yearning. It is about the difference between emptiness as hollowness and emptiness as bliss. It is about regaining balance without forcing straightness and about the paralysis born of trying to hang on to the center. It is about lying down and lying about the truth. It is about chaos and equilibrium. It is about the acceptable skin that hides profound awareness and about standing up, alone and together. It is not a love story, but it is a story about love.

✳ ❂ ✳

Serena and Leo's relationship is shifting in ways so subtle that at first, they are almost indiscernible. The fabric of their connection, the bright threads of scarlet, emerald, garnet, the threads of indigo and silver and the darkest earthy brown have started to fade, just a little. Hardly at all. They are loving with each other, sleep entwined. They garden together in the cherished backyard of the brownstone where they live and they tend the indoor plants. They grow some of these from seeds and pits; they also buy plants and festoon the space with greenery, so it is lush and green all year. They discuss their work, see their friends. Meditate. Leo is still trying to teach Serena to bake bread. But a breeze is blowing, the faintest movement of chilly air that slips under the front door, carries their shared energies out the open windows during the summer and autumn; it flows between them when they make love and their lovemaking is friendly, but the heat is mysteriously dwindling. Only a bit. Then a bit more. It's as if the molecules in the body of their relationship are slowing down, their touch now containing some element soft with loss, their years of eagerness diminishing. It's as if clouds have entered the house, perhaps carried on the breeze; barely visible, they bump and stretch, sometimes light, sometimes darker, a pale bleak gray. Other times, they disappear.

At breakfast one autumn day that is sunny, but full of sharpening cold, Serena asks if Leo has noticed these changes, if anything is wrong. She presses her strong hands together, her eyes, sometimes blue, other times gray, are wide; there are bruised half moons under them, the visible color of her worry.

"Yes, yes I have noticed and nothing is wrong." They discuss possibilities, alternately holding hands and eating.

"Are you less attracted to me?" Serena's question, echoing women's eternal concerns, their forever fear, but not one she thought would ever occur with Leo.

"No. Not at all, Serena. And I would ask you the same question."

"No, no I'm not, but I am starting to feel bereft in this amorphous dissolving. And frightened."

Leo gets up from the table, lifts Serena to her feet and holds her. "We'll figure it out. We will. We'll look at it and track it, stalk it, uncover the causes. Maybe it is an old shadow, unacknowledged, that has slipped between us." The drapes move slightly in the open window and the sunlight vanishes suddenly. An old shadow. Nameless, potent. The breeze slithers around their feet as they hold each other. Serena longs for her guardians, her protectors, the wise ones, and can sense them, but the experience is only mildly comforting. She feels her personal self, full of sadness, is isolating her and creating a barrier. The guardians are there, but she does not have access to their vibrancy. "I cannot find them," she says to Leo, who understands what she means. They have had many discussions about the guardians. "I feel abandoned," Serena says, and laughs ruefully.

Serena calls Rose and Ingrid and they make a date to meet for lunch at Ingrid's. They arrive there two days later, when the weather has turned unexpectedly cold. At Ingrid's street door, Serena notices its dented metal has been fixed, and as they mount the stairs, she sees they are freshly swept. Probably Ingrid's doing. The landlord, another artist, doesn't do much, though he will pay for improvements that Ingrid initiates. Responding to the recent cold snap, Serena is wearing a black coat and a cerise scarf; Rose, compact and quick, climbing the stairs with no wasted motion, wears her old tweed jacket. When they arrive, Ingrid has on her usual black jeans and a tee, once perhaps yellow, now faded with washing to an indeterminate light color. Her thick curls, ashy gold, are pulled back tightly. Ingrid wears no more than a heavy sweater on all but the coldest days, so the heat in her loft is off. Her artwork is, as always, covered, or turned to the wall. "Freezing," says Serena, when she has barely entered the room. If she starts now, maybe Ingrid will turn the radiator on and the heat will come up before lunch. "What are you working on?" Serena asks, knowing she will not get an answer. She and Rose have brought lunch from B&H Dairy, just around the corner. Thick barley soup, bagels lavish with cream cheese, coffee and one very large chocolate cookie. By the time they set the food out on the long table, painted shiny black, Serena can hear the steam hissing.

"Bird's feet," Ingrid says, with a straight face, referring to her work. And who knows? It could be true. "Is today a special conference? It feels as if you have called a meeting. Is there trouble?" asks Ingrid as she begins to eat her soup. She looks with concern at her friend. Serena is scraping some of the cream cheese off her bagel and cutting the whole thing into smaller pieces. This is not a good sign,

Serena managing her food in that way.

"Are you not eating? You seem so sad, Serena." This from Rose, who has been through decades of Serena's relationship to food-as-enemy, which worsens when Serena is upset.

"I am. Eating. Not a lot, but steadily enough. There is a purpose for this meeting, yes. You're right. I want to talk about my relationship with Leo. I mean talk about something specific. Trouble? Yes, I guess so. We have changed in a slow way, but now it has become really noticeable. It feels as if the heat is leaking—our connection is loosening, though it all looks the same and we aren't fighting. It feels bleak and sad, with maybe some anger underneath? We've started to talk about it, but it has gone on for some time unacknowledged. Have either of you experienced anything like this?"

"Distancing," says Ingrid. "Sure. But Max and I fight when it happens. Then we make up. It's not very subtle. Usually Max points it out because I'm not that sensitive to distance." Both women look at her. "Well. Okay, a little insensitive. But better than I used to be. I'm controlling and Max is controlling, so we fight. It isn't mean fighting, but it's volatile. We don't punish each other and probably the fighting warms things up, though there must be better ways. Might be better if you did fight? And how long a time?" Ingrid's old cat, Calliope, jumps on the table and starts to lick the cream cheese on Ingrid's bagel. Rose and Serena know this is all right with Ingrid. "That's a good example," says Ingrid. "Max hates it when the cats are on the table. I don't mind. Who gets to control the situation?"

"Is that the level of your disagreements, the cats on the table?" asks Serena. "Months, it has been going on for months, really. It isn't so much distancing as contact that's weakened. I feel bereft. Maybe it's similar to distancing, a kind of distancing . . ."

"No, the cats are just a simple example of control issues. The hard one is the way that Max wants me to promote my work. Ongoing issue. Painful. We wrestle with it. Months. That's long."

"What about you and Hal?" Serena asks Rose. Serena already knows a lot about her friends. But these questions are specific and related to her own need and distress. The three women have talked for years, their attitudes changing, their sense of healthy entitlement growing, clumsily at first. Their skills have increased and their professional lives have unfolded successfully. The have talked about body image and erotic fantasies, about art and politics, about housework. (Max has always had a housekeeper, which initially embarrassed Ingrid, but she now appreciates it. The other two women share the chores with their partners, though Serena cleans and Leo cooks. Hal and Rose share evenly and with good humor.)

Their conversations have curved through seasons, through years, through changes in their bodies, a narrative that expresses their trust and closeness. The closeness vibrates, a slow steady hum, comforting and enduring. Just now, Serena simply needs to talk about this new, fragile situation in her life with Leo; she feels that she is gathering information. Ingrid turns on the lights; the afternoon has gotten dark, the room, now warm, seems lightless, as if the talk itself has absorbed light. Serena nibbles a fragment of cookie, rubs her finger along the edge of her coffee mug, feeling a chip. Ingrid has made fresh coffee.

"Yes," says Ingrid, "it's chipped. Are you eating that piece of cookie, because I will if you don't." Serena passes her the cookie.

"It's moist," she says, smiling for the first time that afternoon.

"No matter," says Ingrid, eating the cookie fragment. Calliope sniffs hopefully at it. She likes sweets. "We could have used more of these."

Serena turns back to Rose, who sighs. "We have more sadness than what you're describing. You know. We keep trying for a baby and it doesn't happen." Sirens scream by outside. "Exactly," Rose says. She points to the window. "Sometimes I feel like that and sometimes I scream. Yes, surprising, I know. Angry sometimes, too, so not just sad. We have both been tested and there's nothing wrong. Hormones off, maybe? But it isn't showing up. And I don't want fucking fertility drugs. Is this about babies?" she asks Serena.

"I don't think so, but maybe unconsciously. If that were the issue and it was conscious, Leo would say so, we've certainly talked about it before. However, time is passing, isn't it? But being in our thirties is not very old. Late thirties, really, but women have babies much later now." She rolls one of the large oranges from the fruit bowl in her hand, feeling the dense nubbly skin. She looks at its shape and sighs. "Huh. Well, it's good to talk. Always good." She rubs her stomach gently. "My abdomen feels tense all the time, all those feelings gathered there, insisting on recognition. I want to *do* something."

"Well, it's not like cleaning, Serena," Ingrid says, but kindly. She knows Serena cleans when she is anxious; it relieves her need to take action. Ingrid shares Serena's desire to vanquish dirt and she does it efficiently—matter of fact and swift. Different in spirit from the scrubbed house she grew up in, which was disinfected but full of secrets, violence. It is pleasurable, Ingrid's making order and cleaning. Perhaps it is simply her pleasure in shining spareness. It is not like Serena's misery, where keeping things clean and polished winds into her viscera, is a badge of her goodness. And yes, yes. A way to control her helplessness.

"I know it's being and not doing. We're going to see Nick. That should be both being and doing, right?" Nick Christos has been Serena's therapist, mentor and teacher for many years. His work is intense, bodywork linked to an understanding of Spirit, a psychiatrist far outside the mode of traditional beliefs. He is married to a woman who is a skilled intuitive, a channel, which Serena knows, and though it interests her, it has no particular meaning for her yet. That will come later. "I know what he'll say, pretty much, and I need to see him."

"Even I know what he'll say," says Rose. She stands up, her neat figure transformed into Nick's stocky body and energetic posture. "Express what you are hiding! Fight for each other, fiiight for this love. Yell. Fight. This is your life energy we are working with. This is precious vitality." She does a creditable imitation of Nick's voice, his stance. "And Nick loves you so much, Serena, he'll tell Leo to be a maann."

"I know, and we are going to work with him. We need help."

"Maybe Leo's energy really is leaking," says Ingrid. "Sucked into all those cold stones in the buildings he restores. Losing his vital forces?"

"Ah ha. No. But maybe that remote aspect of Leo has strengthened, though. It's always been there. When we first met, I dreamt that he had a lake of tears inside. I think that's so. Somewhere, hidden. Hidden. Private." She puts the orange back in the bowl. "I have mauled the fruit."

"Oh so," says Ingrid. "Iss zat significant? Hmm. Mauled fruit? Ze muzzer's breast?" Sometimes Ingrid jokes about Freudian-type queries. Max was in analysis for years and she has picked up the style; she teases him about it and he is tolerant of her teasing and almost always laughs with her.

"Well, at least it isn't a question of better underwear," says Rose, joking. Serena likes nice underthings; Rose likes clothing that is serviceable, including underwear. Ingrid has discovered that she can buy underwear at Woolworth's, which she does.

"Lingerie," says Serena and laughs ruefully, remembering this old sad story from when she and Rose were thirteen years old and opened the underwear drawer in Syl's bureau. She can still see the drawer in her mind's eye. It was filled with bras, panties and slips in delicate peach and lime, violet and pale jade and white; frills and ribbons and lace adorned the delicate pieces. Serena called it "underwear," and Rose, mockingly, had said, "Lingerie, please," imitating her mother's false, refined style. The drawer also contained an empty diaphragm case, a discovery that shifted Rose's home life forever. That long-ago afternoon ended in Rose's flash of awareness that her mother was having sex with one of the workmen redecorating the house because, since her father was away, where was the diaphragm? Ingrid has heard the story.

"Secrets," Serena says. "Secrets. Secrets are undermining us. Must be what reminded me of that day in Syl's bedroom. Maybe bedroom secrets, though I don't imagine Leo is having sex with someone else. It isn't his style. Maybe secrets are coming?"

Wind leaks through the old windows and the room is chilly, even with the steam up. It is time to go. The afternoon has passed with some silences and some talking, but also feeling their bodies' energies reaching out to each other, the touch invisible and soothing. They have listened to some Coltrane, to some Couperin. Ingrid won't paint anymore that day, she is going to meet Max at an opening. Rose is going home with Serena. They dress for the outdoors; Serena wraps the soft, cerise, wool scarf carefully around her neck and adjusts it. She puts on a little lipstick without looking in a mirror. "Always the fashion plate," says Ingrid and hugs her, holds her in her arms for a long moment. Rose and Serena head downstairs into the early evening, which is filled with the autumn smell of drying leaves and, this night, an aching press of cold.

Serena and Leo do go to see Nick on a day of flamboyant sunlight, the edges of the buildings limned with brightness, everyone enjoying the streets in this welcome sun. The street door to Nick's building gleams, the glass polished. The doorman nods to Serena; he has seen her for years. The elevator man greets her, as well. "We know that *you're* a regular," says Leo.

"Are you nervous?" Serena asks.

"No. Yes, of course." Leo has met Nick and worked with him a bit, so they are not strangers, but he is nervous anyway.

Nick comes out of his office, the sun pouring through his door, and hugs them both fiercely. They go inside and sit on the scooped chairs facing Nick's couch. He listens carefully to what they have to say, sometimes closing his eyes, removing his heavy glasses, pinching the bridge of his nose. When they have come to a stopping point and he speaks, what he says is so close to Rose's enactment that Serena smiles. But he says much more than that, of course. "How is sex?" (One of his favored topics.)

"Fine. Good."

"And I know you communicate—yes?"

"Yes."

"So, what is buried under all the sweetness? You say 'drifting, weakening,' but maybe something stronger is happening. Maybe old, powerful feelings are sucking, a whirlpool draining energy from the places where the feelings are hidden." Nick works with Core Energetics, which engages the body and Spirit, loosening defensive armoring, strengthening the collapsed areas, giving flexibility to the rigid places and using active physical expression and interaction. "So, let's work. Stand up and face Leo, Serena. Turn your fear of abandonment around. Tell him you are leaving him, look at him and tell him." Core Energetics activates the feelings potentially hidden in the reverse of what is expressed consciously, thus statements can be explored at a deeper level. Shadows are revealed.

"I am leaving you?" Serena's heart pounds and her ears ring. "Part of me . . . I don't know? Do you think this is defensive? I will leave before you do?"

"No, stick with the basics. Stay in your body. You are saying this situation is painful and you don't want it, but the statement sounds like a question. Turn it over and make it active. 'I am leaving you!' Look at him. Try again."

Serena does, this time more forcefully. "I am leaving you," she says. "Leaving!" The statement frightens her.

"And Leo? What? 'Leave me! Go away!' Or, 'I am leaving you'?"

"Go away," Leo says, directly to Serena, moving slightly toward her. "I need privacy. Go away," Leo sounds desperate. His hazel eyes widen. "Everyone wants me." It is a wailing roar and he begins to cry; old tears, cracked, ancient tears, perhaps coming from that hidden lake. His long legs are almost shaking, his hazel eyes seem darker.

"Whom are you talking to? I don't think it's Serena." says Nick.

"My mother. My sisters."

"Were you allowed to say that?"

"Not really, no. No, not at all. It's not so straightforward, though. They gave me privacy; they respected the time I needed to draw, to be alone. It's deeper than that."

"But women need you, in ways beyond physical privacy."

(Ah, Serena thinks. Leo as a magnet for women and their needs. But an ambivalent one.)

"And I need them, but I don't want to and I want to be left alone." Leo's voice is loud and carries the weight of what it has cost him to hold all of this back for so long.

"With the stones? They don't need so much? They don't need you?"

"Well. They do, but not in the same way."

"No. And you are in charge of them."

"Yes, mostly." Leo laughs. The session continues, each of them expressing feelings in a more direct way than has been possible. The cracks between them are revealed. Widen. But though there is pain in the awareness, it allows life and heat to flow.

"This is good work," says Nick. "More to be done. Much more warmth than when you came in, maybe even heat, yes? Keep making the feelings active, conscious." And then, "Leo—don't leave her alone so much for those stones. Use your feelings truthfully, they are your aliveness. And Serena, when you need him, say so. So independent, with those needs covered over, but the needs are still strong. Boiling, maybe." He touches her shoulder, his broad hand familiar and comforting. "This is not the moment for that and Leo can learn to say no."

By the time they hug goodbye, Serena feels that she has brightened, moved a bit out of the shadowy discontent and sadness, but she is also dismayed. Leo feels invigorated. "I feel as if I have done something dangerous," he says, as they leave the building.

"You have, because you said, 'No,' to your mother and sisters in ways that you never have. At least not consciously or deliberately." They go home through a salt-scented wind that has risen and blows through the sunshine, edgy, demanding.

"Let's make a big soup," says Leo. "And invite our friends for dinner and feed them delicious food."

"Good," says Serena. When they get home, they take out vegetables and lentils and spices. Fat carrots, succulent tomatoes and celery, striated and greenish-white. Garlic, onions. They put Bach's *Mass in B Minor* on the stereo. In the middle of the preparations, amongst the cut vegetables, they kiss and kiss, warmth arising from where it has been depleted. They get as far as the couch and undress, pressed to each other. There are not enough ways to touch; every part of them needs to be kissed, sucked, stroked. They touch until Serena feels as if the stars have turned into liquid, are flowing everywhere in her body, until she becomes the earth receiving their wetness. The earth cradles her. She wonders if Leo feels the liquid, senses the stars and the soft earth. Sometimes they have shared similar images when they made love. Leo finds a condom in the drawer of the end table next to the couch. Serena knows it is one very old condom, they both know, but say nothing. The soup waits until morning. Their renewed warmth has, for the moment, mysteriously sealed windows and doors and there is no draft, no sliding breeze to weave around the room. The cats arrive and they all curl together under the blue quilt kept on the couch. A full moon half-covered by a streaky haze floats above the city. In the morning they do cook the soup and invite friends for dinner. They decide to continue their work with Nick. Of course.

They see Nick through a biting, splashy autumn and into the winter as the solstice comes. On Christmas Eve all the friends go to midnight services at St. Mark's, which is the church their friend Bart still attends and where he has become involved with performances and poetry readings; it is part of his New York community, and he has invited them to the service. Surprisingly, even Ingrid agrees. Serena wears a red velvet blouse, deep, soft fabric curved around her breasts.

It is a recent gift from Leo. "The return of the light and of our warmth, beloved Serena," he has written on the card. He has made a drawing of their house on the front of the card. In the church, the music is glorious, the air filled with the scent of balsam and the room with a group of glowing poinsettias and stands of white candles, lit and gleaming.

Serena listens to the music and sings carols and celebrates, appreciative of it all and of the coming doorway into light as the days lengthen. At the end of the service, Serena and Leo and their friends walk out into the street, into the stillness of the body of the cold, which seems to be ancient and permanent, as if no other season ever existed. Leo takes her arm. They walk home, warmth around them as they enter the house; they undress and get into bed with the cats snuggled close. Leo falls asleep almost immediately, but Serena is awake and begins to reflect on the past week and on the larger aspect of her work.

❋ ✿ ❋

Serena remembers the late Tuesday afternoon, glittery and wet; the rain over, Twelfth Street bright but strangely shadowless, as New York twilights sometimes are, just flushed rims of color on the western sky above the Hudson and the silver lightness of headlights and long stretched lines of bright bus windows on the avenue and, before Christmas, ornamental lights and twinkling decorations. Unsheathed branches press out from the front of small, brownstone gardens; an occasional rose clings to life, pale and wet and vibrant in the hovering shift of day into evening. Serena walks quickly towards the hospital on her way to visit Anton, who is ill—but this time, not yet, not very ill—with an as yet mysterious complication from HIV. Serena and Anton have worked together for a year, doing —what? A hybrid form of therapy and healing, of meditating and visioning and talking and listening and stillness that Serena developed and practiced and taught long before the slick popularity of the New Age emerged, bringing both gifts and the dangers of a smooth fundamentalist underbelly.

Serena knows her work is, of course, very old, some of it the oldest aspects of healing known. What could have preceded touch? Or sound? But when she began in 1969, it was unheard of, mostly forbidden except, perhaps, in some religious circles: tent revivals, themselves not mainstream, not part of the muscular ruling family of official religion. So she is a maverick and outlaw at the outset and then, in the engulfing swell of the New Age, again misperceived. Or, to her mind, falsely included. This concerns Serena in odd and complex ways that stream in and out of her awareness, sometimes sharp and troubling, but never enough to abandon what she does, what she explores with people, the realms they travel together. In Western culture, her work is non-traditional except in the most ancient concept of tradition. She understands that in many ways she will always be an outlaw.

She has worked with many people who were physically ill and visited most of the hospitals in Manhattan, seen her clients half-undressed in miserable hospital gowns, seen incisions and bleeding, drip bags of various fluids and sprays of tubes entering and leaving their bodies. She juggles the mixtures of her roles, being in a variety of situations, sometimes feeling skillful, sometimes clumsy, and is immune to the constant bells and voices in hospitals and often says, when training students (who request quiet! quiet!) that you need to be able to work in the subway.

They are intimate in a way that includes all this, Anton and Serena; she is familiar with the unfolding, intricate textures of his life, with details of his body as fine as the tiny pulse that beats beneath his left eye when he blinks. And for this year, now a year past his initial diagnosis, he has been mostly healthy, if sometimes very frightened. It is the time before the medications for HIV shift drastically, offering hope to the lucky ones for whom it works and who can afford it. Serena is thinking about this as she enters the hospital, about the disease and her relationship with Anton, which is especially close and tender, roomy enough to contain his rage and his sweetness. The hospital corridors both contrast strongly with the outdoors and are paradoxically similar to it: too hot, rather than raw and damp, lit in the floating opaque way that fluorescent bulbs produce, but also without shadows. The floors are tight and waxy with dirt beneath the surface and the ceaseless pager's voice, always a woman's, calls doctors to one unit or another. Christmas decorations insist that the season be noticed.

All her years of seeing and touching and talking, meditating and chanting and holding are alive inside Serena as she enters Anton's room. He is, in fact, neither prone nor attached to any tubes this time, but sitting at the focal point of a circle of friends, his black curls wild, his eyes wide and perhaps too bright, pupils and irises almost merged into a shiny darkness. Anton is the cherished only son of a Russian immigrant father from Odessa and a Mexican mother from California. His father is emotionally expressive and out-going, his mother a woman who cooks abundant meals and invites everyone she knows for dinner. Their home flowed with at least three languages at any given time and was often a stopping place for newly arrived immigrants from both countries. Thus, Anton is attuned to people and to both sorrows and celebration. In the hospital room, a sort of party is in progress. The friends have brought food and one, a musician, holds a saxophone that he is mouthing, soundlessly. Someone has brought a small bedside lamp with dangling crystal beads at the edge of its shade, through which glows peach colored light. A Merry Xmas garland is pinned to the wall above Anton's head.

Walking toward Anton, Serena notices blood on the floor, a round, wide shape, trailed by distinct drops. She starts toward the bathroom to get paper towels— Serena, the cleaner, the polisher—and realizes immediately that the blood is probably contaminated. No one at that time seems exactly sure how long the virus can live when exposed to air. She says, "Right back," and looks for an aide who, when found, shrugs and says, "It's not my room." No one else is about. She returns to the room, gathers some folded towels, drops them flat against the blood, makes another layer and says, "Watch your feet." Everyone's eyes meet briefly and they nod. Serena moves across the floor and stands close to Anton's bed.

"Baby," Anton is saying, "I'm going to party when I leave here. You better believe it." He tosses his head and grins. "My healer," he says, gesturing grandly toward Serena. "Come sit. Jesse, Bert, Al—Serena. All in the theatre. Like me. All bums." He points at Jesse, who is tall and slender and elegant as a greyhound in soft, tight pants and a sleek, fawn turtleneck. Serena knows that Jesse is one of Anton's lovers and it is likely that Jesse knows that she does.

"Baby, you are a bum," Anton says to Jesse and then laughs, less nicely. Serena can see his agitation, riding below—and not very far below—the laughter and tossing curls.

She kisses him hello. "Sit. Sit down," he says. "Have some food, Serena. Then you guys need to go. Serena and I are going to work together. Right? This isn't just a social call?" She nods.

"We are, yes, in a bit." The friends slowly gather their coats and bright scarves, wooly hats.

"Baby, leave that food," says Anton as he watches them. The assorted dishes seem to contain a combination of macrobiotic food (Serena can smell the seaweed and brown rice) and Danish and bagels from the local deli. "Baby, baby," he sighs toward Serena, "I hate it in here."

She takes off her old, black, down coat, veteran of many winters, and pulls a battered chair up to Anton's bed. She closes the curtain around them, and it rattles softly as it slides along the metal rod. As much privacy as there is to be gotten. Her hands are soft, large for her rather small body; she rests them gently on his belly and they begin to breathe slowly together.

As Serena breathes with Anton, she can sense her guardians around her, guiding her, protecting her. Sometimes they are distant, but now they are close, distinctly present. She welcomes them following the images that unfold about Anton's condition, emotionally and physically—perhaps she will be able to discern the movement of his spirit, his essence—and she listens to the inner sounding of his body; deep interior streams of sound—all kinds of sound, from the shivering fall of rain to the ancient booming of ocean depths and the hissing of fire—that describe to her the functioning of his physical self. The images might be like dream symbols: torn ribbons, overflowing goblets, a bird's bright wing, or moving colors. Although she has been working this way for many years and has complex ways to interpret what she perceives, it is always new, sometimes fragile and shaky, other times bold and clear. Sometimes eloquent. The whole experience is both familiar and surprising. Paradoxically, the comparative fragility or boldness are not themselves indicators of the accuracy of her interpretation or her perceptions. It is risky business, she thinks. Now, with Anton, she is aware of several things: blocked ducts, looking like small, silted channels, leading from his liver. Too much heat, scalding waves of it. A child screaming and screaming, beyond comfort. Serena does not speak yet, but releases the images and sounds, sliding into the purely pleasurable part, opening herself to streaming love, vast and impersonal, supremely intimate. It moves through her and merges with Anton as the dark falls silently beyond the windows and the hospital bells continue to ring and ring.

By the time Serena finishes, Anton is almost asleep, but he opens his eyes as she moves her hands away, regarding her sleepily.

"What?" he says.

"Liver, maybe. What do the doctors say?" The energy work is complete and Serena is commenting on what she was aware of while doing it.

"They say it's okay. I'm not yellow. What else?"

"When you get out, you need to scream some. It seems like pretty early screaming. Old brain. Infant screaming. When you're out; next time we work at my office."

"Baby, you don't have to be psychic to know that," he smiles. "Come on, Serena, am I going to die? Well, die soon?" A slight flirtatiousness skimming over his fear.

"I don't know that," she says, struggling with her desire to comfort him falsely which would serve them both badly. "But no dreams of falling from windows, or anything else," she says. Three times, before his friends have died, Anton has dreamed of their falling: from fire escapes, down elevator shafts, from rooftops.

"No dreams," he says.

"Ask again about your liver. I think it's the source of your physical pain."

"Okay. Okay, I will. Are you going?" She is moving to put on her coat.

"Mmm. I'll come tomorrow." She hugs him.

"Almost Christmas," he says. "Bummer." He slides down under the covers as Serena waves and leaves. Leaving the hospital, she tries to find a bathroom where she can wash her hands, but the only available one has no soap so, failing that, she tucks her hands in her pockets and heads for her apartment, only two blocks away.

Walking home, Serena thinks about the way her work moves her in different ways, unique patterns that depend, she imagines, on all the circumstances she perceives and many she does not: on the moon's phase—which she really may know on any given day—on deer running somewhere in a dark forest; on the position of seeds buried deep in the ground in winter, or pushing though the earth in spring. Food being cooked. Babies sleeping deeply nearby or on the other side of the world. Mysteries mixed with the seemingly ordinary features of life, the flesh on her hands, one tired ankle, the soft, ugly hospital gown of the person before her. At some point the particulars melt and there is a fine, sweet clarity. Or there isn't and she needs to be able to work anyway, to yield. Not to rely on strength, but to stay balanced in the moment. No force. There is no way to force the flow of healing. She simply opens what she thinks of as channels in her body, and the energies move through. In Anton's room that afternoon, Serena knew she was anxious enough to feel the gateways shut. A reaction to her personal fears for Anton, to the sharp bells and endless announcements (which, despite what she teaches, intrude on her, though she knows she shouldn't be bothered), and to her worry about the slippery blood under the towels on the floor. But her fears dissolved as she sat quietly, listening to her breath and his, and the gates slipped open, her hands warmed as her inner vision began to travel through his body, or some facsimile of it that was presented to her. The pleasure of love arrived. Ultimately, no matter that she had initially been anxious. She had looked down at the miracle of Anton's sweaty curls, and at his strong teeth with a sharp thin space between the ones in front. She had smiled and begun to chant softly, moving her hands to his forehead, her arms at an awkward angle. These thoughts comforted her as she walked home.

The day after her first visit to Anton, just two days before they all meet at the church for Christmas Eve services, she made her way back to the hospital, snow melting around her feet. When she reached Anton's room the bed was empty, stripped, and not yet re-made. She stared at it for a moment and then walked quickly to the nurses' station and waited for a while until the nurse on duty finished her phone call. It seemed personal, conducted in a low voice, spattered with giggles. She does not look at Serena as she speaks into the phone. Then, finally. Serena pulls her breath into an even flow.

"Anton Lark," she says. "His room is empty."

The nurse frowns. "Who is it again?"

"Anton Lark. He was here for a few days; he was here last night." She must be a new nurse on this unit. Most of the staff knew Anton and his music and improvised décor and his pools of guests flooding in at all hours. They are very relaxed about HIV patients and visiting hours. Serena feels her heart pounding under her forced calm breathing.

The nurse smiles, but not reassuringly. "I'll check," she says and riffles through computer printouts. "Oh, yes. Home. We discharged him. You must have just missed him."

"He's all right?" Serena knows this question is foolish. "Okay. Thanks." She goes to find a working phone in the hospital, no mean feat. Only Anton's machine responds. A short piece of music and then his lovely voice.

"The cats are here. I'm not. Message now, dear ones."

Serena headed down to the ladies' room she used the day before. She was puzzled and worried. And relieved that he was on his way home. The bathroom sported the same overflowing towel bin, untouched since the previous night. Faucet still broken. What was she thinking?

That night, in bed, Serena's long reflection on Anton and her work fades and she sleeps and dreams about Anton swimming in a warm aqua sea, enveloped by soothing waves, his dark wet curls floating in the water. He is smiling.

✳ ☸ ✳

Their time with Nick turns things upside down and around. "Serena," Nick says, "tell him not to leave, to stay with you. Who is he as you say that?" Snow leaps and flies outside the windows, but the office is warm, Nick's stocky body relaxed, light blue shirt sleeves rolled up.

"Oh, Nick, come on. Not my father. Again?"

"Who else?"

"Maybe my mother, although that would be more, 'Get away from me,' I think."

"Oh, not so easy when you are small and alone." Nick says. "Leo, are you keeping those women away? Making boundaries?"

"Yes, but they aren't very receptive. They push harder, in their gentle ways."

In the ongoing process, Serena connects with parts of her psyche that are like flowers beginning to grow, but some blossoms appear that are torn—and with other parts of her that seem empty until she sees that there is earth there too, neglected, but receptive, earth with seeds planted beneath that are alive, but dormant. As she stays with this and her tears come, the earth softens, the seeds begin to move and press upward. Going below the softening earth, she finds the sharp curve of something hard, imagines it as a chunk of obsidian, shining and dark. Her survivor self, the part that Ruby has given her.

Leo finds anger mixed with desperation to rest from caring—not so unlike Serena's struggles, but he is sturdier. His feelings boil and erupt with Nick; he does not enact them with Serena in their life together, yet their peaceful home rocks and shivers as their pain opens fully to admit more life. One afternoon, exploring the ache of loss with Nick, Leo experiences a pain in his chest, a contracting spasm. Nick, who is a doctor, listens to Leo's description and says, "No, that is not a heart attack," seeing Leo's frightened expression and Serena's terror. "No," he says again and massages Leo's mid-back, pressing into the muscles. "The ego," he says. "Right there, behind the heart center. What wants to come out of your heart?"

Leo stands up straight, hands on his face and yells. "Why did you leave me? Why? You broke my heart!" He is sobbing. Nick doesn't know this story, but Serena does. She wants to break in and tell it, but stays silent; it is not hers to tell. She has never heard Leo yell, except in joy, when they make love. This is a very different sound. She watches his tears and sees them filled with tiny seashell fragments and with glowing bits of rainbows. She sees shards of broken bones, old and smooth, and the lake of sorrow that exists outside of time, yet has inhabited Leo's measured days. His sobs slow as he sits down and starts to tell Nick about Katherine, his first love. Katherine, who died in a freak accident, who—maybe— was pregnant when she died. He will never know. Then the room is silent for a while and the crystals—amethyst and rose quartz, yellow citrine and the darkest green tourmaline—placed around the room stand sentry.

"So, you were left, too. Not only Serena was abandoned." Nick takes his glasses off and pinches the bridge of his nose, that gesture he often makes when he is listening for what he can hear beyond the words. "I think this pain has never completed. No, that is not the right word. It is still lively, yes? You are guilty?"

"I don't know yet," Leo says, "although it is clearly alive, isn't it?"

"Give it room to emerge, now that it has made its presence known."

Serena is both sad and relieved, since she never thought this grieving had completed, had not finished; it might never finish, but could come to a resting place. She thought it affected them both.

It is the end of the session and they gather their things to leave. Nick hugs them, strong and close.

"Don't go away so much," he says to Leo. "Not now." He is not of the might-you-consider? school of therapy.

"I haven't, but I can't always choose. It's my work."

"Change it. For now."

Once at home, they hold each other, sitting on the soft, blue couch, the torn mess and misery painful, but now open between them. Since all this work has started, there has been a lot of holding, hugging, patting, comforting. Well, comfort is certainly needed.

The winter's end is very cold and ice forms in the streets during one bitter week. It is black and treacherous. They drift away from each other again, but this time fight their way back quickly. Nick has taught them to open more deeply and they are now engaging aspects of themselves that are growing and healing. Wounds of old losses getting air and light and compassion, angers activated and described—mostly responsibly. One afternoon, Ingrid is at Leo and Serena's visiting them and a new kitten that they have adopted that very week of darkness and ice. They had found him wailing in their frozen garden. How did he get there? He didn't seem to have enough strength to climb the walls that separate the gardens of one house from another. Perhaps he went up a tree and jumped? "He is ours," they agree, when they find him, taking him indoors and wrapping him warmly, feeding him sips of liquid and small bits of food. They are afraid he has been traumatized and will be wary of people, but once warmed and fed, he is rowdy and adventurous. His marmalade coat fluffs. Ingrid is there to meet him and to supervise his installation into the family of resident cats. They all love cats and Ingrid is considered the specialist. The other cats, Teamster, who loves everyone, and the delicate Miss Charlotte, their princess, are inquisitive and surprisingly friendly and once the kitten has been to the vet and had flea treatments and shots, they mother him and all sleep together, often on Leo and Serena's bed, though when they are making love, the cats might leave, bored and polite. Serena and Leo know the kitten represents their own renewed hope, their wish to rescue and be rescued and, also, their devoted emotional work. They name the kitten Romeo; he has turned out to be an irrepressible flirt.

"That story did not end well," Leo points out when Serena suggests the name.

"No, but it has acquired a popular meaning."

❊ ⊕ ❊

Just as the spring begins, Leo is called for a job in Amsterdam that will take weeks. He knows Nick has advised him not to go away, but he needs to work. He feels miserable and defensive. "Are you all right with this?" he asks Serena on the windy evening that he tells her. The windows rattle and the wind seems to have a presence, even inside the warm house, which now seems vulnerable again.

"No, but I will have to manage. We've made a lot of positive changes and they'll hold for three weeks." She hopes this is so, but feels spiteful and punitive. She does not want to manage; she has always managed and she is tired of it. The youngest parts of her have emerged in their months of seeing Nick; she feels unstable, not enough of her adult energies are consistently available.

"Ours are luxurious problems," Serena says one night when they are watching the news. "I really believe there is only One of us, ultimately, and I hope that the tenderness and compassion we nourish is mixing in the soup of consciousness and benefitting others. There are no individuals, just the web of connection." Serena has understood this web since she was a child and Buddhism and years of metaphysical studies and meditation practice have strengthened it. "Even if I am angry and frightened right now. Not feeling much compassion." She is stroking Romeo's neck and he is purring loudly, blinking his eyes to show his further appreciation. "An outrageous flirt," says Serena. "You fit right into this family."

"What made you think about this?" asks Leo, though it isn't unusual for Serena to link her process to a larger meaning.

"The world's sorrow; my own small sorrows. Hoping I am not adding to the general anguish." She moves close to Leo and puts her hand on his wide brow, looks into his eyes, going deeply into their hazel color, with its tiny lightning flecks of shining brown.

"Oh, Serena, you make yourself responsible for too much; far more than could possibly be true. Can you stop for right now?" He hugs her. "Stop. Please."

"Yes, okay. I know. I'm stopping now." As if it were a process she could simply halt, one that would cease at her command.

The day after that, Leo packs to leave and Serena calls Nick, then makes a lunch date with Rose and Ingrid. In her present sensitive state, with so many young parts activated, she has no real concept of three weeks. Leo could be going to the moon. Even though spring has officially started, it has snowed again and the plows crunch through the streets. The day Leo leaves there is dark rain, all day. Serena says goodbye from home, hugging him as the cats, distressed with this looming change, circle around Leo and Serena. "The airport would be too hard," Serena said, when they discussed the best plan. "I would be all the way out there and need to get home . . . No." Serena has a presentiment that this trip will bring trouble, but as sometimes happens with intuition, it is not precise. It does not seem related to health or physical danger, so she does not talk about it. She is not sure it isn't her anxiety and nothing more. Her bones feel transparent, emptied.

"No," says Leo. "Not a good idea." About the airport.

Ingrid has offered her guest room for the first few nights or more and Rose has offered to stay at Serena's. "Just for company," she says.

"No, I'm fine in the house, it's the fears of separation that are so active—and regressed and scary," she says. Rueful, a little embarrassed.

The snow has melted, the rain stopped, the sun is noticeably warm on the day after Leo leaves. Serena sees her clients, does some chores, but by the evening her throat is scratchy and she feels weak. She goes to bed at eight, cats all with her, and drinks hot herbal tea. When she dreams, it is a double of the physical reality. She is in bed, Leo's side is empty, she is feeling sick and then she sees the shadow of a man who enters the room and sits on the side of the bed. She knows he is not a physical presence, but an energetic one, yet she can feel the bed move as he sits and she wakes. Even awake, it feels as though someone is sitting there, though now there is no shadow. She waits. She has had experiences like this before, so she is not alarmed, but wonders what it might portend, if anything. The cats are asleep, old Teamster snoring softly. The city night is full of familiar sounds; a police car goes by, siren wailing. The pressure on the bed releases and Serena realizes she has a fever—she aches so badly and is dry and hot. She has not had a fever in years, not been ill, not even a cold. She gets water, pulls Teamster up so he is next to her and goes into a deep, now dreamless sleep. When she wakes, it is a bright day and she is really sick. High fever, sore throat, aches. Rose calls to check in and says she will come with soup. "Good," Serena whispers. "Thanks." She does not mention the dream and as the days pass, still does not. But she remembers it vividly.

Serena is sick for ten days, just in bed, wrapped in her quilts, drinking soup and tea. She has had to cancel all her appointments, too ill to work at all. Ingrid comes and reads to her, since her head hurts so badly at the beginning that she can't read. "This is some production," Ingrid says, but not unkindly. "Who is it for?"

"That's the question. Leo is the obvious answer, but maybe multiple layers of meaning here—it's for me, too. Even for Nick."

"Daddy Nick," says Ingrid.

"Daddy Nick, yes. We should all be punished. Leo has been calling regularly, very guilt provoking for him, this illness. Good strategy, just as we get on our feet, here. The fever is down. Maybe I can move into the living room and lie on the couch." They go into the living room and Serena looks out at the garden. "This is a cold, reluctant spring," she says.

"It is, indeed. Only some daffodils starting. I'm going to make a real lunch, just something light. You lost weight."

"Oh excellent. The quick weight loss diet."

When Serena is better, but still a bit weak, she makes arrangements to have lunch with Ruby at MoMA. "Lord," says Ruby, "you lost weight," when they meet in the restaurant. She is wearing her old, dark raincoat, bundled around her small, strong body. The coat is heavily lined with something—maybe wool? No, something fuzzy, synthetic. And she wears a hat she has knitted, a kind of turban in brilliant apricot; it rests on her thick, black hair that has almost no gray, despite her age. She is carrying her green leather handbag with the torn handle. "Worn handle," she says, when Serena mentions it. "Better not to look as if you have too much, makes you less of a target." Serena does not argue. Ruby has never been robbed in her whole life in the city, so maybe she is right.

"I know about the weight. But it's not from fiddling with my food, I was sick." Serena is wearing a good, blue wool coat, her favorite cerise scarf and fashionable boots, with a handbag she has just polished, an expensive one that has lasted for years. One that Leo bought her as a present. The restaurant is crowded on this rainy afternoon, wet on the floor with heavy smells of food cooked a little too long, plus the strong aroma of coffee. It is mostly filled with women, talking, leaning into their conversations. Serena is thrilled to be out and well enough to go to the museum. She and Ruby eat companionably and then look at the permanent collection, saving the best for last. They enter the room where one of Monet's *Water Lilies* is hung and sit on the bench facing it. They are quiet, just looking. They have been looking at this painting together for years. Ruby sighs. She came here when Alexander was so ill. Came after he died, so long ago now. She still visits regularly.

"This is healing," she says to Serena. After almost half an hour, Ruby says she is leaving.

"Ok. I'll sit for a bit longer. Love you." She kisses her mother. When Ruby leaves, a man sits on the bench. He has a solid body and thick straight hair, much of it going silver, though his face is young, tan, his large eyes a deep blue, with strongly curved upper lids and long black lashes, his nose a bit wide, his ears large and sculptural, flat against his head. He has a wide mouth and, yes, a square jaw. It is an arrangement that appears harmonious when regarded together, though only his eyes are remarkable; he is wearing a black trench coat, well-made and much worn, and rubber boots with leather laces. Neither of them speaks until he smiles, turns to her and says, "Not much to say about them, is there? They are beyond speech." And then, laughing, "Do you come here often?"

Serena laughs, too. "Yes, why?"

"You seem very comfortable here; a familiar place for you."

"It is. I have been coming here for most of my life. And you?"

"Not been here recently. I've been in California for a year, but I always check in."

As he speaks, Serena imagines the water lilies loosening from the canvas, floating through the room and at the same time staying still, resting the way they were painted. The experience reminds her of the dream she had shortly after she met Leo, where flowers floated out of a dream into her room. She coughs. It is a serious cough.

"Are you okay?"

"Yes, a bug. I'm mostly over it."

"May I invite you for coffee? Or maybe tea?"

"You may. The question is, will I say yes?" She pauses. "Yes." And this pattern will describe aspects of their communication for the months to come. I am flirting, thinks Serena. No question.

"I'm Jake," he says, "Jake Fein," offering his large hand, smiling in a way that promises things he will never deliver.

"Serena. There's a coffee shop near Sixth."

"Yes? Still? Been there forever."

"Yes, true."

No one else has entered the room as they talked. They sat alone, swimming in beauty and the subtle ambiance of museum lighting. They leave the museum, out into the cold, persistent rain and walk toward Sixth Avenue. Once settled, Serena with tea and Jake with coffee, Jake asks if she would like something else? Serena eyes the muffins—terrible sweet muffins, gummy, full of sugar and fat. Generally, she would not even consider eating them.

"A toasted English?" Jake suggests.

"No, a blueberry muffin. Toasted."

"I'll have a toasted English," Jake tells the counterman.

This man feels very familiar, this Jake she has never met before. If she could verbalize it, what words would she use? She has a sudden, sharp pain in her heart, like being stuck with a sliver of steaming dry ice. Something dangerous here? A warning?

They talk about ordinary things and Serena feels the air spin between them, hears the conversation beneath the words. "What do you do?"

"I'm a scriptwriter; mostly comedy and sometimes I perform my own work. It's satire, not jokes."

No, he doesn't seem jokey, thinks Serena. Not at all. If he performs, might she have seen him, or heard about him? She watches him as she eats the muffin. Long torso, strong legs, graceful. Maybe a swimmer? (Which he is.) The muffin is excellent. Forbidden food, she thinks and smiles. Serena describes her work. They don't get as far as their childhoods, their pasts. "I need to go," Serena says. "I see a client later."

"Would you like to have lunch?"

"Ah. Lunch. I live with someone."

"Well, okay, but it is just lunch. Are you married?"

Serena sighs. "No."

"Should I ask why?"

"No. Or, you may ask, but will I tell you?" Or, do I even know? she thinks. "Okay, then. But it is just lunch." They exchange phone numbers. Jake walks her to the subway.

One lunch turns into three; tulips begin to emerge in Serena and Leo's garden. The days seem to struggle to lengthen in the continuing cold. Leo's time in Amsterdam is finished, but he must go to Florence. Very briefly. "I'm sorry, Serena. I know this is a bad time," he says, on a phone call full of static. Oh, you don't know how bad, she thinks. She is sad and when she cuts her finger chopping vegetables and looks at the streaming blood she realizes she is also very angry. Bloody angry. She watches the blood stream and pool into the sink before she cleans her finger and bandages it. I am giving him the finger? The damaged finger? Drawing my own blood?

Jake knows different and wonderful restaurants all over the city that Serena has never visited. In this way, he resembles Leo, who loves to investigate new restaurants and knows many. They go to a French one on Tenth Avenue, a diner on Clinton Street, a Cuban-Chinese place on Eighth Avenue where they eat octopus salad, this one a restaurant Serena has visited with Leo. Jake does not seem as interested in the food itself as in the place, its ambience and character. During and after the lunches, Serena thinks about Jake and what she is doing. She knows herself—she knows what she is doing. She is being flirtatious, seductive, feeding the part of her that needs a man's attention, his approval. Her desirability confirmed. This is not a mystery. But during all these years with Leo, she has not done this, not even been tempted and now, in the middle of their work with Nick, nourishing their love and pulling honesty from deep, secret places, she is making a dangerous choice. She remembers the seeping chill that had crept into her relationship with Leo. The chill that has warmed some, their aliveness returning. Now? What a betrayal. She is betraying herself and Leo and their relationship. Maybe Jake, too? But no, Serena thinks. Jake is the kind of man who could decide to go to Paris, take his passport, his toothbrush and his credit cards, go to the airport and get on the next available flight, without a word of warning. Am I forsaking our hard work for this? For the kind of man who could buy a car on a whim; the kind of man who could be infatuated with a woman for three weeks or three months and then just disappear. Be gone so fast you might imagine he had never been there. A mirage. Serena is partly right. Jake has disappeared from relationships, but he does not become infatuated and he has an old Mercedes sedan that he babies and plans to keep forever. He imagines traveling on a whim, but has never really done it. But the women who have been in his life might nod at Serena's thought about Jake as a mirage, a man whose charm masks a withdrawn nature and the capacity to vanish.

After the fourth lunch, which is at Jake's apartment, and after some sashaying around, they land on Jake's parrot green rug, Serena's small body stretched out against Jake's long torso and strong legs and they begin what had been inevitable for centuries. At least that long. At least that much thunder and hunger. Touching, they drop into a canyon of passion, hurtling downward through space. Or, as Serena later thinks, she fell, or perhaps flung herself over as Jake stood at the edge, the toes of one foot curled at the canyon's rim, the other foot lifted slightly, feeling the air stir as Serena tumbled through space.

When Leo returns, Serena says she wants to stop working with Nick, at least for the moment. She cannot face telling Nick. Or Leo. Certainly not Leo, at least not now, though part of her wants to tell him so that he can stop her. But she knows he won't. It would not be his way at all. She is deep in her lie. It wraps around her core and tears at her, distracting, insistent. Leo and Serena are affectionate with each other. If he knows about the man Serena dreamt of, the shadow man who is now all too real, it is not a conscious knowing. Serena's heart feels broken; there is a pain in her chest that grinds tightly and mixes with her terrible wild passion for Jake, which will go on for much longer than she imagines.

✳ ✿ ✳

Jake always says that he was born in Brooklyn which is true, but the implication was misleading, since his parents moved to Manhattan's Upper West Side two months after his birth and he grew up in a large apartment whose windows on one side craned west toward the river and the setting sun. An only child, Jake's birth followed a series of miscarriages and his mother, never to conceive again, gave up her life as an opera singer to mother him. Instead of performing, she coached voice students, their sounds protected by the apartment's heavy walls and buffered by deep carpets. Though never a star, she was nonetheless a diva to her students and to her husband, a lawyer whose compact, stocky body hovered around her small, bosomy, powdery one. Since they were not tall people, Jake's height was a mysterious surprise. He sprung large between them, unbalancing their circled harmony. At some point, Serena thinks, as she gets to know him, Jake will go into politics. And one day he does.

Jake believes certain things about himself and about other people. His beliefs are both mythic and, for a man whose mind is so quick, inflexible. He torments Serena with pronouncements about her motives and his insights into her psyche, which she feels are made on the spot because he is intrigued with them at the moment, and her protests only harden the quality of his certainty and make him laugh slightly in a way that makes her feel hopeless. The more he fixes her in his beliefs, the smaller and more remote she seems to herself, deprived of the fluid, smoky, moving shape of her identity, her mystery captured and squeezed. She watches this happen, tries to stop it—and fails again and again.

He has a way of describing situations and people and—especially upsetting to Serena—other women; he elaborates on their startling beauty, perfect breasts, amazing intelligence and creativity. It is this capacity to perceive life in archetypal sweeps that makes him a dramatic, engaging performer. Later a riveting politician. It seems innocent, an appreciative man extolling the virtues of things that intrigue him, but it has a sly quality that undermines the listener; it is not so exaggerated as to be readily obvious; rather it seems believable and, to Serena, curiously indelible. She imagines that she remembers his descriptions of women long after Jake has forgotten them and the women they belonged to. This one's beauty, that one's mind. Sometimes their wealth. Wealthy women like Jake.

Although he is surrounded by people when he performs and has scores of acquaintances, some of who appear at the most awkward moments on the few occasions that they are in public together, Jake requires a good deal of solitude. He has a surprising, deeply-rooted introversion. His skill as a performer seems disconnected from an intricate, internal remoteness.

She discovers that he is indeed a swimmer; even in the most miserable New York cold, he goes to the chlorine-saturated pool at the "Y" and swims laps and laps. No frills, just swimming straight ahead, down and back, for a long time. Once he and Serena went together to a local health spa. She thought it would be romantic, faintly erotic. The hot tub and swimming and being nearly undressed in public, something they had never done, having never gone to a beach. She wanted to experience their sexy relationship encased in steam and bubbles and the bite of hot water, then cold. But the reality of the spa was disappointing, like a food long anticipated with pleasure that turns out to be flat and wrong tasting. When they had undressed and met at the hot tub in their suits, Jake looked at Serena slowly and critically. For once quite pleased with her body, Serena tightened her stomach muscles, squinted slightly and said, "What?" Jake shook his head, shifted his gaze from her thighs—the part of her body she disliked the most—and simply said nothing.

Serena hopped into the tub to hide her legs and thought, He's really nasty, without exactly committing himself to that, either.

They bubbled and soaked for a while in the company of an older man with a fat, humped tummy and a drape-over hairstyle that was fast losing ground and starting to wave toward the ceiling. He hummed softly to himself and stared appreciatively at Serena's round breasts. It was during their time in the whirlpool that Jake mentioned that he was a lawyer.

"This reminds me of when I was in law school," he said. "I joined a health club to warm up, my room was so eternally cold; there was something wrong with the heat on my side of the building. I used to sit in the sauna and the whirlpool." He laughed. "They must have thought I was reptilian. Everyone else was sweating and I took twenty minutes even to feel warm."

Serena was back at the beginning of the paragraph. "When were you in law school?"

"After I was in college."

"I didn't know you were a lawyer. Are you? Did you finish?"

"Oh yes," Jake said. "And passed the bar the first time, but I never practiced. By that point performing had me. Law seems so out of character, doesn't it? I guess it was."

"Oh," she said, "perhaps not so out of character."

Then Serena swam for a bit in the vast pool and Jake swam and swam, looking at nothing, back and forth, over and over. Watching him swim, Serena felt high above her body in an atmosphere that was wet and thin, where things floated, but did not touch. The pool smell reminded her of eighth grade at Hunter and their miserable enforced swims. After the spa swim, they dressed and parted with a small kiss, standing on the street in the wind, headed toward their separate neighborhoods on different subways, Serena toward the Village and Jake to the Upper East Side.

✳ ☉ ✳

During the late spring, Serena talks to Ingrid and Rose and Sue Ann about Jake —after keeping it a complete secret, an almost unknown situation for Serena, who courts transparency, honesty. Spring had finally arrived and, after its hesitant beginning just as she met Jake, Serena feels the cold darkness of her secrets is unbearable. The women are in Central Park the first time Serena confides to them about Jake; she describes their relationship, tries to convey what he is like with her. They are sitting near a wildly blooming cherry tree, it's petals luminously pink in the sun. They all had paper cups of hot tea that mixed with the cardboard flavor of the cups. Ingrid is eating a huge corn muffin, passing pieces to Serena, who, as always, pretends she is not eating. Rose and Sue Ann are eating a bag of Sue Ann's homemade gorp. A large dog, a mix of many incompatible breeds, looks at the muffin with longing, his person on the next bench. Ingrid tilts her head toward the owner to ask permission and then gives the dog a hunk of muffin, having received a nod. "Should I tell him?" Serena says, when she has described the situation and the quality of her relationship with Jake. "I hate secrets." Sun rides in the breeze, in the newly warming air.

"Tell him?" Ingrid says, in her strong, clear voice "Why? So you can burden him with your guilt? No, don't tell him, work it out. It would be cruel, unless you think there is a serious threat. Do you think so?"

"But he knows, Ingrid. He knows something. Having an affair is a serious threat, just in itself."

"Might be, might not be. I'm sure he knows something. Has he asked?"

"No. And both of us are responsible for the relationship. He must have an unconscious part in this."

"Oh please. That's ridiculous and self-serving."

"Why are you with Jake?" Rose asks. "He isn't even nice. You've never liked mean men."

"I don't know why. There's a compelling sexual passion. But the feelings I have are sad, and torn. Or bleak. I don't know what the compulsion is, though. Maybe the fascination of trying to have him love me, when he won't. Or probably can't. But that isn't my pattern, either, until Jake. He isn't mean, exactly."

"Yes, he is," says Rose. "Exactly. Precisely. That's how you describe him. This isn't romance, it's punishment. You're punishing yourself and Leo. Maybe you can break it off, Serena. Tell Leo it happened and it's over."

"I can't break it off, that's the problem."

"Of course you can," says Ingrid. "You can't levitate. You *can* say goodbye, but you don't want to. For a woman who has done so much therapy and meditation and is truly insightful and verbal, your description about the nature of your attachment isn't convincing. What is this doing for you? He sounds like Ruby, withholding and vindictive. And maybe angry. Is he? Angry?"

"He's not obviously angry, he's more likely to withdraw and not communicate. He's not an essentially angry person. He doesn't raise his voice. And we don't fight. No, we do sometimes, and he is nasty, really. Mocking. But quietly."

"Why did you start seeing him?" Sue Ann asks.

"Because I was angry?" Serena sighs. "And no, I am not seeing Nick, in case anyone was going to ask." Nothing has been resolved.

They are all quiet. Serena remembers a recent dream: she was in an empty house, the floors old and swept clean, the open windows scarred. There is a single table in the room where she stands and on it, in a clear glass jug, a fat bouquet of zinnias Leo gave her years before, their colors brilliant red and orange, the deepest coral, creamy white. "Generous Leo," she says out loud in the dream.

The women stay for a while, petals from the cherry blossoms sprinkling them in the wind.

But Serena cannot bear the lies and then, one evening when she and Leo are taking a shower together, the water warm around them, enclosing them, she begins to talk about Jake. "I don't own you Serena," Leo says, when she's finished, wet with tears, with the water still pouring from the shower. "I want to stay with you, but I don't need to control you. And you will never leave me for Jake. I knew something was happening, and I trusted that you would tell me what when you were ready."

"Jesus, Leo. I don't have that kind of trust. I couldn't do that if the situation were reversed."

"No, you don't. You couldn't. And you *are* telling me, so you must be ready to face this."

"Is that all?" Serena asks. He is not going to be angry? Or sad? Or fight for her? She can hear Nick's voice. "You must fight for this. Fiiight. This is precious."

Leo turns the shower off and gets out, gets a towel. Gets Serena a towel and brushes off some water and then wraps her up, holding her close. Every move is precise. "What do you expect me to do? Issue an ultimatum? You don't respond well to ultimatums. This is something you need to take care of yourself. Even if I ask you to stop seeing Jake and you do, you will have done it for me—ostensibly. That doesn't work. It's your responsibility." Moonlight shines in the window, sizzles in a cold arc between them, shatters and falls to the floor. "Maybe having told me is the first step to making a change," Leo says.

They dry off and dress and sit on the bed. "I don't know why you would make such a treacherous choice, Serena; this is miserable. We'll have to see how it goes from here. I'm not leaving, you know that. And I do need to know what part I have played in it. He is silent for a moment, clearly in pain. Is this why you stopped wanting to see Nick?"

"Yes." She says. "Yes. It is the reason."

But in the moment, Leo does leave. He leaves the bedroom and shuts the door. Serena feels chilled, her bones icy, empty, her tears frozen. Finally, she gets under the quilt. She hears Leo playing the cello. Later, she hears the front door close and still later, he is in bed beside her, his arm resting on her back. It is late, the moon long gone from sight.

"Where did you go?" she asks.

"To walk. I had cup of tea. I'm just sitting with this, I can't really think much yet. I'm in shock, really. Have you slept?"

"No."

"Well, let's sleep, Serena." Eventually, they do.

In the morning, his side of the bed is empty and there is a note saying he has gone to work early. Serena weeps until she is breathless, with the cats hovering around her anxiously. Romeo wails.

When Leo returns, he begins making dinner and Serena comes into the kitchen to start cutting vegetables. "Please," she says. Her eyes are still swollen; she hasn't eaten at all, and is weak with exhausted sadness. She feels as if parts of her are separating, are torn, lost. Leo, determination in every part of his tall body, his face grim, prepares a salad.

"Please, what?"

"Please can we talk? We always talk."

"Well, this isn't always and we haven't ever dealt with this before. I don't want to talk. I want to live a life with you; I want to protect what we've created. But I don't want to spend our life talking about this, about your affair and your feelings and my feelings, on and on. I don't see the point."

"How can we not talk? Pretend? I thought you were interested in what part you played?"

"I am not planning to pretend anything and obviously we are capable of not talking, since you haven't. I don't know why you didn't talk to me when you started to be sexually interested in another man. We should have talked then. I am interested in my part and I don't know if I want to talk about that, either. You said this was why you didn't want to see Nick?"

"We should have. I should have. Yes, again, it is why I didn't want to see Nick. I know; that was when we needed to." Serena feels ashamed, a ragged pull in her belly, and she feels sad, and defiant.

"Well, you can bear to have a lover, but not to tell Nick? Or me, until now? I'm going to see Nick alone."

"Okay. Maybe I will, too." But she won't, she knows it as she speaks. She starts to shiver.

"We will do our best," Leo says. "And you will never leave me for Jake. I know that you won't." This statement, assured, yet puzzling, seems true to Serena.

Serena and Leo do manage to live their life, scraped and injured, often loving, but sometimes bitter with each other, their closeness torn, a body ruptured and struggling. They reach for each other through rolling pain that subsides and rises again.

When summer comes they go to France and then Italy. One night in Paris, in the small, lovely guest bedroom of their friends, all cream and different shades of blue, always fresh flowers on the bureau, Serena wakes and sees Leo crying in his sleep; his face peaceful, his wide cheekbones and his cheeks wet as the tears slide through his lashes, course down his face, but he does not wake or make a sound. She touches his chest softly, the strong planes, smooth skin. The lake of tears again, she thinks, overflowing. In the morning, they walk along the Seine and sit on the embankment. Thin sun stings the water, which looks cold, full of secrets. They are talking about a church Leo is working on and then they are talking about babies, with nothing in between and no seeming connection between the two. "What if we had a baby?" Leo asks. "Is this affair to avoid the possibility, push it further away?"

"No, no. It isn't, Leo. It isn't related to babies. But maybe something I haven't thought of? The relationship between . . . This sounds like Nick. Is it?"

"No, it's Leo."

The leaves on the plane trees crackle in the cool wind. Boats wind down the Seine. "I need to think about it; it is possible."

"Do you miss him?" This is the most Leo has ever asked.

"No," Serena says. "I don't." Before she left for France for the summer, she called Jake to say goodbye and she was shaky, which he picked up immediately.

"You sound a little off, Serena." And then he laughed, as if he were having a light conversation with a friend.

"I am going to miss you," Serena said, feeling as if her bones were cracking open, fragmenting as she spoke.

"Oh, I never miss people," Jake said. And that was the end of the conversation. Their summer goodbye. Jake so flat and matter of fact. And she does not miss him, a great surprise and a pleasant one.

At the end of August, when they return to the city, Serena's period is late, but it must have been the traveling. Every month, she worries about being pregnant, more intensely since she has been with Jake. One boiling afternoon, as she is gardening in the back of the house, she starts to cramp and then bleed.

Months pass and she is still with Jake, seeing him only during her breaks in the day, or when Leo is away.

✳ ❂ ✳

When Serena and Jake met, he lived in an apartment on Mulberry Street. But he has moved and now Jake lives in a small apartment on upper Park Avenue, just at Ninety-third Street, below the break where the commuter trains appear, sliding out of the tunnel's mouth at Ninety-seventh. It is an odd place for him to be and is, in fact, an apartment he inherited from his grandmother, Molly. When Saul, Molly's husband of forty-five years died, Jake's father wanted his mother to move from Brooklyn, her longtime home, from the big house where she had raised her children, with its back garden full of energetic thorny roses, abundant iris and two large lilac bushes. "Only to Park Avenue," Molly said, mostly as a joke. She had no intention of leaving the house, full of the sweetness, still, of her husband Saul's pipe tobacco, years of furniture polish and her extensive collection of blue and white china, this an idea she had gotten from a fancy decorating magazine in the early 50s and pursued with her usual dogged tenacity and enthusiasm. Nor was she interested in leaving the garden, which she treasured. "Where my parents came from," she told Jake when he was small, his nose buried in a heavy cone of lilacs, "Jews did not have flower gardens, believe me."

Jake's father, not to be deterred in his plan to have his mother close by in the city where he could keep an eye on her, bought this oddly shaped apartment for a good price. It faced onto Ninety-third Street, but the building was long on that side, so the windows looked over some of the small brownstones, letting in the sun through a southern exposure; it had a compact living room, an enormous bedroom, an adequate kitchen and two baths in the foyer outside the bedroom. It also had a spacious cedar closet, a dumbwaiter sealed shut and day and night doormen who had been there since the flood. Molly moved in, complaining, and decorated the living room, the kitchen and the bedroom with her beloved china. Jake inherited the apartment and left everything in place, including the china, just adding his books, clothes, computer and cats. The cats, Normal and Juniper, are stunned by the size of the apartment after the small rooms on Mulberry Street, but they adjust quickly, roaming around the place in a proprietary way. Blue and white plates wink down at Jake as he develops his material in the huge bedroom, which he also uses as an office, surrounding him with blind porcelain eyes when he makes love, presiding over his life and reminding him of Molly and her kind, determined nature. When Serena describes Ruby, he is in some ways reminded of his grandmother, her valiant nature, though Molly was unfailingly kind. Visiting the apartment for the first time, not long after Molly's death, Serena is as stunned as the cats.

"Are you going to leave it this way?" She is curious, interested in Jake's answer, but not judgmental.

"I don't know. No. I don't know, Serena." He looks helpless. "No, I can't leave it this way. It's like living with my grandmother." But he does, for quite a long time. And it is clean, much cleaner than his Mulberry Street place (where they first ate lunch and made love) ever was. He has also inherited his grandmother's housekeeper, Sophie.

"Keep her," says his mother. "Those are antiques. You'll ruin them." So, he does, out of courtesy toward his grandmother and because he is tired of cleaning and girlfriends don't do that sort of thing anymore. Like the cats, Serena considers the apartment an improvement.

Serena visits this apartment one afternoon right after an aunt's funeral—and the visit is a surprise to them both. Leah, her last remaining aunt on her father's side—that smart, critical, loyal family—dies in the middle of a ravishing October flooded with light and the dazzle of leaves tipped with scarlet so bright that they seem wet. On Serena's last visit to her aunt, in a hospital in Westchester, they face each other in a spacious single room and Leah, breathing with difficulty, raises herself to look at Serena's multi-colored scarf, liquid forms on heavy silk and says, "Mmm. Very becoming. But I'm angry with you." Her face is disapproving, her tone dismissive. She lies back against the pillows. This beloved aunt, who had fed Serena dry bakery cookies with dense chocolate drop centers while Serena watched her make dinner, who had wheeled Serena's stroller down Broadway, pulling chunks of fresh rye bread from a bag when Serena was hungry, delivering it lovingly into the child's small hand. "No need to be hungry," she would say, "but you have to eat dinner, too." The only aunt married to a man who was observant, a Jewish scholar; the aunt who provided Seders, year after year, where Serena, the youngest, asked the four questions. (In English, but still.) The only one in the family curious about Serena's work, about intuition, which Leah called ESP. "I believe it," she would say. "I know when your mother is calling me before I pick up the phone. You know your grandmother had a little of that." Inclining her head. "The ESP stuff. Maybe more than a little." Now she is angry with Serena, here at the end of her long life, a life with sad and curious hardships.

"Why are you angry?" asks Serena. "What are you angry about?" Anxious to set it right with the time they would have melting quickly, understanding how much can turn on a word, feeling that the fate of their love could tip, slide one way or another in these moments. But her aunt is tired and says no more and then, only a day later, her long-steadfast heart fails completely and she is gone, following the unbroken family line of failed hearts. As is the Jewish custom, the funeral is immediate, partaking of the gleaming weather, with its bright sky and gorgeous colors. At the cemetery, Serena stands surrounded by members of this large family, living and dead; graves of uncles and aunts, grandparents and great-grandparents and of course, her father's grave. She picks up a warm stone from the ground and leaves it on her father's grave, then one on each of the other graves. A marker of the visit. Stone of remembrance. This is a family without public tears, Serena has never seen any of them cry, but she breaks the code for just a moment and tears flicker down her cheeks and then are gone into the blue air.

Serena skipped the gathering at a cousin's house on Long Island and headed back into the city on the train, taking whichever one said Manhattan; lost in Queens and eager to get out, not particular about where it landed her. Once across the bridge she decides on an impulse to ride farther uptown, change trains and visit Jake. She does not call, but she knows he will be there, at home, working.

He is surprised, but not displeased when the doorman announces Serena's presence on the all but useless intercom. A blur of static and Patrick's voice saying only, "Your friend's here." But Jake knows who it is. Serena steps wordlessly into the apartment and Jake reaches for her, seeing that she is in trouble of some kind and they lean into each other, Serena starting to cry and then wail, pressing against Jake's shoulder. Holding on to him, she sees the scene at the cemetery, the family together under the round shine delivered by the October sky; she sees their careful faces, serious and contained—always contained. She remembers focusing on her cousin Lillian's shoes to stop her own tears; expensive black suede shoes, dusty from the walk to the gravesite, Lil's broad ankles pressed against her stockings, the shoes looking tight as her cousin stood still in the sun. All the cousins are handsomely dressed, as if this attentiveness might fend off death, Serena thinks. Rough wool, sweet silk and gold, each item with a story attached, Serena is sure. Urban hunting for precious prey. And she knows it is not that simple.

Uncomfortable as he is with her tears, Jake continues to hold her. He wonders briefly where Leo is (isn't this his job?) and almost asks, but thinks the better of it. Serena is aware that she has never been invited to fall into Jake's arms this way before and she doesn't move away, just lets her weight rest against him. Why has she come here? She wonders the same thing herself; true, no one was at home, but she could have called Leo at work and asked him to come to her if he didn't offer. Would he have offered? No, probably not. He had not wanted to attend the funeral. But he would have come at her request, not begrudged her his presence. As her wailing stops, Jake holds Serena away from him and looks at her carefully.

"Where were you? I've never seen you dressed like this."

Like the rest of her family, she is carefully arranged: flared black wool skirt, pale silk blouse, open at the throat, delicate pearl earrings and a single ring with a large, creamy, opaque stone, a ring she has had for years and treasures. A black jacket with velvet trim and yes, black suede pumps, bought in Venice on a trip she took with Leo. Serena feels that in many ways she has removed herself from what she calls the official world—the consensus trance about what is valued. But not in this way, of hiding herself with her choice of clothes—of "passing" she thinks sadly. She looks down at her uniform. It is not the clothes themselves, but her understanding that she is still hostage to her childhood yearning to appear acceptable, this insistent shadow, and she wonders what other sacrifices she accepts, what small lies she tells, to placate the need. It makes her suspicious of other more hidden choices that she might be making.

She brings herself back to Jake. "What does it look like?"

"A funeral is what it looks like, not to mention your tears."

"A funeral is what it was. I need to get out of these clothes. Do you mind?"

"Do I mind if you undress? No, Serena. I don't mind."

"Well, only to my slip, just that far." She starts to get out of her skirt on the way to the living room, then sits on the soft couch, another remnant of Molly's life, and sinks into one corner.

"Do you want something?" says Jake. "Wine? Tea?"

"Tea would be good," she says. One of the rituals that exist in this constrained relationship lived almost exclusively within four walls and frequently horizontally. Serena's tea.

Jake disappears, reappearing with two mugs of tea. He hands her one. "Yours has honey in it. Now tell me what happened."

"My aunt Leah died. She was the last of my father's siblings; I loved her and she was the only one who really accepted Ruby. I saw her just before she died and she was angry with me. I don't know why. No one at the funeral cried, except for me, for about ten seconds. Then I held my breath and looked at my cousin Lil's shoes to stop the tears." Serena stands and slips off her pantyhose, folding them carelessly and then stretching her feet, which are broad and flexible. "It makes me feel desperate that no one ever cries."

"Why?"

She knows this kind of talk doesn't interest Jake very much. She feels full of information about herself and simultaneously blank, or maybe flooded. "Do you want to know?"

"Do you want to tell me?"

Serena is quiet for a moment. "What do you think happens when you die?"

"Is that what you want to talk about?"

"Yes. Yes, I do." She looks at a bowl of fruit resting on the coffee table and then up at Jake. He follows her eyes.

"My mother visited."

"Oh."

He hands her a ripe russet pear and she bites into it, juice running as soon as the skin breaks. So, with her chin wet with pear juice, Serena tries to talk about her understanding of death, about the possibilities she has learned and the related experiences she has perceived directly, mopping the juice up as she continues to eat.

"Well, your consciousness continues when your physical body dies," she begins.

"Your physical body? Is there some other body I don't know about?" Jake says.

"Yes, there is; it's a luminous body that carries the—uh—print of your energy. Your life experiences, your beliefs, your essence." She thinks of the Tibetan Buddhist understanding that part of life includes a preparation for a good death, meaning a conscious one, without clinging or aversion, and of the monks who are trained to escort the dying into the next realm and then return. Not easy to accomplish, a conscious death in a culture where drugs are so readily employed.

"Of what is the consciousness aware?"

"Well," Serena says, "of the life just lived, perhaps not immediately, but after a while; of the presence of other beings who have died . . ."

"You mean like a reunion?" Jake is asking seriously, but he knows the question is funny.

"Well, sort of. I'm sure you've read about near-death experiences and people who move toward a light and are sometimes greeted by people they have loved."

"What happens if you get the wrong greeting committee and are greeted by people you have not loved?"

"Do you have anyone particular in mind?" asks Serena, finishing the pear and looking for somewhere to put the core. She has a vivid memory that floats in brilliant colors in her mind of dreaming of a friend before she knew he had passed, seeing him vibrant and young, smiling at her as they embraced in what looked like a green and misty park and his assurances that he was well, had moved into a new world and wanted her to tell his friends that he was celebrating at the release from a body that was desperately ill, wasted and in pain. And she remembers sitting with a dying woman with whom she had worked; the woman, Claudia, was in a coma; Serena saw her leave her body and appear at the other side of the ugly hospital room, smiling, then nodding once at the figure on the bed, making a gesture with her hand that said, I'm finished. She also remembers being afraid because she was alone with Claudia and if she died when they were together, someone might think Serena had disconnected her from her life-support system. Had hastened her death.

Jake looks interested, even curious; Serena wonders if this will go into his material sometime soon. She decides not to pursue it further, mostly because she is too sad and tired to be articulate and she is unwilling at this moment to feel foolish. Coward's choice, she thinks.

Jake rescues her, perhaps inadvertently. "Is this why you're crying? Because you and your family differ so widely in your beliefs?" He feels Serena is easily capable of crying about this.

"No, no. Because they never cry. No, not that either. Because I never feel they let anyone close to their heart; well, because they never let me close, to be more accurate." She smoothes her slip, a plain black one, and rests her hand against her mouth. Jake moves close to her on the couch and holds her. They are silent as the afternoon darkens and dusk falls on the banks of chrysanthemums planted in rectangles on Park Avenue. The shadows in the room are reddish, tinged with a sliver of light from the street. Sometimes they kiss slowly. As the room continues to dim and lights come on outside, Jake looks at his watch.

"What?" asks Serena, noticing both the movement and catching his air of sudden discomfort.

"I need to move, Serena. I have to shower and change." He hopes for a moment that she will not ask why and knows that with Serena this is so unlikely as to be impossible.

"Ah," she says and then asks why, even though she guesses what the answer will be.

"I have a date," Jake says precisely. "I didn't know you would be here," he says, slightly defensive, which is odd for Jake. "I have a dinner date." He wants to say, Just dinner, but why should he need to placate Serena and lie into the bargain?

Serena smiles in the dimness. She reaches for the lamp and turns it on. "You don't have dinner dates," she says. "And I shouldn't be here." She begins to dress, upset with herself that she is so disappointed. She waits for him to find a way to remind her that she is committed to someone else, but he doesn't. She doesn't ask further about his date. She dresses quickly and carefully and they hug briefly. Jake doesn't ask when they will meet next. When she is gone, he sits in the dark until he knows he will be late if he doesn't start showering. He has a date and they are having dinner, but it is not really a dinner date.

When Serena gets to the street, it is much colder than she imagined given the warmth of the day.

Sometimes, particularly after a time like this of unexpected closeness, however imperfect, Jake imagines putting Serena in his old car and simply driving away with her. He thinks of her packing some clothes, her herbs, some books and the cats and leaving with him. He is imagining kidnapping her, he thinks, when this fantasy surfaces. He has known Serena for months and they have never been alone for long. Ordinarily Jake does not require, or want, extended periods alone with women. He has lived with only one woman, an archeologist with a staggering IQ, a long torso, flat breasts and a lush bottom. He doesn't exactly equate these characteristics, but he remembers them simultaneously. They were together for a year, during which time she traveled extensively. Though he has known many women, some of whom he remembers only vaguely, this is the first time he has had this kind of fantasy. Having it both soothes him and alarms him; he does not ever mention it to Serena, or to anyone. He thinks about the way she fascinates him and frightens him; her extraordinary abandon and her sharp controlling will, her softness mingled with a kind of relentless searching that makes him want to hide. He does hide; he retreats, withdraws. How could he ever contemplate stealing her away? Being with her and no one else?

Occasionally he fantasizes that they will marry. A real wedding with a rabbi intoning in Hebrew, a tumbling architecture of sound, the old words surrounding them, protecting them. He is horrified by this thought; he has rarely been to synagogue since his bar mitzvah and Serena, though Jewish, has had no religious training at all. And he has no desire to marry, ever. Strange concepts, for this large man whose solidity belies his elusive nature.

Serena will say that Jake always longs for the woman he lost and is never completely present with the one in front of him. One day, she wonders, will she be the lost love and thus finally capture his attention?

Working at his computer before he goes to meet Serena one night, creating new material from ideas that have been revolving in his thoughts for days, Jake considers—for the ten thousandth time—what makes people laugh and how to move them into that vulnerable place where sound emerges spontaneously and bellies and shoulders shake, when people recognize some particular truth. It might be something hidden, suddenly, plainly revealed, or sometimes something utterly known and familiar mirrored back in a manner that renders its deeper meaning inescapable. In some way, Jake wants the audience not to be able to escape his meaning. He says things that make his audiences laugh, but he is not a comedian; he does not tell jokes, but deals in what he considers to be social issues: in paradoxes, common lies, cruelty laid bare. Some of his words emerge on the whirling force of his intention, so that the audience is spun in a wind tunnel, left breathless until the words stop for a moment and their laughter catches up with them. Other times he speaks slowly, reflectively, drawing the listeners closer and closer until the borders of their attention press against the stage and then they collapse into laughter as the implication emerges. Jake's performance is not unlike jazz, which he loves and about which he knows a great deal. And of course, the play of his words is like sex, about which he is intentional. Perhaps he is defter in this way than he is sexually, with a woman? For him, the relationship with an audience is an ardent one, whose ending is assured, though it is not without demands, he thinks wryly. Audiences can be very demanding. Demanding and potentially fickle. Socializing with him, people may seem wary, perhaps wondering if he will use them as material, which he does, but not blatantly, he imagines. Jake is mistaken about this. Serena says she has recognized individuals from his act, famous people, since she doesn't know his friends. He is shrewd about people's foibles, their vanities. He is merciless about politicians, so it is ironic when he becomes one. Ironic, but not unexpected, thinks Serena when he moves toward politics, years later.

✳ ✪ ✳

It is winter again. They have been lovers for most of a year and Jake is preparing in the chilly dark for an evening with Serena. Jake washes everywhere and puts lotion on his hands and then, as an afterthought, on his feet. He always has the feeling that she wants him to be completely scrubbed, though Serena has said that she loves the way his sweat smells. And making love, Serena might go anywhere: between his toes, under his arms and anywhere else. Jake, when he is busy with his work, embraced by waves of ideas, lost in them, can forget to change his underwear. Well, not forget, just not remember. But in spite of the dust that accumulates in his apartment and the occasional lapse, Jake is quite fastidious. He irons his own clothes.

By the time Jake rings Serena's bell, she has dressed in dark wool slacks and an old, soft, red blouse and silver hoop earrings. Underneath it all, fragile, white lace underwear, an indulgence that embarrasses her, but she wears it anyway, the lace very white against her skin. She slips into black boots and adds a warm sweater for under her coat, seeing that it has indeed started to snow. Downstairs, Jake is waiting at the curb, sitting in his large Mercedes, which smells inside like leather polish. It is a vehicle so like Jake and his clever, plain, expensive clothes. Serena slides in beside him. A half-empty coffee cup sits between Jake's legs, adding the smell of coffee to the leather polish.

"We're going to buy you a present," Jake says.

"But it's late."

"No, no. The stores are open late this close to Christmas."

"What kind of present?" As far as Serena can remember, Jake has rarely bought her dinner, let alone a gift.

"A surprise present." He starts to head uptown, swinging easily through the streets.

"Where?"

"Fifty-fifth and Fifth."

"What's there?"

"You'll see, Serena. Trust me."

They both laugh a little. Uncomfortable and close as they bump into something Jake says when they make love and he has no condom, which he often does not. (So, Serena uses her diaphragm, which tends to give her cystitis if she isn't careful.) Trust is a raw issue between them, for this and other reasons. It is rarely discussed directly, but present and for Serena, ominous. She does not really trust Jake. Not really at all. Once, on a summery evening full of long light and streaky, peach-tinted shadows, they tried tying each other up, securing wrists to Jake's bedposts with silk scarves, taking turns. Jake laughed and ordered Serena around when he was tied up, enjoying his enforced passivity, but Serena faked it until she got untied and then said she was frightened. She could feel fear pooling in her eyes and in the back of her skull. She was too frightened to say anything until she was free.

"Oh babes," Jake said, very tenderly. "I thought it would be fun, I didn't mean to scare you. What did scare you?"

"I don't know, Jake. It just did. It wasn't sexy or fun or funny."

"Why didn't you say?"

"I don't know; I don't know why." And she didn't understand it, exactly. It made her want to scream. Or weep. She remembers this incident now, as they pull up in front of Fortunoff's. She hasn't thought about it in a long time.

Miraculously, they find a semi-legal parking place.

"Here? Hmm?" Jake takes her hand and they move quickly through the blurry cold. He leads her into the fluorescent swim of the huge store.

Lots of fluorescent light, thinks Serena, in the huge bluish brightness. Cutlery is laid out in precise rows, extravagant displays of knives and scissors, shiny and sharp. Large implements that might be poultry shears. He's buying me a knife? No, this is not possible, even for Jake and his odd humor. But they come, toward the back of the store, to large jewelry counters displaying racks of hanging pearls, rows of earrings laid out on black velvet. Mass produced, but sparkling and pretty.

"You're buying me jewels?"

"Yeah. Yes. Take a look. What do you like?"

Serena is puzzled. She feels both greedy and constrained, her belly tight, uncertain about how to respond, often a problem for her with Jake. She wants so much to please him and never understands exactly how. It enrages her that she cares in this way and that it controls and distorts her behavior. She knows the need is attached to her lost (and therefore permanently displeased?) father and to thousands of years of inherited poison delivered directly into women's bodies, now lodged in her tissues and singing in her brain. She is embarrassed for herself.

"What's the—uh—price range you'd like to consider?"

"I don't know; a hundred. Like that," he says.

They stop in front of a case of earrings; small, semi-precious stones each resting above a tiny diamond. Row on row. Serena feels paralyzed. She looks at them unseeingly and then pulls her gaze into focus. Shoppers swarm around them. Some part of her is angry and thinking, This stuff is pretty trash. She feels miserable with her mean thoughts. She feels like her mother, so scornful of gifts, so accusatory toward the giver. She focuses on the amethyst collection, her birthstone. Amethysts, culled from the earth, untouched for thousands of years. Some of them (all?) hidden in geodes. She imagines them inside a rumpled elephant hide of solid rock, locked in the earth under rain and heat, buried under the moon and splashy starlight, then routed, touched, cut. Stones travelling to factories, to jewelers, arriving in cartons to be opened and displayed this Christmas season among waves of other commodities, meeting Serena's eyes. Leaking into her possession.

Jake is smiling happily, his heavy hair damp and slightly flattened from the hat he's been wearing.

"Those," Serena says, pointing to the amethysts. Small purple rectangles above the diamond. She tries them on, removing the silver hoops. Her face looks pinched and slightly blue under the vengeful lighting. "They're lovely." She watches Jake's smiling face.

"You don't want to look around?"

"Unh unh."

"You buy the way you order a meal; one glance and you know what you want."

"That's right, I do. These are lovely, Jake," she says again, as he pays for them. "Thank you." They leave the store and go back to the car, now partially covered with snow and amazingly still there—with no ticket. "Is there an occasion?"

He kisses her softly. "You're the occasion." They slam the car doors and slide carefully away from the curb.

They are heading toward the Lincoln Tunnel, snow spinning around them and then they enter the tunnel, echoing sounds slapping against the dirty tiles.

"Where are we going, Jake?"

"That's a surprise, too. I told you, my apartment reeks of paint and you're allergic to it. And to the chaos." When Jake is in a creative phase his apartment fills with piles of mail, mysterious folders, mountains of laundry, most of it clean. His cats roam around the mess, shedding blissfully on everything. The idea of brushing them is, to Jake, as far away as the moon. It is true, Serena hates mess.

"Well, okay, but who lives in New Jersey?"

"You say it as if it were Siberia."

"Isn't it?" Serena really has no idea where they are. The signs are clear, even through the falling snow, but beyond Fort Lee, up across the George Washington Bridge, across the river from where one of her oldest friends grew up and where they would bike, stopping for sodas in what was then a small town, Serena is without any thoughts at all about New Jersey's geography. She is more familiar with some parts of Paris.

"A mystery journey." Jake laughs and touches Serena's thigh lightly. After about forty minutes, he pulls off the highway onto a smaller road that seems fairly deserted. Then he steers onto the shoulder and stops beneath some trees, bare branches weighted with new snow. Through them, the darkness is snow-speckled and without stars. He turns to Serena and begins to kiss her very slowly, putting his hands under her coat, on her breasts and then sliding one hand against her belly, slipping beneath the waistband of her slacks, touching her skin. His hands are warm from the heat in the car, but Jake's hands are almost always warm.

"This isn't where we're going," she says, pulling away from him, feeling her own heat but also a surge of hopelessness. She is not going to have sex at some roadside in the middle of God-knows-where in New Jersey in the middle of a snowstorm. No.

Jake laughs. "This is the warm-up," he says, pointing to the snow. "Put your hand on me. Touch me."

Serena does, torn between her own rising sexual feelings and the impossibility of the situation. Tidy, passionate Serena.

"Jake, please."

"Yeah," he says. "Please. Please," his voice is teasing. He hugs her and then starts the car again. They come to a small house, no more than a cabin, really, and they pull in. Snow covers everything, drifts in waves, floats on the roof. A few sparse lights strike the dark, blurry circles illuminating little. Jake goes up the path through the snow. Comes back to the car and opens Serena's door, lifts her down to the white path and produces a key from his pocket. He opens the door to the cabin and then closes it when they enter. Inside the cabin, it is completely dark. The window shades are drawn, so not even the meager light from outside shines in. Without any hesitation, Jake goes to what must be a table near the door, finds a candle and lights it. A glow flutters and reveals the room, wreathed in shadow and wavering light. They take their boots off, leaving them near the door.

"Where are we?"

"A friend's."

"What friend lives here?" Serena is completely puzzled. (Here? Why here? Why are they here together?)

"A performer friend who travels. Shh, Serena." He leads her to a bedroom, quickly finding another candle to light. Serena, who is nervous about fires, has checked to see that the candles are stable, which they are, sitting in heavy glass jars. Jake begins to undress her, standing at the edge of a large bed piled with quilts. Somewhere in the cabin a heater hums. "Slowly," he says. "Slowly, Serena." He takes off her coat and folds it, then her bright sweater, her shirt and slacks, so she stands in her lovely underwear, which is mostly invisible in this dark. The room is quite warm, but she has goose bumps and her nipples push against her bra. Jake takes one full breast out and starts to suck. Then he stops.

"I'll undress you," she says. And does. They stand still for a moment.

"And you," he says. She unhooks her bra and steps out of her underpants. Then they are in the bed upon the soft quilts and Jake blows out the candle.

"Feel me," he says. "Lie back." He sucks on her for a long time, stopping intermittently. "Don't come yet."

Serena is lost in blackness, in seamless dark. Making love, she feels things at the border of memory: lost rapture, abandoned knowledge. Things she needs and has forgotten; things that are necessary, their loss dangerous. Once when they were making love, she felt that they were being born out of the universe, plummeting through eons, lit by passing planets. When she told Jake what she had seen, what she had whispered to him, cried to him, he laughed and said, "Oh, yeah?"

Should have been a clue, she thinks, much later.

Now his passion is trained on her, but is it really connected? Or just his experience of his own energy, moving in the same space that she occupies? No, surely it is more than that? She tries to connect to him, to feel his heart, to sense his eyes, even in the dark. But his energy moves outward, not permitting the waves to flow back into him and although she cries out, she feels turned inward, without a voice.

"Are you wearing it?" He presses his finger inside her, against the edge of her diaphragm.

"I am."

Jake slides into her, then pushes hard and stops. "I'm going to fuck you, I'm going to fuck you." Jake likes words, particularly these words when they have sex. Serena has known other men who liked them, but not Leo, who says he loves her, who says she is precious to him. Sometimes Serena rhymes Jake's words in her head, Duck. Luck, fuck, tuck, pluck, as a way of distancing herself. But this night she does not. She is lost still, connected only to wetness and dark and desire. She strokes his back and pinches it lightly, presses against him, all in this undulating, soft place. This stranger's cabin home. After a while they both come, hard, clinging to each other, and then lie still. Jake breathes quietly and continues to hold her, not moving away as he often does. Sexy, often (mostly) distant Jake. He touches the stones in her ears. "Pretty," he says. He could mean the stones or her. Serena lies against his long body; the dark is like the darkest chocolate, bitter and sweet together. The candlelight barely penetrates it.

✳ ✿ ✳

Serena has had a terror of getting pregnant with Jake. She has always been meticulous about birth control, convinced that she could not bear to have an abortion, though she believes it to be her right and has seen numerous friends through them, both before and after they became legal. There is something about Jake's largeness, the force of his smooth carelessness, that makes her feel endangered. As if he will penetrate all her careful defenses with that insistent and somehow impersonal press; that force moving forward against her wishes and her pleas. Or perhaps he meets some strong and hidden current in her and she will cooperate against her judgment and be overwhelmed. And pregnant.

Sometimes, after they have made love and are drinking a glass of wine, or hot tea, which she loves, Serena will say tentatively (not hopefully? certainly not), "You don't think I'm pregnant, do you?"

"Serena," Jake will say, "we're being really careful. Really."

But they are not really that careful all the time. Jake will enter her before she gets her diaphragm in and tease her, daring her to move away, to bypass her own heat and displease him. He has gotten several women pregnant, has Jake. Unconscious complicity? They all had abortions. No surprise. What really worries Serena is that she will collude with him. To what end? He would never help her care for a child; of this she is absolutely certain. She knows her fears are exaggerated, tangled with fears about being fat, blowing up in many different senses, her terror about helplessness and being powerless. Well, feeling powerless.

What does Jake think about? Serena wonders; she frequently reflects on Jake's inner life, which he rarely discusses. His work? Yes, surely that. He is often writing comedy in his head, he has said so. But what else? What does he think about relationships, other than how to avoid commitment and stay in control? thinks Serena. But perhaps he doesn't dwell on that much at all, just does it without thought. For a man who does not seem mysterious, Jake feels inaccessible to Serena, but she knows that he is really just elusive, which is not at all the same as mysterious. And cagey. Jake is very cagey. When he wants to punish her, he won't commit even to dinner. Or to a definite time to meet. "I think our needs are very different, Serena," he will sometimes say, so that she feels creepy, her needs bulging and uncomfortable. Pregnant with them. When this occurs to her, she laughs out loud.

Serena has always been surrounded by men. Well, boys and then men. She is accustomed to a great deal of attention and though she doesn't take it for granted and pays for this need in a variety of miserable ways, the reality of Jake's emotionally noncommittal stance is an oddity in her life. She still knows her boyfriends from second grade. Yes, of course. Yes. Her absent father, ghostly and perfect and gone forever. She has covered this ground in all the therapy she has done; her fierce longing (Jake is not wrong about that) and her need to be chosen, over and over again. Nestled in the seeming safety of being special. She had a boyfriend when she was two. (Like Leo, who had a girlfriend.) It was a family joke. Did she sense, even in Ruby's womb, that her father had already been ill? Might live for a very limited time? Ruby has often said that she knew she would raise Serena alone, knew and had the courage to have her anyway. This is true. Ruby is courageous; even at her most despairing about her mother, Serena knows this. Perhaps Serena heard Ruby, as her own developing body grew, turning through all the stages of evolution, deep inside Ruby's ferocious belly, pushed along by her mother's fierce will and knew they would be left with only each other.

Jake's hidden heart. He mentions it sometimes. He even has jokes about it in his act. "What do you mean?" Serena said, when he first spoke this way about himself. They were in his apartment on a cool summer day, standing near a window flat with summer light. Just standing near the kitchen, leaning against the wall. Jake wearing a worn linen shirt, the fabric rubbed smooth, creamy against his skin. He had just returned from Italy and was sleepy and jetlagged. His legs were bare, slightly tanned. "My heart feels hidden," he said. "What is there to understand, Serena?"

"I just never thought of it that way, or thought it about you." But she did understand, she just didn't like it. "It's such a definite statement." Jake's voice wasn't scornful or teasing. He sounded completely serious and unsurprised by his own words, so it was something he knew quite well about himself. Thought of often. Serena didn't want to feel the sad implications it had for her. For them. Such a miserable prognosis. A hidden heart; like delicate feet, or long eyelashes. He made it sound non-negotiable.

She thought of Rose, and Rose's childhood question on seeing a chicken's heart. "How can it feel? You can't even find the heart! It's almost hidden."

Many years later, Jake's heart would appear and grind open, not swinging wide or melting, but yielding reluctantly, perhaps in desperation. Or in weariness. When they are together, Serena sometimes feels herself pushing against a membrane of—what? Withdrawal? Longing for a part of him that is slippery, remote, she presses forward, her own ground lost beneath her, balance abandoned. He might seem to offer his hand and then, at the last moment, pull back so that she would need to draw abruptly upright, not wanting to topple forward. She knew she was not invited to fall into his arms.

❂

Holding Serena, Jake is now thinking about Elena, the woman who owns the cabin and her life of traveling, always moving. He has traveled for his work, of course, but it is not a lifestyle. He has known Elena for almost a year, at first fascinated with her stories of her life, much of which turns out to be prosaic and very hard. Unrooted. Demanding, with long hours. He was also curious about how she would be sexually. Passionate, he imagined, though he was not quite sure why he had this fantasy. Wild in some way that he had not experienced before. But she was matter of fact about sex. Not distant as much as practical. Fairly uncomplicated, or so he thinks, and quite happy in bed. Nothing like Serena, who is truly wild and sometimes blissful and sometimes, what? Heartbroken? Elena, the performer, knew as soon as he talked about Serena that Jake was much more involved than he admitted. Maybe more than he knew. "She is very deep in your heart," Elena said. He thought Elena might be from somewhere exotic, with her wild road-life, but in fact she is from New Jersey, not too far from where the cabin is. Her father is a school principal. Jake has her keys so that he can water her plants while she travels abroad—he has offered—and also so he can write in a different environment when he feels the need, which he sometimes does. He doesn't think she would mind Serena being there. She has few attachments and her fondness for Jake is more as a friend than anything else.

In the darkness, time floats inches away from Serena's body. "Jake," she whispers, "what time is it?"

"Mmm. Does it matter? Isn't Leo away?"

"Yes, but I have to work tomorrow. I need to get up early."

"You could stay here. We could sleep here. I'll drive you in the morning. I'll even get up early." An unusual offer from Jake, a night person.

"I can't, Jake. I have no clean clothes."

"And Leo might call in the morning?"

"He might," she says reluctantly, "but I want to go home anyway. I don't know where we are. I feel disoriented."

Jake starts to rub his hand against her. "You're so controlling, Serena." But he says it softly, with nothing mean embedded in the words, half teasing. "We're in a cabin that belongs to someone who goes on the road."

"Who is he? What kind of a performer?"

"She."

"Oh."

"She has an act. Very edgy. One-woman."

"How well do you know her?" Serena noticed Jake's familiarity with the candles, the matches, the rooms. In the dark.

"What difference does it make?"

"Well, some." Serena is ashamed of her possessiveness and her own hot streak of jealousy—a trait of which she disapproves and will often deny outright. "Anyway, I need to go." Now she is really not staying overnight.

"Okay. We'll go. I'll take you home. You are really not adventurous, Serena."

"I am about some things." She is thinking of her work, the deep ravines of the unknown that rest within it; the forbidden aspects of using intuition in the way she does, of using touch and sound.

But Jake presses his finger into her again, smoothly, suddenly. "Some things," he says. Then he moves away from her. The candlelight gleams and they sit at the edge of the bed, alternately kissing and looking for their clothes.

Serena finds the tiny bathroom and, finally, a light switch; she washes and pees, looking at the mirror without really seeing her face. Then she does look and sees the earrings, Jake's first gift to her, clasped to her ears. She touches one gently and smiles. Looking around the bathroom, she thinks of the oddity of this cabin they have just made love in and the traveling woman who lives here. Near the mirror is a snapshot of a tall woman with a thin, flat body, long legs and a short, very black pixie cut. She is wearing a shiny outfit of some kind. Serena turns out the light and makes her way back to bedroom.

Finally dressed, Jake blows out the candles and leads Serena to the door. Except for the bathroom, she sees the cabin only by candlelight. She knows she could have found other light switches, or simply asked Jake to turn the lights on, but she has had no desire to do so. They leave and Jake shuts the door; the lock clicks behind them. The car windows are covered with snow, though the falling flakes have slowed. Somewhere behind their white spin and flutter is the moon, now almost full, Serena thinks, its own round whiteness steady, but completely hidden. Jake cleans the car quickly and lifts Serena in. He kisses her and gets in his side. The car starts easily, moves slowly down the path and onto the road. Serena hears her stomach rumble. "I'm really hungry. We never had dinner."

"We can stop. There's a diner."

"It's almost eleven. Is it open?"

"It is. It's open all night. We'll stop. I'll feed you. I'm a gentleman."

The diner, a kind rarely found anymore, has cracked, red leatherette stools and years of grease clinging to the walls; it is partially filled, mostly with men, some who look like truckers and others who might be salesmen in careful, ugly suits, their shoes wet from the snow. Serena and Jake sit at the counter and order coffee and rice pudding and cherry pie. "That's not dinner," this from Jake, who is vaguely aware of Serena's partially healed relationship to food-as-enemy and is worried that she will not get enough to eat and will not care.

"Do you want a sandwich? No? Just soup?" Serena nods so they both order chicken soup in addition to desserts and sit together quietly, breathing the warm air, resting in the yellow light and the sticky, layered smells. When it comes, the soup is surprisingly good. Rich and full of white meat and vegetables. Serena, who is a vegetarian, waives her preferences and eats all of it. When the desserts come, Jake swallows his pie almost whole. Serena laughs. "It's good," he says. "Want some? Just a taste? You can give me some pudding."

"Okay. Small piece." Serena looks speculatively at the bright wet cherries sitting in thick syrup.

Jake breaks off a tiny piece and feeds it to her, feeling virtuous. Serena eats it, chewing very slowly. Their coffee cools. She begins to feel the pull of leaving him even before the meal ends. One of her demons, this pull. How have they covertly agreed not to speak about this? The waves of yearning toward greater closeness that she feels, a sorrowful ache that she is quite sure Jake does not return. "It's hard to leave you," she ventures.

"But Serena, you're committed." He always draws out the word, half mocking, half something else, she doesn't know quite what. Do you want to change that? is what Jake does not ever say. Never. Nor anything like it, though her commitment —the fact of it—seems to anger him, and though he is in no way an angry person, he keeps this firmly in place, resists her questioning it. And holds it against her.

Quite suddenly, Serena feels heat between her legs, wet heat different from the heat of the diner or the warmth the soup left in her mouth. She feels cramps with the wet. "Be right back," she says and slides off the stool, heading for the ladies' room, which turns out to be hidden behind a group of mops and pails leaning out of a supply closet. She feels a flicker of dread at what the bathroom might be like, but it is amazingly clean. Old white hexagonal tiles, worn and scrubbed, a clean sink and toilet. The smell of disinfectant is potent, sharp and invasive. She feels the heavy flow of blood running into the toilet, enough blood to slide around the diaphragm. Her period. Early. Her cycles wobble depending on the season, her mood and other factors that she has never fathomed. Blood swirls in the white porcelain bowl. She cleans up, splashes her face and stands for a moment, hands on the cold lip of the sink. Her belly feels tender. She is relieved to see the blood.

Serena thinks of her terror of getting pregnant with Jake. Often, with Jake, particularly when she thinks about pregnancy, Serena says she must stop seeing him. It is making her wretched. "Then stop," Jake responds. "We never thought this was going to go on forever." But she has not stopped and Jake has not encouraged their separation.

In the diner bathroom, feeling relief that she is bleeding, Serena knows again how frightened of bearing a child she is, not only of the physical changes. She is frightened that she would, as a mother, recreate shadows of her relationship with Ruby, a thought impossible to tolerate. Leo's feelings about having children are intricate and intense. He has always wanted children, Serena the one who was frightened, unwilling. They are still being somewhat careless about birth control. It is a conscious, but dangerous thing to do, a frightening choice. Leo has entered her when there is no condom, no diaphragm. He hasn't come inside her, but they are not fooling themselves about what they are doing. And now, on this night with Jake, what is all this blood? Jake is waiting for her when she returns, bill paid. He doesn't mention her half of the small amount, which is unusual, nor does he make a half-comical remark that he has paid the whole thing.

Jake has a fantasy that he would like children—but no wife?—he thinks. He imagines being a father and what he imagines about the rhythm and order of it, qualities he longs for and avoids. He wonders how a child would affect the bursts of inspiration that he then molds into order through his work, whether the child would always be in his mind, a solid concern that had priority. It would need to be so, wouldn't it? He wonders whether part of his wish is about impregnating women, rather than living as a parent. This is an idea that he can entertain only for moments, flashes that appear when he is having sex and resisting birth control, hating it, his body sometimes unwilling to use it, refusing hardness. Flashes that appear swiftly and disappear almost instantaneously. There are times when he knows he is daring the woman to resist him. A number of his lovers have had abortions, one woman conceiving twice in succession, very quickly, the second time not wanting to abort; he remembers that he did not want her to, but also that he did not love her and would not agree to take care of a child. He always made this very clear. She had the abortion and never spoke to him again. So Serena's fears with Jake are not entirely imaginary, though he doesn't mention this. Barely knows it himself. He suspects that spending time in the landscape of his own cruelty would immobilize him; instead, he is alert to it in his work, his professional voice steady and merciless about the cruelties of the world.

Once in the car again, Serena's cramps begin in earnest; usually mild, this night the pain is brutal and she feels suddenly lightheaded and sweaty under her coat. By the time they reach her apartment, she knows she is bleeding heavily and feels weak and panicky that no one is home. But she has never asked Jake for help of any kind and certainly nothing remotely like this. The help of his physical strength and the comfort of his presence.

"Jake," she says quietly, "I think I need some help." She explains why. "Could you just walk with me upstairs? I know you hate being here. I'll just get some ibuprofen and a heating pad or something and get into bed."

"Of course," he says, surprisingly. He garages the car—no spots this time and he doesn't even look—and holds Serena's arm, guiding her along the street and up the long, snowy outdoor flight to the apartment door. Then he helps her undress, puts up water for tea and puts the heating pad he finds in the bathroom in her bed. Hers and Leo's. Once she is settled, he undresses and gets in with her. The blood is heavy and thick and Serena feels frightened of so much blood. Where is this coming from? Jake holds her and then rubs her feet and smoothes her hair and sings to her a little.

"I didn't know you could sing."

"A little. I used to. Leo isn't the only musician."

Serena is packed with a tampon and has a towel under her butt. Not only does Jake dislike being there, he dislikes blood, she remembers. The first time they made love, stretched out in wavering spring sun on the awful parrot green expanse of rug that was often studded with long blonde hairs, she was at the very end of her period.

"Does this bother you?" she asked.

"No, no," he said with great certainty and then after a miserable ten seconds went to wash himself off.

"Are you okay?" she says now, eyes closed in the lamplight. "Here, with all this blood?"

He strokes her belly softly.

"Are you staying?" He has never slept there, has hardly ever even been in this apartment at all.

"Yes," he says.

"Thank you, Jake." He curls around her under the soft comforter; shadows of plants drift on the walls, made by the light from the street lamps below. Snow shines on the surrounding rooftops and slurs the sounds of traffic. They sleep with Jake's hand on her belly and far away the moon blinks among dark fast-moving clouds.

When Serena wakes the sun is shining. The snow is shimmering with light. She has been up several times during the night and the blood has slowed to a normal pace. She removes the towel, which is slightly spotted, and takes a gingerly shower before Jake wakes. Leo still has not called.

Jake smiles as he wakes. "Are you doing better?"

"Yes. Thank you. Thank you so much for staying."

"So I'm not so impossible?" Jake doesn't look directly toward her as he says this, but toward the window.

"No." She bends to kiss him. "I have clients at ten."

"I need to go," he says. "Should I call you later?"

"Yes," Serena says. This is so different from their usual goodbye: See ya. Yes. See ya.

The sun is still out, a winter glow, edgy, precise and fleeting. Shadows suck at the corners of the buildings, pulling toward the early dark. Serena goes into the coffee shop on Twelfth Street. Joe Jr.'s. It has been there since her days at the New School, now many years ago. It sits low to the ground, windows on Sixth Avenue, the waiters friendly with the whole neighborhood and welcoming, happy to see you. They follow the threads of their customers' lives and inquire, correctly, about family members and business deals. Gus waves her in. "Hello. Hello, Serena. Beautiful girl, beautiful day. What can I get you?"

She is really not hungry just wants to sit in the warmth in friendly company and drink the terrible coffee. She considers cantaloupe, but the cold, slippery texture doesn't appeal on this blustery afternoon. "Muffin," she says. "An English with butter. And coffee. Hot, please."

"I know, Serena. Hot. Hot."

She sits at the window. The place is uncharacteristically empty—a lull at an odd afternoon hour. Serena feels the sun on her shoulder and sips the burned, black coffee.

She thinks of Jake and his tenderness. Unusual. She feels her yearning and then her wariness. What commitment could he really make? How could she bear to leave Leo, her dear partner, her deep love? And how bad, to leave one man for another. Doomed, certainly? Could she try, even after this messy start with Jake and what would be a heartbreaking leave-taking from Leo? Would Jake want to? Would she really consider him, or is Leo right? She would never leave him for Jake. She looks out the window at the rhythmically moving traffic, at people walking along the avenue and at the heavy row of Christmas trees on the other side of the street. Would Jake ever really be faithful, that strange old word? Would she? She looks down at the slick black of the bitter coffee and then up again. Jake is walking right there, in front of her, just beyond the window. Not his neighborhood; what is he doing there? She realizes that he is walking with a tall woman whose long legs disappear into a red, down coat; her hands are in pale blue woolen gloves. She has delicate, tight, pixie hair, very dark, and wears slim boots with flat heels. Serena's heart starts to shiver with fear. Jake and the woman walk close together, not speaking. And then at the corner, she turns east and Jake continues ahead. Serena realizes they are strangers to each other. She sits very still.

At home, in their apartment, Leo calls from Florence and the phone rings and rings. Finally, the machine answers it.

✳ ❁ ✳

It is the day after Christmas. Leo returned just in time for the holiday, jet lagged and carrying boxes of gifts. Everything has been opened and praised. Serena and Leo spend Christmas with his family at his grandmother's; at eighty-seven, Mary Heffernan still presides over the family: Leo's parents and his two sisters, their husbands and children, Mary's remaining brother, Francis, his children and their children, the children of her other siblings. Francis' wife Theresa, gone this past year, quickly on an autumn Sunday, on the way home from Mass, dropping onto the leaf strewn sidewalk, her kind, round face surprised—the sad note in their gathering. The Christmas afternoon was filled with the noisy fabric of voices, mingled with carols and then respectful quiet for Leo, when he played the cello. There was baked ham, hot, sweet and heavy; mashed potatoes and a platter of mixed greens. Leo and Serena made a giant salad, full of nuts and cranberries and raisins and orange segments. Grandma Heffernan's apple pie for dessert. The apartment bursting with people, rocking with happiness and the mess of family. The day is intensely cold, with broken clouds and streaks of bold sunlight. Leo and Serena go home and go to bed early, Bach's *Christmas Oratorio* playing, and make love slowly, deep into the night. The cats crash around the apartment, high on Christmas catnip.

Now, the day after Christmas, they are preparing for their friends to visit. Serena is sipping from a large cup of tea, now cold, and washing greens for salad. In the middle of the wet greens moving through her hands, she stops, knowing she has just made her decision to say a permanent goodbye to Jake. The certainty comes recklessly, with total assurance, cracking apart months of wavering. The water is still running when her decision becomes final. She turns the faucet off and stands still. She had expected the decision itself to come slowly, with difficulty and yearning. But really, the moments of her choices have always arrived swiftly. It was the misery that was slow, the tearing passion; the commands of her own desire, the disastrous, unfulfilled need to have Jake love her. She can hear Leo cutting vegetables, hear the wind pushing at the garden doors, and then she is standing outside of the physical world, sliding in time. For a moment, she is moving in a dimension where Jake was never her lover, never even existed. But she remembers kissing him, lying with him inside her. Ah, he did exist, insist, demand. She needs to tell him her decision and she will do it the next day, a day when she is not working. As soon as possible. She stops her preparations and calls Jake, leaves a message for him. Could they meet for lunch the next day? Even as she speaks into the electronic emptiness, she knows he will understand why she is calling.

All that night it is quiet, the wind frozen into stillness. In Serena's dream, snowflakes fall, so large that she can see their intricate structure with her naked eye. Jake appears, moving in and out of curtains of heavy snow. When Serena wakes, no snow has fallen; the streets are cold, the sky streaky white and gray, with sun pushing through at intervals. Serena wears the cashmere shawl Leo has brought her from Florence, its dense blue is reflected in her eyes. She wears warm, gray slacks and her old, black, wool coat; hatless, her dark hair shines in the sun, blows around her face as the wind passes. She and Jake meet at a restaurant on the Upper East Side, a place where they have often eaten at odd afternoon hours when Serena has a break in her schedule and Leo is at work. Jake is waiting when she arrives. The room glitters with white Christmas lights, the tables have bouquets of red carnations, small red roses. Jake rises from his chair, kisses her. Spiky fragments, sharp as glass, seem to curve around Serena; brilliant green, electric blue, the shards halo her body, like a doorway announcing her path out of this relationship, away from misery and the passion that does not cradle love.

"Over," she says.

"I know. I knew when I heard the phone message. I didn't think we would last forever, but this stings more than I thought it would. Why now?" To Serena's surprise, Jake looks stricken.

"You mean why not last week, or last month?"

"Yes. What has changed?"

Serena is quiet.

"I'm going to order some food. Tea?" Jake asks. He smiles.

"Yes, and some fruit salad. Please. And a blueberry muffin. What changed is I finally realized that, unlike the other men in my life—and unlike my women friends, too—you were never going to love me. It was a relentless and futile pursuit on my part. Why did I want that? I want passion and love to be together. I didn't like the way you treated me, or I let myself be treated. It was shaming, to be treated that way. And, the most important part, because I want to stay with Leo and be with him completely."

"Ah," Jake says, "full circle. The muffin, I mean." They are both remembering the first time they met and the rain and the tea and the muffin. Life's grand moments punctuated by the mundane. They alternately hold hands and eat. They eat a few of the cookies Jake has ordered and share the muffin and the fruit. "I didn't intend to treat you badly, Serena. I think you encountered me the way I am and those are my shortcomings; my emotional deficits."

"I think they probably are. It wasn't personal, except that it affected me personally, and caused me pain. I allowed it. And I am with a partner and it was a cruel choice for me to make. I don't want that choice in my life anymore." She looks at Jake carefully, watching his reaction. "You look sad and angry." Jake rarely lets his anger show.

"I am. Both. I want to punish you for leaving." Then, "I don't suppose we can be friends?"

"I don't know that we can, Jake. No. I know that we can't. I feel punished enough already. My own choice, to the extent that it was really a choice. Yes, it was a choice, I know that."

They leave the restaurant separately, Serena first.

It will be years before they meet again and then it is by accident at a fundraiser for children with Down syndrome. By that time, Jake will have been married and divorced, with a daughter with Down whom he adores. He has entered the political arena successfully, a liberal, diligent man. They hug and talk for a while and then Serena and Leo leave. The meeting has more tenderness than Serena would have imagined.

When Serena returns home after her meeting with Jake, she waters the plants, remembering Ruby, who often watered her plants in the dark, leaving stained white circles on the wood floor around the pots. Serena streams the water carefully into each pot. When Leo gets home he can feel that something is different, though Serena says nothing. The plants bring to her mind the vacations she and Leo have had in the tropics—not surprising, since many houseplants are tropical. But here they flourish indoors, ebullient and lush. "Let's go to the Botanic Garden tomorrow," she says, "to the Tropical Pavilion." They both love the garden in all seasons. "We'll go to the Desert Pavilion, too and then have a terrible snack." Serena's heart is banging in her chest as she continues to water the plants, using a small ladder to get to the hanging ferns. She is going to tell him there, in that sheltered, glorious place, surrounded by small waterfalls and immense greenery.

Leo gets out his cello and plays softly. "Yes," he says. "That would be good."

The next day, a Saturday, is full of sun, with a cold, sharp wind, a day in the hammock between Christmas and New Year's. Looking at the shining sky, Serena imagines the stars, now invisible, riding there. She plays with words, trying to find exactly what she will say to Leo. They go to the Desert Pavilion first and then to the tropical display. Inside that pavilion, warmth is everywhere, moist, pungent, embracing. A small stream makes a hushed, sighing sound. Sometimes Serena sees white-gold light around plants, but on this afternoon the plants reach and stretch and billow, solidly physical.

They walk along the path, hand in hand and then sit on a wide ledge surrounding the planted area. Before she can speak, Leo knows. "It's over," he says. "It's over, isn't it?"

Serena nods. "Finished forever."

Leo drops his head into his hands. "I could not have stayed with it much longer, Serena. I was about at the end. I wouldn't have left you, but I couldn't see how to go forward." She wants to ask more, but stays silent. "We will talk more another time," Leo says. "Let's just be with this. Just be with it."

Serena kisses his palm. "Yes, just this for now." They leave the green warmth, the garden, the wet blooming world and step into the sunny cold. Two beings who have, according to Buddhism, never been born and never died, walking arm and arm, heading home. Wind rushes through the bare trees. Peace, it says. Rest now.

Loose Change

They start tangled together in their own sweet smells mixed with the scents from outdoors that come through the open window: warm leaves and earth from the trees in their small garden. City heat carrying smoky fumes; a Friday morning in early September, which always feels like the beginning of the year to Serena. Their cats, now only Romeo and Charlotte, are curled at the foot of the bed, have been there all night and morning, now waiting pointedly for breakfast, which is late. The heavy wisteria vine curls around the window, a gateway of leaves lifting gently when the wind blows. Leo kisses Serena one more time and then begins to get out of bed, long naked back, brown from summer, long legs, on his way to make them breakfast.

"Are you coming?" he asks. "I don't have time to linger. Sadly." He comes back for one more kiss and touches her breast lightly. Sunlight reflects in his hazel eyes. The room they are in is large, with high ceilings, cream walls, a heavy antique wardrobe; the sheets are variations of white, with their blue and white patchwork quilt on top. Pillows abound, some in European pillowslips, embroidered at their corners with initials by women long dead. The wide board floors shine. This apartment has come to Leo and Serena through old friends of Leo's family—it was offered years ago, at a startling low rent, with love and gratitude; Serena and Leo are not sure what the gratitude represents, it does not seem shady (Leo's family is a truthful group), but it is mysterious in a pleasant way and the apartment was accepted with eagerness. Even the possibility of having it, before things were fully settled, brought out what Serena called flamboyant greed. She craved the apartment; so did Leo, but more quietly. "Not part of the Buddhist path, this greed," she said, without any real remorse. (Technically, Serena is no more a Buddhist than she has ever been, she has taken no vows; she is a hybrid who has studied many paths and chosen many Buddhist concepts as a way of life, but she does not follow them exclusively.)

It had been neglected, their large parlor floor. Leo, architect and restorer, has fixed it all, painstaking, attentive, a little obsessed. Now the bedroom is filled with billowing ferns and at the moment a large blue jar of sunflowers stands on the dresser. White linen drapes are on the windows—Serena's old curtains from her first apartment, lengthened with carefully stitched, aged linen to become drapes. The owners had made steps down to the garden in back—Leo is an expert gardener, Serena an enthusiastic one—and thus, in this strange way, it mirrors Leo's old loft on East Tenth; they have simply moved west on the same street and are now in the Village. The room has been groomed and tended and holds their love on every surface: the care they have given it shimmers and the air is full of their passion and sexual longing, fulfilled and renewed and fulfilled again. It holds exuberance as well as moments of sadness—closeness and the ache of separating—or sometimes the relief of it. Their shared emotions are vibrant, intense, yet not greedy, but earth and heaven dancing through them, their love opening doorways into deeper wisdom and compassion and the precious nature of each moment.

"Mmm. I'll take a quick shower and be right there." Serena does not really take quick showers, this is a polite fiction. But she does get up and head for the bathroom. An ordinary Friday morning on a day that will split open, pour out excitement and questioning and possibility and shift the curtain between the worlds for Serena and Leo and, ultimately, for many other people. The edges of reality will shiver and widen; accustomed perceptions will twist and spin and pull open into new dimensions.

But at this moment, early in the morning, they have made love, warmth falling on them as they tasted each other and their aliveness. Their bathroom is sunny too, and Serena watches the light catch on the streams of water sequinning her small, long-boned body. At this moment, water running loose and warm, she likes her body, an unusual appreciation. Her awareness stretches beyond the apartment walls and she contemplates the light and water in this city, which has always been her home. She imagines light swimming on the two rivers that frame the island, their briny water bearing river traffic. She imagines blankets of grass in Washington Square Park, a few blocks from where she is, resting in warm light, covering the silence of skeletons in the old potter's field beneath the lawns: people whose stories are many years gone, their remains jumbled under the earth and pavement, their presence mostly unsuspected. Forgotten bones. Layers upon layers of them. Ingrid told her that there were streams that ran in the cellars of some old buildings in Soho, ancient tumbling water, belonging to no one, beyond official responsibility, their flow sunless, persistent. It is an idea that gives her great pleasure. She imagines the fluids in her body: clear ones, sticky ones, the bright fire of her flowing blood, moving in contained darkness, the blood that arrives every month and passes into the outer world. Or does not, if you are feeding a baby. An embryo.

"Serena? Breakfast." Her musings have captured her. She has been in the shower longer than she thought she would be. She puts on her blue terry cloth robe, wraps her dark hair in a towel and hurries to the kitchen. Leo has cut up fruit and made scrambled eggs and toast, the toast for himself. Serena does not eat bread or anything she has decided might be fattening, and she still experiences food as the enemy, still forgoes meals. When she is with Leo she does eat because he insists, sometimes mentioning, half teasingly, that she needs strength if they decide to have a baby, though this topic has not come up recently. Serena always reminds him that she doesn't find this funny and that she needs to be strong just for herself.

"Of course, you know I think that, too. I'm sorry; I know this is a sensitive subject," is Leo's standard reply. "I shouldn't be coy. I'm sorry, Serena." And it rests there, though time is passing and Serena is nearing forty, so the conversation now carries the weight of decreasing possibility, an invisible gate swinging through the seasons; one that will eventually shut, silently and forever.

✳ ☯ ✳

When Serena and Leo met and started their relationship, it was clear that Leo wanted children; he had been planning to have a baby with Katherine, his first love, before she died in that miserable accident. Leo talked to children and babies on the street; he cuddled them when he could, sang to them. He struck up conversations with parents and grandparents, delighted, unselfconscious, with warmth that radiated from his core, the soft bloom of a flame of happiness.

Serena watched him, curious, tentative, a little shy. She knew she did not have Leo's ease and delight with children, but it was not until she started a women's group at the end of their first year together, that she began to drop, week by week, into the dunes of sorrow and terror that waited within; thousands of grains of feeling, which formed the landscape of her deep responses to bearing a child. Fears of her body swelling, losing ground, distorted and appalling—this battering body trauma that had been with her since adolescence, leaking into all the corners of her experience of herself, pervasive and cruel. There were fears of invasive doctors pushing inside her over and over again; fears that she would create a relationship with her child that mirrored the one she had with Ruby. Exploring, she would sink into the dunes, and within their airless, sliding weight she could feel her heart break into roaring fragments, sore and torn. How could she care for a child, bear a baby who would swim in her, in these emotions, as its life developed? What a betrayal to a new life and to Leo—and herself, she realized as she went deeper and deeper. Serena had always believed that she would have a baby, no one imagined or suggested that all women did not want to be mothers. In Serena's youth, childlessness was a sorrow and a shame, always the woman's fault. A barren woman —it was assumed that women who did not bear children must be barren—to be pitied, or worse. Serena told Leo what she was uncovering and he held her and talked about the sorrow he felt, but he did not try to coax her, simply said he hoped things would change as she changed. They would have sporadic conversations about having children—well, a child—and Serena did change, but only slightly, a small move toward imagining holding an infant and the love she would feel. Possibly feel. Mostly she accepted that she did not want a child, that many women didn't, even though they had them.

Long after she heard the story of Katherine's death, Leo told Serena that there had been a question about whether Katherine had been pregnant when she died. That the doctor had mentioned it to Katherine's parents. Leo had overheard the doctor, but had never asked him about it directly, nor did he ever speak with her parents. His failure to reassure them tormented him. Had he been too ashamed? Frightened? Angry? At any rate, he had never managed the question and Katherine's parents had moved away, lost touch. Who would have known better than he, he said, when he told Serena this part of his history, one rainy fall afternoon, watching Tompkins Square Park washed with water, the pavement alive with slippery yellow leaves, the benches soaked and empty. He had made them both espressos, in tiny silvered cups bought on one of their hunts through almost-antique stores. The coffee was satisfying and strong and Leo had put a deep orange throw around Serena's shoulders. They were packing to move to their new apartment and boxes stood open, half-packed. The orderly loft in disarray. Serena was quiet when she heard the story. Her breath felt scoured, her bones suddenly icy as she imagined the hospital room, Leo's feelings as he overheard the doctor, Katherine's strong body, lost forever, now perhaps a lost child as well. Serena felt Katherine's ghost with them—not always, but sometimes—in the first year of their relationship. Now, after thirteen years together, it had mostly disappeared. Because of the nature of their intimacy, Serena asked, when she had these feelings, if she was accurate, or imagining. And Leo responded honestly. Yes, I feel her with me, yes, sometimes there is yearning, but mostly not. We are together Serena, and I cannot change my past, but my relationship to it is changing. An honest man, even when there might be pain. A mostly honest man. A conscious man.

Then Leo, tolerant of silences, simply sat with her. Finally, Serena said, "Why tell me now?" It is all she can think of to say. Her head is turned away from him, tumbled, jagged thoughts careening in her mind, moving through what felt like night in a cold desert whose borders are beyond reach, a place presided over by careless stars scattered in eternity, flung into emptiness. If this was a secret for so long, are there others? She thinks he has planned to tell her at exactly this moment, in this way because he is thoughtful and plans carefully; it is unlikely he would blurt the story, information spinning out from beneath his conscious mind, tearing their world casually.

"I am telling you this now because we are starting a new chapter together, a new home that is ours, we are moving from a place I created alone and then with you to a place that we are starting together. It is a kind of conception that will lead to a birth. It isn't a good time, but it is better than some might have been. Maybe there isn't any good time to tell what has been secret." He shook his head. "No. There are times when it is healing to let a secret be revealed."

"You sound so formal, and that sounds so passive. 'Let it be revealed'," Serena says. "It isn't revealed by some magical process. You are telling me. Actively. Was this prepared?"

"Oh, yes. Over and over again. Prepared and then buried and then prepared again. I have waited too long, haven't I? And you're right it does sound passive. I'm sorry. This is hard, it isn't graceful. It's painful. I'm sorry, Serena." Leo is a man who apologizes gracefully, usually easily. (But not always.)

"Well. I would have been shocked at any time. Maybe the best time would have been at the beginning, when you told me about Katherine. The first time we made love. Then there would have been no secret, but it probably would have been too much information. So, no. No perfect time, but I feel shocked, although it isn't unusual for a man to have impregnated a former lover."

"Yes," Leo says. "Now you sound formal. In this situation it is a shock. Given who you are and who I am. We don't have secrets, so the secret is part of the shock." But this is not entirely true. Who does not have secrets? Leo does. So does Serena. What is the line between privacy and secrecy, the honorable need to hold some things for you alone and the need to hide? This is the path of a discussion Leo and Serena might easily have taken, but they did not move in that direction.

"You don't really know if there ever was a pregnancy?" Perhaps she sounded hopeful, rather that simply curious.

"No. I don't. I don't think the doctor knew and I never understood why he would have asked, even if he thought it might be so. I didn't understand why he thought it." Leo has gone over this in his mind for years. Why would a doctor perform a pelvic exam on a dead woman when there was no question about the cause of her death? What was the point? There was no autopsy, not ever a suggestion of one. It would remain a mystery with piercing hooks, their sharp hold intact until Leo could let go of all of it. Now Serena was hooked, at least for the moment, for right then. The maybe-child in Katherine's body. Katherine, a woman who did want children. But who knew about that either, Serena thought later, sometimes angrily. A young Catholic woman; of course she wanted children, it would have been forbidden to think otherwise. Coming from a liberal home, raised with no formal religion, it was hard enough for Serena to allow her feelings of fear and distaste. If Katherine had similar feelings, they would have been deeply buried. And perhaps she truly wanted to be a mother. The truth died with her, rested in her ornate coffin as the sun shone on the ground where she was buried and the moon lit the cemetery and rain and snow dropped from the sky as the years passed.

✳ ☢ ✳

So, on that warm Friday morning, on a day that will bring enormous changes, when Serena tightens the belt of her blue robe and goes to have breakfast with Leo, all of this has been woven into the body of their relationship. Something purled into its sinews and running in its bloodstream, added to the many experiences they have had together, including the sorrow and rage about the affair Serena had, now in the past, but part of their life as a couple. Despite her intuitive nature, her mindfulness of her dreams and years of meditating, Serena has no conscious hint of what the day will bring. She is inclined to think Leo is going to want to talk about having a baby, though he hasn't said anything about it; but they communicate in their dreams, in the movements of their sleeping patterns, in shifts of breath and infinitesimal changes in tone. Perhaps something about the way he rubbed her belly when they made love?

Serena eats the eggs appreciatively, tasting the light spices Leo has added, the plush, cooked tomato chunks.

"No bread?" asks Leo hopefully. "Really good rye." He knows the answer, but half imagines that Serena's agony about food will pass; he is sometimes simultaneously hopeful and resigned. The two feelings rubbing together.

"Mmm, no." Appearing thoughtful, a faked response, which they both know. It seems to Serena that she has worked on these feelings forever without more than a tiny breath of movement, a slight exhalation. Even that is an irregular shift, unstable. She tries to determine if he seems particularly interested in her eating and then abandons her effort at secrecy and simply asks. "Are you thinking about babies, Leo?"

"Yes," he says happily. "Could we revisit?"

"Now?"

"Soon?"

"Soon, okay." And for the first time, the thought really is bearable to Serena, if not appealing. "You're going to meet Nina and look at fabrics?" Nina is Max's daughter from his first marriage. Only marriage. They spend a good deal of time with Max and Ingrid. It is happy time, comfortable and loving, threaded through with mutual interests in art and music and good food and the enormous ironies of life. Max is older, so perhaps he is the most aware of irony, though Ingrid is not far behind, given her nature. Nina is a designer, living in California, visiting New York to restore the upholstery on the pews in a church, old for New York, one which is much admired in the city and supported by a wealthy congregation. She has been researching antique fabrics that will blend with the age of this particular church and Leo, an expert on restoration if not on fabric, has been asked to assist her. Asked by Nina at the dinner they all shared the previous week. Flirtatious Nina, sleek and subtly sexual in a graceful way, but not so graceful or subtle that Serena missed the cues. She is not disturbed, however, despite her watchful nature, since women flirt with Leo relentlessly, right under her nose. And he is gracious, but does not respond. Ingrid raised her eyebrows slightly at Serena when no one was looking and Max treated them all, picking up the check, saying, "My treat, please." Gracious Max, whose solid body looked unusually tense under his old, well-tailored jacket. Clearly, he is aware of Nina's interest in Leo.

✻ ☺ ✻

Breakfast over, Leo gets ready to leave; he is wearing slacks that fit beautifully, light fawn fabric falling along his long legs; with them, a white, collarless shirt. He and Nina are meeting at the townhouse in the East Fifties, where the fabric store is, in a townhouse where its owner lives and Nina is staying.

"You look lovely," Serena says, fluttering her lashes. "Nina will appreciate the fabric and what it covers, I am certain."

"This is work, Serena." He is unruffled. This issue is a mild joke between them. Almost. Of course, Serena flirts, too, but she is conscious of it. She has never figured out what Leo is doing, if anything. He has never figured it out either and doesn't care much. His love, wide and generous, is focused on Serena. "I'll be back late afternoon. Intact." He hugs her, strokes her still damp hair, kisses her.

Serena goes upstairs to dress for a meeting with Laura, a student from the class she has just finished teaching at a local college that explored the relationship between astrological symbols and psychological states. Laura, a successful singer, asked to speak with Serena privately. She said only that she was studying channeling and wanted Serena to evaluate her work, if she wouldn't mind. She had serious questions about her channeling and valued Serena's opinion. Serena agreed and the day of their meeting has come.

Of course, Serena knows more about altered states than Laura might imagine. All the reading she had done since childhood that made altered states and reincarnation feel like home, like a rhythm central to her heart. Feel like freedom. It was something she and Ruby shared and was deeply rooted in Serena's experience of life and her understanding of reality, an eternal process of unfolding and contemplating and mystery and frustration.

Serena knows her guardians and teachers have been with her since birth, and probably before, sometimes as brilliantly tangible, vibrating presences, sometimes far away, but never gone, these energies that hovered. Her protectors, shining aspects of non-physical realms, their vastness spun smaller to accommodate her. Now, in the 80s, it is possible to have conversations about them, about reincarnation and astrology—at least with some people. It makes Serena less lonely, feels like an extension of the way she and Ruby kept each other company in their explorations.

✳ ✪ ✳

Since the beginning of her astrology practice, when she was twenty-five, Serena has studied Science of Mind, an open-ended spiritual teaching based on the understanding that one loving source is the universal creative essence out of which all manifestation arises; all physical manifestations and experiences are individualized aspects of the source, of oneness. Life, in this teaching, is shaped by consciousness, by awareness and beliefs, which can be changed. Science of Mind is a profound teaching and one that particularly appeals to Serena.

At first, she approaches it with her usual enthusiasm and determination, wants to share it with her friends, wants the good she can see for them, and is impatient when they hold back, argue, are skeptical. It is several years before she begins to understand the importance of shadow, of mystery and not-knowing—or understands surrender. Before she begins to grapple with the subtle complexities of interactive consciousness and the ways in which it is misunderstood, can be badly used. Is sometimes cruel. People come to her to work with cancer and are ashamed they have "created" it, sunk in the misery of blame and self-hatred heaped on what may already be a life-threatening situation. She knows that healing and curing are different, that death is sometimes the healing, but still more years pass before she understands how to hold paradox—can tolerate that healing is frequently uncomfortable, yet simultaneously, surprisingly, calm and fluid.

Serena has studied the Tarot, working with the complex, dream-like symbols of the cards, each one a world unveiling possibilities, and with handwriting analysis, which follows the curves, slides and loops of letters as shaped by the nervous system and the brain, a map of individual reality.

She learned hypnosis—this with a stalwart woman with flamboyant blonde hair and an operatic voice, who would say, in ringing tones of certainty, "You can, you will and you must control your eating." Serena's original interest in hypnosis began with wanting to regress to past lives, but while she was at it, she added weight control, this continuing poisonous issue—her preoccupation with her body's shape. Years later, she will learn Ericksonian hypnosis with its magical, complex and powerful insights, its wild, yet formal structure.

After she begins her astrology practice, she will study Core Energetics with Nick, adding powerful emotional work to her metaphysical practice, guided by Nick's wisdom and his ferocious love.

Learning astrology had been more like remembering, like rippled threads of silk, loose strands carrying information through to her, like the stars that offered a tracery of light from the sky that she saw in her crib, just after she was born, alone in the night. As she studied, the sounds of rustling leaves from some long-ago forest floated into her awareness, whispering ideas when she meditated on the planets; knowledge arrived in her dreams, or at odd times during the day when she was occupied with something else entirely. Sometimes the information came as intricate, wordless forms that sifted into language and understanding. The Tarot felt familiar, but not as strong as her connection to the stars.

When she came to experience that consciousness was everywhere, she felt it as a joyous reunion, a deep sense of oneness that felt essential, utterly known.

In her practice, Serena weaves these elements together, offering people a way to work based on their innate wholeness, on meditation and mindfulness and active attention to their bodies and the stories they reveal. On consciousness as interactive with eternal forces, some mysterious. She feels in her bones and blood that there is a single source, vast beyond imagining, loving beyond the capacity of most individuals to know it—yet ever-available. All beings, all creatures and the earth are individualized aspects of the source. The task is to dissolve, to whatever degree possible, patterns which interfere with that perception so the way opens to live in its magnificence. Her work moves and grows, layers form and collapse, new possibilities emerge and connect different paths, wider realms; in her work there are doorways and trapdoors, fragments as well as integrated experiences of wisdom, compassion and presence. She starts to work with people and then to teach long before the phrase "radical transparency" exists, but had it been available, Serena would have embraced it with celebration. Some of the sharp certainty she starts with will gradually rub away, leaving her tender heart increasingly exposed, and mostly more resilient.

* ✪ *

Once Leo has gone to his appointment, Serena dresses slowly in white linen slacks and a blue silk blouse that is worn and still lovely; she chooses lapis earrings and light makeup. She rarely wears more than mascara and a little shadow on her eyes. She is extremely curious about this meeting, about the channeling.

Serena grew up reading about Eileen Garrett (among others), of whom she was in awe. Garrett, a powerfully gifted Irish psychic participated in various scientific experiments. Serena felt the experiments were intrusive (later, she thought they were cruel and ignorant), but Garrett was determined to find scientific answers. Eventually she moved to New York and Serena longed to meet her, but never did. An independent woman of great intelligence and dramatic flair—she was reported to have worn a purple velvet cape—Serena was fascinated by her work and admired Garrett's courage and the way she dealt with both skepticism and hostility, and—perhaps as difficult—with adulation. She had extraordinary skills and a forthright nature. Until the end of her life, Garrett said she was not sure what she was doing, not sure what it meant. Nor was she convinced of life after death. Her consistent questioning touched Serena. She and Ruby discussed Garrett as well as the books they shared on Buddhism and Hinduism and mystical realms. These talks were times of peace, sweet as a light rain; times of loving connection. "Do you think this is true?" Ruby would ask. "Did we live before?" They talked about places that seemed familiar, about people who were "old friends," people they had known before this life.

Serena was certain that many realms existed, as did reincarnation, though she felt that all descriptions were incomplete. The reading gave her names for what she had known forever. It soothed her yearning to understand what she experienced in the world, allowed her to claim mysterious colors of awareness in shades that she had felt alone in seeing.

Serena's reading and studying continues for all of her life. Most recently, she was reading *Seth Speaks*, a book by Jane Roberts, a contemporary channel who is intelligent, unassuming and humorous; Serena's spiritual teacher suggested it to his students. But she has never seen anyone work in an altered state, save a psychic at the Ansonia, that dreamy, frosted building on Broadway, once the height of fashion, but by that time ragged and down-at-the–heels, with sagging chairs in the lobby and the smell of mold and sad aging. She and Rose went together, unimpressed by his offerings.

Serena goes out to water the garden in spite of the white linen slacks while she waits for Laura. The sun is inviting and she will cut some yellow chrysanthemums for the house. Standing in the garden, the hose spraying cool water, Serena remembers that when she started her practice as an astrologer, she would recall Garrett's courage and the memory would support her when she needed that kind of strength.

"An astronomer?" Leo's Uncle Andrew, a professor of literature, asked when they met—asked when Leo introduced her to the family on that first Thanksgiving, when they have been together a few months.

"No," Leo's mother said to Andrew, her brother, a large, cordial man with radiant pink ears and graying auburn hair. "An astrologer," she said again.

"Oh," said Andrew, looking interested. "Tell me about that." A response unlike that of Serena's family, who were at the least baffled, perhaps politely horrified when she started to practice. Not that they said so. (Of course not.) But over the years, she has been supported in her work, mostly accepted and valued for her insights.

❋ ✪ ❋

Leo decides to walk to his meeting with Nina, realizing he has more time than he thought. It is all the way to the East Fifties, but he walks fast when Serena is not with him. He walks up Fifth Avenue, paying particular attention to the buildings in the Twenties, elegant buildings, carefully ornamented, with robust, pleasing proportions in the manner of the end of the nineteenth century and the early twentieth; buildings of graceful urbanity; many, once hotels for the wealthy, are now shabby, soot scarred, with large show windows stuck onto the building faces at street level. Some offering linens and bedding to the trade, others displaying wholesale china sets, spread unattractively, their surfaces covered with pale dust. Leo is looking at the windows above and at doorways, the old ones replaced by steel and glass, incongruous rectangles; the curvy scrollwork around the upper windows remains, some have plump sandstone rosettes, others have stately swags at the edge of the deep embrasures, but there too, the stone is darkened with neglect. The way a building opens to the outer world fascinates Leo. Some are welcoming, some forbidding, some cramped, reluctant. He has studied the many possibilities for years; his own work pays great attention to these features. Madison Square Park is flush with winos, strutting pigeons and dirty benches, only the old, handsome trees appealing, turning color slightly, a wrinkled gold. (It will be many years before this neighborhood is renovated, the buildings converted to condos, to exclusive hotels. The park, too, will be revived. But it will happen; Manhattan has a very limited amount of space. Everything gets recycled. Eventually.)

In addition to the architecture, Leo is also thinking about Nina and the dinner they all had and her very obvious flirtatiousness. He wonders if his daughter embarrassed Max; he jumped to get the check when they had barely finished the dessert and coffee.

Generally, Max liked to linger. He also thinks about Serena's not-quite-humorous comment before he left the house. It is true; people flirted with Leo, men and women both and he is not sure why, although he assumes he is participating in some way. A disguised way? Why? He doesn't welcome it (does he?). He certainly doesn't follow up. Well, not since Serena—or only once when they were first together and he was in Venice for a project and made love to Angela. Once. (Could it have been twice?) Nina reminds him in some way of Angela, though not in her looks. Nina is tall and has her father's wide bone structure, but even with that, she is all lightness: amber eyes and short, glowing hair, almost blonde, a flat bosom and long legs, long narrow feet—a smooth skin over restless inner movement. She has a sharp mind and a sharp tongue, quick and definite. Angela was an architect, passionate about her work, passionate about life, curvy and physically compact, sweet to touch. (Angela's physical presence was something like Serena's, which he knew at the time.) He and Nina will meet and look at expensive fabrics, muted rose and green stripes, smoky blue brocade, and he will communicate—either verbally, or more obliquely—that he is unavailable. An image of Serena in her blue robe floats up, his love, his jewel and he can feel his hand on her belly, feel himself inside her, making love to have a baby and then he stops, suddenly knowing how much he wants that. He looks up and realizes he is in front of Saint Patrick's Cathedral and laughs. He was never a practicing Catholic (though his grandmother certainly is) but his Irish side is rueful and amused. It must be the end of a mass, because people are streaming out, the heavy doors open. Some are obviously tourists, but there are couples and families with small children who seem local and Leo's amusement changes to sadness. He notices that a number of the women leaving the cathedral are pregnant. If Katherine had lived, they would have had children by now, probably more than one—and probably she would have insisted on church. The mother church. Leo sits down on the steps of the cathedral and waits quietly as people pass him. Then he sighs and stands up; he doesn't want to be late for Nina. He is always prompt.

They go together to look at fabrics at the exclusive shop housed in the brownstone owned by Nina's friend. They describe the intricacies of fabric quality and design to Leo. It is not, as he told Nina, his area.

"The colors need to harmonize with the church's interior and exterior," Nina says. "Silvery gray stone with some shadows in it and antique oak pews." She is looking intently at the fabrics, touching them carefully. "Greens, I think," she says. And after more than an hour, Leo sees one that he thinks is remarkable. Deep green, with the warmth of a summer forest touched by sun. It has a pattern of leaves woven into it as part of the inviting texture. He looks at it and remembers the fabric on the cushions in the church he attended as a child; a deadly maroon, heavy duty, made to last forever, kin to the rock on which the church was built, he thinks. Nina is delighted; her amber eyes rest on the cloth with appreciation. "You may not be an expert," she says, "but that is the one. It is your eye I wanted. Now you must let me take you to lunch. Late lunch." So, while the foundations of Serena's life are shifting, slipping into a wider focus, Leo is eating an elegant late lunch with Nina, who, in the middle of the meal, covers his large hand with hers and asks, "Are you and Serena married?"

"No," Leo answers. "Not yet."

"But soon?"

"Probably." Leo is not going to explain Serena's political objections to marriage.

"Does 'probably' leave room for anyone else?" Nina continues.

"No."

"Is that an absolute no?"

"Yes, Nina. It is. I don't have lovers. We don't."

Nina sighs. "Well, sad for me. Might you change your mind?" She is a persistent woman, unused to not getting what she wants. Their colorful salads wait; restaurant noises, voices, music, accompany their conversation.

"No, not a chance."

Nina sighs again. "Well, the food is extraordinary here and you have chosen a perfect fabric and I will just enjoy what I have."

"Sensible," says Leo. "Happy to have helped, at least in one way." They finish lunch and order strong espressos. As they walk to the door, Nina rests her hand on Leo's waist, her fingers slightly below.

"Maybe at another time or another place," she says. Leo smiles and shakes his head slightly, no. She smoothes the fabric of her skirt. "I will contact you about the fabric, though," she says.

"Of course," Leo says. Not much choice here, he thinks. I should have seen this coming—the obvious flirtatiousness at the dinner. But he had already agreed to meet during their phone conversation, which preceded the dinner. It would have been awkward to cancel.

They part and Leo decides to walk back downtown and to go slowly. He would like to understand why the scenario with Nina has repeated so often in his life. He would like to think more about babies and perhaps marriage. He wants to marry Serena. Maybe he will stop in the cathedral. Light a candle. His grandmother would surely approve.

✳ ✿ ✳

Laura arrives bringing a bunch of russet mums. She and Serena go into the kitchen so that Serena can add them to the bouquet she has cut and they talk while Serena arranges the flowers carefully and takes them into the living room, bringing lemon tea she has made and a plate of ginger cookies with her on a tray. They settle themselves on blue floor pillows, the paisley pattern of the Oriental rug spreading under them in soft violets, cream, touches of red. The room is full of sun, dust motes floating in the light. Laura is sturdy and sits with her strong legs folded in a lotus position; she has a broad, calm forehead and high cheekbones with wings of brown hair framing her face. Her narrow, light blue eyes are frilled with dark lashes and her gaze is direct, a solid, handsome woman. Her loose skirt is tucked around her, almost the same color as Serena's shirt and she is wearing a white peasant-style blouse. They both notice their matched colors and smile in acknowledgement of this small synchronicity. In the years to come, in their unfolding friendship, they often wear the same colors when they meet. Laura is an accomplished singer, which Serena admires. She has an air of competence and Serena trusts that quality will inform her channeling.

Laura starts to describe her experiences learning to channel, working with a teacher in a small group. "For months, there was nothing," she says. "I have never considered myself particularly intuitive until recently, when I began having strong predictive dreams; I thought I needed to learn more about all of this. That's why I joined the group. Then, one afternoon when I was practicing, my voice felt as if it wanted to change and the feeling got stronger and stronger until it did change and what sounded like another voice began to speak. It—they—they always say, 'we,' talked about my life and my musical gifts and said they were there to assist me and that Florence, my teacher, would support me in this exploration. This new work."

Serena listens carefully, finding Laura modest, making no effort to impress. She seems practical, grounded in her life and in the work she is describing, curious about it, but not distressed. Serena realizes that despite her interest in altered states and her years of reading about it, it would never occur to her to study channeling.

"So," Laura continues, "I have gone ahead with Florence and the group and now several others have started to channel. We ask questions of each other—no fortune-telling. I would like you to ask me some questions because I want an outside evaluation." Laura laughs. "I do, really. And I thank you for doing this."

Serena smiles, noticing that the flowers have a distinct herbal scent that floats in the warmth of the afternoon. She sips her tea, a little nervous, somewhat to her surprise. "I've never seen anyone channel," she says. "I'm not sure I know how to evaluate it."

"I'm confident that whatever you offer will be valuable," Laura says calmly. "You're knowledgeable about these experiences; I learned so much in your class about altered states, even though that was not specifically the topic."

Serena can see the garden through the long windows that front it and she can see the heavy pots of chrysanthemums, clusters of white and deep purple with red undertones, yellow and terra cotta all massed together. The climbing roses, still vigorous, curve up the garden wall, scarlet against the worn bricks. She lets her nervousness flutter, excitement mingling with it. Charlotte, their delicate calico with the air of a politely demanding princess, spreads out between Laura and Serena and stretches.

"Shall we begin?" asks Laura. She closes her eyes, but not quite all the way and her arms open out, her hands swaying, her fingers tapping rhythmically in the air. She begins to speak, her voice a ribbon unrolling in peaks and troughs, the tone one of humor and delight. Serena asks questions about her personal life, but is careful not to be too revealing with someone she doesn't really know. She asks about Leo, though, and their relationship; asks what Laura's guide might offer to enhance their relationship in ways Serena has not thought of. She inquires about her perfectionism, how to move away from it. It does not occur to her to ask if channeling might be an option for her. As she listens to the guide's responses, she is aware that her mind is scrambling around, wondering where Laura has dug up all this intimate information about her. She feels a shimmer of defensiveness rise in her belly at the depth and accuracy of the responses the guide gives, though the words are spoken gently in an atmosphere of kindness. Her defensiveness gives Serena a sharp understanding of one of the reasons people might be eager to discount (or disparage) intuitive information. It is unsettling to have an almost stranger speak about personal matters with such clarity. But Serena is also pleased and intrigued, grateful for the insights, which are shrewd and, she thinks, will be useful. Laura emerges from the trance, is silent for a moment and then looks at Serena, who thanks her and says the information was accurate. They talk for a while about Laura's feelings when she channels and Laura says she hopes they can meet again.

"Certainly," says Serena. "I am very interested in your work. You seem completely natural in the altered state, nothing dramatic beyond the obvious drama of shifting your awareness and the change in your voice. I was wondering if channeling always results in an altered voice? Or speech, really. Your responses were accurate and skillful. A little unnerving sometimes," Serena laughs. "Having a stranger know so much about me."

"The people I work with all have different voices when they channel. Different from their own and different from each other. But I don't think it is always so, no. And I am not sure why it happens."

"Let's make a time to follow up," Serena says. "Let's do it now, so we know it is definite." They arrange a time and Laura collects her things to go. They hug briefly and Laura leaves, petting Charlotte on her way out.

The whole session and their talk have not taken long and now Serena is alone with Charlotte, who is napping, and Romeo, who is in the kitchen rattling his food dish. She still has no idea that her life is about to change in ways both blissful and profoundly challenging. She sits looking out at the shifting light in the garden; darkness curls slowly into the daylight, though it will not be fully dark for a while. There are deepening shadows of late afternoon as the earth spins away from the sun. Laura's channeling is striking, inviting. And then, with no more than an imperceptible tilt of the plane of her existence, Serena thinks, Maybe I can do that. What if I can channel? She knows that the delicate personal ecology of the psyche can lose its bearings, shift the convergence of interlocking agreements that form ordinary reality and be unable to reconfigure them. But now she is determined to try and once determined in this way that feels aligned with her heart, Serena goes forward, riding on her heart's wisdom and propelled by her will. She sits quietly for a few more moments. Then she begins to chant, letting each sound emerge spontaneously, and her heart races and her mouth feels sticky and slightly numb. She has swiftly flying images whose outlines gather into words and then she is speaking. The first words are ones that she will say a hundred—a thousand—times in years to come: "We greeet you, dear friend." There is a pause and they continue, "We have been waiting for you, waiting until you could manage this without alarm." She imagines the empty, whirling space of atoms, drawing the illusion of solidity around themselves, ancient, unknowable emptiness coalescing into the familiar rub and shine of ordinary objects: the squish and sigh of flesh, the hurtling of heartbeats as a river of blood swims through her.

The content of the first communication is unremarkable, but the experience of it is entirely new. The aura of the trance is comforting—the steamy density and compassion of the voice is like a sigh being released from some interior well of mercy and soothing. The visceral quality is reassuring, though the speech—swaying, the words elongated, the volume rising and then falling almost to a whisper—half dismays and half amuses her. Laura's channeled voice had been unusual, too, different from her normal voice. As Serena speaks, her eyes roll back and the lids flutter wildly, so that a curve of trembling light presses the bottom rim of her vision. Her body feels emptied of weight; the room's edges hover timelessly, though the floor is solid beneath her. When she returns to her accustomed reality it is on a flushed wave of exhilaration and, in its wake, a swirling pool of questions. It takes a few moments to realign with her usual self, to re-enter the gateway into her ordinary world and when she has, she does a quick reality check. Her thoughts are orderly and familiar, if—now—flooded with curiosity and doubt, pleasure and dismay. Her broad feet, still slightly tan from the summer, look as they always do; the walls hang neatly from the ceiling, folded in shadow at each corner, the room holds her, steady and safe; nothing wobbles. But the edges of her world have melted, expanded, she has done something she never imagined for a moment that she would do—it will change her perception of reality and of herself, of other people's view of her and sometimes she will feel more like an outsider, even more radically different than she has often felt. It is a challenge that will braid gossamer wisps together and tear other aspects of her personality apart. All this while the sunflower petals in the bedroom glow, the teacups sit half-empty on the floor, the wisteria leaves that had greeted her and Leo that morning move in the late afternoon breeze; her heart beats steadily, her breath rises and falls. The elements the same, the context shifted forever.

The voice, Serena will realize later, as she experiments with it, feels more like a shape given to pulses of information, an architecture of impressions as they are received energetically and then relayed in speech. It is not so much hearing a voice and then speaking and more like being the voice in order to deliver the information and the feeling that so often accompanied it. For months before she started to channel, Serena had watched shapes transform from solid patterns into fiery transparent ones. Trees, especially, revealed their brilliant underlying spin. She vaguely remembered seeing lights around trees when she was a child, a living aura that breathed color. The recent seeing—or perhaps it was sensing—fascinated her and also made her anxious. The world sliding, glowing, inhaling and exhaling. She had told Leo about it and he was interested and calm; she confided in a Buddhist friend, who simply said, "Just keep breathing." But that didn't seem to cover it, although she understood the suggestion. She had also noticed that in her work as a Science of Mind spiritual practitioner (she had studied for three years and received her license), her spoken meditations, done with each client, had become more insightful, spontaneously organized and purposeful, detailing the healing intention with grace and joy. Her personal meditations had deepened as well and though she noticed these changes, she in no way anticipated the coming events. As she moves forward in her channeling practice, explores the possibilities, taps at the edges of a new reality, the physical world remains reliable, lets Serena see its transient brilliance without ever failing her. She is delivered onto a path part invention, part memory, part gift from all her teachers: an expanded expression of herself as an urban mystic (a term she will use later, only half-humorously). A path sometimes smooth, sometimes scraping and bumping, one of stunning and undiluted paradox and one that opens her further into perceiving signals from shadows and strategies through dreams.

It would be a long time before Serena thought about the relevance and the irony of shifting her focus toward disembodied energies—or, if not disembodied, alive in a manner different from the apparent solidity of the physical world. She, who had fought her own weight and density with such intensity. When she does realize this possible connection, she appreciates it and sees that it has a certain humor and also some sadness.

When the first session is over, Serena writes down what she said and the experience of doing it. She is eager for Leo to come home and talk about it. While she waits, she waters all the plants and then sits on the sofa, reflecting on her past and what she understands now was a search for a spiritual home.

Between the vision of her father's light body watching over her at night when she was four and he was very ill, and the moment this afternoon when she sat with the cat, chanting and diving through the web of reality, bouncing through skeins of consciousness into an enlarged geometry of awareness, she had studied widely, seeking what was behind the physical world.

❋ ✹ ❋

When Serena was fifteen she and Ruby moved from Central Park West to an apartment on East Seventy-sixth Street. Two large, bony rooms with wide windows facing south and a small kitchen and bath. Referred to by the realtor as a 'three-and-a-half,' they would joke about where the missing room was supposed to be. The light switches glowed in the dark and moved up and down soundlessly, another of the agent's selling points. Serena asked that they paint the living room, where she would sleep, creamy beige and her mother's room a soft lemony yellow. She arranged the move and she and Anna, their housekeeper and Serena's surrogate grandmother, packed the old apartment while Ruby read or went for walks in the hot summer afternoons. In the wisdom of her fifteen years, she gave away French lamps, elegant flowers painted on glass, and a handsome pottery lamp, to replace them with speckled, beige, glass lamps from a large department store. Her idea that things should match. When her Aunt Marion discovered the loss (she had chosen the lamps) she folded her lips and sighed. Another strike against Ruby, letting a child take charge. But nothing to be done. Once moved, she and Ruby bought a huge Kentia palm that they named Alfred. Living as two, Serena and Ruby were forever missing the magical third that would make them a 'real' family. Serena took her normalcy where she could find it, smoothing surfaces, matching paint chips and ordering upholstery, with Ruby seeming sour and resigned at the money being spent (but the finely made bedspread for Ruby's room would be intact fifty years later). The apartment satisfied Serena's love of order and beauty and soothed her with what she later called her addiction to surfaces, not understanding when she was young that the soothing was false and dangerous. Ruby said this way of being calmed was genetic, an inherited trait. From Serena's father Alex's family.

Their windows faced a Catholic church and the adjoining rectory. A loud bell called the fathers at five each morning. Was it a bell to wake them? A bell for mass? Neither Ruby nor Serena knew, but it sounded every day. The church windows were spotty stained glass protected by wire mesh. When Serena and Ruby's windows were open in the summer, music and the soft swell of voices were audible along with what sounded like a small bell. One early morning in February, Serena crossed the street in the icy darkness to attend Mass. People sat in their overcoats surrounded by the smell of incense, then unfamiliar to Serena. Gritty melting wet was everywhere underfoot. She did not understand more than a few words of Latin and the translated text seemed ominous to her, full of shame and pleading; agonized apology. The church was full of candles, their flames stretched and pale in the morning light. Serena loved the candles and the murmuring, sleepy voices and the mysterious lifting and dropping down as people stood and then knelt in response to the priest, who was almost inaudible to her. She learned the rosary and would stop into the church to light candles, kneeling on the stone step in front of a tilting bank of small flames, praying in her own anarchistic way, but she never returned to mass.

In the summers, she and Ruby stayed in a small town in New Hampshire. They began going when Serena was eight and continued until she was sixteen, so she grew with the children of the town. The Congregational church at one edge of the village green was a steady feature of those times. Their services were mild and plain, comforting. Serena loved the hymns, though she was always puzzled by the line in one hymn that said (about Jesus and the church), "With His own blood He bought her and for her life He died." The congregation sang it with bland contentment, that violent strange thought floating unrecognized through the atmosphere of the room. Later, she would wonder about the militaristic nature of so many hymns, but at the time, in the bright morning light coming through the church windows, they seemed simply a celebration of belief.

Some years before going to the church across the street, Serena had tried Temple Emanu-El, another place of worship where she did not understand some of the language. The text, although different from the Catholic devotions, was stormy and threatening. Beseeching. She went to services several times, finally asking Ruby to go with her, which she did without protest, surprising Serena. But Ruby was critical of the rabbi and they were both clearly outsiders. They did not return. Serena passed through the time of her friends' bar and bas mitzvahs cheerful and unmoved.

Serena remembered herself as a child with spiritual yearning and no religious training; she was hoping to connect, to be nurtured and received. In her adult life this emerged as a passionate pull to create a community, a heart-family, a group that was home.

On Sunday mornings, the year Serena was fifteen, Ruby started to listen to one Raymond Charles Barker on the radio. Dr. Barker. Serena found the plummy voice comical. "One Mind," he said, "One Divine Intelligence in All, as All and through All." Serena cruised through the *New York Times* entertainment section and made her face up endlessly, trying new and different combinations as Ruby listened to Dr. Barker.

"Interesting," Ruby said, about Dr. Barker.

"Oh mother," Serena sighed. "Really."

She was not yet interested in Science of Mind and Dr. Barker, or in the idea of an interactive reality. Reality by participation. When she is twenty-five, she will meet her teacher, when Ruby invites her to hear him speak and she goes, with reluctance. "A younger man," Ruby would say. "He was in the theater and majored in psychology." He will become both her teacher and beloved friend in a relationship that flourishes until he dies when Serena is sixty.

✻ ◎ ✻

When Leo returns, Serena is still sitting in the living room with Charlotte on her lap. He comes and sits with her. "How was it?" he asks. "What was the session like?" Serena holds her arms out and Leo hugs her and she rocks in his arms for a while. His beautiful Serena; sometimes a silvered lily, washed by the rain; other times the blazing velvet crimson of an anemone petal. Sometimes as untouchable as a translucent shell of ice polishing a smooth stone. He has determined on the walk home that he is going to ask about marriage, about a baby. He doesn't know how to interpret the hug. "Serena, what?" he says. "Are you all right?"

"Yes. Yes. I had an extraordinary afternoon and you won't ever guess what happened to me. So I will tell you right away." She describes the session with Laura, how impressive it was, how accurate. Laura had, in channel, described the relationship with Leo in some detail and highlighted the crossroads Serena felt she was at. She had received invitations to teach in Paris and Amsterdam, and to meet for sessions with individual clients as well. This would be exciting and challenging and Serena wants to accept the offers, knowing they will bring changes that she cannot yet imagine. She talked about Serena's mother and the complications between them, about Ruby's rages, how afraid Serena had been as a child. And then Serena tells him that she herself channeled after Laura left. She describes the weightless sensation and the sliding voice, the speech stretched and then rapid, sounding unlike her own, the sense of being cherished and held with love. The gentle humor and robust pulse of energy. "I know," she says, at the end of her description, "I know it can be dangerous. Believe me, I did look around when I was finished to see if things seemed normal, whatever normal is." She knows how carefully she had looked at the room—saw that the plants were the same, the furniture in place. And, most importantly, the cat was relaxed and purring. She had experienced a profound shift and the physical world had held her reliably, to her relief. Her experience of her ordinary identity remained intact. She very much wants Leo's support and feels that if he is critical or unkind—or afraid—it will be troubling and she is, along with her excitement, troubled enough.

Leo has listened quietly and then says, "Pursue it. It's fascinating. I don't think there is anything to worry about, you'll go carefully and you're skillful and grounded. I want to see you—what?—in trance. Entranced. Not now, I know. Too much for one day." The gate between the worlds swings open to include them both as he talks and holds her. "Let's eat and talk," he says. "I'll make dinner." Their years of intimacy shiver and expand to include this new aspect of life. The marriage and baby conversation he had imagined has ended before it begun. Too much for one day. Maybe too much for quite some time.

"How was Nina?" Serena asks, as they cut vegetables. Nothing, not even the worlds opening, would cause Serena to forget to ask this question. She is from what she refers to as "the Doberman School of Sharing."

"About what I expected, after the dinner."

"And that was?" Their knives go up and down neatly; Leo is faster and neater than Serena, who cuts slowly, the results always pieces in mixed shapes and sizes.

He resists sighing. "Were we married? No? Was I available? No? Maybe some other time?"

"Oh, cute. Not too subtle." Serena stops cutting. "So, while I was having a transformative experience that will change my life forever, you were being propositioned by Max's daughter? Are there hidden parallels here?" She bites into a carrot.

"No, no hidden parallels. I assume that's a joke?"

"Yes, it is. Did she mention marriage and babies, while she was at it?"

"No. What makes you ask that?" Everything goes into the sizzling pan.

"I don't know, really. Has anyone ever gone that far?"

"No, Serena." Leo wonders whether to mention what he had been thinking and wonders if Serena, who is very intuitive, quite apart from the channeling, might have intuited his thoughts.

"What is it that happens with you?"

"I don't know; I was wondering that on the way up. I must be participating in some way, but certainly not consciously."

"Has this always happened to you? Since you were small? A little guy with all the lovely girls following him around." But Serena knows it has always happened. They have talked about it together and with Nick.

The question stops Leo. He looks out at the garden, at the shadows turning lavender as the light drops away. Has it been this way? Always? He should certainly know the answer, but for a moment he does not. And then he remembers his family teasing him about it; why would he forget that? "Our own Romeo," his grandmother would say. He disliked it, disliked the fuss—though he liked the girls and then the women. The memories arrive and then bloom in flamboyant color, rising from the dusk of whatever he would have liked to forget. There was a rolling cast of characters.

Leo laughs out loud. "It has always been so," he says. "It also seems to have a lot attached to it that I haven't really—uh—accommodated consciously. Is that the right word? Could we come back to this later? I'd rather talk about your afternoon.

Let's eat outside." They have a tiny café table in the garden and the night is warm.

"Good. Let's. I'm sorry, Leo. I know I'm hyper-vigilant. I embarrass myself. All the abandonment fears, still so powerful. They come from so far down, all the way down in my cells." Serena, who is fearless in so many ways, bold in her work, resilient and peaceful with people who are ill and dying, courageous about her beliefs, but still frightened of impending loss in this primitive way, despite the efforts she has made to heal. They take the fragrant platters out to the garden and light two candles for the table. Leo heaps his plate; Serena takes small amounts of everything and then cuts things thoughtfully into tiny portions, which she eats slowly. Both cats station themselves as close as possible to the table. Romeo jumps into Leo's lap, noses into the food, without quite touching; a whisper away.

"Okay, tell me more, Serena."

"I wondered, when Laura left, if I could channel, though it had never occurred to me before, with all the reading I have done about altered states, I didn't imagine myself being part of that kind of work. I chanted first—as I always do before I meditate—and then I was quiet and then a voice spoke through me. Or I spoke in another voice. I don't know yet what is happening. The state was astonishing, not only because I was speaking, but because the feelings of being loved and held gently were so—what?—not unfamiliar, exactly and not blissful—but very present. Vibrant. I've told you this part."

"Yes. And I want to hear it all together," says Leo. "Was it like your experiences of your guardians being around you?" Serena has told Leo that she has often felt presences near her, protecting her. When she first talked about it he asked if she meant something like a guardian angel, his association from Catholicism and Serena said she didn't know. But maybe.

"My heart was beating fast, but I didn't feel frightened. Maybe excited? Then, when it was over, I did a reality check, as I've said. No, the guardians feel different. They are around me, but not within me. Then I remembered all the stories I have ever read about possession and dissociation, being overcome. I didn't feel overcome, though; I felt a sense of respect from the energy—or whatever it is—no flicker of fear or possible harm. That was my thinking self, later. I do need ground rules, Leo. The first one is that I only channel when I want to and I am not on call. Not available at random times. I don't want to imagine I could be swept away in the middle of a sociable restaurant meal, rolling my eyes and croaking, 'We greeet you,' as neighboring tables signal distress and my fork dangles loosely from my hand." She laughs at the thought. Even at this early time, the very beginning, Serena is starting to use her humor to protect her tenderness, her wildness and her vulnerability, her courage in following this path, which is both grace and, she

283

knows, filled with difficulties she cannot foresee. She understands that she has ventured past the frontier of the socially plausible and she is thrilled and cautious. Laughter and irony will remain two of her defenses for years.

Leo brings out a bowl of pears and carefully cuts two. He gives Serena a gingersnap and eats several himself. "I want to meet with everyone," Serena says. "With Rose and Hal and Ingrid and Max and Sue Ann and Sept and Bart. I want to do this with them all and see what their reactions are."

"Stephen?" Leo asks. Stephen is more Bart's friend, but he is often part of their close group.

"Uhhh. Stephen." Serena thinks of his coolness, how caustic he can be and how clever.

"If you do this, you'll be with people who might be critical."

"I know that," Serena says, slightly defensively. Any one of the group might be critical. Ingrid. Max? Although Max wouldn't be unkind. None of them would, even Ingrid, who doesn't mince words. "I don't know how they'll feel. I'm not sure yet how I feel. Too soon? Should I wait and not share this until I feel more secure?" Serena looks worried and imagines how hard it would be to face harsh criticism at this point; perhaps especially from people she loves. Then, with one of the sudden shifts she makes, she says, "I want to do it. If they are critical or can't tolerate it in some way because it's strange, then I need to know. These are the friends I trust most in the world."

"Sept won't have a problem," Leo says.

Sue Ann's partner, Sept was a detective with the NYPD for more than twenty years; he is highly intuitive and comes from a family that gave intuitive gifts an honored place. He says his great-great-grandmother took her family along the underground railway using what she called her guidance. And she brought them to safety. Once, in the Tarot class where some of the friends first met Sept, Rose asked if he had used his gifts in his police work. "Now that wouldn't be proper," he said. "Wouldn't be impossible that I did, either."

The candles burn low and the lights of the city flicker beyond the garden, signaling that nightlife has begun and will continue until dawn. City children, they find the lit nights reassuring, an arena that holds them safely, though both also love the country and stillness. A curl of moon presses through the gathering clouds and the sweet scents of the phlox and late roses from their garden drift in the city air, along with the sharper accent of the chrysanthemums. Leo and Serena gather their dinner things onto a tray and move inside. The cats follow hopefully, Romeo meowing loudly. Technically they don't feed the cats leftovers, but this is a mere technicality. "Well, tomorrow I'll call Ingrid and Rose and we'll arrange a get together. I know Ingrid is preparing for her show, so maybe after that and not tomorrow. I want to tell everyone together. Ingrid's opening is on Thursday." Serena knows that Ingrid has prepared everything down to the last detail and will supervise at the gallery when the show is installed. The preparation is psychological as well as physical, a grim duel within her to appear in public and not flee. Which would be her preference. Serena and Leo start to wash the dishes, having doled out scraps to the cats, and part way through, Leo stops and rubs Serena's back.

"Would you like a massage?" he asks.

"Tight?"

"Mmm. Very."

"Yes, and who knows what glorious pleasures might follow? This isn't a ploy, is it?"

Leo laughs. "I don't need a ploy," he says. They leave the dishes where they are and go into the bedroom.

"Oh, such confidence," Serena says. "But deserved."

✳ ◉ ✳

Ingrid does have everything ready for the show, for the opening, which she dreads. It is the day after Serena's experience of channeling and she is pacing in her studio. She dreads it no less now that she did all those years ago in Iowa, at that first show. Maybe it is more intense now, because her work has "caught on," a phrase she loathes. It is, to her, meaningless and demeaning simultaneously. Art as fashion, or the fashions in art. (Soon she will be invited to pose for glossy magazines; she will decline and then agree, reluctant and somewhat resentful, but determined to have her work go into the world and do whatever is necessary to have that happen.) Her reputation is growing swiftly; now the openings are in large rooms filled with people, with eyes and moving mouths, careful clothing (fashionable) and the smell of wine and mingled perfumes, the snicker of high heels and the snap of costly purses. With greed and posturing. Yes, there are always some who come for the work, who are appreciative and, perhaps, knowledgeable. Max consistently reminds her of this as she gets more and more desperate as the date approaches. "I can't see why I need to be there," she says repeatedly. "My work is there. They aren't coming to see me. It isn't a performance." But they are coming to see her and it is partially a performance. Has always been. She dislikes hurrying and is precise and careful about her work; she knows where she wants each painting to be hung in the gallery and hopes the gallerist will agree with her. Ingrid is neither flexible nor accommodating. The openings are so far from her experience of herself, the solitude of her work, with only the sounds of her own body, of moving and breathing and painting, with the smell of coffee, the restless city outside, the empty studio floor, shining, black. (Ingrid paints the floor periodically. It is a restful task and satisfying.) She does not answer the phone when she is working, which distresses Max. She does eat—Ingrid always eats—making runs to the deli in all weather, coatless even when it snows.

Sometimes Max simply appears at her studio, carrying lunch; a hint of when they first spoke, years ago, both carrying paper deli bags, riding in the elevator in the building where they worked. Max's family owns the building, but Ingrid did not know that at the time. She thought he was a well-dressed functionary of some kind. The building was full of them, though the others were not as assured as Max. He had commented that she must have a hearty appetite. She always carried a substantial amount of food upstairs. When Max visits the studio, they spread out a picnic lunch of fat sandwiches and garlicky pickles, Danish and lots of good coffee. At home, they cook healthy food, but these visits are an exception, a private party in the midst of the guarded sacred solitude of Ingrid's studio. Occasionally now, they eat lunch and then Max undresses her and they make love on the narrow daybed: heated touch, intimate rituals and excitement—still. Max has brought soft quilts, pillows and scented soap, adding them to Ingrid's spare studio space. Ingrid does not know why she permits this particular interruption, but she does, knowing that Max would never pressure her if she didn't.

Ingrid's new work has surprised her. Flowers have appeared, or parts of them. Some scattered petals and leaves of bright garden flowers: intensely blue delphiniums, the deepest pink peonies, apricot roses, a few splashy orange zinnias. Other flowers are pale, from hidden places, like Indian pipes. There are delicate ferns that grow only in the shade, some painted in one place with their fronds half-broken, the whole fern appearing in another part of the painting. She has brushed lightly across many of the forms, so they are visible, but somewhat remote. Some paintings include mushrooms with vivid caps, floating upside down and sideways. Small images are half-hidden behind other forms: babies' teeth, a claw tiny enough to belong to a mouse; there are images threaded through mazes or strung loosely in garlands; there are occasional words that are almost indecipherable. The colors vary from muted, barely present, mysterious, to touches of flamboyant sparks, like punctuations of sound. The canvases are a good size to hang in a home, unlike some of her earlier work, though this was not a conscious choice, but seemed dictated by the material.

Ingrid has studied some botany in order to do this work. She has read current books and very old ones, doing research at the main branch of the library on Forty-second Street. She is careful in her representations, correct and accurate. The intensity of her research does not disturb her, she is always intense, but some of the subject matter is surprising, even as she paints it. It comes from a source that is unfamiliar, particularly the flowers, since she is not especially interested in flowers. (The claws and teeth are not a surprise, and make her laugh, alone in her studio.) She lets herself be surprised and continues to paint what presents itself to her.

One canvas is filled with blues: blue to almost purple, to indigo. There are rounded shapes, apparently abstract, but viewed a certain way they could be full, rounded abdomens, pregnant bellies with protruding navels and moon-sliced silver marks rippling along their sides. Here, too are flowers: these dark, almost black, but not quite. The petals are of no known blossoms, surreal and yearning.

Her dreams have changed, as well. More flowers, growing profusely in fields, on hot summer roadsides, gathered in formal vases. Or there are babies, sucking at the breast of a goddess (but which one?); lips fast on the nipple and Ingrid can feel the sensation of the baby, the pull, the tightening in her groin as she sleeps.

When she tells Max about the dreams he laughs. "Lest my years of therapy go to waste, these dreams are not exactly mysterious," he says.

"They are to me," Ingrid answers. She is clearly puzzled. Sharp Ingrid.

Max kisses her. "Flowers and suckling babies and pregnant bellies. What does that suggest?" he says.

"Well okay, yes, I understand that part, but I am not interested in having a baby. We have talked about it and you're not interested either. Right?" Max is quiet. Too quiet, thinks Ingrid. "Are you? You have two grown daughters."

"I do. But I don't know. When I imagine it now, it feels possible, I would be a much better father now."

"Max, I do not want to be a mother. Ever. I hope all our friends have lovely babies and I can be an aunt. That's as far as I want to go." Ingrid feels slightly agitated, as if the tilt of her world has moved.

"That's fine," says Max. "My feelings are a surprise."

"Yes, like these paintings. And my dreams. Big surprise. There are a lot of interpretations. I could be giving birth to new aspects of myself and flowering." Ingrid is pleased with this interpretation. "Right?"

"Yes. Right. Let's go out to dinner."

"Yes. Good. Let's." That ends the conversation, for the moment. The next day, Serena will call with her news. She does not wait until the show has opened.

❋ ✲ ❋

On Saturday, Serena and Leo garden together in the morning and Serena talks about her knowledge of trance work: about Jane Roberts, and Eileen Garrett, and about Helena Blavatsky. Serena talks about the Bible, what she knows of it, which isn't much, and the trance states that she feels are part of Biblical lore. Leo adds to this, since he studied the Catholic Bible at his grandmother's insistence, until he rebelled, absolutely and with his parents' support, when he was eleven. They deadhead spent blooms and pull weeds, sweaty and happy, and go on to talk about Shamanistic practices in cultures where they are a deep part of the fabric of life; where they value these practices and cherish the skills to reach them with care and precision. Leo takes in some lettuces that he has grown in a barrel and reseeded during the summer and they eat a big salad for lunch and then shower together. "Just showering," Serena says, "I want to call Rose."

"Of course," Leo says, soaping her breasts carefully. "No question. I have work to do."

Serena dresses and then calls Rose. Rose is always the first one she talks to about personal matters, intimate experiences, spiritual conundrums; they have been together since they were twelve, since their breasts and periods were new. They have traveled together through the 60s, through lovers and short storms of random sex, which Rose treated with practicality and amusement and Serena explored because she did not want to realize at some later age—say, forty—that she had missed a variety of experiences. (By the time Serena is forty, she feels she could have skipped a lot of it.) She and Rose enter the feminist movement together. They are, to each other, the sister they never had. Of course she calls Rose first. They have shared so much for so long that they can finish each other's sentences. Often, they speak in shorthand, referring to events familiar to them both, but not, necessarily, to someone else, should another person be listening. Rose, now an attorney working for an organization that aids women in a variety of legal crisis situations, lives with her partner Hal, just outside of Woodstock, where he is a vet —mostly large animals—and she commutes to the city three days a week. She stays in the apartment she and Serena once shared. Serena and Rose have meditated together and studied the Tarot in a group with Frieda, whom Serena still regards as a Spiritual mentor—though Frieda would deny it. Rose is not really drawn to mysteries, is sometimes edgy and skeptical, but she is always curious and will always listen carefully.

"Hi," Serena says. "How are you?"

"Thinking about getting a horse. To keep the dogs company." Rose laughs. She loves animals with her whole self; loves them with generosity and abandon.

"A horse? Really?" Serena's tone implies they might just as easily be getting a unicorn, though she knows that Rose and Hal both ride and of course Hal cares for horses in his practice. Actually owning a horse is beyond her imagination, not part of her worldview. She is not sure whether she has ever touched a horse. "That's exciting. Is it? Must be."

"Yes," says Rose. "It's amazing." And that is true. She is amazed and happy.

"You?" She hears something in Serena's voice that tells her that Serena has news of some kind.

"I had a very odd experience. The woman who came over yesterday . . ." Was it only yesterday? Only twenty-four hours since this enormous change?

"The one from your class? The singer?"

"Yes. The one who channels. She did a session for me and her voice altered and she responded to the questions I had with great insight. She only knows me from class, not anything personal at all. She was very matter-of-fact. She just sat down and was quiet for a bit and then began to speak." Serena is sitting on her bed and gazes at the bunch of sunflowers, lost for a moment in their brilliant spiky petals, and the dark center of the blooms. She is quiet and hesitant, which is unusual in her relationship with Rose. They have talked about their secrets, shared their daily lives, trusted each other since they were twelve. She lets herself stay quiet.

"Serena?"

"Yes, yes. I'm here." She moves past the silence and describes what has happened; her description loosens bundles of questions, hers and Rose's. What it is, how it felt, what it means. And the question that will arise again and again, Is it real? The question that will thread itself in and out of Serena's work for years, sometimes a pleasurable quest, sometimes stinging, sharp as a cut. Why, she wonders later, when she has been working in an altered state for a while, would she do this demanding, exuberant, profoundly challenging thing that, for her, carries vast responsibilities, probably even beyond those she could identify, if it was not authentic? Even if she cannot explain it fully, not ever, she can see that it is valuable to many people on their journey and that must be enough for her to keep the commitment.

"What did it feel like?" Rose circles around again.

"My body felt light, but grounded, I didn't feel as if I were floating, but the physical edges were soft, or open. Something. My arms and hands moved as I was speaking—almost like sitting still and dancing simultaneously. I felt embraced. Happy."

"Nervous?" asks Rose.

"Not when I was speaking, no. After I came out, or back, or whatever it is, I looked around the room to see if things seemed normal and they did. The cats were calm, which I took as a good sign. It wasn't like after an acid trip," Serena tried acid only once, "when the whole world seemed altered. The voice—I don't know—it was my voice, but sliding and the speech was distorted. No, just different. Laura's speech shifted, too. It seemed to go with the whole state, the embodiment. I want us all to meet so you can see it. Experience it? After Ingrid's show, of course."

"Who is all?"

"You and Hal and Ingrid and Max and Bart and Sue Ann and Sept. All of us."

"Stephen?" Stephen, a weary, shining man. The cousin of someone who had been Serena's love, years ago.

"Funny, Leo asked me that. I'm not sure. He can be so caustic and I feel vulnerable. And I feel—how? Not fragile, but tender."

"Mmmm. Maybe no Stephen. How long after the show?"

"Next weekend," Serena says. "Here. We'll make dinner."

"Okay. I'm excited to see it. I've never seen anyone channel."

"We saw that psychic, though—you know . . ."

"Oh, at the Ansonia. Bertram." Who was a jumpy, fast-talking man who took questions from the audience written on slips of paper and waved his finger as he responded, rapid-fire. Who sounded like an auctioneer.

"But it isn't like that?"

"No, no. Nothing like it. I certainly hope not."

They are both quiet again. The information settles.

"Speaking of the show," Serena says, changing the subject, "what are you wearing?"

"I haven't thought about it." Rose, whose mother, Syl, is obsessed by clothes and ornaments, shoes and hair and glistening skin had not passed her frantic focus on to Rose.

"And you?"

Serena details several possibilities, with great concentration. She has her own obsessions about how things look. How she looks. "I think the lavender, in the end. I will call everyone about Saturday." Rose has listened with the patience of love and long practice.

"Good. See you Thursday."

"Love," Serena says. By Monday, she has called everyone to invite them for Saturday. She says she doesn't want to describe what happened, wants them to experience it first. She calls Stephen, too, and considers calling Frieda, but realizes she is not ready yet and that she will meet with Frieda soon.

✳ ☺ ✳

Thursday arrives with dark clouds and wind, but by late afternoon the sun is out and there is only a mild breeze.

For the last month, Max has been asking Ingrid what she wants to wear for the opening. Ingrid calls him her dresser. "Or maybe your costumer," Max says, unperturbed. Max, who loves fabric and style and color, who is passionate about Ingrid and takes such pleasure in her beauty.

"I don't know or care," is her standard answer.

"Nothing pale," he says, musing. "The works are dramatic, you need to be dramatic, part of the pageantry." They have been having varieties of this conversation

"Ai. Max. Please." She sighs. "I have that black silk, remember?"

"Only too well. No, and nothing in the orangey-gold range." What is it, wonders Max, that fascinates him about this: the openings, dressing, display. Ingrid's stature, her flat belly and large round breasts, her shining tangled hair. Her wildness, so carefully controlled in her work. And in this show, suckling babies, teeth. Claws. Ingrid, the creator, severe among the paradoxical shapes. He does see it all as a pageant. But there is something else, something hypnotic, he thinks.

"Why are you so focused on what I look like?" Ingrid asks. "You seem hypnotized by the whole drama. What are these conversations really about?"

"You read my mind," Max says. "Maybe I really wanted to be an artist, not a— whatever I am. A collector?" Technically, he is an importer of fine objects; gathers them for people who admire beauty, people who display their wealth, companies that include what he brings them in their regal offices.

"Did you?" Max has never, to her knowledge, drawn or painted.

"I don't know. It's in my dreams, sometimes." Then, "Green," he says. "The color of dark sea glass. Very plain. Severe." (That word again.)

"Fine."

"I'll have Maurice make it," Max says. "We have all your measurements."

"Thank you, Max." Ingrid has learned to be gracious; it gives her pleasure to appreciate her lover. She never expected anyone like him.

✳ ☺ ✳

On that Thursday, in the warming evening, Ingrid wears the new dress. Max takes her arm and they walk from her studio to Soho. She is still dreading it, as she always does, her dignified fragility carefully hidden beneath glowing confidence, her apparent nonchalance.

Max and Ingrid get to the gallery early, and by the time the gallery opens, people are crowded in the street, leaning against cars, smoking; there are clouds of talk as they move through the doors, waves of perfume, a loose excitement floating around a tighter focus of curiosity, eagerness and adroit, competitive pushing. There is an abundance of white wine and servers cruise the room with elegant food in tiny portions on garnished platters. Ingrid is too tense to eat and she does not consider this food. She and Max have eaten a late lunch. All their close friends are there. One young man with a curly auburn ponytail stands still for a long time in front of a single painting. Bart, who has been Ingrid's friend since college, looking at him from behind, imagines that it might be Jeremy, his first lover, who is far away in San Francisco. (Maybe it is Jeremy? A surprise visit?) But no, the man turns, smiles at Bart and continues around the room. There are women and men with babies close against their chests, riding in baby slings; there are a number of people in sunglasses, even as the light drops and dark approaches. The doors are open and noise from the city mingles with the other sounds and becomes part of the pageant. (Max is right. It is a pageant.)

The art sells so fast that many of the pieces have red dots even before all the special invitees and their friends have arrived. Ingrid is appalled. Her popularity and success still seem impossible to her. How can anyone decide to buy a piece of art so quickly? It is a sure sign that she has become a desirable commodity in this world shaped by opinions, mood, history, by rivalry and jostling trends. Her stomach begins to clench, reminding her that her wholly reliable period is late and she lets the thought stay with her only a moment before pushing it sharply away, a feat at which she is skillful. Her friends are moving through the gallery, looking intently at the work. Ingrid does not let anyone except Max see her works in progress. Max is delighted. Thrilled. He believes that Ingrid is inspired, truly a genius. He greets people with pleasure and warmth, arms open to offer hugs. His large, dignified head, topped with full silver and black curls, nods. He knows Ingrid's feelings, but wants to enjoy all of this without marring his sympathy for her; it does not seem that mirroring her feelings will contribute in any way. He does touch her as she moves around the room, his hands offering a moment of comfort. "This is like a lettuce sale," she says, at one of those moments.

"A what?"

"A lettuce sale, at a supermarket, with people waving coupons and poking the produce. That kind of atmosphere."

"Is that a play on words?" Max is baffled.

"Why?"

"Lettuce? Lots of money?" He knows this is a mistake as soon as he has said it.

Ingrid looks grim. "No, I mean it literally. I feel shopped."

Max says no more, touches her shoulder and moves away. There really is no way to comfort her in this paradoxical reality of creating art, and wanting it to go out to be seen and feeling betrayed by the process, beset by a sense of loss and violation. He does understand the art world (very well indeed) and Ingrid's feelings, but there seems no resolution. Certainly not at that moment.

Having made the tour, Sue Ann and Serena stand in the quietest corner they can find. Sue Ann is talking about wanting a baby. "Are those pregnant women in Ingrid's paintings?" she asks. "Or am I just imagining it? In Ingrid's works? Does not seem possible." She rubs her back and legs. "Tired of standing," she says and folds into a squat, a robust woman, leaning against a perfect white wall.

Serena is startled, for a moment thinks she hasn't heard Sue Ann. "A baby?" She hasn't heard Sue Ann even mention a baby since her divorce from the terrible Richard and that was years ago.

"Mmm. Yes. I would like to have a child. With Sept, I mean. Not just in the abstract. Yes, he has grandchildren, in case you were going to remind me." Sue Ann smiles. Then there is just the noise of the gallery. Serena is completely quiet.

Serena and Leo, Rose and Hal, Bart and Stephen gather themselves to leave the show. Ingrid does not go out after her shows. No celebratory meal. She will go home with Max, shower, and make a cup of espresso. So they all hug her and Max and move out into the cooling, moonless night.

Ingrid takes her espresso to bed. She takes a sip of Max's small tumbler of scotch and shudders as she always does. "Awful."

"It was a great success, Ingrid," Max says. Always careful not to use superlatives with Ingrid; their effect is that she backs away and then disappears inside herself. He would like to say something extravagant, though, maybe, *incroyable*, because it sounds more dramatic in French and the event was incredible. All the paintings sold and there were private requests for studio visits, murmurs of commissions. A usually canny reviewer went beyond himself with personal compliments, an unheard of display of admiration before the review was written.

"It is in the air," Ingrid says, swallowing more espresso.

"What is?"

"My work. Work like it. There will be more and more that is similar, I am sure. Things, ideas, configurations, float in the air—or float somewhere—and at a moment that arrives mysteriously, people want that idea, or thing, or music, or food. Or art. Or lifestyles and everything else, too. Think of the late 60s and early 70s. Maybe if you studied it, it wouldn't be mysterious, but a concatenation of forces, a shift in awareness, a need that gets activated, the sensed movement to a new direction, unconscious fears that are soothed—or not—by the new creations. Maybe it is an awakening of vibrant curiosity. I don't know, but it isn't personal, except that I am personally involved. It is mysterious, really. I don't think there is a rational explanation, though plenty have been found."

"Ingrid, your work is extraordinary." He risks that much.

"Oh it is, yes." Modesty is not driving her thoughts at all; she is not modest and considers it pointless. "But how many people are aware of this phenomenon? It doesn't really matter, I'm going to do my work because that is what I do." Her coffee cup is empty and Max has finished the scotch. He turns out the light and holds her and she is asleep in moments. He strokes her hair, kisses her large lovely hand and knows that he needs to review the evening and what Ingrid has just said before he sleeps. He imagines meeting with Serena on Saturday and how what she is doing might be involved in what Ingrid has just said.

✳ ✪ ✳

On the Saturday of the gathering at Serena and Leo's, the day she will share her new work, Serena's thoughts are similar to what Ingrid's were on the night of her show. It is in the air to shift consciousness, to meditate. (Well, that started in the 60s in America, and Fritjof Capra's book, *The Tao of Physics*, linking Eastern mysticism to contemporary physics was published in 1975.) Serena remembers when it came out and how she read it voraciously and then had to start again: a meal she had gulped, but not digested. She has always known that what she does is ancient, with humans forever in some form or other, knows that it only appears to be different, clothed in different beliefs, but is essentially the same awareness of a connection to expanded realms of consciousness, areas beyond what most Westerners consider normal. Acceptable. She knows that this work has been dangerous to engage in, might still be so for some people strongly attached to what she considers "the official world." An American politician who channeled—and she does not much like the word and will like it less as time goes on—would not last long, would be vilified, maybe be in danger, the prospects ominous. Unlike Tibet, now in ruins, but with the traditions continuing, where ceremonial trances were used as guidance, brought the Dalai Lama out of danger; the ceremonies still intact, though so many people were dispersed, or killed. She is not comparing her meager awareness to that of highly trained monks, but considering what she is doing in a larger context. (In the years to come, a member of the president's cabinet will consult her and, sadly, she will think, not take her suggestions, though he listens with great seriousness and respect. A lovely man who supports violence and lies, who will become involved in a massive scandal.)

Serena does not feel endangered, but she knows she will be questioned, not always in a friendly way, knows there will be sly comments as well as appreciation and probably people who want to believe wholly in what she is saying in trance, the desire to believe completely a danger she has encountered in her work in astrology and healing. Serena is excited about the evening, very much wants to share this new aspect of her life with her closest friends. Leo has prepared the menu, this one of his great joys. He is making poached salmon, served cold, with broccoli rabe and a platter of the last tomatoes from their small garden, with mozzarella and basil. In the morning he bakes bread and a lemon cake. Serena assists, which means she is the sous chef, but really she does a little preparation and trails around the kitchen talking about the evening as Leo cooks.

"Are you nervous, Serena?"

"No. Maybe a little. Excited, for sure. I could be nervous, if I thought about it, but I'm not going to."

The group starts to arrive at five-thirty for drinks, which means some wine and some homemade lemonade. The day is warm and very bright and the sunset, when it comes, will be all violet and peach, with streaks of dark orange; it will start the display of color just before Serena goes into trance. Rose and Hal bring a huge bunch of wildflowers from upstate, carefully held in a large, glass jar. Ingrid and Max bring bars of bitter chocolate, a group favorite. Bart and Stephen arrive together with several special cheeses that Stephen has chosen with great care, commenting that Bart, alone, would have brought Swiss.

"No? Okay, goat cheese, then." Still teasing Bart about his Midwestern origins, his innocence and lack of sophistication, an old game with them. Ingrid, who has known Bart for so many years, looks at them together and wonders, again, if they are lovers. But no, Bart would tell her. (She is right. They are not, have never been, though Stephen has always remained vaguely hopeful.)

After dinner, they bring the lemon cake and coffee into the living room. "Can we eat dessert while you channel?" asks Bart, always sensitive to feelings, to the ambiance.

"Yes," says Serena. "Why not?"

"You might be distracted," he replies.

"I guess I might, but I don't think so." Serena, it turns out, is not easily distracted when she channels, unbothered by fire engines, hospital noises (when the time comes that she does a lot of work with people who are ill), the cats, who like to be near her when she is in trance. Her awareness woven into a non-physical realm, the physical world is present, but not intrusive.

They sit in a circle and Serena is quiet and then starts to chant softly. Her heart is beating fast—pounding and banging in her chest—and then she relaxes and her heartbeat slows and she can feel the voice emerging, loud and welcoming, arriving through her as one stepping through an inviting doorway, saying what it will always say. The tone contains seriousness blended with great good humor. Serena's facial expression shifts, the organization of her face moving quite noticeably. Her voice changes, as well, the speech sliding and swooping, the volume raised and then almost a whisper.

"We greeet you, dear friends and we are most pleased to be with you and, in this case, to meet the family." There is soft laughter from the group, an exhaled pleasure at being acknowledged. A brief silence, then, "You have been here together on this earth before; not in this room, but in other rooms, in forests and wide fields, on scalding deserts; on sailing ships and in castles, in huts and temples. Not all of you together each time, but always connected, if only as passersby who caught each other's eye and moved on. So it is no accident that you are here tonight. We understand that some of you feel that you have lived before, some not. You can think of what we say as a teaching tale—we are not here to foster particular beliefs. Take what interests you and leave the rest. Nor are we strangers to each other. This one", Serena touches her heart, "is gracious to allow us passage. Becoming acquainted with this work as a creative possibility in this life is part of the plan for each of you. A plan chosen—in the largest sense—by you. Some," she nods at Sept, "are already acquainted with altered states."

Sept nods. "Yes. Yes, I am."

"And you," to Max.

"Yes," he says, somewhat to everyone's surprise.

"We know you have come with questions, many questions," laughter. "So please begin."

And they do ask their questions. "Who are you? May we ask that?" From Max.

"Yes, yes. There is no one, single answer. This is a response for the moment, because it will evolve as this one does." Serena touches her heart again. Apparently her given name is not used in this context. "For the moment, we are a representative from a non-physical realm to which this one can now attune. And to answer what might be the next question, no, we have never been physically incarnated." (Unlike Seth, channeled by Jane Roberts, who had had physical lives, Serena thinks, noticing that her ordinary self can think in this altered state.)

"Let us also note that as soon as we speak in this way, we are caught in your language, based on space and time, so there will be distortions, since we are not in that frame. Let us also note that this information needs to be evaluated, like any other, and with care, so that the fabric of the communication is not torn. We are not, as we said, fostering certain beliefs, or seeking 'true believers.' That is what this one calls people who believe without questioning, yes?"

Some laughter from the group and a sense of appreciation.

The questions continue. At some point, near the end of the session, Serena is aware of Sept's heart and has the image of a small bird, maybe a sparrow, resting there, then struggling, then resting again. She will think about it later, not yet skillful enough to catch an interpretation in the moment. She is then drawn to Sue Ann and sees a glow around her abdomen and is quite sure she understands it, but says nothing about either impression, which brings another realization: she can choose what to say, at least in this circumstance. The session ends, as they most often will, with words of appreciation. "So, we thank you for this invitation and bid you a very good, warm summer evening." Serena's face slowly moves back into her own characteristic expressions, the other countenance vanished.

The group's reactions vary widely. Bart has thought, uncomfortably, of the church he was raised in and what they would make of this: the Devil's work and possession. He is surprised that these thoughts arrive. He is so many years away from that teaching. But they are not gone, apparently. He has appreciated being there, and assumes the old beliefs will fade again. (In the years that follow, as Serena's work becomes known, she receives a few letters from strangers warning her of hell.)

Ingrid thinks it is like her art; this, in some way, in another form, is related to the source of her inspiration, which she does not believe is her imagination alone. She enjoys the session and finds it familiar, though she has never seen anyone in trance.

Stephen wonders if Serena would see him privately. He has some serious questions about how to proceed with his health, with the purple stains that have appeared on his abdomen.

Max and Sept feel that Serena has a real gift. In Sept's background, altered states are not unusual and Max's mother, that dignified lady, took Max to mediums—good ones—when he was a young boy; she sought guidance for herself and her son. And Max has traveled a lot, has spent time in India, though he doesn't speak of it often.

Rose and Hal are quiet, Hal understanding that awareness beyond the physical is part of his deep connection to animals. Rose, always practical, hopes Serena is not going to make trouble for herself. She does not doubt that Serena has been in a trance, that another energy has accompanied her. She has known Serena for a long time and this is completely in character, and she knows, more or less, that Serena was very intuitive when they were not much more than children, would come up with odd, sudden insights that would prove correct.

Leo is happy and proud of Serena's courage in venturing into this. His love, his mystical love. He remembers that his mother said his grandmother had "the sight," though he was not aware of it in himself.

They eat a little more lemon cake, re-fill their coffee cups. Stephen takes Serena aside and asks, softly, if she would see him alone. Serena, who was intuitive long before she channeled, knows what is happening with Stephen. Though she realizes that you would not really have to be intuitive about his request in these times. "We can talk, Stephen; I can't channel with you yet. I'm too new and too unsure." She realizes that she needs to proceed with strong intention to hone her skills, investigate them; whatever she can contribute will be needed.

And then the evening is over, with hugs all around. As they are leaving, Serena looks at Sue Ann very directly and receives a smile and a slight nod in return. Then the group is going down the steps and the door closes. Leo kisses Serena and holds her and they go to the kitchen to clean up and talk.

"It went well," he says, as they move around the kitchen. "How did it feel?'

"Both natural and familiar and daring, though that is a strange word. I could feel the seep, right through the trance, of wanting all of them to approve in a fundamental sense. Not agree, just support me. Too bad; I hoped those feelings would not combine with the trance state—maybe just be held for later?" Serena laughs, a bit rueful, a bit sad that her personal needs are not going to disappear so easily. "Well. I guess it just goes with—at least for now. I want to see Nick really soon."

She will start to consult with him regularly about her work, possible blind spots that she has, techniques to refine or expand her knowledge. His wife is a widely respected channel, a dynamic woman; she has been a guide to many people, though at the beginning of her work, it was held as private—almost a secret—within the community. Now it is more public, with transcripts available and used in the training program that Nick heads.

"Yes," Leo says. "See Nick. Absolutely."

"I think Stephen is in trouble," Serena says as they prepare for bed. They look at each other for a long moment.

"Oh no. No"

"Yes, he wanted me to do a private session with him, but I can't. I'm too unskilled and it's too soon for me to do that."

"It is," Leo agrees.

But now that Serena has started, the requests will come quickly. She will call Nick first thing on Monday.

Leo sleeps immediately; Serena lies awake for a while. She imagines the cats that roam the Village, imagines the perfect blue of a robin's egg and sun shining through the timeless Rose Window in Notre Dame with the gargoyles crouched outside. She rests her cheek against Leo's back and falls asleep.

Sunday passes quietly and on Monday morning, Leo and Serena eat breakfast and Leo leaves for work; it is raining steadily, a dark day with yellow leaves pushed onto the streets by the rushing rain and wind. Serena calls Nick's office and, miraculously, he has an open appointment at two that afternoon, which coincides nicely with her break, although she would have found a way to go no matter what. She dresses in a light wool skirt and a sweater almost the color of the robin's egg she imagined the night of the gathering. She knows she dresses up for Nick, a man who appreciates women and finds meaning in the way people dress—well, women more than men. She teases him about being sexist, which he probably is, and enjoys his pleasure. The rain is unrelenting and she wears her long raincoat and high boots, both fashionable, but not quite waterproof, an extravagance, but she hates rain boots and these are her excuse to stay dry, knowing she is vain and not approving of it, but accommodating it with some sadness and—sometimes—humor.

On the way to Nick's, when she is waiting at Sixty-eighth Street to cross Second Avenue, she sees the back of a compactly built man with brown curls and a light, but focused stride. He is with a woman Serena's height, whose heavy dark hair reaches most of the way down her back, as Serena's did years ago; the woman is wearing high heels and Serena notices—just in a flash—that her feet are dry in this teeming rain. They walk with their arms around each other's waists and she can hear that they are speaking French, the only language Serena speaks in addition to English. Serena's heart races. The man so strongly resembles her first lover, Michel, now and for many years living in Paris, his birthplace. No, it is more than a resemblance; she can feel the man's essence, unmistakably Michel, here, walking ahead of her. And the young woman is her earlier self: long hair, dreadfully pinching shoes and all. They do not seem even slightly transparent, or different in any way from the other passersby, except that they are not wet from the rain, yet they carry no umbrella. No one else notices them.

She and Michel had separated in a sad way. No, she thinks, a terrible way. They were to be married and he was in the army in France. Serena had promised to meet him, purchased her one-way ticket and then did not go and did not ever explain why. She made a promise she could not keep. She had been too young, too frightened of living in another country, with no one but Michel, and she had never resolved her feelings for him, or forgiven herself for being cruel. On the other side of the avenue, Serena starts to run to catch up with them, turns her head for an instant and when she turns back he and the woman have vanished. She stops and stands still in the heavy rain, looking up and down the avenue. People dodge around her. They are gone. Tears come, mingling with rain. She begins to walk forward, weeping soundlessly. Has she seen an apparition on this day, so soon after embarking on channeling? Is she going to see other things, events that have passed, perhaps people who are no longer living? Is she going to see them in this way, intruding into her ordinary life, slicing her reality so that it is unreliable? She hurries toward Nick's office, almost running on the slippery street.

Nick's office is welcoming, with soft chairs and crystals placed together on a dark, polished table; the windows are large, now sluiced with rain, and the carpet is thick, a dark blue. There is a round vase of frilled white chrysanthemums on another table and books range along the walls, some neatly ordered, some stacked unevenly. Nick hugs her, his aura of authority and his love rolling together in the hug. She rests for a moment in his arms, head on his shoulder. A stocky man with a large handsome head, a prominent nose and flyaway gray hair. They sit down facing each other and he takes off his substantial glasses, closes his eyes and pinches the bridge of his nose. "Something has happened," he says. "Something new . . . You are curious about it and also a little perplexed? Distressed?" An intuitive man who knows Serena well.

Serena describes her experiences of the past week and Nick just listens and nods, unsurprised and then says, "I am not surprised. Are you?"

"I am. I didn't imagine I would ever do this and I had no particular desire to do it—or it wasn't something I aspired to. Maybe that's more accurate. May I show you?"

"No, just shift into the altered state and let me spend a little time with your energy."

Serena breathes softly, deeply and then shifts. They are both quiet for a while. Then Nick says, "It's good, Serena. It feels strong, vibrant, full of possibilities. And this is a big responsibility, but you know that, yes?"

"Yes, yes, of course."

"Your first responsibility is to care for yourself well. This will move faster than you imagine and the demands will increase. Don't get caught in your ego, or in false humility and pay attention to your needs." This is an old issue for her, which they both know, and it touches on Nick's life, as well. His wife, Miriam, who has channeled for years, a fierce and passionate woman, a woman who escaped from Nazi Germany moving through frozen forests enduring unimaginable horrors, has recovered, just recently, from breast cancer. She is well at the moment, but the prognosis is not good. Nick has said that she did not care for herself enough, that her illness came in conjunction with a weariness that she ignored. He has spoken of his helplessness and rage. Serena knows all of this. She remembers how many healers and intuitives struggled with illness: Eileen Garrett, Edgar Cayce, who had been warned by his guides to slow down and did not, and died, Maria, a healer who has worked with Nick for years and had myriad health problems. For the first time, Serena feels the potential heaviness of the tasks ahead and she sighs, putting her hands over her face.

"I would like you to meet with Miriam when she is stronger. Will you do that?"

"Nick, it would be an honor." And it is, in that community, an honor to speak privately with Miriam. But they do not meet, ever. In two months, Miriam will be dead.

"Should I continue with this?"

"I can't answer that for you, and I think it will be good. The energy moves all the way from your pelvic harp, the sacred bone, at the first chakra, through your crown and then beyond. The harp is the gateway. Your nervous system will take some time to acclimate, and your life will need to change in ways you cannot yet imagine as this develops, and I can see that you are grounded in the midst of this newness. Leo supports you, your friends, too?" He lifts her up from the chair and holds her. "We are always in touch. I am here."

Before she leaves, she describes the incident in the street. "What was that? It really unnerved me."

"Time dancing," he says. "Don't worry about it. Time bends, we are just not usually aware of it. Go home and rest."

The rain has subsided when Serena leaves, but the sky is gray and impenetrable. She wonders whether Michel will appear again, but he does not, the street is full of hurrying strangers. Nothing like that ever occurs again, though time will dance and slide in different ways and Serena will accommodate the changes.

Two days later, she goes to visit Frieda. Frieda is writing a book. Something she has not mentioned to anyone. A secret? Private? More a secret. An accounting of her life and a compilation of what she has learned. She puts the papers she's working on away before Serena comes. Frieda does not have Nick's kind of certainty, feels much more the illusion of it all, the flimsiness behind which are truths larger than she can imagine.

Frieda and Miriam, Nick's wife, share similar histories and know each other, but more in passing, though Frieda is familiar with Miriam's work and has read transcripts of her sessions with her guides, said the work was solid (but not remarkable?) and has discussed some of them with Serena. Frieda has also said, in an almost neutral tone, that they seemed vaguely Christian. On the day Serena visits it is hot, boiled September heat, and Tenth Street seems grimy, the sandstone steps, with bits of light shining in them, are badly worn and tired in the end-of-summer sun. Frieda serves iced tea with lemon and offers Serena a bowl of fruit. Serena describes the channeling again and Frieda listens, then sits, silently, for what feels to Serena like a long time. The cats cruise; the street noises rattle and sigh. "Well, I am not really surprised," Frieda says.

"That's what Nick said. Exactly. I was surprised. I was shocked."

"Well, maybe it is easier to see some things from the outside. You have always altered your awareness naturally in a number of ways: when you read the Tarot, when you interpret a chart, even when you speak. Sometimes I see you do it, bits of particular wisdom floating in. It's a gift, Serena and it is all a play and this is a serious undertaking. But you know that." Serena nods. "Explore it with caution? No, perhaps not. Enter it with abandon and evaluate the results with a kind and critical eye. Keep conscious track of your feelings in the altered state as well as before and after you enter it. I think what you are describing is called conscious channeling. That is, you are aware of the physical world as you work; you are not dissociated and unconscious of what you say. Always ask for feedback because it is a conversation, not a pronouncement. I know you will not tell fortunes, but sometimes events will appear as strong probabilities in what we call the future. How will you deal with that?"

"I will say what I think is appropriate. So far, I seem to be able to choose."

"Yes, so far, but leave it open. You don't know so much yet. 'So far' is not very long at this point. Don't try to be remarkable."

"No, of course not." But sometimes it will be more of a temptation than Serena initially imagines. An urge to lean forward and fly into brilliant spangled extraordinary awareness. She imagines that she wants to stay plain, unadorned and, mostly, she does. The work is so humbling that it is not difficult. The garden of this realm she is sharing with other energies floats with her, its landscape awesome.

Then Serena is silent, contemplating what Frieda has said earlier about her perceptions often containing bits of wisdom floating in. She supposes Frieda is correct, though she has never perceived it that way. Not at all. In some way, she feels caught out, or embarrassed. "That feels disorienting," she says, going back to the observation Frieda has made. "Embarrassing, or tricky."

"It isn't all right for me to notice something you have not been consciously aware of?"

"I guess not."

Ruby assessing Serena, tormenting her with her accusations. "You don't know how to love; you don't know what love is. I can see you," all in a low voice with a hiss embedded in it. A refrain Ruby repeated through the years. And Serena believed this was true, even after she had grown and worked in therapy and meditated, the wounds were there, sharp slivers, painful and alive. Something is recapitulated in Frieda's act of observing, even though it is praise. It is the very act of being observed that is dangerous. She tells Frieda what she is thinking and Frieda, who, like Nick, knows Serena's history, nods. "Yes, of course. Offer yourself some compassion, perhaps? So, you must decide whether you want to continue this path, though you needn't decide this minute."

"Nick was very positive about it. I know, I know, I am the only one who can decide." Serena really does know this; she is consulting with two of the people whose opinions and thoughts she values, but she is not asking for permission. She wants to speak with Carlo, her other teacher, as well. Then, in the flashing way that is characteristic of her, she says, "Yes. I am going to continue." She simply understands this is true. That she will go on to explore this path, give it her energy and love, her questioning and reluctance and whatever else emerges.

Sept comes to see Serena late in September and they stand for a moment at her front door and then hug, his strong frame curving around her slight one. It is raining again, the heat vanished, a chill, light rain, a pearly insistent whisper. Sept has a large umbrella, which he shakes out carefully and puts in the stand. It is as if she and Sept are enacting, in the physical world, something that has already transpired, walking down a corridor that fills the luminous with the pulse of the physical, or maybe drawing a dream sequence into solidity. They have had this kind of relationship almost from the time they met, years ago, in Frieda's Tarot class: loving and practical, with a dreamy, spinning center that embraced other realms easily. She has known Sept longer than she has known Leo.

Frieda and Sept were old friends when the class began, close, with a deep appreciation for each other, the origin of their friendship mysterious and never referred to. Because of the intimate nature of the Tarot, its mythic scope made personal, the class members got to know a great deal about each other. Sept, many years a detective with the NYPD, was retired. He was a detective when there were few blacks among the detectives. He spoke of himself as driven, self-critical, intolerant of his own mistakes and the mistakes of others. "Harsh," he said. "I guess I needed to be, or that was the only way I saw to manage." His wife dead young of cancer, he raised his two boys with the help of his Aunt Etta, who moved up from Georgia and stayed. He began on a spiritual path when his eye caught a book on Buddhism in a bookstore window and then started what would be years of change, moving toward mindfulness and vulnerability. And he met Frieda early in his studies, seemingly by accident, in Central Park. A man whose personal needs had been submerged, but not crushed, and a woman who had lived on the rim of death and escaped the Nazis. They both held ancestral sorrows as well as personal experiences of profound loss. He carried a hard rind of anger and, beneath that, depression; it was not unconscious, but it was not addressed, either, until he met Frieda and began to work with her. Yes, when they met, he admired her round bosom, soft in white summer linen, and her tanned, sturdy legs; he admired the way she spoke to his sons, direct and interested. Yes, they became lovers, but the lasting force was their inner journey, the paths they explored, the techniques they discovered to melt into compassion while holding clarity and discernment. By the time Serena met them, Sept's hair was gray and Frieda's was determinedly aubergine. When Sept spoke in class and described his journey, he said he had wanted something. "Not church," he said. "I left all that when I was young, though Etta took the boys. I learned there were other ways." He spoke plainly, did not elaborate much. "Scared me though, to let go of all that protection. Armoring." He smiles at the irony. So his harshness had loosened, his criticism softened and that was the man Serena met, though there were still edges, warning. Signals that he was not someone you would want to cross.

Serena has a newly made pot of coffee on the stove and pours a mug for each of them. They sit next to each other in the living room, on the large, soft couch, not speaking for a while. "You know why I'm here," Sept says. It is a statement more than a question.

"Yes, I think so, but go over it so we are both sure."

He sighs. "I believe you saw my heart," he says. "The condition I have. When you were channeling."

"Yes, but I saw it as a symbol, a struggling bird."

"Yes, and that Sue Ann is pregnant?"

"Yes."

"But you didn't say."

"No. I discovered, right then, that I could, to some extent, choose my words. The trance seems to encompass several levels of activity. This is really new, Sept. I am just at the beginning of the exploration. Did I make a mistake that way? Not speaking?"

"No, no. Don't apologize, if you are. I want clarity, maybe. I want some further guidance, if that's possible. And I don't want to push you, you know I don't."

"I do know. Thank you for saying it."

"Sue Ann and I have talked at great length about this child and I agreed to have it, knowing that I may leave them alone."

"The way you were left?"

"The leaving is the same, but the circumstances are different emotionally, as well as financially, of course. My wife and I were not really close emotionally. Loving, but not revealing ourselves. Is that possible? I don't know. Anyway, this is different. And I know a lot about raising children; this is her first. I don't think you really understand parenting until you've done it, though there are all kinds of parenting, God knows. I'm babbling. Nerves."

"I don't know," says Serena. The air falls loose around them, a shawl of the finest invisible fabric. The windows drip with silvered rain.

"Can you look at this? I don't want our fortune told."

"No, I know."

"Just whatever is available." All of it is so plain between them. Momentous. Unembellished. Serena takes Sept's large hand.

"My heart's been acting up for years," he says, sipping his coffee. I figured if I went, I went. The boys were all grown. But these years with Sue Ann, it's been different. She wants that baby so much and I'd be pleased to raise another child under such different circumstances, but there's doubt here beyond the ordinary nature of the unknown." He smiles slightly. "However much we accept even that. So what do you think, Serena? Can we do this?" Serena had refused to work with Stephen but with Sept it seems—what?—transparent?—available?—she feels no pressure to accommodate him. It seems possible.

"All right. I don't know what kinds of things I can see; I can't promise anything at all, except my good intentions." Serena will never promise anything, in the years she works with her intuition, there is always the unknown, the mysterious, the elusive. The questions she has shift focus, but continue. Even when she has had years of practice, understands most of the symbols she is given and can interpret them. Even when she speaks in trance with humor, in the spirit of curiosity and can feel the depth of her state and its nuances, she will never promise. It is always an exploration.

Serena and Sept move and settle themselves on the floor, facing each other. She shifts her awareness, greets Sept. That rolling voice, "Weee greeet you, dear friend." Behind her eyes there is a play of shadows—gray and lavender, almost black, shining curls of darkness that open to a full, rosy glow. She feels it is Sept's heart, its physical state perhaps supported by some greater strength. The shadows move and the glow persists. What comes next is surprising. "You must create new patterns," Serena's trance voice says. "Send blessings to the people you have encountered in your work—men who were criminals and acted out of deep pain, who caused further pain, men and women who were scarred by desperation. They need release; you need release. You have not completely forgiven them or yourself and it burdens your heart."

Serena continues, "In the physical realm, the body realm (though it is a false separation, all is consciousness), your heart can be supported by certain foods, nutrients. By acupuncture and massage. You do exercise now. You need to stay consistently hydrated, a seemingly small thing, but relevant to bodily wellness." She has been both seeing images and hearing words given to her. Then there are colors and images, but no sound. She sees them together, Sept and Sue Ann and a small girl. Is she willing the images? Imagining them? No way to know, so she just reports what she sees. Sometimes the session seems smooth, rolling easily; other moments it has irregularities, like water running over heavy stones, rippling, diverging, returning. As her voice changes, so the quality of her connection to the energy shifts, this movement more like wind than water, wind gathering splashes of light, sparks of brilliance behind her eyes and among the words. At the end, only words, drumming a steady rhythm. There is information about what seem like past lives Sue Ann and Sept have spent together, their roles changing, but the connection always deep. "Before you were born," Serena's trance voice says, "you agreed to meet again and perhaps to have a child. You met at a time when you were free to be together, when you were open to this deep love. And you cherish the love between you, it is a first time for both of you in this life."

Serena stops speaking and sits with her eyes closed as her face moves back into its ordinary contours, into the expression of her personality. She opens her eyes, blinks several times and she and Sept regard each other in silence. Then Serena says, "Do you think that part about forgiveness was relevant? It seemed presumptuous, but that was the impression I had. And who knows about the baby? I want it to be good. How much is that influencing me?"

Sept nods his head. "Yes, it's relevant. All of that went into my heart, though I wasn't aware of it in those early times. After I met Frieda and started to study, I did the Tonglen practice, the prayer of giving and receiving that is directed toward alleviating suffering, but there was a lot of ground I didn't cover." He smiles sadly, this resilient, tenderhearted man who spent so many years involved with violence and tragedy. "It's grueling work and no one in that environment deals with it the way we are discussing. They might be horrified. They might also feel relieved. We don't know about the baby and this sounds hopeful. We won't base any final decision on it. That's our responsibility."

Romeo, with large paws and the nature of a tornado, settles quietly on Sept's lap and taps his face gently with a hefty front paw. Sept gets up, holding the cat under one arm and hugs Serena with the other. Romeo is unresisting and curls onto Sept's shoulder. "You have done me a great kindness," Sept says. Serena is not so sure, but she hugs him fiercely with one arm. The wind has risen and branches tap-tap at the window, a reminder that something has reached in to offer comfort; that comfort beyond the obvious is always present. Sept clears the coffee cups, retrieves his umbrella and kissing Serena goodbye, goes out into the rain.

Serena continues to practice and to ask friends to sit with her and ask questions. She invites people who work in areas where she has little or no understanding, so that she can investigate her scope and discover whether she will receive useful information about a subject of which she has no knowledge. Her first choice in that arena is her friend Jed, who is a physicist. Serena studied both chemistry and biology and excelled at chemistry, but she avoided the courses in physics. The books on the relationship between quantum physics and mysticism have been available in recent years, and she has devoured them with great excitement. However, she is absolutely certain that she is ignorant about physics and she is certainly not acquainted with the level of physics that would interest Jed. He comes to Leo and Serena's with his wife, Gaby, an artist and a close friend. They are both deeply involved in meditation and work with Nick and his wife, so they are familiar with channeling. The state itself will not be an issue, not something that Serena needs to explain. The evening is unseasonably warm, with leaves floating down, golden, through hazy air, the fading light hovering soft as a whisper. Leo has made espresso and cinnamon buns, filling the apartment with their dense, rich scent. Leo's hospitality seems shaped into the atmosphere of the apartment; Serena is always warm, but it is Leo who cooks, planning each meal and snack as carefully as he plans his building restorations.

They all gather in the living room, which is becoming the ritual place for Serena to work in trance. Romeo touches the plate of cinnamon buns pointedly and Leo feeds him a small piece, theoretically against the rules. They drink coffee and eat and Serena describes her channeling to date, something still so new to her. "Sometimes," she says, "it is like wading into sweet familiar water. It feels soothing and full of tenderness; other times the energy is electrical and sharp, dissonant. I am just at the beginning, you know. I know you know that," she laughs a little. "Just experimenting, a bit awed and slightly shaky."

"Yes," says Jed. "Whatever happens is fine. We're with you."

"I want to start," Serena says. "I'm too nervous to wait. Jed, I think you need to ask the questions so that I understand them, not in technical language, and I will respond in language I understand. I was hoping I would be the kind of channel who could speak languages I don't know, or maybe play Bach, but so far, that is not the case and I don't imagine it will develop in that direction."

Outside, dog owners are taking their evening stroll, bits of human conversation and canine interjections rise from the street. A police car howls and the dogs join in.

They put their cups on the coffee table and meditate for a few moments, eyes closed. Serena takes a deep breath and begins to chant softly, whatever sounds come to her; she waits, her heart racing, and then she can feel the shift, a tide moving delicately and precisely as her back straightens, her eyes flutter and her head drops backward and then lifts to face her friends. "Weee greeet you," says the voice, hearty and welcoming. "We are so pleased to be with you this evening." Her inner world is filled with rolling spheres of light in dark turquoise. They move randomly, feathered in between with splits of bright yellow. The spheres begin to vibrate slightly, moons rotating slowly within them. The whole of it rumbles as it moves. These images, accompanied by the low sound, are different from what Serena has so far experienced. She does not begin by asking questions, but talks first about Jed, as she did with Sept.

"A magician," she says. "An alchemist and a priest. And now a scientist." She laughs gently. "You pursue the same interest in different ways, always pushing against authority, against the accepted path. You do so now, too. A scientist who meditates and explores alternate realities and ancient healing modalities. This is a lifetime during which you are moving toward the union of heart and mind—mind in the personal sense—seeking to join all with the larger consciousness and you are doing well. We congratulate you."

Jed laughs. "Good. Thank you." He looks pleased, nods his head, which is large for his body and has the aspect of a falcon. One leg crippled by polio, he has worked with different healers, always curious about the nature of energy not yet officially identified in Western culture. When he asks his questions, Serena receives the answers in blocks of words, which has not happened before. There are some images, colored geometric shapes that slide together and precede the words. She has no understanding of the questions, or of her responses, but the words come easily and fit comfortably in her body. "Yes," Jed says as she speaks, "yes, I understand."

When she is finished and opens her eyes, Jed says, "Very helpful. I asked about a project I'm working on and the information is insightful. It resolves several dilemmas I have been facing about the structure of the work and how the parts fit together. This gives me a way to move forward with confidence on a path I hadn't considered. Thank you. And I am gratified to hear that my life is on the right course. The alchemist-magician element feels deeply connected to my heart. I'd like to ask about my health some other time, if I may?"

"Yes, we can do that. This was a real test for me and I'm glad it's useful and relieved, too. Could have been a disaster." They go back to the espresso and buns and Leo brings out some fruit; the conversation moves to the work Nick's wife does, which Jed and Gaby have experienced many times. Jed speculates on the nature of channeling itself and then the evening is over and Leo cleans the kitchen and undresses Serena simultaneously. "My beautiful mystic wild woman," he says. Romeo and Miss Charlotte, the lovely calico, accompany them up to the bedroom and all four get on the bed in the lavender dark and noisy New York night.

* ☼ *

Leo gets a call from his office that the project they are working on in Paris, delicate restorations in Saint-Julien-le-Pauvre, will require his expertise. It is one of the oldest churches in Paris and is close to the oldest tree in the city. They knew this was a possibility and both Leo and Serena are excited about it; Serena has been to Paris many times, but never in this season, the dark edge of winter, just before the solstice. Leo has been there in all seasons. They prepare quickly, Serena telling her clients she will be gone for almost two weeks, back before Christmas. Bart will cat-sit and water the plants. Leo hovers over Serena as they pack. "Take layers," he says repeatedly. "The heating is terrible and the weather is damp." He knows Serena dislikes the cold and that being cold affects her mood in dismal ways. "Layers. Socks. Long underwear. Sweaters. Waterproof boots."

"I have no waterproof boots."

"Yes, you do. The heavy black ones. The rubber ones."

"In Paris? Are you joking?"

"Well, we'll get some and you can wear them on the plane, they'll be too heavy to pack. Very fashionable waterproof boots." They make an expedition to an upscale department store and buy expensive boots. Serena agonizes over the price, but Leo is casual about it. "Business expense," he says, trying not to imagine what his mother would say about such a costly item. His mother is a fan of stores that offer outdoor gear and durable clothing. "Anyway, we're staying with Jacqueline and Jean, so no hotel bill, though it would be paid for anyway. Just enjoy them, sweet Serena." The couple they are staying with are friends Leo has made in Paris, through his work. Now they have all become friends, the Parisians staying with Leo and Serena when they visit New York.

They leave on a Monday night, the air freezing and still. Leo sleeps deeply, falling asleep in, what seems to Serena, minutes after takeoff. She asks for a cup of cocoa and the stewardess brings her a cup of sweet, steaming chocolate, something sticky in it—maybe fake marshmallows. Serena sips it slowly, it is so messy and delicious. When they darken the plane, she looks out the window; it feels as if they are tunneling through something solid, as they move through icy space, only the wing lights winking a steady rhythm, crossing over the black, empty sea rocking far beneath them. She thinks of Sue Ann and Sept's baby, growing silently in the darkness of Sue Ann's womb and her eyes spill tears, for no reason she can understand; they are as salty as the ocean. The engines growl loudly in Serena's ears and whatever talking there is becomes amplified with her eyes closed. She hypnotizes herself, but does not sleep; she never sleeps on planes.

When they arrive, Paris is wet and cold, with wispy heat in the café where they stop for a quick breakfast—croissants and coffee. Jean and Jacqueline will be at work and have left keys for them, so they eat a bit before heading to the apartment on rue Beautreillis. "Are you warm enough?" Leo asks. Serena has that pale, tight look that she gets when she is cold.

"No, but the coffee will revive me. And I don't do well on no sleep." She feels regretful about her sensitivity, which appears in so many areas; Leo is robust, can go without sleep, though not so well without food. While he had slept for most of the flight, he would be okay if he hadn't.

"I think it's a package deal, Serena. Your sensitivity gives you your gifts."

"I don't see why they have to go together. I'm particularly sensitive now, with the channeling and all these changes. I feel both peeled away from ordinary life and, more deeply buried in its magic. A delicate balance, I guess." She sighs and bites a piece of croissant. "My feet are warm, though. Thank you for getting the boots."

"It is a balance and I imagine it changes all the time, maybe more so right now."

"I started to cry on the plane, when I was thinking about the dark and the ocean below us and Sue Ann's baby in its own wet darkness."

Leo knows better than to ask whether this might mean that Serena is longing for a baby herself. He just waits.

"No, no I don't think it's that," she says into Leo's stillness. But maybe? A sliver of yearning beneath an awareness that opened her tears?

They leave the café and get a cab, which hustles, with the other cars, through the damp morning, lights blurry in the wet air and the cobblestones dimpled with moisture which seems like it must turn to ice any minute, it is so cold. But it does not.

The apartment, when they get the various doors unlocked and step inside, is warm and scented with pine from branches in a large green vase. They set their bags in the guest room, put a kettle on and Leo makes a fire in the large fireplace, its mantel's carved edge garlanded with cupped lilies and curling vines. "We're supposed to walk around outside in the daylight to ease the jet lag," says Leo, "but there is no real daylight, so let's drink our tea and get into bed and nap and who knows what else." Serena is on her way to the guest room before he has finished. Leo brings the tea with him, honeyed and very hot. They drink it slowly and kiss. Love in Paris, in the featherbed, Serena finally warm and then asleep in Leo's arms. By the time Jean and Jacqueline arrive home from work, Leo and Serena have showered and changed and Leo has gone out and shopped for a little food, though he knows their hosts will have prepared ahead. He likes to buy treats.

Jacqueline is a printmaker and Jean a writer and editor, deeply engaged with mysticism, occult philosophy and the lure of darkness and its role in creation. When they come home, there are hugs all around and wine offered and some cheeses and nuts. They sit in front of the fire. Jacqueline is petite, an appealing figure in a long, warm skirt and a stole of almost transparent lemony wool, embroidered delicately with mythic figures: goddesses and magical objects. Jean is compact, but not muscular. He is smooth and agile, with a narrow face and deeply set blue eyes behind delicate glasses that have almost no frame. He often wears a paisley scarf tossed casually around his neck. They are sleek, well-groomed people.

Sitting with them as the fire glows orange with flashes of blue, Serena is reminded of the first time she visited Paris with Leo. "The French," Serena had said, "not so warm and fuzzy. I feel a complete outsider. And the women! I despair." Serena is embarrassed by her interest in fashion, in putting herself together in a particular way. "No contest," she said miserably. "These women have been steeped in style since birth. Maybe prenatally. They start with *soin* and whatever in nursery school," she said, looking at the many salons for facials and regular beauty care.

"Serena, you're so beautiful," Leo would respond. Her loyal love.

One afternoon, they passed a lingerie shop and Leo wanted to buy her something. "No, no," she said. "I can't. I feel gross." The worst of Serena's body fears rising, an explosion of sadness and streaky rage. Oddly, Parisians often think that Serena is a native and are surprised she is American. "I'm a New Yorker," she would respond. "That's different." Serena's feelings about herself as a woman have changed only marginally, but she no longer feels such a stranger in Paris. There they are, with Jean and Jacqueline and they have other friends, as well.

Jean is an accomplished astrologer and later, at dinner, he tells Serena about Lilith, the dark moon, the demon goddess of antiquity. He says he will find the placement of the moon in her chart and in Leo's; it represents an area where vengeful feelings are aroused and must be confronted, making it possible to take responsibility for them. Serena is intrigued, Leo less so, but astrology has never particularly engaged him.

As Serena tells Jean and Jacqueline about her new experiences, her channeling and her thoughts and feelings about this still very new development, Jean, particularly, is immediately interested, wants to experiment with something, if Serena is willing. Ah, Serena, still innocently willing to try so many things, to experiment with her altered state and find its depths and its edges.

"I want you to hold a ring," Jean says. "Is that all right?"

"Yes. Yes. Psychometry. Holding an object or token and attuning through it to the owner's past, or a past event. I haven't ever tried it, but yes." Really, if Serena had thought a moment, she would have realized that she did something similar on a regular basis, something that was a strong thread of her natural awareness. She is sensitive to rooms and how they feel, to events she feels have occurred there. And of course, to people, to their nature, their patterns. But she doesn't associate all of this when Jean asks his question. She simply thinks she has never tried this formally, this holding an object and letting it communicate with her.

"I need to get it," he says and goes to the bedroom, returning with a delicate silver ring set with a green stone swirled at its center with a slender white spiral. Sprightly Jean, with the firelight winking at the edge of his glasses.

Serena takes the ring between her palms and holds it, shifting her awareness as her eyes flutter. Then darkness swallows her, darkness that is nothing like night, but soaking and impenetrable, filling her throat so that she begins to choke and shiver. There is no voice, just these sensations gripping her. Oh, she is in water. She is going down, hardly able to breathe. "Drowning," she whispers, not in trance, just her natural voice, but weak. Jean takes the ring from between her palms; slowly, her breath returns and she feels sick to her stomach.

"What is that?" Leo asks. "What did you give her?" He is angry, though his voice is quiet. He goes to Serena and holds her hand.

"It was my first wife's," Jean says. "She drowned herself in the Seine. I'm so sorry, Serena, I didn't imagine you would feel it that way."

"No," she says. "I never have, but I've never done this, exactly." Leo hugs her, envelops her small, still shivering body. He draws her close to the fire.

"I am so sorry," Jean says, again. He takes the ring, looking sad and concerned. Jacqueline rubs her feet, which are very cold.

"You didn't know. It's all right. I am experimenting, after all." But could he have guessed? Serena wonders later, when her body has calmed. Jean knows a lot, really. She doesn't say anything to Leo about why Jean gave her the ring, but she is never sure and though this was a frightening experience she will try psychometry again, with no ill effects. Each time she holds an object, she will remember, for a moment, that plunge into chaos.

The rest of the short visit passes pleasantly; Leo investigates the work he has been asked to do and knows he will need to return for a much longer time before he even starts. They return to New York and the cats and the plants, Serena to her practice and Leo to his work.

✳ ✵ ✳

In the winter, Ingrid is working on a new series; portraits that reveal the person's shadow self, aspects usually hidden from view. In one, there is a darkness, with small eyes, splintered into fire, scattered around a formal, complacent woman; tiny spiders are embedded in some of the burning irises; a vase of crimson tulips with heavy, nodding cups is on a nearby table and glowing moths flutter downward in a wobbly line. In another, a bright shadow, all brilliant colors, appears behind a drab figure that is bent and mean and frightened, shabby and ominous. This androgynous figure is dressed in a rumpled gray garment, perhaps a robe, that also appears discarded on the ground at its feet, next to it a cornucopia of full, ripe fruit lies on its side; in the background, a spilled glass of wine floats in shadow. The surfaces on all of this collection are smooth, inviting, drawing the viewer into the confusion. Ingrid is enjoying painting these images; she understands them better than the series showed in the autumn. The pieces from the autumn show are gone, all sold, and Ingrid has not kept any for herself and Max. Her popularity has exploded, with requests for photo shoots and interviews. She avoids whatever she can until Max points out that she is sabotaging herself and acting out her ambivalence. He suggests therapy and Ingrid laughs. They compromise by getting an assistant to make appointments and talk to her eager collectors.

She and Max make love often, even more than usual in this time, in the frozen winter that has invaded the city. In February, there are two snowstorms, vast amounts of snow, endless trucks scraping the streets and cars buried in the snow banks. It reminds them of the snow on the first night they spent together. On these days, Max arrives, always with food and they will be undressing as he closes the door. He presses far into her, moves in different ways inside her, holds her breasts to him. An hour can pass in their lovemaking and Ingrid loses track of the time. They eat the food slowly, wrapped in sweaters and blankets, her studio never quite warm enough.

One afternoon, when the storms have passed, but the streets are still full of snow, now battered and gray and frozen into lumps and Ingrid is picking up lunch at B&H, a small luncheonette that has been on Second Avenue seemingly forever, she watches a mother and her baby. The baby is bundled into a blue snowsuit and smiling as the mother feeds him warm soup directly from her finger, which he sucks eagerly. Watching them, they strike Ingrid as eternal, vast, the gladness of the earth itself right before her. Shocked by her thoughts, Ingrid gets the food, hurries through the brilliant density of the cold and into her studio, where she eats her soup and bread in deep silence, turning her experience of the baby's smile over in her mind, examining all its elements. She will add babies to this series, different ones from the mysterious, implied babies in the last series. She feels disoriented, unmoored from the self she recognizes. Can this be? Just from that one moment when her world split suddenly, and perhaps forever, like a violent tear in the familiar fabric of her beliefs, or an explosion delivered from within. A force that had been waiting apart from her conscious awareness. She has never been interested in babies at all, not in any way. When, at her last opening, she realized her period was late and she might be pregnant, she was horrified. She understands them mostly as a permanent obstacle to her work, time vampires. She begins to sketch the baby she has just seen, staying with it until the early dark is full, using her clear, passionate skill to portray the marvel of this baby. The next day, Ingrid returns to the sketch, makes others of imaginary babies and children. She didn't say anything to Max at dinner, but he asked, several times, what she was thinking. She didn't say it was nothing and she didn't describe her experience. He let it rest, knowing she would tell him in her own time, if it was important. She is working on an image of a child, on that next day, which is still deeply cold, but sunny, when she realizes she is crying and it is now early evening and she has not eaten. When she becomes aware of her tears, she gets up without hesitation and calls Max at work. "Can you come down here?" she says.

"Yes, of course. Is everything all right?" Ingrid has never done this.

"No. Nothing wrong. I just need you to come here."

Max has his coat on in minutes and takes a cab, rather than taking time to get his car. Ingrid has never made this kind of request before. When he enters the studio, Ingrid is sitting on the daybed; she is very still. "What is it?" Max asks.

"I think we have a change of plans here. With your agreement, of course." But she knows that Max would like them to have a baby. "I want us to have a baby. Could we do that?" By the end of her sentence, they are undressing each other. They make love and then lie holding each other. Max has not even asked what caused Ingrid's change of heart. It all seems clear between them, this is the time. She believes she conceived before they had finished making love, believes she sensed the raucous conjoining of egg and sperm, though she knows it isn't instantaneous. By nine, when a few hours have passed, she knows she is pregnant. That night, they wrap themselves in quilts and sleep in the studio. On Seventh Street, the steeple of the Catholic church pushes its icy length into the sky; across the street, their friend Bart is asleep in his apartment, an empty mug of cocoa on his nightstand. He will be the first to hear the news, when they are sure, and he will be overjoyed. He has already bought a stuffed bear with plushy fur and a camel with long eyelashes and put them in his closet for Sue Ann's baby. Now he can start adding to the collection. The moon gate of his longing for a child glows white in his dreams and since he will never have one, these will be his children. It will be years before gay men can adopt.

Ingrid is not surprised when she misses her next period; her breasts have already started to swell, which Max noticed. "Is this what I think?" he asks.

"Mmm. Must be."

He rubs her gently. "Do you feel different?"

"Mmm. More sensitive. Do some more of that."

Many things that Ingrid does amaze Max. But this is not an act of will and Ingrid is on the older side to have a first baby; in addition, he and Evelyn, his ex-wife, had tried for months and months with no success. There was temperature taking and special positions and loose boxer shorts and frustration and what became sad sexual encounters on demand. By the time Nina was conceived they were both exhausted, with spiky, wounding anger at each other that eclipsed the celebration of conception. With Grace, their second daughter, they had nearly given up when Evelyn became pregnant, and the pregnancy had been delicate, was several times in danger. But it is characteristic of Ingrid, he thinks, to begin the process of pregnancy five hours after deciding she was ready; the force of her relationship to reality is majestic.

By the beginning of March, Ingrid has tested herself twice, not that it was necessary, since she can feel her body changing daily. She has invited Bart to her studio to tell him, and he hugs her and begins to cry. "It's happiness," he says. "I never thought you wanted a baby."

"I didn't until I did." Ingrid considers telling Bart about her experience in the deli and decides she will. He listens, hypnotized. "You still think there isn't much beyond the human personality?" he asks. This is an old discussion between them.

"No, I never said that, exactly."

"No, just very, very close. Never mind, it doesn't matter. Here we are and it's happening."

"And since I never said what you think I said, would you be the godfather?"

"Oh, Ingrid. Yes. Yes. But, you're not going to . . ."

"Have the baby baptized? Hardly. And Max is Jewish. No, this will be a family ceremony. I want Serena to be the godmother."

Bart sighs with contentment, a soft, long sound rippling from his heart.

Max and Ingrid call everyone, even Ingrid's family, with whom she has little contact. Her parents sound pleased, to her surprise. "Probably it's the closest thing to their idea of normal that I've come," she says to Max after they have all spoken. They have never come to her shows, never met Max, though they have seen photos.

"He's an old Jew," her father, Arthur, said to her mother, Dossie, when they saw the first picture of Max. Dossie pursed her mouth in what was meant to be disapproval, but there was no force behind it.

"A very well-off man," Dossie replied. "Well educated, worldly."

Arthur honked through his nose. "Worldly. Well, that should suit Ingrid."

But they are happy about the baby; they have five grandchildren and love them all, very different as grandparents than they were as parents. "Maybe we should visit after the baby's born," Arthur now muses. "See the big city. After all, she's sort of famous, right?" He is sure she is, but will not admit it in this casual way, as if he really has been noticing, all these years.

"You know she is," Dossie says. "And yes, I'd like that."

✳ ✪ ✳

Spring comes hesitantly, with leaves budding, green and furled against skies that are often pale and cloudy, and then in the middle of April, there is a flood of warmth and the brilliant tulips planted in beds on Park Avenue shine: red ones and gold, striped ones and purple ones and in the park, the cherry trees blossom, those particular shades of pink and cerise and shadowed white, petals floating in sunlight. Ingrid and Sue Ann, pregnant together, walk in Riverside Park. Ingrid is looking at the river, which comes right to the edge of a bank sprouting new grass. It always startles her that the river is right there; you could put your feet in it. No barriers or fences, just the cold, salty water sliding at the rim of the land. Sue Ann is wearing maternity clothes. "I feel as if I must be having twins," she says. She has been big since the beginning of her pregnancy and rocks slightly as she walks. She has read stacks of books about pregnancy and birth and she and Sept will attend a birthing class together in May. Ingrid does not show yet and will never be big; she wears jeans and even in the later months, she will wear Max's shirts and regular jeans until Sue Ann takes her to get some slacks with room in front for the baby.

Sue Ann passes her books along to Ingrid, who says, "It can't be this complicated, Sue Ann. My mother did it." They pass homeless men and women as they walk slowly along the path. "Some of the many beneficiaries of Reagan's economic policies," Ingrid says.

Sue Ann and Sept eat carefully. Sept has changed his diet, goes for acupuncture and cooks pots of Chinese herbs that waft into the building hallway and can be smelled in the elevator as it rises to their floor. He has had two more sessions with Serena and she has made these health suggestions, which he and Sue Ann take seriously. (Serena is discovering, in her new work, that she has a special sensitivity to health issues. "No surprise," she says, when this starts to emerge as a particular skill.) Sue Ann and Sept both meditate—which Sept has done for years—and he works out, long a part of his daily regime. They cook large, organic meals and Sue Ann packs some into containers for Ingrid, who tends to revert to bagels and lox and dark chocolate, despite Max's own careful meal planning.

Bart brings her homemade bread. "What do you think it will be like to be a mother?" he asks one afternoon, when they are eating slices of the new loaf, loaded with sweet butter and marmalade.

"Like a partnership," Ingrid replies, her mouth full.

"I don't think so, Ingrid," he says.

"Babies are very intelligent," she says.

"They are not partnership material."

"Well, we'll see. I want the baby here while I work. We'll work together and inspire each other. Max will take the baby half the time, he has a flexible schedule."

"Max will probably hire a nanny to help out."

"That's okay."

"Ingrid, we are from Newton, Iowa. Do we have nannies?"

"I wasn't from there when I was there, so why start now? We'll hire a nice young artist who could use some money, who loves babies."

"Remember, I'm right across the street when I'm not at work," he says. He has said this before.

"I'll remember. I appreciate it, Bart." She hugs him, still chewing.

✳ ✪ ✳

Serena and Leo are at the Whitney on a Thursday afternoon at the end of April, the weather has stayed warm, and that day is full of rousing wind that hurries full, white clouds across the sky and seems to clear even the New York air. "Let's sit for a moment," Serena says and when they do, she touches Leo's cheek gently. "I have really decided," she says. People mill around them; the room is perfumed with a mixture of different scents and filled with murmuring opinions. They hear snippets of conversations.

"So dynamic."

"No, I think he's just repeating himself. Greta told me . . ."

"The colors never wear out, do they?"

Leo knows immediately what she means. "You don't want a child," he says quietly.

"No, I don't."

He is still for a moment, letting the slender hem of hope drift away from him. He thought maybe, with Sue Ann and Ingrid (Ingrid!) pregnant that Serena would be what? Inspired? Encouraged? No, he hoped it, but did not think it a reality. He takes Serena's hand. "All right," he says. "All right. Let's walk, okay?" Still holding hands, they walk slowly down Madison Avenue. But it is not their final conversation, after all. Serena will change her mind in the autumn, near Thanksgiving—Leo has never completely given up hope, so he is not entirely surprised—and they will try, but she will never conceive. No one can find a reason why and she chooses not to boost her hormones, not to experiment with IVF. The healer she works with, Maria, a skillful, intense and authoritarian woman, says there is nothing wrong, that Serena is afraid. Serena can believe this with no problem.

✳ ✪ ✳

Sept and Sue Ann are walking in Riverside Park, close to where she and Ingrid were the previous month; the park is near their apartment and they walk there frequently. It is May and the colors are flamboyant; the later cherry trees are full of blooms and some old lilacs, their panicles deep purple, nod on a low hill, here in the upper reaches of the park. Dogs, bicyclists mingle. Some people are picnicking on the grass. They are admiring the cherry trees when Sept feels a pain in his chest; he has had these before, so he ignores it until he is almost overcome. He doubles over and Sue Ann begins to yell, "Call an ambulance! Call 911!" By chance, or perhaps not, a police car is cruising slowly along the path behind them and they stop and make the call. Then they move quickly to Sept and Sue Ann. One of the policemen recognizes Sept, who has given lectures to members of the department since his retirement.

"This is Detective Lewis," he says to his partner, "get this going fast." The ambulance arrives sooner than seems possible, moving quickly along the path and then Sept is lifted onto a stretcher and Sue Ann gets in the ambulance with him. The siren howls and they depart in a flurry of blossom petals, which are drifting in the wind. Sept is taken to Columbia Presbyterian and then it is all movement: the stretcher, doctors, Sue Ann running with them and then not allowed any further.

"We have him," the attending doctor says. "We will tell you as soon as we know anything."

In the corridor, Sue Ann calls everyone, starts to run out of coins and gets some from one of the nurses. The baby kicks and kicks. All the friends arrive and wait, with no information forthcoming. They bring food up from the cafeteria; it smells bad and is overcooked and accompanied by terrible metallic-tasting cups of tea and coffee. In the early evening, the doctor emerges and says Sept is unstable; they are still working. There is that sporadic talking that takes place in hospitals: "Not sudden, but still. A shock."

"Was he feeling bad?"

"Other symptoms?"

There is great concern for Sue Ann, who was shaking by the time her friends arrived, but has stopped. One person after another holds her hands, rubs her back. There are silences. The night deepens. Ingrid falls asleep briefly and wakens to flooding tears. Max has initiated a round of phone calls to all the important doctors connected to him and his wealthy, doctor-oriented family. Serena walks, sits, walks. She meditates and tries to remember her last session with Sept. She knew he was fragile, he knew it, it was not a secret to anyone, but had she seen this? She had not. Was she spared? Inadequate to the task? And what would she have said? The waiting room is bright, but bleak. She doesn't even imagine channeling now and no one asks.

A little before midnight, Frieda arrives; she, too, has been crying. "Nothing?" She can tell from their faces that they don't know anything yet, except that Sept is still alive. Frieda has brought a huge thermos of good sweet tea and another of coffee. Everyone sips gratefully. She has brought bread and butter sandwiches and muffins with heavy raisins embedded in them. "Eat," she says. "Even if you can't imagine swallowing food. Eat anyway." They know life has made her an authority on this and they eat, slowly, carefully.

At 4 a.m., the doctor comes to them smiling. "Going to pull through. Sue Ann, you can see him for a short visit. Go home," he says to the rest of them. "Sleep. He's going to live." Finally, after hugs and plans to call the next day, they leave. The air is warm and still, just waiting for dawn to come, for the light to ruffle the sky and climb higher and higher.

They all sleep, much to their surprise, and no one calls.

Sue Ann stays at the hospital and when the sun comes up, she goes to the cafeteria and tries to eat, sitting at the scarred table, using plastic utensils, the windowless room soaked with the smell of old food. She looks around and sees a large man getting coffee. He is broad and heavy, but stands straight and it looks as if the stance is taking effort. For a moment, Sue Ann stares at his back before realizing the man is Richard, the ex-husband she has not seen in many years. Before she can decide whether to greet him, he turns and sees her, walks toward her and when he reaches her, she stands. He puts the coffee he is carrying down on the table. They look at each other, silence streaming around them, an active force, until Richard reaches out and puts his arms around her, leaning slightly to allow for her belly. "What are you doing here?" he asks, still holding her.

"My partner has had a heart attack. Today, just today, well, no, now it's yesterday it happened, but he's going to pull through. They said he would. I know he will."

Richard lets go of her. "My son," he says. "Cancer. They let us sleep here sometimes." To Sue Ann, he has the feeling of a man whose defenses have cracked, been plastered together, cracked again.

The child who started before he and Sue Ann separated. Whose mother was the pregnant woman Sue Ann saw with Richard in a restaurant. The child who was the reason Richard let her go, was uncharacteristically generous and supportive. But it all falls away for Sue Ann; angry memories tear apart and float in ghostly fragments to disappear in this ugly room as the sun shines out of sight beyond the heavy walls. "I'm sorry, Richard." She does not ask for the prognosis. She can tell from looking at his face that it isn't good.

"And I am sorry," he says. "Sorry. I wish you the best," he says, taking her hand for a moment and then letting go, picking up the coffee. "My wife," he says. "She's upstairs." Sue Ann nods and he leaves.

She goes into the lobby and then out for a moment to feel the sun. Slightly warmed, she goes back to Sept. On the way up in the elevator, she feels a contraction, slight, but noticeable. Too early, she thinks. Too early. It's only May. Please, baby, not now. You're coming in June. June. The sensations stop. She reaches Sept's floor and walks toward his room, praying. The early morning rituals of the hospital, full of ordinary liveliness and purpose, are in motion around her. "Strong," she says out loud. "He will pull through." The days lengthen and Sept improves, but slowly, and at first he is weak and struggling.

Visiting, Serena remembers the image she had of the small bird, on that first night she channeled for all of them, the bird's wings beating fervently, its energy collapsing and then reasserting itself. It rains on and off for a week in the middle of May, the new leaves heavy with water, glowing in the pearly light. Everything seems sodden. At the end of that week, the rain stops and Sept improves suddenly, miraculously, as if his strength has built slowly and then surged. The doctors are sending him home. All the friends have brought food for Sue Ann and Sept during his hospital stay and they now start to cook, en masse, each taking an assigned dish for his arrival home and more to store for the weeks ahead. He comes home at the end of May and settles into the big apartment that Sue Ann has filled with flowers. The friends are there to greet him, but don't stay long; they pack things they have left there, since they took turns sleeping over when Sept was in the hospital, keeping Sue Ann company, cleaning and shopping, the efforts of a small and loving community to ease the pain.

Sept is walking every day, then climbing stairs, then working out slowly, starting his exercise regime, grateful for his body, for his newly mended heart and his steady breath. He feels his meditations deepen and the prayers he has said in the hospital stay with him, increase as he and Sue Ann hold hands and bless their life and the baby to come. Frieda suggests that they all meet to meditate at Sue Ann and Sept's and they do. She arrives with her favorite tea and prepares it, insisting no one else does it correctly. She does not allow anyone to add ice, even as the weather warms substantially. "Forbidden," she says, smiling. "You will ruin it with this tea."

Sue Ann and Ingrid shop for baby things and Serena and Rose are planning a shower for Sue Ann for the first weekend in June. The baby's room is painted the yellow of daffodils, the furniture already delivered. During her time with Sept in the hospital, Sue Ann has embroidered the hems of curtains with a wild display of blooms: multi-colored pansies in mauve and gold, glowing gerbera daisies, sunflowers and budding crimson roses next to others in full bloom. "Do you want to start the baby's room?" Sue Ann asks Ingrid one day, when they are deep in tiny overalls and tee shirts.

"No. No. Too soon." Ingrid rubs her fingers along the edge of a soft shirt. Her thick, ashy curls are pulled back, showing pale, flat ears, beautifully shaped. She is wearing her favorite orange shirt, now faded and frayed at the collar, and her usual black jeans, with the top button open and the zipper half undone. Other customers look at her obliquely; is she familiar? Someone they should recognize? Even though her picture has now appeared numerous times in magazines and newspapers, people had this reaction to Ingrid before she was a celebrity in the art world.

"It is not too soon," Sue Ann says firmly. She smooths her hands along the blue A-line blouse she is wearing, the baby pressing far out, almost reaching into the world. "There are a lot of decisions to make. Does Max believe in that Jewish custom of not buying anything for the baby until he or she is born?"

Ingrid laughs. "Hardly. Just not ready yet." They pick a few things to buy.

"Are you and Max planning to get married?" Sue Ann asks, pretty sure of the answer, but curious.

This time, Ingrid doesn't laugh, but she says no. "I can't see the point. We are certainly committed to each other. Every once in awhile Max brings out his grandmother's diamond and asks me to at least consider it."

"Do you?"

"I do. And I come to the same conclusion."

"We are," Sue Ann says. "Getting married. In October."

Ingrid puts down the little bundle of clothes she has chosen and hugs Sue Ann and then holds her hands against Sue Ann's curls, still golden as a child's. "Good," she says.

✳ ✦ ✳

On the sixteenth of June, a little before three a.m., Sue Ann starts contractions and they quickly become steady as she and Sept time them. They take what they have packed and ready and head for New York Hospital on what becomes a windless day of hot sun, going in through the doors at the end of the curving driveway. The building's tall, gothic-style windows flicker with light. "No hurry," Sept says. "I've done this before; you're fine. But this time I can stay with you and see that child come into the world." He feels his heartbeat quicken, now in a pleasurable way. They go to the maternity unit and Sept calls Serena, who starts the telephone tree. Here they are, in a hospital again, under such different circumstances. He can feel his eyes fill as he breathes with Sue Ann and rubs her back. The friends arrive in groups: Serena and Leo and Ingrid and Bart and Max together. Stephen alone. Rose and Hal come when Sue Ann is halfway through her labor, having driven down from their farm, going above the speed limit. When he was ill, Sept spent time imagining the other patients, their particular suffering, perhaps their death; he imagined surgery and incisions and blood and the blood of birthing, the babies arriving into the world of wind and stars, spinning planets and rolling oceans. Now he is fully focused on Sue Ann, no thoughts of the others and their situations. Just this baby and his beloved. Sue Ann's labor is fast, especially for a first birth.

The group of friends is in the waiting room, drinking iced tea and eating greasy doughnuts, stale and crumbly, when Sept comes out of the delivery room. He is jubilant. "A girl," he says. "A beautiful girl. Our daughter. You can all see her soon. She is Etta Elizabeth, after my aunt and Sue Ann's grandmother on her mother's side." Serena remembers the little girl she saw with Sept and Sue Ann in that channeling session, how it worried her that she was simply imagining what she wanted to see. And perhaps she was, but here is the child, she has come. Bells ring, doctors are called, announcements of all kinds instruct, repeat, instruct again. Other expectant families wait, patiently or restlessly, sharing food companionably. People arrive with flowers, with plump stuffed animals, and smiles and tears mingle.

They squeeze into Sue Ann's room, where she is already nursing this baby born into the miracle of her father's spared life; Etta is sturdy and queenly, sucking at her mother's nipple on this, her first day under the sun on this magical planet that is overflowing with love for her and where bliss and tragedy are often dancing partners.

Everyone has been shaken by Sept's illness. Though they knew he had heart troubles and it was always possible, the fact of it fostered a different kind of urgency—to treasure this birth, which could have been so different, and to be grateful, each in their own way, as they move through the rough and ordinary magic of their daily lives.

As Serena looks at Etta, she shifts her vision slightly and sees the baby's form as streaming shapes made of liquid, transparent light: gold and a shimmering blue, rose and violet, the palest green. The light opens from the center of Etta's body, stretches out and then coalesces in a rhythm that ripples through it. Serena watches for a moment and then simply looks at Etta, at her perfect roundness, her head resting on Sue Ann's arm, seemingly unmarked by its journey through the birth canal. She wonders if Etta senses her guardians, as Serena believes she herself did. As she is considering it, Sept looks at her and says, "Yes. They are there. Frieda is coming later. I know she will see them." He nods slightly. No one else notices their exchange.

Sue Ann will go home the next day, so the group does not stay long, plenty of time to visit later. Sept's family is arriving in two days, his sons and their wives and children. His grandchildren and his newborn, together. Sue Ann's family will come the following week. Whatever feelings they have about Sept's being black have been blanketed under a flat, Midwestern calm. Perhaps they are really happy for Sue Ann— once married to a rich, mean white man and where did that lead?

Leaving, Ingrid and Max head downtown. Ingrid wants to work and Max will keep her company; Rose and Hal go to Ingrid and Max's apartment, where they will stay for a few days in its roomy elegance. Bart and Stephen go to Bart's. Leo and Serena go home and sit in their small garden, where pink roses are blooming in abundance, along with pansies and impatiens in white and coral. They have made coffee to take outside. "Remember the impatiens?" Leo says, referring to the first night they made love.

Serena, laughs, remembering. "Impatient?"

"No," says Leo, laughing in return. "Impatiens. The flower." He has picked a small bouquet of the coral impatiens. He turns to Serena and, dropping one of his long legs into a kneeling position, offers the flowers to her. "Serena, my dear love, will you marry me?"

"Yes," she says, with no hesitation. Like Ingrid, Serena has not wanted to marry, but with Etta's birth and Ingrid pregnant, she knows she longs for a family. She and Leo could be a family. "But will it change everything?"

"It will change some things. Do you mean will you start to do the food shopping and cooking, instead of my doing it?" He is only half joking.

"No. I mean will I become 'a wife,' in some mythic sense?"

"Will you? Not to me."

"No, and not to myself either, and I have never cared much about the rest of the world. So, yes, Leo. I will. I will." And there, amidst the flowers and warmth, in a world of birth and passion, loss and misery and renewal, uncertainty and impermanence, they begin to plan their wedding.

About the Author

Julie Winter is a psychospiritual therapist based in New York with an international practice via the internet. She is a teacher, astrologer, channel and ordained Minister in the Helix Healing Ministry. She co-founded both The Helix Training/Helix Ministry and Healing Works, a not-for-profit organization dedicated to serving, at no cost, the marginalized population of New York through a wide variety of healing modalities. She is a charter member of the Association of Transformational Leaders NYC.

Her award-winning cable TV program, *Micciah Channel, Julie Winter,* produced by Jon Child, ran for ten years in the United States and Europe. Those programs and her current work can be seen on www.WinterChild.com/julie.

CPSIA information can be obtained
at www.ICGtesting.com
Printed in the USA
FSHW011114151119
64080FS

9 781889 471334